The Bestselling Novels of
TOM CLANCY

THE TEETH OF THE TIGER

A new generation—Jack Ryan, Jr.—takes over in Tom Clancy's extraordinary, and extraordinarily prescient, novel.

"INCREDIBLY ADDICTIVE."

—*Daily Mail* (London)

RED RABBIT

Tom Clancy returns to Jack Ryan's early days—in a gripping novel of global political drama . . .

"AN OLD-FASHIONED COLD WAR THRILLER."

—*Chicago Sun-Times*

THE BEAR AND THE DRAGON

A clash of world powers. President Jack Ryan's trial by fire.

"HEART-STOPPING ACTION . . . CLANCY STILL REIGNS."

—*The Washington Post*

RAINBOW SIX

John Clark is used to doing the CIA's dirty work. Now he's taking on the world.

"ACTION-PACKED."

—*The New York Times Book Review*

continued . . .

THE CARDINAL OF THE KREMLIN
The superpowers race for the ultimate Star Wars missile defense system.

"*CARDINAL* EXCITES, ILLUMINATES . . . A REAL PAGE-TURNER."

—*Los Angeles Daily News*

CLEAR AND PRESENT DANGER
The killing of three U.S. officials in Colombia ignites the American government's explosive, and top secret, response.

"A CRACKLING GOOD YARN."

—*The Washington Post*

THE SUM OF ALL FEARS
The disappearance of an Israeli nuclear weapon threatens the balance of power in the Middle East—and around the world.

"CLANCY AT HIS BEST . . . NOT TO BE MISSED."

—*The Dallas Morning News*

WITHOUT REMORSE
The Clancy epic fans have been waiting for. His code name is Mr. Clark. And his work for the CIA is brilliant, cold-blooded, and efficient . . . but who is he really?

"HIGHLY ENTERTAINING."

—*The Wall Street Journal*

Tom Clancy's
NET FORCE®
THE ARCHIMEDES EFFECT

Created by
Tom Clancy and Steve Pieczenik

written by Steve Perry
and Larry Segriff

BERKLEY BOOKS, NEW YORK

THE BERKLEY PUBLISHING GROUP
Published by the Penguin Group
Penguin Group (USA) Inc.
375 Hudson Street, New York, New York 10014, USA

Penguin Group (Canada), 90 Eglinton Avenue East, Suite 700, Toronto, Ontario M4P 2Y3, Canada
(a division of Pearson Penguin Canada Inc.)
Penguin Books Ltd., 80 Strand, London WC2R 0RL, England
Penguin Group Ireland, 25 St. Stephen's Green, Dublin 2, Ireland (a division of Penguin Books Ltd.)
Penguin Group (Australia), 250 Camberwell Road, Camberwell, Victoria 3124, Australia
(a division of Pearson Australia Group Pty. Ltd.)
Penguin Books India Pvt. Ltd., 11 Community Centre, Panchsheel Park, New Delhi—110 017, India
Penguin Group (NZ), Cnr. Airborne and Rosedale Roads, Albany, Auckland 1310, New Zealand
(a division of Pearson New Zealand Ltd.)
Penguin Books (South Africa) (Pty.) Ltd., 24 Sturdee Avenue, Rosebank, Johannesburg 2196,
South Africa

Penguin Books Ltd., Registered Offices: 80 Strand, London WC2R 0RL, England

This is a work of fiction. Names, characters, places, and incidents either are the product of the authors'
imagination or are used fictitiously, and any resemblance to actual persons, living or dead, business
establishments, events, or locales is entirely coincidental. The publisher does not have any control over
and does not assume any responsibility for author or third-party websites or their content.

TOM CLANCY'S NET FORCE®: THE ARCHIMEDES EFFECT

A Berkley Book / published by arrangement with Netco Partners

PRINTING HISTORY
Berkley edition / February 2006

Copyright © 2006 by Netco Partners.
NET FORCE® is a registered trademark of Netco Partners.
Cover illustration by Gallucci Imaging Inc.

ISBN: 0-425-20424-3

BERKLEY®
Berkley Books are published by The Berkley Publishing Group,
a division of Penguin Group (USA) Inc.,
375 Hudson Street, New York, New York 10014.
BERKLEY is a registered trademark of Penguin Group (USA) Inc.
The "B" design is a trademark belonging to Penguin Group (USA) Inc.

PRINTED IN THE UNITED STATES OF AMERICA

10 9 8 7 6 5 4 3

Acknowledgments

We would like to acknowledge the assistance of Martin H. Greenberg, Denise Little, John Helfers, Brittiany Koren, and Tom Colgan, our editor. But most important, it is for you, our readers, to determine how successful our collective endeavor has been.

—Tom Clancy and Steve Pieczenik

PROLOGUE

Fort Stephens, Oklahoma
January 2015 C.E.

Every time he had to work guard duty on a night like this, Stevens's respect for the pioneers in their covered wagons went way up: That bone-chilling Oklahoma winter wind cut through you like a razor. How they could travel across the country on nothing but rutted dirt roads, no running water, no electric heaters . . . Amazing.

Stevens, Sergeant Theodore M., whose name wasn't spelled the same as that of the base's, but who caught all kinds of crap about it being "his" base anyhow, wasn't going to step out of the nice, warm kiosk into the teeth of that howling gale without a damned good reason.

*Some*body was going to have to, though. . . .

"Car approaching, Sarge," Billings said. "Coming pretty fast."

"I'm not *blind*, Billings."

The private shrugged.

"But since *your* eagle eye picked it up, you can step out and check his ID—"

The rest of what he was going to say was cut off by the screech made by four radial tires under a full-sized hunk of Detroit iron as the brakes locked. The car, a black Ford, skidded to a stop ten feet short of the gate's bumpers, a smoking trail of rubber behind it.

"Jesus!" Billings said, coming to his feet.

"Side arm!" Stevens said as he drew his pistol.

Billings also pulled his Beretta, but like Stevens, kept it low and pointed at the floor.

A soldier in an Army winter dress uniform and coat leaped out on the driver's side of the Ford, waving his hands. "Wounded, we got an injured *general* in here! Open the gate!"

The voice came through loud and clear over the state-of-the-art electronic sound system. Great. An injured general?

The car's interior dome light was bright enough to show a man in the passenger seat, sure looked like an officer, with blood running down his face to soak into his uniform. That's all they needed; some shiny brass hat got drunk in a bar and thumped by a local Okie who didn't like his looks.

Well, crap, looked like Stevens was going out into the winter night after all. "Call Medical," he ordered Billings. He holstered his pistol.

Fort Stephens, a high-tech installation and the newest jewel in the Army's crown, wasn't fully manned yet, but there was a working infirmary since the place was at least half-staffed with a couple thousand boots-on-the-ground. Not to mention asses-in-chairs . . .

Stevens thumbed the lock's reader on his console. The reader matched his thumbprint to the one in the computer's files, and the heavy electric steel door slid open noiselessly on its Delrin track.

The wind hit Stevens with an icy, take-your-breath-away slap as the door slid shut behind him. Damn! The antiram bumpers, squat chunks of rebarred concrete as big around as bridge supports, would stop a tank, but they didn't offer any protection at all against the freezing breeze.

He went around the bumpers and toward the car.

As he got closer, he could see that the injured man had a star on each of his shoulders. Crap, it *was* a general.

"Don't you die on my watch," Stevens whispered under his breath.

He pulled the passenger door open. "Sir—?"

He found himself looking into the bore of a very large handgun. Muzzle big enough to stick your finger into it.

What the hell was this?

"Stay cool, Sarge," the "general" said.

If these scumbags thought they were going to be breaking into the base by *his* gate, they were mistaken.

"You can't open the door or the gate from out here," he said to the "general." "Especially on a 'Code Alpha' like this."

He smiled. The outside of that armor-plated steel door didn't have a knob; it was as smooth as a baby's butt. The windows in the kiosk, including the door's, were armor-tempered optical-grade Lexan, six centimeters thick, and nobody was shooting holes through *that* with small arms, not even the big honkin' revolver this guy had pointed at him. Those windows would stop an elephant gun. You could plink at it with a .50 BMF and it would eat the slugs without shattering—for a while, at least.

The seven-ton steel gate and double-brace bars of more than two tons each would halt an eighteen-wheeler rolling at speed to a dead stop in its retreads.

Plus, Stevens was wearing a LOSIR ear-button with a mike pinned to the inside of his shirt collar, and unless Billings had gone completely deaf and stupid back in the kiosk, he'd hear this conversation and that "Code Alpha" and realize something was wrong.

As soon as he did, plus about forty-five seconds, a couple Hummers full of MPs armed to the teeth were gonna come roaring toward the gate, at which point Sergeant Theodore M. Stevens was gonna hit the dirt flat on his face so as not to get shot when the MPs lit up this car and these two losers. Code Alpha meant come shooting. Gonna be a most active war zone around here, and somebody was gonna get hurt.

The man smiled like he could read Stevens's mind. "Have a look at your PFC in the kiosk, Sarge."

Stevens frowned. He glanced back at the guard shack.

Billings was thumping the edge of his right hand—the one holding his side arm—into the comlink handheld with which he was supposed to be calling for Medical and MPs.

"I do believe your phone is, um . . . out of order," the fake general said.

As Stevens watched, the man who had leaped out of the car took a couple quick steps to the kiosk door, and pulled the pin on some kind of grenade. He had what looked like a TV remote in his other hand, and he thumbed it.

What was he gonna do with that? It wouldn't dent the kiosk wall, and it might scratch and fog the Lexan, but that was all it was gonna—

The kiosk door slid open a hand span and stopped. Billings dropped the comlink and swung his pistol up, but the driver shoved the grenade through the gap and moved to the side before Billings could fire.

The door slid shut again.

What the hell—?!

Billings saw the grenade, and he tried to get out through the other door—

There was a muffled *whump!* and the kiosk filled with green smoke.

Without thinking, Stevens reached for his side arm.

"Belay that, Sarge! It's just puke gas. You behave, you'll be telling the story to your buddies over beer tonight. But move crooked, and you bleed out right here and now. They don't pay you enough, you know."

Stevens nodded. "Yeah. I hear you." He moved his hand away from his gun's butt.

Twenty seconds later, the kiosk door opened. The night wind cleaned out the vestiges of the greenish smoke to reveal Billings on his knees, heaving his guts out, the partially digested remains of his most recent meal splashed all over the floor in front of him. Stevens hated emetic gas. It was worse than pepper spray, though not as bad as DG—diarrhea gas. Put that together with PG, the dreaded P-G-D-G double-ended spew combo? Oh, that was messy, messy. . . .

The driver ran into the kiosk, and used a cuff-strap and manacle on the still-vomiting Billings.

"Turn around, put your hands behind you."

Stevens did as he was told. He felt the cool touch of a plastic wrist-cuff wrap around his wrists. He thought about lunging backward and trying to knock the guy silly, a head butt to the nose, but even as the thought crossed his mind, a second car skidded to a stop to his right, and five guys piled out, hooded and goggled and dressed in black, armed with submachine guns.

His mama didn't raise any foolish children. Sergeant Theodore M. Stevens lost the idea of further resistance in a big hurry. These guys knew what they were doing. *He* wasn't going to do anything stupid, no, sir. The Army didn't pay him enough to die for nothin', for sure.

The massive gate swung open.

How could they do that? The gate, like the kiosk door, was keyed to thumbprints—this watch, his, Billings's, and those of the OOD back in the MP HQ, plus their relief. Nobody else was supposed to be able to open this kiosk or gate if they weren't in the system.

Somebody's head was gonna roll for this, for damn sure. He sure hoped it wouldn't be his. . . .

1

Four-Star Army General Patrick Lee Hadden—should have had five stars, but the continuing War on Terror wasn't an officially declared conflict. There hadn't been one of those for a long time, not since WWII.

The Chairman of the Joint Chiefs of Staff was a most unhappy man. He said, "Okay, you've seen recordings we did with the MP sergeant and his PFC, and other personnel inside Fort Stephens. You've seen the reconstruction as put together by our computer people. What you did not see were the actual recordings from the gate camera, or any other security cameras on the base, because the attackers shut those off just as easily as they did everything else, including opening the gates and getting into the base."

Net Force Commander Thomas Thorn nodded. "Yes, sir. And you want to know how they did it." They were alone in Thorn's office, which was pretty amazing— Hadden could have called the meeting in his office. There was no way Thorn could have turned down that invitation.

"No, I don't give a rat's ass how they did it. What I want to know is *who* they are and *where they live*. If the way to get that information is to figure out how they did it, fine, if that's what it takes. Those men got into my shiny new high-tech Army base and did damage to it. Not much, but *any* is too much. I want them, I want their heads on a platter and their bodies roasting over a slow fire, and I want it *yesterday.*"

Thorn didn't smile. When the Chairman of the JCOS said something like this, he might be joking. Then again, he might not be. And since Thorn and all of Net Force had left civilian control, shifted from being a branch of the FBI to the military, General Hadden was their master. Thorn didn't like it, but he had to either live with it or leave, and he wasn't ready to walk out just yet.

"The Army's computer people tell me what happened, and even how it happened, in theory, but that's not what I need. I want these bastards tracked down."

"You've got some pretty good people in the Army."

"That's right, we do. But your people are better—and *you* are in my Army now. What you did to break up that Chinese thing? That was outstanding work. I need you to get me these people, General."

General. The man forgot who he was talking to. Thorn was a civilian, and a "Commander," but no way a general.

Hadden must have seen it on his face. Not that it would have taken a particularly perceptive man to see that. Thorn's surprise—and his anger—were undoubtedly very apparent. "It's a new technicality," Hadden said. "You're heading up a military outfit now, son. And besides, we've promoted Abe Kent to general and he reports to you. You need a commission and a rank higher than his, so no more 'Commander.' You are now 'General Thorn.' Two stars to Abe's one."

Still stunned, Thorn said, "You can't do that! You can't *draft* me!"

"Son, if I want, I can get a million GIs, swabbies, jarheads, flyboys, and National Guardsmen to stand on their heads and whistle 'Dixie' in four-part harmony. The President will have to sign off on it, of course, but the new Terrorist Powers Act gives me all kinds of leeway. I'll have the paperwork put through—it's a done deal."

Thorn blinked. Whoa. This was getting really strange. But, as he thought about it, it did make a certain twisted sense—from their point of view, anyway.

"Can you do this job, Thorn?"

"General" Thorn gave him a little half smile and nod. "If it can be done, yes, sir. I'll have Jay Gridley contact the Army computer experts and pick it up."

"Good." Hadden stood. Thorn stood, too. "My aide will provide the information. Your man will go through you and General Ellis."

He turned and marched out of the room, leaving Thorn standing there alone.

"*General* Thorn? Sweet Jesus."

A thought hit him. Some of all this, now that they were no longer part of the FBI, was tolerable because he knew he could walk away if it ever got too bad. But now that he was in the military, could he still quit if he wanted to?

Damn.

Marissa was going to *love* this.

Fort George H.W. Bush
Clinton, Arkansas

There were two guards inside the kiosk at the south entrance, and a third man outside.

Lying in the wet grass in his gillie-suit, Carruth watched the guards through powerful binoculars, the magnification such that he could see the faces of all three. They looked bored.

You'd think the Army would be on high alert after the hit in Oklahoma. But that was the Army—they weren't the Navy. . . .

The ex-SEAL grinned. *Don't worry boys, your lives are about to get interesting.*

He thumbed the LOSIR microphone to narrowcast a message to Hill. The light used to transmit wouldn't be detected by a radio scanner, and it was a different spectrum than the Army guys used in their own LOSIR systems.

Patrick Hill was the gearhead, an über-geek who could build most of the electronics they carried from scratch, but who also could kill sixteen different ways with the soldering iron he'd use to do it.

"Any eyes?"

"No, Boss, clear canopy for the next twenty. No sonics, radios, or LEDs active. Passives either, as far as I can tell."

Good. They were clear from satellite recon, and no active sensors were operating. Of course there weren't supposed to be, according to the specs that the chief had given them, but a man like Carruth didn't leave things to chance. Weren't-supposed-to-be could get you killed quick.

"Give them the sig," he said.

"Roger."

Hill would signal the other two men on their team, and start the clock ticking.

Carruth slid forward on the wet grass, letting the cold soak into him, doing his best to become part of the landscape. Smooth movement, slow and steady was what won this race. Leaves and twigs pressed against him as he moved.

Damn, it was wet. He could use a mask and snorkel. . . .

Twenty-five meters. Twenty. As he slid forward, he could hear the sound of the ambulance as it rolled up to the gate.

The guards looked a little more animated. One of the men in the guardhouse stepped outside, exactly as Carruth had expected—and the scenario had predicted.

That left only one inside the shack.

Carruth crawled faster now. The slowly moving vehicle had captured the attention of the guards—they'd be looking southwest.

When Stark stopped the ambulance and started to talk to the guards, Dexter, his copilot, would shoot the guards, using an air gun firing special hypodermic darts. Once they hit, lightweight capacitors in the darts would release several thousand volts. Low-amperage, but it didn't take much under the skin. Zap, the guards would go down, out and probably not dead, though that didn't matter, and no big bang for anybody to overhear.

The ambulance slowed to a stop at the entrance.

"Howdy." Stark's voice, flat and nasal. "We're here to pick up a Major Kendrick—seems he busted his hand up pretty bad, and the base doctors wanna send him out."

The guard seemed to relax. It wasn't uncommon for such transfers. "Yes, sir," he said. "I'll just check with the OIC—he didn't tell us you were coming."

Two dull *whuuuuft!* sounds punctuated the guard's words.

Carruth was at the guardhouse now, low, so he wouldn't be seen. The ex-SEAL slid smoothly upward and saw the guard inside turning toward a monitor.

"Hey, Sarge?" Carruth said as he stepped into the room.

"Yeah?" The man started to turn.

Carruth darted him. "You lose, Sarge. Sorry."

The guard fell heavily to the ground.

Carruth and Hill slid into the ambulance with Stark. Dexter had already taken his place in the guard's hut. The gate slid open. Not as heavy as the one in Oklahoma, but stout enough so that ramming it would have been a waste of time.

Ahead was the barracks.

Stark had been telling the truth at the gate—they really *were* here to pick up Major Kendrick. The principal lock on the armory was a biometric palm scanner. The device used infrared light and ultrasound to read the pattern of veins underneath the skin, a signature as unique as a fingerprint or retinal scan. They hadn't been able to get the matching file from the camp's computer, so they had to do it a different way.

The problem was that the scanner also read the temperature of the hand while the ultrasound checked on the arterial flow. Dead hands tended to cool pretty quick, and no blood circulated, so they needed Kendrick alive. Microwaving a hand to body temp might be a viable option, but faking the live arteries was impossible. Different than the hit in Oklahoma, but you had to adjust, that was the name of the game. Roll with the punches, and don't get caught flat-footed . . .

The three of them entered the building. Stark pushed the collapsible stretcher. They made no attempt at stealth. One of the oldest tricks in the book—look like you belong, and you won't be questioned. The three moved down the hallway to Kendrick's room. Once there, Carruth opened the door and stepped in. Kendrick was asleep, and the quick injection he gave the man would keep him that way.

They rolled Kendrick to the ambulance without incident.

They drove to the armory. The building was a large warehouse within a carefully guarded perimeter. It was good security—human guards outside and technological ones inside.

Again, they darted the guards. Stark took over at the kiosk, while Carruth and Hill drove inside.

At the outer door, Kendrick's hand worked exactly as advertised. Patrick did some kind of geek-magic and opened the electronically controlled inner door.

"You ready?" he asked.

Carruth nodded.

Things were about to get hot.

The warheads couldn't be removed without activating indicators well away from the armory. Such alarms were active at all times, part of SOP for keeping track of the weapons. So they had to move fast.

"Go."

The target they were after was a big one—approximately three hundred pounds. They pushed the stretcher—now clear of Kendrick—close to the rack, and rolled the device onto it. An audible alarm went off.

Hill smoothly tightened two nylon safety belts as Carruth pushed the nuke toward the door. They hurried.

They made it to the ambulance. Carruth drove while Hill locked down the warhead.

Go-go-go—!

They sped toward the armory perimeter, hearing sirens approach. Stark ran, hopping in while they were still moving.

They were halfway to the gate when the world flickered and jumped, making Carruth slam on the brakes.

"Damn machine!"

Carruth smacked the side of his heads-up display and the image stabilized.

This is what happens when you buy cheap.

Carruth thought VR training was for shit—no amount of pretending to crawl through the forest prepared you for the real thing. The cold, the bugs—VR just didn't cut it. Sure, the spacing of the base, the time factors, and the movement could be worked with their setup, but the little random things—Kendrick deciding to go pee, or being out on a date—those could never be factored in accurately.

But their current operations budget didn't cover full-scale mockups. Or as the boss had put it, "You can spend the money on your field gear or your training gear, you choose."

So they'd compromised. The system they were using wasn't full VR—it mixed real-time computer graphics and a heads-up display with simulated models. The guards and base were all VR, spun on the Kraken Cluster back at camp, and 'cast to their headsets. But the crawling through grass, climbing, and driving were for real.

They hadn't bothered with much training for the other attack. That had been simple hit-and-run—get in, do damage, and get out. And there, they'd had all the computer codes. Because this one was more complicated, training was a necessity.

But it was worth it. The attack would drive the price of their U.S. military base information through the roof. And on a more personal level, Carruth was looking forward to the black eye it would give the military.

Teach them what happens when they mess with me.

They made the entrance and picked up Dexter without

any problems. By then, the ambulance sirens and flashers were running.

Code three, and they were out.

Hill called out the time. Armory-to-exit was the best they'd done yet.

They were just about ready.

2

Jay Gridley, head of Net Force's computer section, leading expert and master of virtual reality in all its intricate, complicated forms, couldn't remember the last time he'd been this tired. His eyes burned, and felt gritty when he blinked. His body had that brittle feeling, like a piece of glass, as though something would shatter if he moved too fast.

The days when he could sit up in VR all night long, then go all the next day without sleep were gone. When had that happened?

That'll teach me.

Little Mark, his darling baby boy, had run out of milk the night before, and Jay had gone out to the local 7-Eleven instead of the supermarket where they normally shopped. It was closer and faster. That's why, he had explained to his wife, Saji, they called it a convenience store. . . .

Apparently, as it turned out, however, 7-Eleven cows weren't the same as Safeway cows.

So at 3 A.M., when the boy ~~~~~~~~~~
gas pains, Jay had to get up and ~~~~~~~~~
pissed off. "What was it you sa~~~~~~~~~
milk, no big deal? Tell it to your so~~~~~~~

Nobody got any more sleep. The t~~~~~~~
to a convenience store had not been~~~~~~
Nosiree . . .

To top it off, he'd been scheduled to br~~~~~~ al Ellis
on the computer problem at 7:30 A.M. at the ~~ntagon Annex. Why so early? Why couldn't they do it in VR? Because the military said so, that's why. Screw 'em all. Jay
liked being the honcho at Net Force, he'd gotten to match
himself against some sharp players, but this military crap
was for the birds. Maybe it was time to start thinking about
changing jobs.

Jay hadn't met General Ellis before, and was curious to
see what his boss's boss looked like, although he wished he
could have been a bit more rested.

Although if what Thorn was saying was true, *he* was
about to be a general, too. Couldn't swing a dead cat without hitting one of those these days. Jay wasn't sure he liked
any part of that.

"Sir, the general will see you now."

Jay stood up and followed the far-too-fresh-looking secretary through a short, dark hallway, and then into the general's office. Jay's personal guard and escort stayed in the
waiting room.

A picture of the President hung on the wall, along with
several photos of an older man shaking hands with various
dignitaries. Books cluttered dark-grained bookshelves, and
small trophies occupied those areas that weren't held by
books: ammunition, models, and other pieces of hardware.
A painting of a bayou that could have come from one of
Jay's own VR scenarios hung on one wall, cypress trees
thick with Spanish moss crowding a red-hued waterway, itself tinted by a setting sun.

Eclectic.

d the desk sat a man in his mid-fifties, fighting the
e of the bulge and losing. He was pale, and had hair
going from gray to white.

"Mr. Gridley."

The words were stretched out: "Mist-uh Guriddleeee."
A song of the South. Texas? Louisiana? Somewhere down
there.

"That's me," said Jay.

"Your boss tells me you're the best bug-squasher we got."

Jay couldn't help but grin. He'd never heard that precise
phrase put to it before, but it fit. Always nice to hear the
word "best" associated with his name, anyway.

"I guess you could call it that," he said, "although I
don't think that's what we've got here."

"So, tell me, what do we have here?"

"Well, sir, basically someone has put together something that I call the 'Archimedes Effect.'" Jay saw the
blank look on the general's face. "From Archimedes'
quote. 'Give me a lever long enough, and a place to stand,
and I will move the world'?" The general still looked
blank. "It's technically called a Distributed Computer Project, or DCP, a piece of software that runs on thousands,
maybe tens of thousands, of different computers. The program hunts for answers, or, in this case, scenarios, for how
to crack Army base security, and when it gets them, it spits
them back out. Those are the 'lever long enough,' if you
see what I mean."

General Ellis nodded. "Tens of thousands?" he asked.
"How does it do that?"

"The software is distributed by a server. After it gets run
on the host computers, it sends partial work-packets until
the job is complete. At that point, the server redirects the
packets back to the server, where pieces of the solution are
put together."

The general frowned.

"The idea was first used in the late nineties. The Search
for Extraterrestrial Intelligence sent out a DCP that worked
to search streams of radio-telescope data they'd collected

for signals. They'd send out a block of information that was a portion of the search area, and the software on the host machine would process it whenever it wasn't busy doing something else."

The general was still frowning. *Better reset the listening clock here, Jay, or you'll put the man to sleep.* "The result was like having a huge supercomputer, but broken up into lots of small units."

"Okay, I got that part—but where are these machines?"

"All over the world. The way it works is the attacker put the thing on the Internet, and people who thought it might be amusing downloaded it. And the interesting part is, whoever did it put it out in the open, disguised as a computer game—a science-fiction scenario called *The War Against the Bugs*. Only, the designs of the alien bases, in a galaxy far away, were the same as those of Army bases on Earth."

"How did they get the specs of the real bases?"

"That's the real question, isn't it? I'm working on that." Which was true. He still didn't have a clue, but he was working on it.

"Um. Anyway," Jay continued, "the computers sent their information back to the originator, automatically taking advantage of their Internet connection. With most of the civilian high-speed cable and dedicated phone lines, you are linked to the the net all the time. Firewalls stop stuff coming in, but not a DCP going out. That's the beauty of it."

The general nodded.

"Since the game is pretty high-tech, it appealed to hardcore gamers, people who have fairly powerful machines, and people who are used to playing games where cracking security is part of the, um, fun."

"Go on."

"This is how you set it up: Okay, here is an alien military base on the planet Alpha-Omega Prime. Here are the specs for its computers, security devices, the timing of its patrols, all like that. You are the leader of the terran underground forces on this world, and they are getting ready to attack Earth. Your mission is to bypass their security and delay their plans by crippling their bases. How would you do it?"

"You tellin' me our Army base was cracked open by a buncha *video-game* geeks who know jack*shit* about military procedures?"

Jay gave a little cough to cover a grin. The general seemed to be forgetting that Jay himself was a video-game geek. "Well, yeah, basically, that's it. The average game player might not be too knowledgeable about such stuff, but give ten thousand of them a few dozen cracks at something? A solution, if it's out there, is apt to come out eventually. Whoever ran the program had the stats on what was most likely to work, and exactly how to do it."

General Ellis shook his head again and looked at Jay. "Game players are breaking in the Army's bases for fun. Crap. What next?"

Jay nodded. He had to admit, it was brilliant. And the attacker who came up with the idea? He had to be pretty sharp. This was the first such DCP Jay had seen used this way. Once word got out, though, there'd probably be others.

Jay continued: "The bad news is, half-a-dozen other 'alien enclaves' are in the game, so I'm guessing maybe some or all of those are cloned from real military bases, too. The Army better change security protocols on these before anybody makes another run. I don't know which alien base corresponds to which real one, or even if they are all real, but somebody needs to work that out."

"You talk to the Army's computer security so they can do that, PDQ."

" 'All your base are belong to us,' " Jay said.

"What"

"Sorry. It's an old joke, from my college days."

"Son, there ain't nothing about this is remotely funny."

"No, sir." Jay kept a straight face, even though he thought it *was* pretty humorous. But then, it wasn't *his* ox getting gored. . . .

"So, son, is there any way to figure out where these games were sending their answers?"

Jay gave the general a little shrug. "It's tricky—if this had been Real World, it'd be kind of like a bloodhound trying to follow a convict who jumped into the river, then split himself into a thousand pieces the next time he came out onto land, spewing red pepper behind him all the while. He wasn't making it easy."

Ellis nodded.

"Plus, he sent the incoming signals back to other gamers to cross-check the results before they were eventually routed back—so, basically, they go back and forth like balls at a championship tennis match. I'll take a closer look at the code, and we've got folks already trying to track 'em, but if I had to guess, I'd say somebody smart enough to set this up was probably smart enough to use cutouts and bounces—leapfrogging from one server to another, changing comsat repeaters, and winding up on a private server that is shut down by now anyhow. We might not be able to untangle it, and even if we do, the physical location could be a rented apartment in Boring, Oregon, that's been empty for a week. Might have to go at it another way."

Ellis looked grim. "Stay on this, son. It's a big deal. We can't have folks attacking our bases, blowing things up, and hurtin' people. See my aide, get the contact information for our computer people."

The general stood. The audience was over.

Jay also stood. Well, he had gone up against a lot of clever bad guys, and he had always come out on top. He figured he'd manage to run this one down, too—well, maybe once he got a nice, long nap in, anyway. . . .

Net Force Shooting Range
Quantico, Virginia

"What you shooting there, General? An old hogleg?"

John Howard smiled at Abe Kent. "Well, General, sir, it is a revolver, but it's not exactly an antique."

Kent moved over to stand next to Howard, and the two men looked at the handgun Howard had just put on the shooting bench. Before he had moved on, Howard had held the position Kent now had—head of Net Force's military arm. Though now that they were being run by the Marines instead of the National Guard, it was a horse of a different color, sure enough. Kent and Howard went way back. The reason Kent even had the job was that John had gone to bat for him.

Howard lifted the pistol and held it out to Kent. It was deeply blued, almost black, and had a barrel that appeared to be rectangular rather than round, with some fancy engraving on the cylinder, which was unfluted. The grip was carved wood, with finger grooves.

"Nice."

"It's a Skorpion," Howard said. "Made by Roger Hunziker and finished by Gary Reeder. Reeder puts out some of the best custom guns in the country, if not the world. This one is multicaliber. It'll shoot .38's, .38 Special, 9mm, .357 Magnums, even .380 auto if you're desperate—got these neat spring devices in the chambers, lines the ammo up properly. The original design was a little different, called a Medusa, from Phillips & Rodgers, down in Texas. They got into other things—our electronic hearing protectors? Those are made by Hunziker, same guy who built the Medusa. They realized they could do better by producing parts and electronics. Most of the DoD's headphones come from them. Crank up the electronics, you can hear a mouse sneeze across the street, yet still cut off the noise of a shot. Great if you're a hunter out in the woods listening for game. Smart move on his part, given the diminishing gun culture. But the revolver design was good enough that Reeder picked it up for a little while. I had a Medusa, but I lent it to a friend in the Army who got posted to South America as an advisor in one of the drug wars."

Howard paused for a few seconds. "He didn't make it back," he said.

"Sorry."

"How it goes when you put on the uniform."

Kent nodded. He knew.

"Anyway, I went looking for a replacement, and found this. Captain Fernandez is always giving me a hard time about old tech, but I'm a wheelgunner."

"Nothing wrong with that. If it comes down to side arms in battle, you're gonna be in deep shit anyhow, doesn't much matter which one you have."

"I dunno. You ever read Ed McGivern's book *Fast and Fancy Revolver Shooting*?"

"Can't say I have."

"He was a trick shooter, back in the 1930s. He could throw a big juice can up in the air, nail it six times with a double-action revolver before it hit the ground. Used to have two guys throw up two cans each at the same time, he'd hit all four of 'em on the way down. Could cut a playing card thrown at him edge-on in half in the air. When he was in a real hurry, he could crank off five rounds into a hand-sized target in two fifths of a second, using a standard S&W .38 Special right out of the box. Not nearly as much gun as this one." He waved at the Skorpion.

"No kidding?"

"That was just the fancy up-close stuff. With a little more power—a .357 Magnum or a .38-44? He could keep all the hits on a man-sized target at more than two hundred and fifty meters. Man says he can't hit anything with a handgun? Not the gun's fault, nor God's."

"Don't start that again," Kent said, but he smiled to show it was a joke.

Howard returned the smile. "I'm telling you, Abe, our church is different."

"I've heard that one before. Right up there with people trying to set me up on a blind date saying, 'She's got a great personality.' "

Howard laughed. "Speaking of which, my wife has this friend. . . ."

Kent groaned. "Don't go down that road, John. Please."

Howard laughed again.

"So, let's see if you can shoot this here antique."

"You ain't got much room to talk, old son. That slab-side Colt has been around for a while, too."

Both men laughed.

Gunny's amplified voice said, "You better leave that fancy shootin' iron with me to get the smart-gun electronics installed, General, sir."

"Bullshit I will," Howard said under his breath. "Mess up a perfectly good gun with all that safety crap?"

"I heard that, sir," Gunny said. "It's regulations."

"Not for me, it isn't!" Howard yelled. "I don't work for you anymore. The rule doesn't say any piece that comes into the range has to be screwed up, only the ones that Net Force ops carry! And I'm not even sure that applies to the military anyhow!"

"I don't think you have to yell, John," Abe Kent said. "I do believe our shooting bench is bugged."

"He's right," Gunny said. He added a nasty smoker's laugh.

"Them cigarettes are going to kill you, Gunny, if I don't beat them to it!" Howard said.

"Let's shoot. We can pretend the targets are Gunny."

"I heard that. Sirs."

3

With Marissa Lowe seated next to him on the bleachers watching the fencers, Thorn was about as happy as he figured a man could get. A beautiful woman who loved him and was willing to marry him, a warm seat watching a bunch of top competitors fencing with foils, épées, and sabers, and no place else he had to be. Life was good.

"When is Jamal supposed to come up?" Marissa asked.

"Pretty soon," Thorn said. "Ah, there he is now—over there." He pointed.

"He's black," she said.

"So are you, last time I looked."

"You didn't mention that before."

"You didn't know you were black?"

"I *will* hit you, Tommy."

"Okay, okay, I didn't want you overcome with adoration." He smiled, but she punched him in the shoulder anyhow.

"Ow. You CIA types are all brute force and violence, aren't you?"

"With a word in the right ear, I can have you knee-capped, Tommy."

He laughed. Funny. Smart. Beautiful. Couldn't get much better than that, could it? She even liked fencing, though she had just started learning herself.

"Jamal is warming up. His match'll start in a couple minutes."

"This is a good thing you're doing here, Tommy."

He shrugged. Jamal had real talent. He was good with a foil, but outstanding with an épée, and for an inner-city D.C. kid who came to the sport at the ripe old age of twelve, only four years at it, without access to world-class teachers, that was pretty amazing.

Thorn had made a lot of money with some of the software his companies had developed before he went to work for Net Force. Sponsoring a few poor kid fencers around the country so they could get good teachers and gear, and covering their travel to tournaments? That wasn't much. He'd grown up poor on the rez himself; he knew what it cost just to learn to fence, to say nothing of what it took to compete at a high level. He'd been sent across country a couple of times with money raised from bake sales and car washes. This was the least he could do to pay that back.

Jamal walked toward the piste, the metal mesh-covered strip laid out on the floor.

"Here he goes. Watch."

Some of this Thorn still hadn't gotten used to. In his day, all the equipment was pretty much the same as it had been for decades: a blade, connected to a body cord running up your sleeve and down your back, plugging into a floor reel you had to watch out for on fleches or quick re-treats, which in turn connected to the scoring box. These days, though, everything was pretty much wireless—well, almost. The body cord still ran up the sleeve and down the back, but now it plugged into a little box each fencer wore at the small of his or her back.

Used to be one of your teammates helped hook you up, spoke some encouraging words in your ear, maybe rubbed your shoulders before you fenced. These days you were more like a Christian sent out to face the lions—on your own. . . .

Jamal stepped up to the en garde line. His opponent, another youth of about the same age, did likewise. The director, a young man who looked to be in his early twenties, told them, in French, to salute, don their masks, and come to guard.

Jamal brought his épée up to his chin, saluted his opponent, the director, and the scorers. He also gave a quick flick toward the spectators before pulling his helmet into place.

"Êtes-vous prêts?" the director asked.

Both fencers nodded.

"Allez!"

"Watch this," Thorn said.

There were a lot of ways to approach épée: fast and furious, slow and cautious, subtle, strong, leverage, speed. Jamal, like most fencers, could use a variety of techniques and styles, but he preferred slow and cautious. He excelled at capitalizing on his opponents' mistakes—and he was very, very good at helping them to make mistakes.

So far, throughout the previous bouts, he had been very slow to strike. Now, however, as soon as the director gave the command, he closed the distance as fast as he could, his tip licking out and around his opponent's blade and landing solidly in the middle of his mask.

"What happened?" Marissa asked.

Thorn chuckled. "Took him by surprise," he said.

"I could see that. But how?"

Thorn smiled. "Set him up. Most fencing matches are pools—round-robin in the early going—and all fencers watch their upcoming opponents, sizing them up as they face the other people in their pool. Jamal simply changed his tactics here. He knew that this guy had him pegged as a counterpuncher and would be looking for him to once again be cautious, to wait until he had a sense of his opponent before really taking the attack to him. So he did what any good fencer would do: He crossed him up, setting up an expectation in his opponent and then using that to his own advantage."

Marissa frowned. "Seems kind of dangerous, doesn't it?" she asked. "Seems like the other guy could do the same thing."

Thorn grinned. "Exactly. And that's what makes it so fun."

On the strip, the director had awarded the touch to Jamal and resumed the fencing. At his command to begin, Jamal once again took the attack to his opponent. He took two rapid steps forward, his blade already engaging his opponent's, pressed once, twice, and a third time, inside, outside, and back to the inside, then released the blade with a spank.

His tip shot toward his opponent's inside wrist in a feint, then darted down toward his foot in another feint. As his opponent thrust toward his head, Jamal brought his blade back up, meeting his opponent's in a partial bind. Deflecting it to the side and ending up striking the wrist.

Touché, Jamal.

"Nice touch," Thorn said.

Beside him, Marissa smiled. "Hey, I could see that one!"

Thorn laughed. "Yep, that was style over speed all the way."

"So," Marissa said, "you want to predict this next touch?"

"Aw, this one's easy. Jamal will revert to form. His opponent started out expecting him to be cautious and he scored two quick touches by surprising him. Now his opponent will be looking for another quick attack. Jamal will take advantage of that. Watch."

The director signaled the touch, reset the fencers on their guard lines, and again gave the command to fence. Once again, Jamal rushed forward, but this time his whole advance was a feint. His tip circled his opponent's, darting in as though he were setting up for another mask shot.

His opponent thrust forward, expecting Jamal to continue pressing and aiming to strike his forearm as he came in, but this time Jamal pulled up, his blade pressing up and out in another bind.

His opponent's tip brushed harmlessly past the outer edge of his sleeve, while Jamal's tip circled completely around the blade, maintaining contact and pressure the entire time, and ended up landing solidly on the inside of the wrist.

"See?" Thorn said. "Anticipation will get you killed. My first—and best—teacher taught me that. Jamal is setting up expectations and taking advantage of them."

Marissa nodded. "So how do you avoid that yourself?" she asked.

Thorn shrugged. "Depends on your philosophy. Western mind-set: Anticipate everything. Eastern mind-set: Anticipate nothing. Me, I used to follow the Western way. Very active mind, always thinking, always rethinking. These days, I'm much more Eastern: calmer, flowing, more in the moment."

He looked over at her and smiled at the expression on her face. "Keep fencing," he said. "You'll see."

The rest of the bout went quickly. Jamal had his opponent off guard and on his heels, and took full advantage of it.

Thorn and Marissa went up to him at the end of the bout.

"Hey, Jamal—great match."

"Mr. Thorn! Thanks for coming!" He looked at Marissa, and there was no disguising the teenager's appreciation for her.

"Jamal, this is Marissa Lowe. My fiancée."

God, he loved saying that. He'd never seriously considered getting married before he'd met her. Now, the idea of not having her around most of the time was painful.

"That's too bad," Jamal said. "You being taken, I mean."

Marissa laughed. "Jamal, I'm old enough to be your mother!"

"No, ma'am, I can't see that at all. You twenty-five? Twenty-six maybe? My sister. Stepsister."

She laughed again. "Twenty-five? Not for a long, long time. You don't have much trouble with women, do you?"

"No, ma'am, I haven't so far." He flashed a bright smile at her.

"When you get through making moves on my girl, I'll buy you a soda," Thorn said.

"Yes, sir, I could use one. Hard work, waving that sword around. Maybe I could show Ms. Lowe how, if she's interested?"

"Down, Jamal. I'm way ahead of you."

They all chuckled.

Gibson's Sporting Club
Quantico, Virginia

"Jesus H. Christ! What are you shooting over there, Carruth? It sounded like a damned bomb going off!"

Carruth smiled. "What's the matter, Milo, a little noise bother you?"

"When it about blows my damned ears out through my headphones, hell, yeah, it bothers me!"

Milo, a short fireplug of a man, ambled down the firing line. It was just the two of them at the range on this rainy Saturday morning. Milo was ex-Army, a green hat who'd done his time before, during, and just after the second Gulf War, and so Carruth had respect for him, even if he was Army and not Navy. The man had been shot at, he had shot back, and that was worth something in Carruth's world. They bumped into each other at the range now and then, but they weren't drinking buddies or anything, though they could slap coins at one another.

Carruth held up the new handgun. "This here is your basic 500 Maximum, aka the BMF. Custom-made by Gary Reeder, down in Arizona."

"I heard of him. BMF? I bet I know what that stands for."

"Best-made firearm," Carruth said, his face serious. Then he grinned.

"Looks like a Ruger Bisley," Milo said. "Stainless steel?"

"Yep, about a five-inch barrel, but the frame is heavier, and stretched a little, on account of the round being a tad on the large side." He tabled the revolver and picked up a round of the ammo. "Fifty-caliber. This particular specimen is a 435-grain LBT-hard-cast gas-checked bullet made by Cast Performance—developed by John Linebaugh—for the elephant herds in Wyoming."

"Ain't no elephant herds in Wyoming," Milo said.

"Exactly."

Milo shook his head. "I stepped right into that one."

Carruth grinned again. "Forty-eight grains of powder for a muzzle velocity around sixteen hundred feet per second."

"Christ."

He handed the round to Milo.

"Lord, it makes a .45 auto round look like a runt. Bigger around and twice as tall. You expecting to run into a rampaging water buffalo out on the Mall?"

"I wouldn't use one of those if I did." He nodded at the cartridge Milo examined. "*That* sucker will punch right through a water buffalo from beak to bunghole and knock down a lion standing behind him. It's a bit stout for everyday use. Here."

He picked another round up from the bench and handed it to Milo. It was a little shorter. "This is the carry load. The 510-GNR, an itty-bitty 350-grain LBT bullet, a mere thirty-three grains of powder pushing only thirteen hundred and fifty feet per second. That's Reeder's proprietary load. The big one is the elephant-stopper. There's a medium version, halfway between, pretty good for brown bear. The littlest one? That's the sissy load—for people only."

Carruth picked up the revolver and offered that to Milo.

Milo said, "You ever tap anybody with it?"

"So far, no."

"Not all that heavy," the ex–Green Beret said. "What's it weigh?"

"Right at three pounds empty. Got five ports milled into

the barrel to help with the recoil, though they kinda make it look like a dragon sneezing flame. Piece costs a couple house payments in a good neighborhood. Want to cook off a few?"

Milo hefted the piece. "A 435-grain bullet with forty-eight grains of powder? You got a crowbar to pry it out when it recoils and buries the front sight in my forehead?"

Carruth laughed. "Yeah, it's a wrist-breaker, all right. Your basic .357 Magnum? Six foot/pounds of recoil, with a 125-grain round. Clint Eastwood's Dirty Harry .44 Magnum? Fourteen foot/pounds. Casull's .454? Thirty-one foot/pounds. This honker? Talking about . . . *seventy-two* foot/pounds."

"Damn," Milo said. He handed the revolver back to Carruth.

Carruth laughed again.

Milo shook his head. "What's the point, man? I mean, it's way too much gun for anything around here—hell, on the whole continent, the one below us, and those across the nearest two ponds."

"Better to have it and not need it than to need it and not have it," Carruth said.

"Yeah, uh huh, right." He gave the taller man a look.

"Okay. I'm six-two, two-thirty-five, and I can bench-press four hundred pounds. Fifty-caliber is the biggest round allowed by law for a handgun. It's a man's piece and I can handle it. No matter what's coming down the alley in my direction? I can stop it. Lion busts out of the zoo, I can drop it faster than you can blink. Guy in body armor wants to play? I can knock him down and break something even if it doesn't penetrate the weave—it'd be like getting hit with a sledgehammer. If I need to shoot somebody, he will *stay* shot. I like that."

Milo shoot his head again. "You fuckin' SEALs, you're all fuckin' crazy, you know that?"

Carruth nodded. "Oh, yeah. Big-time." What he didn't tell Milo was that he had a custom-made horsehide holster and belt made by Kramer Leather for the BMF, and that it *was*, in fact, his carry gun. Of course, in D.C., any gun was too much—they frowned on concealed carry, or even owning the suckers unless you were in the employ of the local police or some federal law enforcement agency, or were willing to fill out a shitload of paper, get printed, and wait a year for the FBI check to come back. . . . Well, fuck 'em. What they didn't know wouldn't hurt him.

Yeah, the piece was a bit heavy on his right hip, but he was big enough to hide it under a jacket or windbreaker. Milo was right, it was too much gun for anything he was going to run into, but he carried it, and the real reason?

Because he could. And someday, he expected he would get a chance to cook with it when it counted.

He expected that would be pretty soon, too.

4

Abe Kent sat in his new apartment in the city and stared at the guitar in the chair. He had taken it out of its case and set it there and, no doubt about it, it was beautiful. He had done enough research when he'd been chasing the Georgian, Natadze, so that he knew what a good guitar looked like, and he liked listening to people who were adept with them, but he had no musical talent himself.

And yet here he was, with a ten-thousand-dollar guitar.

He sighed. He had taken the instrument out and looked at it a dozen times since he'd gotten it. He didn't know why, but he felt as if he somehow owed it to the man he'd killed to . . . make use of the thing. He could sell it, or give it to charity, but neither of those felt right. And if he was going to keep an instrument worth that much? It ought not to be sitting in the corner in its case gathering dust.

He sighed again. It didn't make any sense, but he knew what he had to do. He stood, picked up the guitar, and put it back into the case.

* * *

The store was small, in a sleepy neighborhood on the outskirts of D.C., in a little commercial strip mall backed by a residential neighborhood. It was called the Fretboard. It had wrought-iron grates on the windows, curvy patterns made to look like a design element rather than bars to keep thieves out. There were several neon signs in the windows advertising products whose names Kent mostly didn't recognize.

A bell chimed as he entered. The place smelled like fresh-cut fir, and there were a couple of customers at the counter talking to a long-haired clerk of eighteen or nineteen. The clerk had a soul-patch that had been dyed green, and maybe nine piercings in his ears and nose.

A third man stood nearby, picking out tunes on an electric guitar—he was pretty good. The guitarist was playing a collage, a medley of old rock numbers Kent mostly recognized, and the clerk was laughing.

He looked up and saw Kent with his guitar case. "You lookin' for Jennifer?" he asked, still smiling.

Kent nodded.

"In the back, down the hall, door on the right."

"Thanks."

Kent moved down the hall. He opened the door and stepped into a small practice room with thick egg-carton soundproofing on the walls and ceiling. The sound of the electric guitar went silent as he closed the door behind him.

A woman sat on a stool with one foot propped on a little metal stand, and she would be Jennifer Hart. He had found her through the local classical guitar society. She was at least fifty, and even though that was a decade younger than he was, she was the closest teacher he could find locally anywhere near his own age. Somehow, the idea of it being somebody younger than some of the boots he owned just didn't seem right. Certainly not some kid with lip hair dyed green and enough hardware in his face to build a waffle iron.

The woman was trim, dressed in tennis shoes, jeans, and a button-up long-sleeved white shirt. Her hair was to her shoulders, brown, with a fair amount of gray in it. She had a lot of smile lines on her face. A classical guitar rested on her left leg.

"Mr. Kent?"

"Yes." He was in civilian clothes and he hadn't mentioned that he was in the military, much less a general.

She put the guitar onto a stand, stood, and stuck out her hand.

She was short, maybe five-two or -three. "Hi. I'm Jennifer Hart."

"Pleased to meet you." He transferred his guitar case to his left hand and shook hands with her. She had a strong grip.

There was a second stool and she pointed at it. "Have a seat."

He set his case down and then perched on the stool.

"That's an expensive case," she said. "Is the guitar handmade?"

"Yes, ma'am."

"Please, call me Jen. Could I see it?"

He popped the six latches open and opened the lid, lifted the guitar free, and offered it to her.

She took it. "What a beautiful instrument! What kind of wood is that?"

"Port Orford cedar on top, Oregon myrtlewood on the sides and back. Made by a man named Les Stansell, out in the Pacific Northwest."

"May I?" She put it on her leg, preparing to play.

"Sure."

She did a little run on the fretboard, adjusted the tuning a hair, then played some kind of Spanish-y thing, short but impressive.

"Good tones. Nice basses and trebles, clean mid-range, great resonance. Sounds more like spruce than red cedar, though." She handed it back to him. "The top hasn't opened up yet. You haven't had it very long, have you?"

"No, ma'am—Jen."

She smiled. He liked the way her face crinkled.

She picked up her own instrument. It had the same color top, but the sides and back were much darker than his guitar, all brown and patterned. "This is also a cedar top, different than yours, but I've had it a while. See if you can hear the difference."

She played the same piece. It was warmer this time, darker, not as bright. Both sounded great, but there was a definite difference. The bass notes seemed deeper, fuller, and the high tones somehow richer.

Done, she said, "My instrument was made by Jason Pickard, it's got claro walnut sides and back—makes it a little mellower."

"What did you mean about the top opening up?"

"Well, that usually applies more to spruce than cedar, but basically, up to a point, classical guitars sound better with age. A brand-new one that sounds pretty good will, after a few years of playing it, usually sound better."

"Ah."

"How far along are you in your studies?"

He smiled. "What I know about playing it you could carve on the head of pin with a battle-ax."

A slight frown flitted across her face. "You're joking."

"No, ma'am. I don't even know how to tune it."

He had a pretty good idea of what bothered her. This guitar he had was expensive. Why would a man who didn't know how to play the thing put out big bucks for it until he was able to do it justice?

"The guitar was . . . a gift."

Now she frowned. "Somebody gave you a handmade guitar that runs what?—eight, ten thousand dollars?"

He nodded. "Yeah."

She raised an eyebrow. "They must really like you."

"Not so you'd notice in this case, I don't think."

She just stared, not speaking.

"It's a weird story."

"I'm not on the clock, Mr. Kent."

"Abe," he said.

She didn't even blink. "All right. Abe."

She waited.

He thought about it for a moment. He didn't know this

woman, he had no reason to sit here and spill his guts to her, but something about her manner invited intimacy. She seemed genuinely interested.

He took a deep breath. Who would it hurt? "The man who gave it to me was moments away from dying when he did so. The reason he was dying was because I had just shot him."

If that bothered her, it didn't show. "I thought you looked like police or military. Go on."

He wanted to grin again. He remembered a story he'd heard, about an ex-GI who had been involved in a shooting at his home. Guy had been jumped by some local bikers, so he'd pulled a piece and fired three rounds, killing one of them. Friends called later to talk to the shooter, and the comments ranged on one end from folks saying how awful it must have been to have to shoot and kill a fellow human being, to old soldiering buddies who said, "What kind of grouping did you get?" Jennifer Hart's comment sounded more like the latter than the former.

"I work for a government agency. The man—who was shooting at me when I shot him—was a hired killer. He was also a very good classical guitarist."

"And you feel that you need to learn how to play it? I don't see the reason."

He didn't blame her. He didn't see the reason, either, exactly. And what could he tell her? Would she understand that Natadze was a good enemy? Smart, tough, adept.

He shrugged. "It seems like the right thing to do."

She nodded, as if understanding exactly what moved him, though it may have simply been acceptance. For the moment, anyway. "Okay. Let's get started, then. Can you read music?"

He smiled again. "Not a note."

"TAB?"

"That a soft drink?"

She laughed. He enjoyed being able to make her do that. "Not exactly," she said. "It's a kind of notation for stringed instruments—guitars, lutes, like that. We'll get into theory as we go. Let's do the basic stuff first. There are six strings on your guitar, numbered usually from the thinnest and highest to the thickest and lowest. When you hold the guitar on your leg—I'll show the basic position—the lowest bass string will be up. Going down from that toward the floor, the strings are usually tuned to E, A, D, G, B, and E, in that order. Here's a way to remember them: Elvis Ate Dynamite, Good-Bye, Elvis. . . ."

Kent grinned again. He could remember that. Hell, he could remember Elvis Himself. Saw him once, in Las Vegas . . .

Louisiana Jay's Dig
Whispering Dunes, Egypt

Jay stood at the top of the tallest sand dune, looking at the huge archaeology dig below. Hundreds of natives wearing flowing white robes toiled in the hot sun, carefully unmasking the ruins of the temple beneath the sand. Some used shovels, some used small hand trowels, and others used whisk brooms made of papyrus to brush away dust on the stones.

Right out of an old adventure movie. Or maybe one about mummies and tomb raiders . . .

Like most of his VR scenarios, it wasn't really a temple but a metaphor for something else—in this case a huge comparison database.

The work hadn't been easy, and the pressure was on.

Because the distributed program had mixed and matched various features of U.S. military bases around the globe to create the alien bases, the question was: How many more bases had been incorporated into the alien designs? How many more potential targets were there?

He would be passing on what he already had to the Army's computer people pretty soon, but another run wouldn't hurt.

If Jay could deconstruct the game and identify features
of the bases that hadn't been attacked, the good guys might
be able to get ahead of the bad guys.

Unfortunately, as with every solution, there were problems.

First was finding copies of the game software. The program hadn't been released all at once—new bases had
been constructed and sent out to the game players in in-
stallments. To complicate things, the game server that had
sent the files out had shut itself down when the first base
was attacked. In addition, the game files were coded to stop
working after a certain date.

So not only did he have to find copies of the software,
he had to keep them from shutting down as well.

Big problems are our specialty.

His grin grew wider, and the desert wind blew pieces of
sand into his teeth.

Several servers on I2's West Coast backbone had been
taken off-line for maintenance a week or so before. He'd
managed to snag the game variants by copying their hard
drives and sifting them for the program. He'd changed the
computer's date before starting them up again.

He'd also gotten several copies from a VR site that
billed itself as a multiplayer on-line game museum. The
site had used similar tactics to freeze the alien games.

After all of his efforts he figured he had about thirty
percent or so of the games that had been released. He'd
popped them onto a closed network loop and then had
gone after problem number two.

Jay looked over toward the main encampment. White
tents fluttered in the desert wind. One was larger than the
rest, and in front of it stood dozens of glass tables, each
one covered with models. Scores of heavily armed guards
patrolled the areas around the models.

In order to figure out which military bases made up the
alien bases, he needed their specifications, security, entrances, and exits.

And no one had wanted to give him the information. He turned and spit the grit out of his mouth.

It was a classic military move, closing the barn door after the horse had gotten out. Here he was, trying to track down terrorists who had attacked their bases, but no one would give him information to do it.

He'd been tempted to hack their database, but had decided that it wasn't worth the trouble. So he'd e-mailed General Ellis instead, taking him up on his offer of more resources. In the meantime, he had gone after the information through conventional means, compiling lists of military bases from FBI archives and gathering site plans filed with land-use and planning commissions.

After all, one could take many paths to the same destination.

He'd started a team of techs transferring the data to VR, and then he'd adapted the desert scene to actively deconstruct each of the bases in the game.

And then, wonder of wonders, Ellis had come through. True to his word, the old man had freed up stats on every Army base in the country: buildings, security orders-of-the-day, and even electronic passwords—all as of the date of the first attacks, of course—nothing current. Still, it wasn't a bad compromise, all things considered. Jay had his data, and the military kept its secrets.

Right now his VR scenario was running on the first or second iteration of the game. The sun beat down and white-robed workers measured features of the temple—which was actually the alien base—and scurried to carry those measurements to others who were near the models. The measurements would be adjusted to scale, and then compared to each model, one piece at a time.

It was a huge amount of information to process, exactly what VR was best at.

"Dr. Jay, Dr. Jay!" One of the natives by the model waved.

Jay headed over, feeling sweat bead on his back in the hot sun.

The man pointed at one of the models, a squared-off
base set against a hillside. There was a main entrance, well
guarded, and along the side was another entrance, which
looked like it was used for vehicles.

The native gestured at the entrance and handed Jay the
piece of paper.

Jay read the measurements on the scrap of paper and
looked over at the entrance. He pulled a set of calipers
from his pocket and measured the doorway.

It was a match.

The VR jock looked down at the base designation. It
was in Germany.

Then, as he watched, it flickered slightly, the doorway
shifting size, shrinking. It held for a few moments, and
then shifted back to being larger.

He frowned. The models weren't supposed to shift—
unless—

Jay paused the VR scenario, and everything froze while
he focused on the model. He triggered some code and
abruptly the model on the table grew larger, until he was
standing at the entrance, scaled to appropriate size.

He walked forward and tapped the left side of the entrance. A tiny window appeared midair, spelling out the
gate's dimensions. Underneath the black figures were
blue ones.

Let's see. . . . Aha—

The blue figures were the ones he'd pulled from public
sources, and the black ones were from the files that General Ellis had arranged for him to receive. He'd kept the
public records in the few instances where they differed.

And they were different. The black figures read sixteen
feet, eight inches. The blue ones read eighteen feet six
inches. A simple transposition.

Could it be the wrong base?

He checked the other parameters—distance to the rock
wall, thickness of the door, composition of the wall. No.
The match was good.

Which was very interesting indeed.

Whether it was the military's measurements that were correct, or whether the public records were right, wasn't what was important—the difference of twenty-two inches didn't matter. What was important was that the figures from the *game* matched the military numbers.

Whoever had coded the game had used the *military's* files.

Nothing like finding a clue to brighten your morning. The devil was in the details, and today Old Scratch was on Jay's side. He'd take it. But the general was sure gonna be pissed off about this.

5

Carruth frowned. "I was lookin' forward to collecting that nuke. What happened?"

Rachel Lewis, dressed down in civilian clothes, smiled. Collecting the nuke had never been in the cards, though she hadn't bothered to let Carruth in on that. They were in a booth in a small cafe on a dead-end street behind a new strip mall. Lewis liked to find places where the service was terrible and business was slow, but hadn't found anything like that here in Alexandria. She'd chosen this place instead because it was frequented by locals, not tourists, and was quiet during this time of the day. You could dawdle here for an hour and nobody would bother you, or likely sit close enough to overhear you.

She said, "The Chairman of the Joint Chiefs pulled on Net Force's leash sooner than I expected. Jay Gridley, their best guy, is on it, and by now he will have figured out how I set the game up, and he will have run with it. The brass are peeing all over themselves, they'll give him whatever he asks for, and he's quick. He'll track the DCP—he's bound to be able to pick up early copies of it—and he'll know which bases we used."

"Is he any threat?"

"Not to me. Oh, I'll admit that he's got some moves, but so do I, and I have the advantage—I know who he is."

"Well . . . crap. So that means we can't use any of the stuff we got?"

"Not from the original game scenario. We have two sets of follow-ups. Gridley will get the first game, and, eventually, he'll think to look for more DCPs, but those are almost ready, another day or two, we can harvest them and trash the rest. He can't backwalk any of them to me."

Carruth nodded, sipped at his coffee, frowned. "This tastes better than most coffee you buy me, Lewis."

She smiled. "I aim to please." She didn't bother explaining her choice of diners to him.

"So, what now?"

"I'll get you the stats on the next target the day after tomorrow. The Army will have upped security everywhere, but we factored that in. Gridley will give them a list of the first round of targets and they will think that's it, so that's where they'll beef things up. They are as predictable as winter snow in North Dakota."

Carruth shook his head. "You really got a hard-on for the Army, don'tcha, hon?"

She fixed him with a stare that could etch glass. "First, that's none of your business. Second, you call me 'hon' again, you are going to be looking for your balls."

He chuckled. "You want to wrestle, I got a hundred and thirty pounds and a whole lotta muscle on you, Lewis, plus I'm a trained Navy SEAL killer. You some kinda kung-fu master, you gonna toss me around like a beach ball?"

"Look under the table."

He bent, looked. Laughed.

"Not much gun," he said once he'd sat back up. "Little snub-nose like that. Not very accurate."

"This close, a .38 Special with +P hollowpoints is as

much gun as I need. I'd have to try to miss, and that monster piece you carry? By the time you haul it out, I could put five in you, reload, and be halfway through the next cylinder. Even a big strong guy like you would find it passing uncomfortable picking the bullets out of your crotch."

She didn't mention that she could shoot well enough with the little snubbie to keep all the bullets on a man-sized target at fifty meters all day long. If he didn't think the gun was dangerous farther away than under a table? That might be to her advantage someday. A lot of people underestimated how accurate a snub-nosed revolver could be—in the right hands.

"I do like a beautiful woman who talks dirty," he said. But he didn't call her "hon."

This was her show, and if he behaved, he would come away rich, and he knew it. Otherwise, she was pretty sure he'd have already made a move on her. Guys like Carruth thought with their little heads for most things, most of the time. He could blow up a bridge, sink a ship, kick ass, and take names fine, but outside of his narrow range, he wasn't a thinker. He needed a leader, and he was smart enough to know that much. Which was just what she needed in a lieutenant—not too smart, not too stupid—so she couldn't complain too much—as long as he knew his place. And that place *wasn't* lying next to her in a bed. . . .

"So, what, in the meanwhile?" he asked.

"Stand by," she said. She stood and dropped a five-dollar bill on the scarred Formica table to pay for their coffee. "I'll call you on the secure cell."

"Yes, ma'am," he said. He gave her a snappy salute, grinning all the while.

He might be a problem eventually, but "eventually" the sun was going to go nova and Earth was going to be turned into a burned-out cinder. Worry about that when the time came.

As she headed toward her car, a politically correct hybrid import, Lewis considered the situation. She had anticipated Net Force's involvement, of course. General

Hadden had co-opted the organization, taking it away from the FBI, for just such problems. And she knew Gridley's rep—he had been two years ahead of her in school, already the boy wonder, and at this level, it was like playing chess against a master at the top of his game—you didn't make a mistake and hope it would get by, because it almost never would. But she could handle Gridley. What was important was that they be able to sting another Army base or three, and soon. Once was a fluke. Two or three times, those were selling points. Some terrorist who wanted to make a big statement by knocking over a U.S. Army base and who could get funding? She'd have to beat them away with a stick. . . .

Revenge—and money for doing it? That was as good as it got. .

U.S. Army's MILDAT Computer Center
The Pentagon
Washington, D.C.

Jay walked down another seemingly endless corridor on his way to see his liaison with the Army's MILDAT. His escort this time, a buzz-cut trooper with "Wilcoxen" etched on his name badge, led the way. Another boots-on-the-ground reality trip, and why couldn't they do it in VR? The horse was gone; closing the barn door now wasn't going to help. You'd think that a computer guy, even an Army one, would be comfortable in VR.

He wasn't looking forward to the meeting, since he was going to have to tell this Captain Whoever that his network had been compromised. There was little doubt that it had been—the military records matched the specs he'd found in the alien game too cleanly for there to be any other option. Which meant that either the security work protecting the data had failed, or that someone inside the network had sold out. Social engineering was usually cheaper than hiring a first-class hacker, and a lot easier just to have somebody give you the stuff than working for it. Not as much fun, but easier.

And while being the bearer of bad news was a part of his job, the process of pointing out security holes and finding fault with a colleague's work was never fun. People tended to greet such news with less than cheery smiles.

Oh, Captain, by the way? All this expensive and dangerous crap everybody is running around trying to figure out? It came out of your *unit. Sorry, pal . . .*

"Here we are, sir," said the guard, indicating a frosted-glass door. The guard knocked.

Things could always be worse—I could be escorting people into the Pentagon, wondering when and if they were going to attack me.

A gorgeous and very well-built short-haired blonde opened the door. She was Jay's age, maybe a few years younger, and she smiled at Jay and his escort. The woman wore an Army uniform with captain's bars, and a name tag:

R. Lewis.

Whoa! When he'd seen the name in his datafile, "Captain R. Lewis," he had naturally assumed it was a man. There was a dumb mistake—he knew better.

"Another stray? Thanks, Willie."

"Anything that gets me to your door, ma'am." He nodded and left.

Lewis turned to Jay and all the focus was on him.

"Well, well, if it isn't Smokin' Jay Gridley," she said, "although I seem to recall that you never inhaled. Come on in."

Jay frowned. "We couldn't have met. I'd remember."

"We haven't. I'm Rachel Lewis. I was two years behind you at MIT."

"No shit?" Jay had actually attended most of college electronically, and right around the time MIT and CIT did their e-merge. He liked to joke about CIT being better, but in truth, he was technically a grad of both.

Jay followed her into the office. He noted how neat and tidy it was: books, shelves, everything in place. On her desk was a state-of-the art VR setup that rivaled his own, with a pair of Raptor-vision VR glasses hanging off the side, the word "prototype" stamped on it. They looked newer than the ones he had. He didn't much like that.

"No shit. I heard all about you in my classes."

"How'd you wind up in the Army?"

She sat at the desk and stretched, sprawling on her chair with an unself-conscious sensuality.

"Family biz. My father was career Army, my grandfather, great-grandfather, like that. I didn't have any brothers, so it was up to me."

Jay nodded absently. "Nice gear." He waved.

"I know one of the guys at Raptor—he keeps me up-to-date. Helps to know people."

She paused. "So how are things in crime these days?" She smiled and leaned forward. The top button on her uniform was undone and the gap, although small, was eye-catching.

Hello? Jay was surprised to find himself wanting to look. He'd had colleagues flirt with him before, and it usually took more than a pretty smile or nice hooters to call to him. Lewis was attractive, no question. A chemical thing, that was all.

"Exciting, Captain—a lot more than school."

"No need for formality here, Jay. Call me Rachel."

Hey, he was married now, with a son. No harm, no foul.

"Okay, *Rachel*." He paused. "Actually, I'm here—"

"Wait, wait—let me guess. You're here about the lost data." Had Ellis told her?

"You know?"

"You're not the only player in the game. One, I run a top-security network. Two, you are the top VR guy for Net Force, and your jurisdiction has recently changed to include the military. You could have come here to compliment me on a job well done, except, three, you don't look happy to be here, and—"

She leaned forward again.

"Four, I've been going over my security logs cross-checking traffic—and I noticed some extra packet requests from one of our nodes. It's a zero-sum dead end, a shuck. So we have a leak. I don't know how or who, but it's there."

"You already found it?" Well, well. Point for Lewis. Might be a little late, but at least she knew it before he told her. Competence had always been more attractive to him than just hot looks. Though those didn't hurt.

Yeah? You're married now, so it doesn't matter how much more attractive this makes her, now does it? Back away, goat-boy.

There was nothing wrong with *looking,* was there? Plus it was part of his job—he hadn't sought her out.

So why did he feel this little stab of guilt?

She reached down and pulled a second pair of Raptor goggles out of a drawer.

"I wanted to investigate it more fully myself before calling it in, but since you're here—feel up to a stroll?"

Jay didn't hesitate.

"Sure, let's go."

Who did she think she was talking to here? Did *he* feel up to it? He definitely felt up to it. Be good to get into VR anyway. No question who the better detective was here, after all, was there? As she'd soon find out.

Jay took the goggles.

It would be fun, showing her just how good he was.

Jay slipped the VR shades on his head, adjusting them so that the extra weight of the other gear—olfactory unit and tiny Harmon Kardon sound inserts—were balanced. Then Lewis handed him a small silver box with a strap attached.

"One of my new toys," she said, "Tactile Feedback Unit. Uses an inducer to stimulate basic skin sensation. They're not too good yet, but it adds."

Jay had heard about the units, but hadn't seen one yet. The basic principle was electric induction via magnetic fields. Unlike a full feelie suit, which used electrodes and localized temperature control to give sensation in VR and covered the entire body, TFUs were designed to do the same thing—without the suit. Nerve pathways were stimulated with magnetic fields and induced to create sensation. He'd heard they were being developed at the MIT media lab—apparently she'd kept close ties with the old school.

"It pays to support your alma mater," she said, grinning.

Despite the fact that he didn't want to be, he was impressed that she had the unit—units, plural.

She handed him a set of VR gloves and he finished suiting up.

He started to say something about his VR analogue, but decided to see what she'd come up with. Entering the Pentagon to see a computer specialist meant surrendering all data containers, and a close search of anything going out, so he'd had to leave his virgil and his data watch at the front desk. He carried copies of his usual VR avatars in them, along with his VR settings. Going into her scenario without them put him at a slight disadvantage, but it also meant she had to come up with something for him to wear in VR.

It would be interesting to see what she did.

"Ready?"

He gave her a thumbs-up, and activated his gear.

He was on a beach. The sun was nearly straight overhead, which put him closer to the equator, and it was hot. Apparently, the little TFUs worked fairly well. He could feel the sun's rays warming him, and it felt *right*. Impressive. A slight onshore breeze tickled his skin, cooling him—everywhere.

*Every*where? He looked down.

Naked as the proverbial, well, bad pun, jaybird.

He looked back up and to his right, and there was Rachel Lewis, also naked, walking in front of him. Her skin was slightly more tanned than she'd been in RW, but other than that, she looked exactly the same. Her figure, as seen from behind, more than delivered what her clothes had promised.

Whoa!

Most VR programmers tended to incorporate some aspect of fantasy in their avatars, particularly for a given scenario. When he played big-game hunter or 1930s pulp hero, Jay would amalgamate his own body's features onto other bodies, becoming someone else, rather than just himself.

The fact that she apparently didn't meant something. What, he didn't know, but it was interesting. *Very* interesting.

She turned and laughed.

"Oh, sorry, Jay," she said. "I'd forgotten the naked part—I usually run this one by myself."

Her front was just as spectacular as her back. Tanned skin, kissed lightly by the sun, had resulted in a beautiful spatter of freckles that topped, um, a bunch of other, um, most attractive attributes he probably ought not to be thinking about.

Jay was struck yet again by how much she looked like her RW counterpart. No enhancements that he could see. As far as he could tell, this was her for real.

He swallowed, feeling even warmer. *Cool off, Jay.*

"No problem," he said. "My wife Saji and I spent some time in Europe on a couple of clothing-optional beaches."

Managed to work Saji's name in there pretty good.

Still, he could feel himself starting to, ah, *react* to the sight of her, the surprise of it. Any second his avatar might begin registering his interest in a visible way.

Shit. Got to stop that.

She motioned for him to follow her, and turned, showing him her backside again as she started to walk.

Yes, that's it. Keep looking the other way.

"I've found that this works pretty good for tracking data packets."

He listened with half an ear as he reached up and tapped the side of his head. It felt slightly *wrong,* since he was not wearing VR goggles in the scenario, and he slid his hand along the earpiece to what he knew was the box under it. He felt the catch open and felt for the tiny dip switches inside. Back in college he'd played VR chicken with other students. It was a game of sensory overloads—who could last the longest listening to things like fingernails on blackboards, swimming in containers of beetles, or the like.

Whoever showed the most reaction in the scenario would lose. He'd sometimes beat the system by learning how to disable the RW sensory interface while in VR.

Like now.

He counted over three switches and turned the next two off. Now he could see and feel everything in VR, but the system couldn't read his nerve impulses.

Any excitement his body registered in RW wouldn't show in VR.

He looked down, just to be sure.

There was that little brown mole, right there on his— Jesus! He was wearing *his* real body. How had she done *that*?

Lewis was still talking.

"The carrier waves are the people on the beach. My scenario shows them naked, so that I can see if they're hiding anything."

She must have used an old copy from the MIT lab, used an aging algorithm to extrapolate the rest. Pretty sharp, Lewis.

They reached a set of sunbathers on green reclining chairs. Lewis sat down on a chair nearby, motioning to Jay to do the same. She straddled the chair as she sat down, giving him something more to see.

"Take a look," she said.

He realized she meant the couple next to them, and saw that there was a slight discoloration on the man's body. And a bulge wiggling under the skin of his belly, like some implanted alien monster about to erupt.

The man stood up and walked away. Jay looked around.

If the scenario had him as a metaphor to a data pipe, anything he was carrying was data. Hidden data, in this case.

Nice.

"Clever," he said to Lewis.

Jay and Rachel followed. Strains of brassy music with bass and guitar drifted across the beach. The music added to the scene, but there was no immediate explanation for it.

Jay looked at Lewis and raised his eyebrow. "That a five-five-five, Lewis?"

She grinned. "Nope—ahead on the right. Hell, I haven't heard that term in years. Professor Barnhardt would be proud."

Jay looked ahead. There it was—a radio on a piece of driftwood next to the beach bar.

Barnhardt had been a drama instructor who'd transferred to the VR department. There had been some controversy about that, since the old man had hardly had any programming experience. But he'd been *smart*.

His specialty was teaching the programmers how to be more real. He'd termed anything that threw you out of the VR illusion a "five-five-five"—taking the name from the fake phone number prefix used in movies and TV. Every time you see that, he'd say, you remember you're looking through the third wall.

Her code was sharp, she'd figured out she had a leak on her own, and she created VR as good as—well, *almost* as good as—his own. He was impressed.

The man stopped at the beach bar. He looked behind him, saw them, and then jumped over a large piece of driftwood and ran.

Jay and Rachel hurried to catch up. Jay marveled at how well the TFU worked—he'd swear wind was rushing over his naked body, and he could feel parts of his body swinging.

When they reached the driftwood and looked on the other side, the man was gone.

Well.

It looked like this might take more trips to the beach. Jay looked over at Lewis and saw her looking at him.

He wondered if that was a good idea or not.

6

Alice's Restaurant
University Park, Virginia

"You jivin' me," Jamal said.

Thorn smiled. "Nope. You get on the American team, I'll cover your expenses to the World Games. Airfare, hotels, food, walking-around money."

Jamal shook his head. "I appreciate it, but—why?"

"Two reasons, Jamal. One, I can afford it. Two, it's not every day I get to sponsor a world-champion fencer."

"I ain't even got on the national team yet, Mr. Thorn, and you got me winnin' the worlds?"

"Aim high, hit high," Thorn said.

Jamal shook his head in wonder.

Thorn's smile slipped into something more serious. "Look, Jamal," he said. "Up until now, if you lost a big bout, you could just shrug and say, 'Well, so what, I couldn't have afforded to go anyhow.' Now, you have to come up with another reason."

Jamal looked at him for maybe five seconds without saying anything. "You a mind reader, too?"

"I grew up on a rez in Washington State, and we didn't have any spare change lying around. 'No money' was my favorite excuse—until my grandfather went out and hustled enough from the tribe my senior year of high school to pay my way to the nationals."

"You win?"

"Nope. Came in third in épée, fifth in foil, didn't place in saber. Bronze wasn't gold, but it might as well have been when I brought it home. No kid from our rez had ever won squat against a room full of white guys. That medal is still hanging in the trophy case outside the principal's office."

Jamal laughed. "They put a trophy case in my school, the whole thing would be gone the next morning, right down to the bolts holding it to the floor."

"Yeah, yeah, your school is bad. You ever scalp a white man?"

Thorn kept his face deadpan, and for just a second, Jamal looked at him as if he was serious.

"Get out my face with that," the young man said.

Thorn laughed. "Had you for just a second there, didn't I?"

"No way." But he grinned, too. "So, Mr. Thorn, what's the deal with you and the fine sistah? You serious about getting married?"

"Oh, yeah."

"Salt and pepper. You gonna catch grief on both sides of the table."

"It's the twenty-first century, Jamal. Fifty, a hundred years from now, it is gonna be like Julian Huxley said, we'll all be tea-colored, and the world will be better off for it."

"Uh huh."

"You don't sound convinced."

"I don't think the world is as far down that road as you do."

Thorn shrugged. "It doesn't matter. Marissa is worth any amount of grief anybody else has got to offer. Screw 'em if they don't like it."

Now Jamal's grin got real big. "That's what a man says about his woman. You all right, Mr. T."

Thorn grinned back. He hoped so.

U.S. Army Recon School
Fort Palaka, Hana, Maui, Hawaii

The Army base at Hana was brand-new, small, specialized, and nobody local much liked it being there. Some kind of land swap with the government was the only reason it was. It wasn't enough that the tourists filled the narrow road leading to Hana so you never could get anywhere. Now there were soldiers clogging things up—that's what a man paying attention at a local cafe would hear, and certainly Carruth was a man who paid attention. . . .

As he lay in the lush growth ten meters away from the still-shiny chain-link fence surrounding the base, Carruth wasn't so sure this mission was worth the trip. Still, it was what Lewis wanted, and it was her command. On the one hand, she was a fine-looking woman and he'd love to get to know her better; on the other hand, she was a cold bitch and he didn't doubt she would shoot a man just to watch him bleed. But for the moment, he was willing to go along with her, because if things went the way she planned, he was going to walk away with enough money to buy his own tropical island and stock it with as many good-looking women as he wanted. He could put up with a little ball-busting for that.

Carruth had only two men with him on this one—Hill and Stark—and they were backup. Carruth was the only guy going onto the base proper.

Into his LOSIR headset, he said, "Two minutes, mark."

"Copy," Hill came back.

"Affirmative," Stark added.

The fence patrol guard, a PFC who must have done

something to get on somebody's shit detail, strolled by in front of Carruth's position, M-16 slung over his shoulder, not even bothering to look at the fence most of the time. Once he was past here, it would be thirty minutes before he came back to this spot, and if Carruth wanted to bother to try and hide them, the doofus probably wouldn't even notice the clipped links in the wire.

Speaking of which . . . On the two-minute mark, Carruth crawled to the fence, came up to a squat, and applied the wire-cutters to the links, snipping out just enough of a gap to slide through. This position was one of many that wasn't covered by security cams, and was far enough away from anything so nobody but the perimeter guard would likely see you come through.

Once he was inside, Carruth moved fifty steps to the SSW, then altered his direction and did thirty-six more steps directly east.

This kept him out of any security cam's view—so the intel said.

At that point, he started walking as if he owned the place. He was dressed in the uniform of the day, Army tropical, and wearing the insignia of a master sergeant. Anybody who saw him on a cam probably wouldn't call out the MPs—they'd figure he belonged here.

His goal—another stupid one, far as he was concerned—was the enlisted soldiers' mess hall, at the south end of the complex, a three-minute walk from his entry point. At ten-thirty hours, the place should be relatively empty—breakfast was long over and lunch wasn't being plated yet.

The maps he'd studied and the photographs he'd memorized were accurate—he had no trouble recognizing his route to the target.

A few enlisted soldiers passed along the way, none close, and he offered a snappy salute to the one officer who came within range, a young lieutenant, who returned the salute and did not speak.

The hall lay just ahead.

Carruth circled to the back side of the place, where the Dumpsters were lined up. He opened the lid of the largest, using a handkerchief so as not to leave prints. He caught the spoiled-milk reek of food rotting in the steel bin. Phew! What a stench!

He removed the device from his pocket, started the timer, and dropped it onto a mass of overcooked scrambled eggs, *splat.*

The bomb was a simple composition device— RDX/PETN blended with dense wax and a little oil, a C-4 knockoff from India stabilized for hot climates, cheap and untraceable—at least nobody could trace it to him. The electronic timer was a throwaway quartz runner's watch he'd bought at a Kmart, no prints anywhere, and if he built another one, he'd do it differently, so as not to leave a signature the bomb guys could read.

Ten minutes from now, the Dumpster was going to pop the lid and spew a goodly portion of its stinking contents into the air—the steel walls would almost surely hold, it wasn't that big a boomer—and the result would be a nasty mess for some poor bastard on kitchen patrol to clean up. Come all this way to blow up a garbage can? Well, it was what Lewis wanted, and probably she had some reason, though he damn sure didn't know what it was.

He turned and started to walk away. In ten minutes, he'd be halfway back to where they'd anchored the boat. By the time the Army figured out what happened—he wouldn't put it past 'em to blame it on methane gas—he and Hill and Stark would have sailed away.

He grinned. Stupid Army wonks . . .

"Sergeant," came a masculine, if somewhat high-pitched, voice.

Startled, Carruth turned. It was that shavetail second lieutenant he'd passed earlier, standing three meters behind him. A big mistake on his part. He should have been paying better attention. "Sir?"

"What is your unit, soldier?"

Carruth repressed the urge to sigh. Just his luck to run

into a kid officer who apparently had a eye for faces and didn't recognize Carruth's.

"My unit, sir? I'm on loan from the 704th Chemical, Arden Hills, sir. USASOC. I just arrived this morning to teach a class in decontamination procedure." He took a step toward the lieutenant.

The younger man—he couldn't be more than twenty-two or -three—frowned. "I don't recall seeing a posting about that."

Carruth stole another step. "I wouldn't know about that, sir. I just go where I'm told and do what they say. I have my orders right here." He reached toward his pocket, as if to remove them.

The lieutenant waved that off. "What are you doing messing around back here with the garbage cans?"

"I got lost, sir. Saw some trash on the ground and picked it up." He didn't have time for this. The clock was ticking.

He was close enough now, but maybe it wouldn't come to that. If this idiot would just leave it, he'd be on his way.

"Show me."

"Sir?"

"The trash you picked up. I want to see it."

Aw, *shit*. He had a problem. This conversation had gone on long enough so that buzz-cut here would remember him once the can went *boom!* and that was bad. Plus the fact that when he opened that Dumpster lid, that ED lying on the bed of yellow egg residue would stand out like a red flag.

"Yes, sir." And with that, Carruth clocked the lieutenant, a short hammer-fist to the temple, putting his hip into the hit.

The lieutenant fell like his legs had vanished. He was out cold.

But he was gonna wake up in a few minutes and probably his memory would work just fine. That wasn't gonna do.

Carruth picked the unconscious officer up, shouldered him, and carried him the Dumpster. He lifted the lid and dropped the lieutenant into the bin. Wiped the lid where he had touched it, then latched the top shut.

He walked away. Too bad for the soldier, but risk went with the job. Probably the explosion would kill him; at the least, it would mess him up enough that he wouldn't be talking anytime soon.

Better him than me . . .

Net Force HQ
Quantico, Virginia

Jay Gridley sat in Thorn's office, looking, as he often did, like a teenager late for a date.

"You got the report on the base in Hawaii?" Thorn asked.

"I haven't read it yet," Jay answered. "It was in the spool when you called."

"Somebody cut through the fence and blew up a Dumpster."

Jay laughed. "Whoa. Big-time assault."

"The bomber apparently decked a second lieutenant and put him into the garbage bin with the bomb."

"Jeez. Kill him?"

"No. The trash somehow partially muted the blast. Blew out his eardrums, gave him a major concussion, ruptured spleen, collapsed lung, burns, and cuts. He's in bad shape, but he's still alive."

"Poor bastard."

"I'm expecting my phone to ring any second with an irate general on the line wanting to know what we have done toward catching these people. So—what have we done?"

"I'm grinding, Boss, you know how it goes. It's like looking for one line of bad code in a million-line program—you don't see it until you get to it."

"I understand, Jay, but they won't. Give me something. Anything."

"The computer game is intricate and well built, so we're dealing with a serious programmer, plus one smart enough to put it out there and then trash it without leaving an easy trail. I'm working with Captain Lewis at MILDAT, running down leads."

Thorn nodded. "Whoever is doing this is trying to make a point. I don't know what, but blowing up a Dumpster doesn't have a lot of strategic value, any more than the raid in Oklahoma, where they knocked down an armory door, blew some windows out, and then turned around and left empty-handed. It looks to me like they are trying to show that they can get into these bases and do whatever they want."

Jay said, "Selling keys to the candy store, maybe."

Thorn nodded. "Yeah. Could be. There are loons running around out there who would pay big money for that. Demonstrate that there is an easy way into an Army base a few times, and the crazies will line up to buy your key."

Jay said, "Or maybe these are just feints, designed to convince the military they don't really need to worry, and they plan on something a lot worse. One of the bases in the bug game has tactical nukes on hand, and from the part of the DCP we got, there were ways to get past the first level of security. Hard to tell what is in the bits we missed."

"You've told the Army about this?"

"Oh, yeah, it's all in my report, ought to be in your in-box somewhere. They've changed security procedures on all the bases I matched, new codes, new guard routines, beefed-up whatevers. We might have short-circuited them." Jay frowned. "Wait a second. You said a base in Hawaii?"

"Yes, a new one, not much there but a recon school. Near Hana, on Maui."

Jay shook his head. "I don't recall cross-referencing a base in Hawaii." He paused. Then: "Shit!"

"What?"

"The guy has another game running!" Jay stood. "I have to get on the net. I should have thought of this before!"

"Go," Thorn said.

After Jay was gone, Thorn sat at his desk. Net Force spent a lot of time stamping out little fires, and every now and then a big one, like this, or the Chinese general. And Thorn felt as if he had gotten better at running the agency, even with the switch in command. Still, it wasn't what he had thought it would be when he left civilian life to do it. He could have retired a few years back and sat around thinking up creative ways to spend his money. He wasn't super-rich, but he could live pretty well just off the interest his millions generated. Working for the military hadn't gotten onerous yet, but he feared that it would eventually. If Hadden was right—if he was going to be made into a military general, even if it was more technical than real— what would that mean?

He didn't want to be part of the problem. He'd taken the job as commander to give something back to his country, which had been pretty good to a poor boy from an Indian rez in Washington State. The tribe was doing better these days— they had a casino outside of Walla Walla, and were dickering for another one near the Idaho border, in a land swap with the feds. Not enough money coming in to make everybody rich, but enough so nobody would be poor. That was good.

Once he and Marissa were married? What then? She could quit her job at the CIA if she wanted. Or not. That would be up to her. And maybe he would quit if she did. He wasn't getting any younger. They could travel, see things, do things together, enjoy life. Outside of his fencing and his collection of swords, he didn't have any expensive hobbies. He had a nice house, was about to hook up with a fantastic woman. Life was short—he could get hit by a truck, a tree could fall on him, and all his money wouldn't matter. Maybe it was time to pack it in at work and enjoy whatever time he had left?

His com buzzed.

"Yes."

"General Hadden on one."

Of course. "I got it."

He reached for the receiver. This would be a fun conversation.

Retirement sounded better all the time. . . .

7

General Abe Kent had something he wanted to show to Thorn.

They met at the quartermaster's warehouse, a nice brisk ten-minute walk from Thorn's office. The pair of armed guards didn't salute, but they weren't supposed to—they needed to be able to open up with the subguns they held at a moment's notice if somebody who didn't belong here somehow showed up.

He saw Kent coming across the concrete, not quite a march, but more than a stroll.

"Abe," Thorn said.

"Sir. Right this way." General Kent nodded at the two guards.

"What am I going to look at?"

"A SWORD fighter," Kent said.

Thorn blinked. He thought he knew about such things, but certainly there weren't actually guys in the military these days who still used swords. . . .

"Excuse me?" he said, frowning. "Did you say 'sword fighter'?"

"S-W-O-R-D," Kent said. "Stands for 'Special Weapons Observation Reconnaissance Detection Systems.'"

Thorn smiled. "I see. The military sure does love those acronyms, don't they?"

"Yes, sir, they surely do."

"You don't need to 'sir' me, Abe."

"That's not what I hear, *General* Thorn."

Thorn shook his head. "Hasn't happened yet. What is it, the SWORD?"

Kent led him to a cleared-out spot in the warehouse. Except for what was parked in the middle of the space.

"What on earth—?"

Kent said, "Basically, sir, it's a robot. About a meter high, rides on tracks, like tank treads—even looks kind of like a stripped-down tank, doesn't it? This model weighs about fifty kilos, runs on lithium-ion batteries. It has a working range of a thousand meters, can go about thirty-five klicks on a charge, or sit parked and watching for four or five hours before the battery runs down, and you can swap that out in a couple minutes. What you have is four cameras—a wide-angle and zoom facing front, one facing to the rear, and one lined up as a gunsight. Mounts an M240 light machine gun, the ammo belt rides in a can, holds about three hundred rounds."

Thorn stared at the device. It looked deadly just parked there.

"You need more punch, you can get one that comes with an M202-A1 6mm rocket launcher."

Thorn glanced at Kent, then back at the SWORD device.

"SWORD is radio-controlled," Kent continued. "Take some kid who grew up playing with a Gameboy or Xbox, put him in a VR helmet. He holds a controller, and it's just like playing a video game. He can roll it down a street, look this way and that, and engage enemy targets from inside a protected location up to a kilometer away."

Thorn shook his head, unsure whether he was impressed or simply depressed. "And what does this toy cost?"

"Starts out just over a quarter million, runs to three hundred fifty, four hundred thousand, depending on the bells and whistles. There's one with an ordnance sniffer good to a few parts per million—it'll nose out an ammo dump a walking soldier might miss. Or you can get one with a chemical/radiation detector. There's another one with a flamethrower—you park it, a little tube comes up and spins around spewing fire in a complete circle—covers three-sixty for fifty meters. Pretty good for stopping a major shooting riot in its tracks. For less-lethal encounters, there's a model that will spew gas the same way—tear, pepper, puke, whatever, and it comes with an extra battery that charges a capacitor which gives anybody foolish enough to lay bare hands on it about ninety thousand volts of low-amperage charge that will knock them onto their ass in a hurry."

"Nice."

"Yep. They started rolling them out in Second Iraq, Stryker Brigade. They were an outgrowth of the bomb-defusing Talon robots built by Foster-Miller, up in Massachusetts. Somebody said, 'Well, if we can defuse a bomb, why can't we put a gun on it?' So they did."

Thorn shook his head again. He was pretty sure he wasn't impressed after all. "Sounds like some kind of science-fiction movie."

"It does, doesn't it? There were some worries about it at first. What if the bad guys got the radio codes and turned them on our people? They use coded, random-shifting opchans, so that hasn't happened, and isn't likely to anytime soon."

"They durable?"

"Better than a GI in body armor. New ones use ceramic plate and cloned spider-silk weave. A lucky shot might take out a camera, but it'll resist small-arms fire fairly well otherwise."

"I bet the first enemy combatant to see one of these coming must have needed to change his pants."

"I expect so. Probably didn't get a chance to do that. Some of the kids running the gear can drive tacks with the guns. If they can see it, they can hit it. There are several hundred of the things on active duty, and another hundred on order."

"So how did we get one?"

"Courtesy of retired Captain Julio Fernandez."

Thorn smiled.

"Best scrounger I ever saw," Kent said.

"He's still working with John Howard, isn't he?"

"Yes, sir. Man can get blood out of a stone. I don't know how he managed it, but it wound up costing us some equipment we aren't using and about twenty thousand dollars."

"The question is, General, what are we going to do with it?"

Kent shrugged. "I don't know for certain, sir, but it's better to have it and not need it than to need it and not have it. Worse comes to worst, we can sell it to the Army and make a profit."

"I suppose," Thorn said.

"That concludes our inspection tour, sir."

Thorn nodded. "What are you up to these day, Abe? Other than collecting props from old Schwarzenegger movies?" For a while, Kent had been showing Thorn how to use a *katana,* a Japanese blade. Kent's grandfather had taught him *iaido,* and Thorn was interested in all kinds of blade work.

"Learning how to play the guitar," Kent said.

"Really?"

"I . . . inherited one, as you probably recall."

Thorn remembered. The Georgian hit man, what was his name? Natadze?

"How is it going?"

"Slowly. Very slowly. But I have a good teacher. She's very patient."

Thorn thought he caught something in Kent's voice when he mentioned the guitar teacher, but he didn't follow it up.

"How about you?"

"Marissa is planning the wedding. I'm supposed to go meet her grandparents soon."

"Congratulations, sir."

"You'll get an invitation, if they ever get a date set."

"I look forward to it."

"Me, too."

Both men grinned.

"You ever married, Abe?"

"Long ago. She passed away a few years back."

"I'm sorry."

"Me, too." A beat, then: "Any luck on the Army base break-ins?"

Thorn shook his head. "Nope. I just left Jay Gridley. He was running off to check on something. General Hadden is really unhappy."

"In his shoes, I'd be, too," Kent said. "He lobbied hard to get the newer, smaller, high-tech bases built and running. Trying to bootstrap the military into the twenty-first century faster. That somebody was able to bust into a couple makes him look bad. Not a good idea to make the Chairman of the Joint Chiefs look bad."

"I hear that."

Blue Parrot Cafe
Miami, Florida

"You're a woman," the man said. His incredulous tone of voice was probably the same he'd have used to say, "You're a dog."

"Yes," Lewis said.

"Your master sent a woman."

Lewis had figured that he'd be one of those—a lot of the fundamentalists were. He was offended, of course, even though she wore a scarf covering her hair, along with dark glasses and a long-sleeved and modest dress, so he wouldn't be further offended by any display of skin.

They sat at a small round table at the Blue Parrot, a tiny, mostly outdoor cafe in Miami—no way she would meet somebody like him in Washington, or even as close as Baltimore. The day was warm, the air damp, and her clothing wasn't particularly comfortable. At least the table's umbrella kept the direct sun off her. It was winter in the rest of the country, but down here, you could lie on the beach and cook. Had she been here for pleasure, she'd be wearing shorts and a halter top, and plenty of sunblock. She could see why so many people retired to this state. Snow three feet deep in Chicago, and people running around in thongs in Miami—old bones might prefer the heat.

The man—maybe forty, tall, dark, with a thick moustache—used the name Mishari Aziz. He wore a dark red Hawaiian shirt, white linen trousers, and sandals, and was certainly better dressed for the climate than she was.

"Mr. Aziz, it is said that a man looking for wolves will walk past a fox."

Aziz blinked at her, as if astounded she could speak. If that line wasn't in the Koran, something like it probably was.

He was a fanatic, but not stupid. He took her point. "Ah, yes, perhaps that is wise." He didn't trust women, but he was the buyer and not the seller. If he wanted to deal, he had to deal with her. Let him think she was a pawn pushed by a man, if that would put him at ease.

He sat on the aluminum chair across the table from her.

"Tell me," he said. It was a command.

"My employer can deliver any of a number of Army bases—codes, guard routines, all the security measures in place. Included among these are some with nuclear weapons on hand."

She saw a fanatical light flare in his eyes.

"A careful seeker will have seen examples of our ability to invade the Army's bases at will."

"Oklahoma and Hawaii," he said.

They were paying attention. Hawaii was hardly past. "Just so."

He leaned back in his chair and affected a posture of

skepticism. "Blowing up garbage cans and knocking down doors? Not impressive."

"Mr. Aziz, do you know the saying about the dancing bear? It's not that he dances well, but that he dances at all. Our operatives were able to penetrate the Army's defenses—they could just as easily leveled a barracks full of soldiers or stolen whatever they wished. That is what we are offering."

"You could have struck a blow—"

"*You* can strike a blow," she said, cutting him off. "We are businesspeople; we do not concern ourselves with politics."

His jaw muscles flexed. He didn't like being interrupted, especially by a woman, nor did he like people who didn't take sides—especially *his* side. But she had something he wanted. He would swallow his anger.

"The amount of money you are asking for is great," he said.

"One must consider what one is buying. For a working atomic weapon, ten million is not such a great amount."

"You are not selling such a thing."

"We are selling the key to the store wherein it resides, and a map of the pitfalls between it and the man who wants it. The rest is up to you."

Aziz nodded to himself. "My backers will require another demonstration."

"What will it take to convince them?"

"Something substantial. Entry, and acquisition of a thing of material value."

"We aren't going to deliver a nuke."

"That will not be necessary. But they would see you recover something more heavily guarded than a trash can."

"We can do that."

"When?"

"A few days, a week, it depends." She stood. He came to his feet, too. "You will see evidence of it when it happens, and we will contact you as before."

She didn't offer to shake hands. Neither did he.

As she left the Blue Parrot, Lewis knew she would be

followed by Aziz's operatives. She didn't bother to look for them. She hailed a taxi, and told the driver to take her to the Dolphin Mall.

It was a bit of a drive, and she smiled to herself as they headed that way. Of course Aziz would have her followed. Knowledge was power, and if he could track her, perhaps it would give him leverage.

The mall, a few miles west of the Miami International Airport, was a huge place, hundreds of stores, a million and a half square feet. If she couldn't lose a tail there, she didn't deserve to be playing this game.

She enjoyed the air-conditioning in the cab. This dress, plus what she had on under it, was passing warm.

Finally, they arrived. She paid the driver and entered the mall. It was crowded, even on a weekday—shoppers, elderly walkers, mall rats. She walked purposefully to Lace and Secrets. She had been here to check it out before the meeting with Aziz. He would not have brought a female op to their meeting because he would not have considered the idea that he was going to meet a woman. A man alone in a woman's lingerie shop wasn't exactly rare, but he'd stand out. The help would be all over him—if the op was stupid enough to come into the place.

She browsed lingerie until she spotted her tail. A short, young, swarthy man with a moustache stood by one of the benches outside the store, pretending to look at a newspaper. He wore a white shirt and gray trousers. A few meters away, a second man, cut from the same cloth, pretended to be talking on a pay phone.

Both kept stealing quick looks at the shop.

They were amateurs. Might as well be wearing neon signs proclaiming them as undercover operatives. Here— look here!

Lewis would have grinned, but she was in persona now. So predictable. If Aziz was as smart as he ought to be, he'd have hired a blond surfer-type in shorts and a tank top for a sub-rosa op, or a barely dressed woman with a tan, who couldn't have possibly spent her whole life under a burka.

But these guys liked to keep things in the family. Lewis would bet that both of the young men out there were related to Aziz—brothers, cousins, nephews, like that.

She went to find a clerk. A young woman with a nose ring and a pierced eyebrow, about nineteen or so, was behind the counter.

"Yes, ma'am?"

Lewis tried to look frightened. "I wonder if you might help me? My ex-husband is out there, he's following me, and I'm afraid he's going to kill me."

The clerk blinked. "You want me to call Security?"

"No, I don't want any trouble. He's—he's a violent man. He beat me when we together. He carries a gun. I have a restraining order against him, to keep him away, but that won't help. If I can get away from him without him following me, that would be the best thing. Is there a back way out of here?"

She already knew that there was, but using it would set off an alarm—unless the alarm was deactivated.

"There is."

"If I could go out that way, I could get to my car. I'm leaving town, going to stay with my sister in Houston. Can you help me, please?"

"No problem," the clerk said.

Once she was in the hall behind the shop and the clerk had closed the door behind her, Lewis stripped off the dress. Under it, she wore shorts and a T-shirt. She pulled a pair of sandals from her bag, then left the dress, sensible shoes, and bag in the nearest garbage can. She headed for the parking lot and her rental car. With any luck, she'd be on a plane back to D.C. before Abdul and Sayed back there realized they had lost her.

There were, of course, other potential buyers. And she would contact them if Aziz didn't work out. The next time they met, she would have Carruth and a couple of his troops backing her. You couldn't trust a fanatic, and once Aziz realized that she could deliver, he would certainly try to avoid paying for it if he could. That was expected.

Lewis had reasons to hate the Army, but she didn't hate her country. There was no way she would put an atomic weapon into the hands of a zealot who would kill hundreds of thousands without blinking, in the name of some warped sense of reality. He had to believe that she would, he had to know that she could give him what he wanted, so she had to demonstrate it, but it wasn't going to happen. Not to mention that the target such a man would select might well be the town in which Lewis herself happened to be. Sure, she'd sell him the key—but there would be a nasty surprise waiting for Mr. Aziz when he tried to open that door. And the Army would give her a medal for it. How ironic was that?

8

Thorn was sweating, and he hadn't expected that.

He was fencing Jamal, just the two of them, in the small, threadbare *salle* he'd opened up a little while earlier.

This was his dream—or at least it was one of his dreams.

Thorn himself had come up the hard way, from a hardscrabble existence on the reservation, and fencing had been an escape for him. He wanted to help make it an escape for others, too.

So a few years ago he'd quietly bought this tiny gym in D.C., refurbished it slightly, and reopened as a *salle*. Then he'd put the word out on the street that he was open and looking for people who were interested in fencing.

Jamal was one of the few who'd responded.

Thorn toyed with the idea of putting in more time here, really putting forth the effort to grow this place into something big. Something like what had happened in New York City a few years back. He could hire a coach, reach out to the community, and put together something that could really make a difference in people's lives.

But not now. A coach alone wouldn't be enough. It would take a tremendous effort by someone with vision, with commitment to the dream. And since it was his vision, his dream, it pretty much had to be him pushing it. But he couldn't. Not now. Not as long as Net Force demanded so much of him. But maybe, someday . . .

Jamal came in fast. Thorn threw a quick high-line parry and riposted to the open wrist, but the wrist wasn't there. It had been a feint.

Jamal's point dropped, circling beneath Thorn's bell guard, then pressed lightly on the outside of Thorn's blade, guiding it further inside and then leaping off for a quick strike to Thorn's shoulder.

Thorn smiled and leaned back, letting Jamal's point fall short. That had been a good try.

As he leaned back, he allowed his guard to drop further, then brought his own point up sharply, striking behind Jamal's bell and landing solidly on the heel of his palm.

"Hcy!" Jamal said. "How'd you do that? I should have had your shoulder!"

Thorn grinned. He was aware of Marissa seated on a bleacher off to the side, but he wasn't fencing any harder just because she was watching.

Well, maybe he was fencing a *little* harder. . . .

"Nice try," he said. "You set it up beautifully. The thing is, you can't think too much. If I'd been paying attention to what you were doing, trying to anticipate your next move, you'd have had me."

Even through the mesh mask, Thorn could see his young opponent frown. "What, then?"

"It's like I've said, Jamal, anticipation will get you killed—as it would have cost me a touch just now. No, there's a different approach I want you think about. When you fence, what do you focus on? With your eyes, I mean? Where do you look?"

Jamal shrugged. "I don't really focus on anything. You

taught me that. I keep my eyes pointed pretty much straight ahead, but by not focusing I allow my peripheral vision to see more."

Thorn nodded. "Exactly. Look at nothing, see everything."

"Yeah."

"It's the same thing with your mind. Don't focus. Be. Don't react to the blade. Be the blade. Be the parry. Be the touch."

Jamal shook his head. "You've said this before, but I still don't get it."

"You will. I've brought some books I think you're ready for." Thorn gestured over to where Marissa sat on the bleacher. There was a backpack on the floor next to her. Inside was a small selection of books he'd chosen specifically for Jamal. Heugel's *Zen and the Art of Archery*. Musashi's *A Book of Five Rings*. Smullyan's *The Tao Is Silent*. A few others.

What he didn't say was that he'd been bringing those same books now for six months, waiting for Jamal to reach the point where they would do him the most good.

Thorn also had two other stacks of books set aside, ready for the next steps in Jamal's growth.

"Don't think, huh?" Jamal asked.

"That's right. Don't think. Be."

"Got it. All right, let's try it again."

And the dance was on once again.

Washington, D.C.

Carruth didn't see it coming, there was no way he could have. Once there, he had no real choice.

He'd driven to a new rave club in Southeast, the Cairo Mirage. Carruth wasn't a fan of such things, buncha idiots taking drugs and dancing until they fell over, but he'd met a drop-dead gorgeous redhead who ran some kind of program for troubled kids in Anacostia. She liked to party down at clubs, and she had told him she was gonna be there, so if he wanted to get next to her—and he did—he had to go where the action was.

A woman who looked that good was worth a little noise and effort.

Southeast wasn't exactly the best section of town, but he wasn't worried about street trash bothering him. He was big, strong, trained, armed, and could pass for a cop. The wolves usually had better sense than to bother a lion when there were so many sheep around.

The car was a rental, so if somebody boosted it while he was inside making nice with Ms. Red, it was no skin off his nose. He found an empty spot—a no-parking curb, but if he got a ticket, so what?—and wheeled the car into it. He got out, adjusted the heavy revolver on his hip under his sport coat, and cheeped the car's alarm. The club was a block east, and it was still early, not yet 2100; ought not to have any problems at nine o'clock on a weeknight.

He was halfway there when an MPDC cruiser angled to the curb in front of him and the cop inside tapped the siren.

Carruth stopped and stared at the car. It was white, with the stylized American flag on the side. The door opened, and a pair of cops got out. They weren't unsnapping holsters or anything, but they were definitely coming to talk to him.

"Evening, Officers," he said. He smiled. What was this?

The nearer cop, a beefy guy almost as big as Carruth, probably about thirty, finished slipping his side-handle baton into his belt loop, watching Carruth all the time. "Need to ask you a couple of questions, buddy."

Carruth kept smiling. "Sure, no problem." But he was worried.

He was dressed in a nice jacket and slacks; he ought to look like a citizen. No reason to brace him. And no "Good evening, sir." MPDC cops were usually polite to citizens. Not a good sign.

The second cop, shorter and thinner than the other one,

and with a thin moustache, said, "Did you know there was a robbery a couple blocks back a few minutes ago? Somebody hit a convenience store."

"I didn't see anybody," Carruth said. "I'm parked about half a block back, on my way to meet a lady at a club."

The two cops approached a bit closer, but stayed well apart from each other. "Well, thing is, the robber was a big white guy in a sport coat."

Jesus Christ, they had to be kidding—they thought he'd knocked over a 7-Eleven and he was just strolling down the fucking street like he owned it?

Carruth laughed. "Wasn't me. I'm not a robber, I'm just on my way to meet this woman."

"Yeah, you said that," Beefy said. "Mind if we see some ID?"

"No problem. My wallet is in my back pocket."

"How about if I get that for you?" Moustache said, still smiling.

"Excuse me?"

Beefy put his hand on his Glock's gun butt.

Nine-millimeter Glocks were dangerous guns—no safety, save for the split trigger, they often went off in the hands of a nervous cop when they weren't supposed to go off. A lot of lawsuits had been settled by big cities where badly trained police accidentally cooked citizens with those Tupperware side arms, even with the heavier New York trigger. Carruth had no use for Glocks.

"You're making a mistake," Carruth said.

"Turn around, put your hands on the wall, walk your feet back, and spread 'em," Beefy said. "We'll apologize if we're wrong."

Oh, shit! If they found his revolver, he was gonna be in a world of trouble. Illegally concealed weapons were a big no-no in D.C., and at the very least, they could confiscate his BMF and put him in the local slammer until a lawyer could bust him loose.

That would not do. Lewis would have a conniption. And he didn't want to lose his gun, no way.

"Okay, okay, no problem, take it easy." Carruth started to turn to his right. When his hand was covered by his body, he snapped it down and grabbed for his revolver—

The two cops started yelling, clawing for their own side arms, but Carruth had the jump on them. He cleared leather, cocked the hammer as he drew, shoved the big revolver toward Beefy, who was all of two meters away, and pulled the trigger—

Even knowing how loud it was, the sound and vibration almost paralyzed Carruth. It was a big bomb going off in your face; the shock of it blasted your skin like a hot wind, and shooting one-handed, the recoil damned near jerked the gun out of his hand.

The protective Kevlar vest didn't do the man any good. It was a center-punch shot, and even if it didn't penetrate, it would be like being hit in the chest with a cannonball—the impact would break his sternum and ribs and concuss the heart like a sledgehammer.

Moustache cursed and brought his Glock up, but it went off while it was still pointed at the sidewalk. The jacketed slug ricocheted off the concrete and spanged into the wall behind Carruth as he dragged his revolver down from where it pointed at the sky. He grabbed it with his other hand, moving like a turtle, slow, oh, so slowly. . . .

Moustache's Glock fired again, this time almost lined up, but the bullet went wide, to Carruth's left, and he got his muzzle pointed and fired the second chamber—

Moustache collapsed, another center-of-mass hit the vest wouldn't protect against, to join Beefy supine on the sidewalk.

Holy shit!

It was like the wrath of God. Two up, two down. He had most likely just killed a pair of Metro cops.

It was way past time to leave.

He looked around. Nobody else on the street close enough to ID him, not that he could see. But this place would be thick with police in five minutes and he needed to be *gone*!

Carruth holstered his weapon. He bent down, pulled a pair of surgical gloves from Beefy's back pocket, put them on as he ran to the cruiser's front door, and climbed into the vehicle. He hit the siren and light-bar controls and screeched away from the curb.

He had to get as far away as fast as he could.

This was bad. Very bad.

9

Lewis was on her way home, driving the politically correct Japanese hybrid car she'd picked up second-hand a year past. At this stage of the game, she didn't want to do anything that might call attention to her, and the little automobile, which she privately thought of as a "Priapus," was as innocuous as they came. Even so, it still used a certain amount of gasoline to augment the electric motors, and the tank was nearly empty. She pulled over to a self-serve station a couple miles away from her house, got out, pushed her credit card into the reader, and started to pump fuel into the little car. A year or two from now, she'd be able to send her butler to buy her gas, if she felt like it. . . .

An ambulance pulled into the lot and parked next to the mini-market. The EMT riding shotgun alighted and went inside.

Of a moment, Lewis found herself riding a quick surge of memory. Like the best VR, it was almost reality—sights, smells, the feel of the air. . . .

The night her father died, Lewis had been in the hospital with her father's mother. Granny had, after Grampa passed away, slipped slowly and quietly into senility. One day, she seemed fine; the next, she was talking about men coming out of the walls of her house to chase her around the bedroom. It was sad—Granny had been a strong, smart woman who had raised two sons and a daughter, while working as an accountant, and run her household like a drill sergeant, which Grampa had been, but had given up when he'd retired.

Her doctor wanted to do tests to confirm what everybody already knew, that she had Alzheimer's and she had been successfully hiding it from her family. Nobody was happy about it.

The room had been unbearably hot. It had been August, in Richmond, the summer days almost tropical and the nights cloyingly warm and muggy, but even so, Granny had been cold, and they had cranked the heat up so that it was eighty-five degrees in the private room. The family had been taking turns going to sit with her—her mother, Rachel, two of her cousins—and on that night, it had been Rachel's turn.

The room was hot. Granny was in and out of reality. One moment, able to talk about what she'd read in the newspaper and comment on it intelligently, the next moment, wondering how a cat had gotten into the room and onto her bed.

Lewis, just turned eighteen, was herself something of a wreck. Her father's court-martial had gone as expected—he was guilty, never any question of whether he had taken his side arm and shot Private Benjamin Thomas Little in the head with it, killing him instantly. Her father was waiting for his sentence, and everybody knew it was going to be life or something just short of it, depending on how much the judges sympathized with Sergeant Lewis because two of them also had daughters.

Benny, the bastard. He had been her boyfriend, from the base, doing his first tour, a private. Tall, handsome, funny, and she had thought she loved him. Two, three more dates, she would have given him what he wanted.

But he couldn't wait. He had refused to take no for an answer when they'd been kissing in the backseat of his car, and had held her down and forced himself into her.

When she'd gotten home, her shirt torn and her face streaked with tears, her father had taken one look, grabbed his gun, driven to the barracks, and shot Benny dead.

So there she was, cooking in a hospital room with the heat turned up in the middle of a hot August night, listening to her poor old grandmother ramble on about a cat that wasn't there, and feeling like shit because it was her fault that her father was going to spend the rest of his life in a federal prison. Things didn't seem as if they could get any worse.

Until her mother showed up at Granny's room with the news.

Rachel's father had just killed himself. A different pistol, but the same results as Benny . . .

The hurried slamming of the ambulance door brought Lewis back to the present. The driver lit the lights and the vehicle squealed out of the mini-mart's parking lot, the siren kicking in as it reached the street.

Lewis topped off the tank of her car, feeling disconnected from the act. She had blamed herself for her father's death for a long time, but as the years went by, she had shifted much of that blame to the Army. Benny had been a soldier—why hadn't he been taught that forcing himself on a woman was wrong? Why hadn't the Army looked at what her father had done as something any father would have done? Made allowances for a man who was only dealing justice to a criminal? Had she gone to the MPs, they would have thrown Benny into the stockade, and in a just world, it would have been Benny who went to prison young and came out an old man.

Yes, she had gone into the Army—her father's suicide note had specified that she still should, as they had always planned—but eventually, she had realized that the Army needed to pay for what had happened to her father. And since they weren't going to do that voluntarily, she would *make* them pay.

She climbed into her car, dropped the gas receipt on the seat, and started the machine's anemic little engine. It had taken years to get into a position where she had enough power to hit the Army hard enough to cause it pain. It would never be as bad as what she had felt, the Army was too big to deal that kind of blow, but it would sting. It would be embarrassing, it would cost them in time and effort and money, and they would never know who had done it, or why. Maybe she would leave a time capsule somewhere, to be opened after she died, explaining it all. Or maybe she wouldn't.

She pulled out onto the street. It had taken a long time to set it up, but it was coming to pass, just as she had planned. If vengeance was a dish best served cold, then hers was certainly that. But she expected that it would taste perfect when it was done.

The Fretboard
Washington, D.C.

Jennifer Hart said, "How are your fingertips?"

It was nearly nine P.M. Given his job, it was hard for Kent to take off in the middle of the day for guitar lessons, but Jen was willing to meet him here at eight. The shop was closed, but she had a key, and they didn't seem to mind her teaching whenever she wanted.

The first time he'd showed up, he'd apologized for cutting into her evenings.

She'd laughed. Most evenings, her social life consisted of sitting in an overstuffed chair trying to read a book with her cat curled in her lap, she'd said.

Kent said, "Fine." In truth, the fingers on his left hand were all sore—the ends felt blistered, and his thumb ached from pressing too hard into the back of the guitar's neck. He figured it would pass as he developed calluses and more specific strength in the hand. No point in making a big deal out of it.

She grinned at him, and he enjoyed watching the smile lines form around her eyes and mouth. "Uh huh. Going to be stoic, huh?"

He smiled in return. "Too late to change now," he said.

She took a black silk cloth and began to wipe the fretboard and body of her guitar. He had a similar scrap of cloth in his case, and he did the same for his instrument. Even with clean hands, there was a certain amount of natural oil and grit that worked their way into the strings, causing, she had said, corrosion. A quick wipe with a cloth after playing helped slow that down.

Kent had learned about strings, tuners, humidifiers, all manner of esoterica connected to maintaining a classical guitar in some semblance of form, and he had no problem doing what was necessary. His grandfather had taught him how to sharpen a knife and keep it oiled when he'd been a boy; the old man had never had any patience for a man who didn't take care of his tools.

"You're coming along pretty well," Jen said.

"It's a lot harder than you make it look," he said.

She finished wiping her instrument, and tucked it into the case, then latched it shut. "Of course. Anybody with a little skill in anything makes it look easier to somebody just trying to learn."

"So, am I ever going to learn enough to justify owning this beast?" He held the guitar up in one hand, then lowered it into his case.

"Truth? You probably aren't ever going to sit on a concert stage and make people want to go home and toss out their Segovia recordings. But if you practice and keep learning, three or four years from now you'll be able to play some very nice things that people will enjoy hearing—and you won't have to worry that your instrument is holding you back."

He nodded. "Good enough. Though that's hard to see

after a fumbling rendition of 'Twinkle, Twinkle, Little Star,' or 'Scales on an E-string.' "

She laughed. "Everybody's got to start somewhere. A few lessons ago, you didn't know the names of the strings. Now, you can tune the guitar, and pick out simple melodies, plus you know a few basic chords. Most of what people play on acoustic rhythm guitar these days can be done with what they call 'cowboy chords,' maybe ten or fifteen or so."

"Odd name," he said.

"Think of those old cowboy movies you probably watched as a kid on late-night TV—Gene or Roy or whoever and his buddies sitting around the campfire, somebody with a guitar, somebody with a harmonica—I think that's where the name came from."

Kent nodded. He could see it.

"For a lot of blues," she went on, "you can get by with three or four, and for most rock and roll you only really need half a dozen. You don't have to be a world-class player to enjoy making music."

She stood. "Same time, Tuesday?"

"Works for me. Walk you to your car?"

"Think I can't make it there on my own?"

"I'm parked close to you," he said. "In case I fall down, you can help me up."

She laughed again. He liked making her do that.

"You used to be married, didn't you?"

He nodded. "Yes, ma'am. She passed away a while ago."

"I was married once myself. But my husband was more interested in work than me. Twenty years ago, he took off and went out to conquer the music world."

"Did he? Conquer the music world, I mean?"

"He did, actually. His instrument is the cello. He can sit on the same stage and keep up with Yo-Yo Ma. Played first cello with a couple of major European orchestras, formed his own chamber group that puts out a recording now and then, usually goes pretty high up on the classical charts. Married three more times since we split. I believe his current wife is a twenty-six-year-old daughter of some German baron. Beautiful woman, and if I had to guess, probably can't keep time in a waterproof basket—Armand prefers to be the only musician in a marriage."

Kent heard just a trace of bitterness, and a hint of ugly history, but then she laughed again, and that seemed real enough. "Lotta water under that bridge," she said. She turned and headed for the shop's exit. "No reason to go back there and fall in."

He didn't speak to that, only followed her to the door. Maybe he would check on-line and see what he could find about this "Armand" character. Might be interesting to know what kind of man would leave a woman like Jennifer Hart. The more he was around her, the more relaxed he felt. That was interesting, too. . . .

10

Carruth knew he should get rid of his handgun. They'd recover the slugs, and ballistics would cook him if they ever
got hold of the revolver. There probably weren't that many
fifty-caliber handguns kicking around, and fewer still of
the custom-made Reeders. But the gun had cost almost
three grand, and he liked it. And now there was certainly
no doubt that it was effective. It had dropped the cops fast
enough, even with vests.

So the trick was to make sure the police didn't get the
gun until he could afford to buy a new one to replace it.

The bored waitress, a skinny twenty-something with
short hair, nine earrings in each ear, a nose stud, plus an
eyebrow- and a lip-piercing, refilled his cup of bad coffee.
She didn't smile at him.

Must be a lesbian, he figured. Or a doper. Or both.

It had been a freak accident, the cops coming on him
that way. What were the chances that would happen? What
were the chances it would happen twice?

Yeah, he'd left the rental car, but even while he was on the boogie in the police cruiser, he had called one of his men and had him haul butt there to fetch the rental before the cops had time to shut the whole neighborhood down, so no grief from that. The car had been leased under a shell-company name anyhow. He had never been to that neighborhood before, and God knew he was never going back there again.

A first-class snafu, but he was clear.

So, yeah, the gun would have to go away, eventually, but it ought to be safe enough for a while.

He was rationalizing, he knew that, but he liked the piece a whole lot.

It wasn't as though he'd never shot anybody before. He'd knocked over a few "insurgents" as they called themselves—aka "terrorists" to the rest of the world—on his second tour, but never a civilian, and certainly not a cop. That was bad business. Cops pulled out all the stops to catch guys who took out one of their own, but even with their fire lit, they had to have some place to start, someone to focus all their righteous anger on, and they didn't know to come looking for him.

The big thing was, Lewis couldn't know anything about any of this. Nada. She was twitchy enough as it was. If she had any idea he was the guy who had cooled two of D.C.'s finest and made the front page of the papers and the Six O'Clock News on every local channel, he'd be in a world of trouble. She couldn't turn him over to the law, he knew too much about her and their mutual business, but she wouldn't want him risking the project. And she would really have a heaving fit if she knew he hadn't ditched the gun he'd used. . . .

The cops, that had been a one-in-a-million thing, not his fault, there was no way you could have planned on it. It would never happen again. No point in worrying about it.

He looked up and saw Lewis come in. This was another crappy mall cafe thirty miles away from the last place. She was careful—and he didn't really mind that. No three-on-a-match business for her. You didn't want to be working with somebody who wasn't careful when it was your ass on the line. Carruth didn't mind cowboys, as long as they didn't shut off their brains when they went rodeo-romping.

Lewis sat down. If the waitress were true to form, it would be ten minutes before she noticed enough to bring Lewis any of the crappy coffee. That's how long he'd sat there waiting. Easy enough to see why the place was empty except for him and Lewis and an old guy sitting at the counter. Probably all the old guy's taste buds were dead.

"You look nervous," Lewis said.

"Nah, just tired. I worked out this morning, maybe pushed the weights a little hard." That was actually true. Whenever he got himself into trouble, he'd hit the gym and try to burn out the tension. Sometimes it worked. Not this time, though. "What's up?"

"Our buyer wants a little more convincing. We need to fetch something that will make him drool."

"Yeah? What?"

"I know just what will do the trick."

The pierced waitress hustled over. Hustled. Jeez, that hadn't taken long.

The waitress gave Lewis a big smile. "What can I get for you, hon?"

Yep. Definitely a lesbian . . .

When the waitress was gone, Lewis told him.

"Damn, that's ballsy. You think that will sell it?"

"Oh, yeah. This guy is so macho he makes you look like a sissy. If we pull this off—meaning if *you* pull it off—then I think he'll fall all over himself to make the deal."

"I'm up for it. When?"

"Soon as we can. Plug the stats into your VR program and run it a couple times. Whenever you're ready, we'll go."

He nodded. It was good to have something to do. Take his mind off the other stuff. Dead cops and all . . .

* * *

Net Force HQ
Quantico, Virginia

"Can you get off work, Tommy?"

Thorn nodded at the image of Marissa on his desk's phone screen. "I don't see why not. The DoD can breathe down my neck just as easily over my virgil if I'm in Georgia as they can if I am here."

"Good. I'll tell my grandparents we're coming."

"You want to take the jet?"

She laughed. "The jet? Oh, yeah, they get a lot of those landing on the red clay road running to the Pinehurst farm. Chickens would stop laying eggs for a year. Jet, right. We'll take my car—I wouldn't want your pilot or chauffeur to get lost. When can you leave? Tomorrow?"

"No reason not to. Will the CIA let you take a vacation?"

"I expect so. I could quit, given as how I'm about to marry a rich guy, but they owe me six weeks. Nothing I'm doing can't wait a few days to finish. Pack warm—it's chilly down there this time of year."

"Yes, ma'am," he said.

When they discommed, Thorn called his assistant. "I'm going to be out of the office for a few days," he told her. "Emergency calls can be routed to my virgil. I'll check e-mail and messages while I'm gone."

"Yes, sir. Where are you going?"

"Georgia. To meet Marissa's grandparents."

Bugworld
Bug Base #13

Jay lay on a slope covered in tall and thick red grass, over-looking one of the alien bases. The sky was a swirly orange, with a dark blue sun and fluffy, electric-blue clouds. Down below this hillside was his target, and the alien base was itself mostly a study in bright green. The visual contrasts were stunning. There was an odd, ozonelike smell to the air, and strange sounds—creaks and cracks, and animals-but-not-as-we-know-them noises—added more layers to the illusion. Jay felt as if he really were on an alien world.

It was just coming on dusk on this part of the planet. The blue sun cast long and eerie shadows. Given the local star's hue, he wasn't sure what the real colors would be, but that didn't matter.

Almost time.

Jay had planned his attack for a hair after sunset. This would provide some cover, and the guards might be less wary, with it only just getting dark.

He peered through the sniperscope, and zoomed in on the guard shack beside the gate. Almost two hundred meters away, the two dark-purple aliens stood there, creatures from a nightmare, each holding a futuristic carbinelike weapon. Their heads were huge, and reminded Jay of Venus flytraps—flat and slightly rounded with huge jaws. Bony ridges sat atop the heads, guarding three eyes—two in the front, and one in back. Sneaking up on them was a bitch.

They were big suckers, too. Had to be at least two and a half meters tall, with three thick stumpy legs and three arms each.

The bugs looked altogether wrong in a human biped's view.

Which was part of the fun of the game. After all, how hard would it be to want to knock off such creatures? It added to the immersion factor, the being-there aspect of a top computer game, by giving the player an attractive goal.

Earthling versus the u-u-ugly monsters.

Jay double-checked his own weapon. It was an Accuracy International AW-SP with a heavy barrel and suppressor, one of the most accurate of all sniper rifles.

This was his third time at this base. He'd tried getting closer with shorter-range weapons, but he'd been unable to do so unseen by the guards.

So this time he'd come up with a long-range attack.

The War Against the Bugs had an extensive database of weapons built into the game, ranging from swords and knives to modern firearms. Anything that might be available on Earth to somebody trying on an Army base, you could use here. Which made sense.

The game allowed for team play—either with other VR players or AI-bots—but Jay liked playing solo.

This time he thought he had the gear and his strategy right.

The trick was timing. Every twenty minutes roving guards cycled past the gate. Jay wanted to time his attack so that he'd have the maximum window before the dead gate guards were spotted by the rovers. He had tried to take out all the guards at once, but he hadn't been fast enough—one of them had always managed to get a call for help out, and that was no good. Two at a time was his limit—they were fast for big bugs. . . .

Once inside the base, his goal was to blow up the armory vault. He had all the explosives he'd need in his kit, but to destroy the target he'd have to break inside—it was protected by armor plate and a heavy steel door. One of his gadgets was an electronic code descrambler. Intelligence he'd gained on the alien base showed it to have a high-bit encryption lock. This meant it could take up to five minutes to break into the vault.

The time factors—twenty minutes before the guard came back, minus the five through the door, plus the time required to get down the hill and *to* the armory—put him on a short clock. At least if he wanted to get back out again.

He *could* take out the roving guard once he was inside, but there was no way to know how many other checkpoints that guard passed, or when *he* would be missed.

There went the roving guard, his three legs moving him along at a solid *thump-thump-thump*.

Jay waited until he had stepped out of sight, and counted to twenty. As he did so, he dialed the magnification up on the scope.

There . . .

Bammff! The gun wasn't completely silent, but the noise wouldn't carry far. Guard one went down, yellow blood spraying from his head.

Guard two stood there in shock for a moment before turning toward the perimeter alarm button.

But Jay had timed this carefully—the remaining guard was three meters away from the alarm, giving time for another shot—

He got guard two in the upper chest, spinning him around—fortunately *away* from the alarm.

But this guard was made of sterner stuff, because he still tried crawling toward the control panel.

Jay fired again. The guard sprawled.

And then Jay was up, running down the hill, the backpack with explosives slung over his shoulders—

A countdown timer in his peripheral heads-up vision began running—

18:50 . . . He was at the guard station. He ran past.

The VR was flawless, maintaining a fluid frame rate so that everything stayed sharp and clear. Nothing on the left or right.

Over the simple lift-arm that blocked the entrance . . .

He looked to his right and could see the backs of the roving guards, hundreds of meters away. He slowed slightly, not wanting to draw attention to himself, but needing to keep his speed up—

17:45 . . .

He made his way past several buildings toward his target. No one in sight.

He hadn't made it this far before. He drank in every detail. Pale blue pole-mounted lights had begun coming on as the sun set, and he stayed in the pools of shadow surrounding each one as he moved toward the armory.

Almost there.

He readied the descrambler, pulling it off his belt and mashing the on button. His other hand held a silenced HK USP .45. An infrared laser sight provided an aiming point that, in theory, only he could see, the aliens having vision similar to men.

16:10 . . .

Jay's heart pounded. It was often this way when he made a leap in a game. He might play a single level dozens of times, getting stuck at the same point over and over again, but sometimes he'd break past the bottleneck and make it the rest of the way on the next try.

And it looked like that might happen. . . .

He glanced right and left, scanning for trouble. The problem with getting so excited was that it made you sloppy. Still clear.

He was at the armory.

Go, go, go—!

He slapped the descrambler onto the keypad lock and activated it. Ha!

Bright flashes of light blossomed in his vision—

Dammit!

Jay watched as his VR viewpoint shifted backward from his body, rising to a point three meters overhead.

An alien wearing a guard's uniform popped out from behind a doorway twenty or thirty feet away. It was grinning. If that hideous expression could be called a grin.

Crap.

He hadn't seen that one coming. Part of the problem with having never made it this far before. He'd gotten careless trying to beat the mission. Bright green letters from the VR menu popped up, accompanied by a deep bass techno theme:

Mission failed. Try again?

Jay checked the RW time. 12:45. If he didn't quit now, he'd miss lunch. He looked at the game timer. 15:23. He could have made it if the damn guard hadn't gotten him.

Yeah. And if your aunt had wheels, she'd be a tea cart. . . .

Screw lunch.

He used his VR hand to reach for the try-again control, but had a sudden realization and stopped. *Playing the game to* win *isn't why you are here, monkey-boy. Did you forget that part?*

He shook his head.

He had to hand it to the guy who'd put this together. It was easy to see why it had gotten the results it had—it was addictive. But what he needed to do was figure out who had built the scenario, and how to run him down—not beat the game. He was here to drain the swamp, not wrestle the alligators. . . .

He smiled at himself. He could always play video games for fun. This was serious business. Best he remember that.

11

The terrorist—or "freedom fighter," depending on your sociopolitical or religious belief—Abu Hassan was a Palestinian by birth, but raised in the U.S. as Ibrahim Sidys. He took his war-nom from, of all things, an old Popeye cartoon about Ali Baba and the Forty Thieves. That's not where it came from originally—the name was not at all uncommon—but that's where *he* got it.

Only in America . . .

This Abu Hassan had never been a cartoon version of Bluto, but a cold-blooded killer responsible for the deaths of hundreds, in bombings, shootings, and even a couple of poisonings. For nine years he had led one of the most radical factions in the Middle East, and was wanted by just about everybody for capital crimes—even the Syrians hated him—for Abu Hassan did not discriminate when he dropped the hammer. Almost everybody was his enemy, and he had no problems with collateral damage if he got the job done. Allah would know his own, and as for the rest? Who cared?

As it happened, one Sunday morning in May of 2012, Terry "Butch" Reilly, then a major in the United States Army, had been having coffee at a Starbucks just outside the old Green Zone when Abu Hassan's group rolled up to machine-gun a police station across the street. Four cops and six civilians went down initially in the hosing, but something happened to Hassan's Land Cruiser as it was pulling away—later it was shown that a return round, probably from an Iraqi policeman, penetrated the car's hood and broke off a battery terminal. The car died and wouldn't restart, and the assassins, five of them, piled out and took off on foot.

Abu Hassan, waving an AK-47, ran into the Starbucks to obtain another automobile, assuming at least one of the patrons owned a car. Calm as you please, Major Reilly, in civvies and crouched low with the other patrons when the shooting started, drew his Beretta side arm from under a sleeveless fishing vest and put two rounds into Hassan from four meters away, one in the chest and one in the head.

Apparently, nobody was more amazed at this action than Reilly, largely because he was, and had been throughout his military career, a paper- and photon-pusher—he worked in PR, information services, and was doing a tour in the "semiactive, advisor-status-only" war zone only because he couldn't get any more rank without it. He hadn't fired a gun since basic training, except for recertification once a year, and had barely qualified doing that.

That the most wanted terrorist in the region was taken out by an armchair computer geek who barely knew which end of his weapon put forth the bullet eventually got much play in the press.

When Reilly went over to make sure the terrorist wasn't going to be getting up and shooting anybody, he saw that the dead man carried a pistol along with his AK. Quite a striking gun it was: a blued-steel Walther PPK .380, with ivory grips, hand-tuned, Butch would eventually learn, by a master gunsmith in Laredo, Texas. The gun, Butch would also find out, had been a present from a fellow terrorist who had once been very high up in the PLO and a close associate of the late Yasir Arafat.

The major didn't see as how Abu Hassan would be needing the piece any longer, and it would be a shame to have such a fine talisman wind up in some Iraqi evidence locker, so he stuck the gun into his pocket. If any of the stunned Starbucks patrons noticed, or cared, none said anything.

Taking out one of the most wanted terrorists in the world in a one-on-one didn't hurt an officer's career any. A few months later, Major Reilly was promoted to Colonel Reilly, and eventually assigned a base command back in the States. This turned out to be one of the new high-tech installations built to house a partner organization for Fort Huachuca. The fort and the partner organization, coming up just ahead, were north of the Mexican border off SR 90, outside of Huachuca City, Arizona. Colonel Reilly's command was responsible for information management, DISA, in conjunction with JITC, mainly interoperability C4I support, operational field assessments, and technical assistance to various combat commands and assorted related agencies.

A buncha desk commandos, Carruth knew. Spin-controllers.

But: Behind his desk on the wall, mounted in an oak shadowbox, Colonel Reilly kept a souvenir from his one active afternoon in the field—Abu Hassan's pistol.

All of this was public record, and Carruth had read about it, seen it on television, and heard stories about it when he'd still been in the Navy. Be in the right place at the right time, and even a pencil-neck could be some kind of accidental hero.

There was still some residual shame amongst terrorists that the deadly Abu Hassan had been taken down by someone who was less than a glorious warrior. It was one thing to be Goliath slain by a sneaky and treacherous David fielding superior weaponry; it was something else entirely to be potted by David's dweeby little four-eyed Starbucks-coffee-drinking brother.

Despite the recent attacks, all you needed to get onto this particular base was a driver's license, proof of car registration and insurance, and a copy of your orders or TDY. Carruth knew a printer who could make *money* that would pass, so ID was nothing.

Carruth flashed his phony orders and ID, drove onto the base, made his way to the adjunct run by Reilly, flashed more phony orders there, and during lunchtime, just strolled down the hall as if he owned it to the colonel's office.

There was a keypad lock on the door, which was not much—he could have booted it open, but that would have set off an alarm. Since he had the code for the lock, which was supposed to be changed weekly, but which was changed maybe twice a year, Carruth just tapped in the combination and walked in.

Security. What a joke.

He took the shadowbox down, opened it, put the gun in his pocket, and replaced the stolen one with a BB-gun copy of a PPK he'd fitted with fake ivory grips. It wouldn't pass inspection up close, but if you just glanced at it, you might not notice immediately. That could be fun, the next time the colonel showed it off:

Abu Hassan was carrying a BB pistol *when you shot him? What was his AK-47, a* water gun . . . ?

Carruth had to hand it to Lewis, this was brilliant. This particular trophy would be worth its weight in gold to a hard-core fanatic—it was practically a holy relic. . . .

Carruth smiled as he left the office, the building, got into his car, and drove away. How easy was that?

It was criminal, that's what it was. Fucking Army.

But the terrorist wannabe Lewis had on the line didn't have to know how simple and easy it had been, now did he?

Just in case nobody noticed the substitution until after he was long gone, Carruth would make an anonymous call, once Lewis had things set up. Not to Colonel Reilly, who might be disposed to keep the theft to himself, but to the news media. Lewis's buyer would pick up on that quick enough. And he'd fall all over himself to give Lewis money once he saw the Walther. . . .

Things were going along pretty good so far.

Churchill, Virginia

Kent pushed back a little from the table. "Best pasta I've ever had," he said, smiling.

Nadine Howard returned the smile. "Uh huh, I'm sure."

"Well, okay, best pasta I've had all week, then."

"Better," she said.

John Howard said, "I've got a couple of Cuban cigars left." He looked at his wife. "Leave the dishes, hon, I'll get them before I go to bed."

"Go smoke your noxious weed," she said. "I'll clean up."

Kent had given up cigarettes thirty-five years ago, and never gotten much into other forms of tobacco, but Cuban cigars two or three times a year probably weren't going to kill him if they hadn't yet. Plus he was living on borrowed time anyhow.

"Don't light them until you get into the garage," Nadine said. "I'm not having my new house stunk up by those nasty things."

Howard and Kent both smiled.

It was cold out, but Howard had put a little space heater in the garage, which had room for two cars but only held one, and there was an old couch and a couple of end tables with ashtrays on them there, too. He cranked the heater up and handed Kent a sealed, clear-plastic tube with a fat cigar, maybe twelve or fourteen centimeters long, inside. Kent broke the seal, and there was a *whoosh* of escaping gas.

"Inert gas to keep it from going stale," Howard said. "Helium or argon, something like that. Better than vacuum, so they say."

The aroma of the tobacco filled his nostrils.

"Hermoso Number Four," Howard said. "Hand-rolled from Havana. Got them from a British diplomat who buys in quantity."

"Thanks."

Howard produced a cutter they both used, then a wooden match, scratching it and allowing it to burn for a second before he lit Kent's cigar, then his own.

The two men stood there for a moment, puffing. The blue-gray smoke filled the air, wreathing their heads in the fragrant odor.

"It's a nice house," Kent offered. "Big yard."

"We have to hire a gardener, come spring, to take care of it."

"Tyrone can't mow the lawn?"

Howard smiled. "When he comes home from Geneva. That exchange-student thing runs until June. If I wait until then to cut the grass, it'll be knee-deep and full of weeds. I ain't disposed to do it anyhow. I did enough of that as a boy. Easier on my back to hire somebody."

"Civilian consulting pays pretty well," Kent observed.

"Oh, boy, yes, it does. You want to chuck your jarhead job and get in the pool, the water is just fine. I can point you to some folks'd love to have an old warhorse like you educating them. Make two or three times what you make now."

Kent smiled at his friend. "If I had a wife and teenaged son, I might find that appealing, but I don't need a house, and I don't spend the money I make now. How much room you figure an old Marine requires?"

Howard took another long drag from his cigar. He blew the smoke out in a big ring toward the ceiling. "You might get married again. Have some little ones running around to call you Daddy."

Kent laughed, nearly choking on the smoke as he did. "Yeah, right. Have somebody to push my wheelchair around when he gets out of grade school?"

"You think you'll make it that long, doing stuff like this?" Howard waved the cigar.

Both men chuckled.

"Nadine met this nice lady at church, just moved into the area. A widow, few years older than you, but a very nice personality, she says . . ."

Kent laughed yet again. "Tell your wife I don't need any help in that department."

Howard must have caught something in his tone. "Really? You dating somebody?"

"Not exactly. I am seeing a woman, but it's more of a . . . professional relationship."

Howard blinked.

Kent let him worry about that for a couple of seconds. Then he grinned. "It's not what you're thinking, John. She's a guitar teacher. I'm learning how to play the thing—after a fashion."

"No kidding?"

"Well, if you heard me fumbling at it, you'd think it was a joke, but I am taking lessons. Twice a week."

"That's not exactly the same as painting the town red, Abe."

"At my age, partying tends to be a little more reserved. Sitting in a nice, sturdy chair strumming a guitar is about my speed."

"You're not that old."

"Come back and see me in fifteen years and say that. Assuming I'm still around."

"I will. Assuming I'm still around. You want a beer?"

"Sure."

Howard leaned over the couch.

"You got a fridge out here?"

"Just a little one," he said.

Kent shook his head.

Howard produced two bottles of beer. "How's the thing going on the Army base attacks?"

Kent took one of the bottles, raised it in salute, and swigged from it. "How is it a civilian consultant knows about such things?"

It was a rhetorical question. The old-boy network worked as well in the military as it did anywhere else.

Howard had retired a general in the Army—well, technically, the National Guard, which had been running Net Force before the DoD took it over—but you didn't get to that rank without knowing a lot of people you could swap information with, to your benefit and theirs.

When Howard didn't respond, Kent said, "Gridley is on their trail. He's like the Royal Canadian Mounties—he always gets his man. Far as I can tell, anyhow."

Howard drank from his own beer. He held his bottle up. "To our men in uniform, including yourself."

"Hear, hear."

They drank. "So, tell me about this guitar teacher."

"Not much to tell. She's about fifty. Divorced, plays well, teaches well. Says she has a cat."

"Anything romantic?"

Kent shrugged. "She's nice to look at."

"But you're interested?"

"I said I was old, not that I was dead."

"Gonna make a move?"

He shrugged again. "I don't know. Maybe."

Howard toked on his cigar, letting his silence speak to that.

Kent took a couple puffs of his stogie. He had checked out Jen's ex—at least he was pretty sure he had the right guy. There couldn't be that many cello players named "Armand" who had recordings out and had just gotten married recently to a much younger woman. Or maybe there could and they didn't have a presence on the net. He'd known a guy once, Ted McCall, who wrote a book about, of all things, barbed wire. Apparently there were thousands of different kinds produced over the years, and a bunch of folks snipped off foot-and-a-half pieces and mounted them on boards and collected them. Paid real money for some rare kinds. McCall had quite a collection, so he'd written a book about how to identify the various kinds. He'd called it *Twist and Shout: Putting a Name to Unusual Varieties of Barbed Wire.*

One day, ole Ted had logged onto the Internet site that

sold his book and tapped in his name to see how sales were doing. Up popped the title *Barbed Wire Varieties,* by Ted McCall. Look at that, he'd thought, the stupid sons of bitches had gotten his title wrong! He'd clicked on the link to see what else they'd screwed up, and found himself looking at a picture of somebody who wasn't him. Seemed there was *another* Ted McCall who had written an entirely different book on the same subject. McCall wasn't that uncommon a name, but what were the chances that there would be another man with the same name who was also a collector of fence wire *and* who had written a book on it? It boggled his mind.

So it was possible that there were two Armands—or even more—who fit the bill, but it was highly unlikely. The closer the match, the more likely it was that this guy, this Armand, was Jen's ex. So Kent had read all about him. There were some indications that Armand was "somewhat difficult" to work with, and something of a perfectionist, and that went with Jen's description of him.

Why had Kent bothered if he wasn't interested in Jen? He wasn't sure about the answer to that one.

12

Greenville, South Carolina

"I'm glad we decided to drive," Thorn said.

"Good thing I know how," Marissa said. They were in her SUV, a small and sporty Honda, with enough weight to make the ride comfortable, on the highway between Charlotte and Greenville.

"Just because I don't need a car doesn't mean I never learned how. Having a chauffeur lets me get a lot of work done while I'm in transit."

"So would taking the bus or a train," she said.

"What, and ride with you rabble?"

She laughed. "I'm glad to see you loosening up, sweetie. I'd sure hate to have my grandparents think you were a stick-in-the-mud. Bad enough you are so melaninly challenged."

"I'll work on my tan," he said.

"Even with your Native American blood, you're always gonna look like a pale pink sock mixed into a load of new blue jeans, at least around my family."

He chuckled.

"You travel much by car before you got so rich and started taking private jets to buy your hamburgers?"

Thorn smiled. "Oh, yeah. You want the condensed version? Or the full-length travelogue?"

"Tell all, Tommy. We have a ways yet to go to Grandma's house."

"Okay. When I was young and heading toward the height of my stupidity—this was the summer I turned thirteen, so I was still a couple years away—my grandfather took me on a road trip. Though our people were mostly from around Spokane, we had some distant cousins and great-aunts and -uncles who were Choctaw, and Grampa allowed as how I should meet them.

"I don't know if you know the history. Along with the Cherokee, Chickasaw, Creek, and Seminole, the Choctaw got rounded up and sent along the Trail of Tears to Oklahoma, as part of the white man's land grab. My distant relatives somehow managed to escape into the swamps along the way, down in Louisiana. There, they hid out and pretended to be black Dutch or something. Nobody ever came looking for them, people left them alone, and most of them became farmers or fishers. Nobody got rich, but nobody died cooped up on a dust-bowl rez in Oklahoma.

"Anyway, my grandfather decided it was time to go and introduce me to them. So he loaded up his old Chevy pickup truck, and off we went."

Thorn smiled again at the memories that floated up.

"It was a long trip. About twenty-five hundred miles each way. My grandfather didn't have much use for the Interstate system, so we took state highways wherever possible, sometimes county roads. Went through Idaho, Utah, Wyoming, Kansas, Oklahoma, and Texas on the way to Louisiana, and added in New Mexico, Arizona, Nevada, California, and Oregon on the way back to Spokane.

"My grandfather did a lot of knocking around as a young man. We'd be tooling along at sixty in the middle of Nowhere, Kansas, and all of a sudden he'd pull over. We'd get out, and he'd talk about the place: 'These are the

Smoky Hills. That over there, that's Pawnee Rock. The Spanish came here, the French. The Americans didn't show up until 1806. The wind always blows.'

"We'd stretch, pee, hop back in the old truck, and hit the road again. Hot and sunny, pouring rain and thunderstorms, saw a tornado once. We made stops like that all across the country. We'd pull into a country store, buy a loaf of bread and some cheese and lunch meat, make sandwiches, have an apple, drink a soft drink, like that. At night, we'd crawl into sleeping bags, either in the back of the truck or on the ground. Look at the stars, and my grandfather would tell me stories. Places he'd been. People he'd known. Bars he'd gotten drunk in."

The memory was fine and green in Thorn's head. He smiled.

"There was a long and rich history here long before white men sailed the Atlantic. My grandfather knew some of it, and told it to me. I missed a lot, being full of myself, but some I remember."

Marissa nodded. "The white men were hauling my people here belowdecks in chains back when they were slaughtering your kin," she said. "Come Judgment Day, a lot of them will have a lot to answer for."

Thorn nodded in return. "Bad times for a lot of people.

"Um. Anyway, I didn't really understand how big this country is until I spent a couple weeks driving across it. Passing through the little towns, the long stretches of nothing between them. We stopped at Cherokee trading posts in Oklahoma; stopped at bars in Texas; we camped on the prairies, in the woods, fields, once in an old one-room schoolhouse that had been boarded up for years. One of the highlights of my life, that trip."

"You loved your grandfather."

"Oh, yeah. We didn't talk about such things, being men and all, but he was always there for me. I miss him."

"I'm sorry. I'm happy my grandparents are still around."

"You didn't tell them I saw those pictures of them on your wall, did you?"

She laughed. "Tommy, they know you and I sleep together, being as how they taught me that when it was time to get married I needed to be sure things worked in that arena before I tied the knot. So they'll know you've spent the night at my place, and they know I've got those paintings on my walls."

He nodded. "Yeah, I guess." The paintings in question were of her grandparents, Amos and Ruth, as young adults, and her grandmother was altogether undressed in the one of her. Quite the looker as a young woman.

"Granny's in pretty good shape for a woman heading toward eighty" she said. "Maybe if you ask, she'll take off her clothes and let you see how well she's aged."

"Jesus, Marissa!"

She laughed. "Still a little bit of stick-in-the-mud there, sweetie. We'll have to work on that."

Circle S Ranch
Oatmeal, South Dakota

Jay guessed he must have been an Old West pioneer in some previous incarnation—either that, or he was more of a romantic than he liked to believe—because of his hand-built scenarios, several of his favorites were cowboy sequences.

In this one, Jay was a wrangler who was going to watch other wranglers ride bucking broncos. Yeah, sure, it was yee-haw kinda stuff, but information flows and datasets could be snorers, and anything that made them more interesting to parse was to the good.

But as he was climbing up onto the split-rail wooden fence to sit and watch, he glanced over at the weathered barn and saw Siddhartha Gautama, aka the Buddha, in a saffron robe, leaning against the faded wooden barn, smiling.

Jay laughed. Saji. She was the only one who had unrestricted access to his scenarios. Even Thorn had to knock. . . .

He climbed back down from the fence and ambled toward the thin and smiling figure. Buddha was sometimes depicted as a laughing fat man—the Hotai—but historically speaking, Siddhartha had been an ascetic at one point, barely eating enough to survive. Even after finding the Middle Way, the man who became the Realized Buddha had never given in to dietary excess. Jay knew this because Saji had taught him the rudiments of the philosophy and its history, even though he had not exactly embraced it. . . .

He strolled up to Saji in her Buddha form. "Hey, Buddy. How's it goin'?"

" 'Buddy.' You make that same bad joke every time. And you're a terrible cowboy—way too much corn pone in that accent."

"Ouch. You got a mean streak, O holy one. What's up?"

"Nothing much. We're almost out of milk, and I wanted you to stop and pick some up on the way home."

"Sure, no problem. And, uh, I'll get the right kind, this time."

"You better. Otherwise, it'll be you up all night trying to calm the boy down."

He laughed.

Buddha smiled enigmatically and then, like the Cheshire Cat, vanished, leaving only the smile, which faded shortly thereafter.

Jay shook his head, and headed back toward the corral. Mommas, don't let your babies grow up to be programmers. . . .

Pinehurst, Georgia

Ruth was, as Thorn's grandfather used to say, a pistol. After she hugged Marissa, she did the same for Thorn, and long past seventy-five or not, she had strength in her grip. She leaned back and looked closely at his face. "Good

THE ARCHIMEDES EFFECT   109

bone structure," she said. "Must be more Indian than
honky in you."

Thorn laughed. "My mother's doing," he said. "The
white man in our family woodpile was earlier."

Ruth laughed, a loud, raucous rumble from deep down.
"He doesn't seem like such a tight ass to me."

Marissa grinned, real big, and Thorn shook his head.
"Well, I see where Marissa gets it from."

"Come on in, you lettin' the heat out. Amos has gone to
take Sheila for her PT; he should be back in half an hour or
so." She closed the door behind him.

The house was a lot warmer than the blustery, raw
Georgia morning outside, a big woodstove installed in
front of the fireplace providing a radiant heat. "I just put
biscuits in the oven. Stick your stuff in the bedroom and
come on back down, I'll fix you some breakfast. You look
like a man who could use a few pounds, and Lord knows
you won't gain any weight from Marissa's cooking. I hope
she warned you."

"Yes, ma'am, she allowed as how she wasn't much of a
cook."

"I tried to teach the child, but she was always more interested in climbing trees and beatin' up on the boys. Go on
upstairs, let me go fetch some eggs."

Ruth hurried away.

The house was fairly large, and probably well over a
hundred years old. It was a big living room, a high ceiling
with wainscotting, and had a dark blue couch eight feet
long facing the woodstove. There was an overstuffed chair
and a couple of end tables, and a coffee table, the latter
three of which looked like cherry, matte-finished and
waxed or oiled rather than shiny. A matching cabinet stood
in one corner, and the door was ajar enough to see a fair-
sized TV screen behind it. Must be a satellite dish out here
somewhere; it was a long way from town for cable.

One entire wall was nearly all taken up by bookshelves,
floor to ceiling, fifteen feet wide, at least, filled to over-
flowing with mostly hardbacks and a few paperbacks.

The house immediately felt like a home—lived in, comfortable, full of life.

There was a hall with a room off to the left, and the kitchen straight ahead. It was clean, the painted and wallpapered walls looked fairly fresh, and the smell from the kitchen was great—biscuits baking. His own grandmother had been big on cooking breakfast, but Thorn had fallen out of the habit of eating much in the morning years ago.

As they headed up the stairs, Thorn asked, "Who is Sheila?"

"The dog. She's got a bad hip. My grampa takes her in a couple times a week for PT."

"The dog?"

"You didn't have pets on the rez, Tommy?"

"Yeah, sure, but we didn't have any *doggy* therapist, only a vet who mostly took care of horses and cows. Who would put out that kind of money on a dog?"

"Here's another big gap in your education."

They reached the top of the stairs, and Marissa led the way into a bedroom with a large window that allowed in a fair amount of light—or would if it wasn't so gray and overcast as it was today. The bed was a double, with a brass headboard shaped like a big letter H with a second crosspiece, and there was a heavy patchwork quilt covering it. It was somewhat cooler than downstairs, and Thorn reckoned that the woodstove was the primary, if not the only, source of heat. Close the door here and it was apt to get pretty chilly on a winter's evening.

"The little bathroom is at the end of the hall, and there's a space heater in it—it gets cold. You can shower there, but the tub is in the big bathroom downstairs."

"Nice."

"This used to be my room. Fortunately, my grandparents didn't make it into a museum after I grew up, so you don't see the Wesley Snipes, Denzel Washington, and Tom Cruise posters I had up when I was fourteen."

"Tom Cruise?"

"Even then I had a weakness for cute white boys."

Thorn chuckled. "So, you were talking about Shelia?"

"Anybody who says, 'It's just a dog.' has never really gotten to know one. My grandparents have owned—or been owned by—Sheila for ten years. She's family. Before that, they had others: Titus, Laramie, and Winslow are the ones I remember."

"I never had a dog as a kid," he said. "Too many cousins in and out of our house, wasn't enough room to keep a hamster."

"People love their companion animals. They feed some of 'em better than a lot of people in this country eat. They take them to the vet when they get sick or hurt, give them medicine, have surgery done. Pretty much anything you can do to a person with a surgical scalpel, somebody has done to a pet—they fix torn tendons or broken bones, take out tumors, even replace bad hips. X-rays, MRIs, whatever tests you need. I knew a man once spent six hundred dollars on treatments for a budgie for a broken wing. Bird cost him thirty dollars originally."

"Jesus."

"So if your dog tears up his hind leg running through the field, you can get it repaired by a top surgeon who specializes in doggy orthopedics, and then you can take him to someplace like Canine Peak Performance, where a vet who does rehab will put him in a tank full of water with a treadmill in it and strengthen the muscles without putting as much weight on the injury as it would walking around your neighborhood. That's what Sheila is doing."

"Really?"

"It's a coming thing. Been around for years, started out for rehab on show animals, or dogs entered in athletic competitions—catching Frisbees or agility competitions and the like—and once people started seeing how well it worked, they started bringing in the regular critters who were just ordinary door-blockers, like Sheila."

"I had no idea." Thorn shook his head. "And there is one of these places out here in the Georgia boonies?"

"My second cousin runs it," she said. "She got trained in

it out in Raleigh Hills, Oregon, by a woman vet named Helfer, who had flyball dogs. Cousin Louella has enough customers so she keeps busy, even out here."

"I guess I need to get out more."

"That's for sure, Tommy. You are woefully lacking in general knowledge about the world. All those years as a computer geek. I'll shape you up, though, don't worry."

He smiled. "Yes, ma'am."

They heard the sound of an approaching vehicle. Thorn moved to the window and looked out. An old, dark green Ford pickup truck arrived. A tall and fit-looking black man alighted, reached back into the truck, and collected a large, short-haired, black and tan dog. Thorn didn't recognize the variety. The man—that would be Marissa's grandfather, Amos—squatted and set the dog gently onto the ground. She wagged her tail and headed for the front door, favoring her right rear leg.

Marissa said, "Let's go down and let you meet Grampa and Sheila. If the dog bites you, you and I will have to re-think our relationship."

Thorn grinned. For a second, Marissa kept her face serious. Just when he was getting worried that she *was* serious, she cracked a smile. "You're funny," he said.

"I am. Try and keep up. Nobody likes a slow white boy, even if you are cute."

13

Lewis had elected to meet the potential buyer, Mishari Aziz, in New Orleans this time. It was much cooler here than in Miami, downright chilly, temperature maybe forty, with gray skies and a turn-your-head-around wind blowing. Even in the cold, the place smelled damp. When her plane had come in for a landing the first time, a couple days earlier, she'd halfway expected to look down at the swamps surrounding the airport and see dinosaurs lumbering around.

Assuming, of course, that they all hadn't drowned in the most recent flood. New Orleans was still right in the middle of Hurricane Alley, and a deluge was always lurking to fill the bowl that was the city.

No dinosaurs down there today, either—if you didn't count Aziz and his hidebound antifemale attitude.

She drove her rented car to the FedEx place at the airport and collected the package she had sent to herself before leaving the District. Back in the rental car, she tore open the box and removed her little gun—an S&W Chief snub-nose in .38 Special. Packing a gun for air travel was still possible, of course, but you had to declare it, and several of the airlines would put a big tag on the suitcase with "GUN" to identify it, and she didn't need that connection. Plus, there were thieves at the baggage carousel who hung around waiting for such tidbits. People who thought their checked luggage was safe on an airliner were wrong.

She slipped the revolver into her jacket pocket, then fished out the Walther .380 PPK, which she had gift-wrapped to look like a birthday present.

She hadn't seen Carruth yet, but he was supposed to have gotten to the airport three hours before she arrived, and he was no doubt following her. Playing it cute by staying hidden, but that was the point.

She pulled a cell phone from her belt and thumbed the button for the programmed number.

"At your service, ma'am," Carruth said.

"Where are you?"

"Other end of the FedEx lot, in the white van with the magnetic sign on the door."

She looked. Saw the van. The sign on the passenger door said SPEEDY COURIER SERVICE.

"All right, let's do it."

"I'm on my way. Give me forty-five minutes' head start so I can get set up."

"Go," she said.

She tried to sound calm, but the truth was, she was nervous. This was where the rubber would meet the road. Up to now, Aziz had been playing it cautious, maybe not as sure of her as to believe she really could deliver the goods. The more he became convinced of that, the more dangerous the game became.

And while it shouldn't matter, she had embarrassed him in Miami by losing the surveillance team he'd sicced on her. A reasonable, rational man in the game would accept that and move on; of course, a reasonable, rational man wouldn't want to do what Aziz wanted.

There was a chance that once he believed she could give

him the keys to the armory he lusted after, he would think he could just take them instead of paying for them.

She didn't know how smart he really was and, unfortunately, the only way to find out was to put herself in a somewhat risky position. She didn't trust the man as far as she could walk on water, but at least she could keep the risk minimal.

Proper planning prevents piss-poor performance. She grinned at the memory. Her father had told her that—but failed to pay attention to his own advice, in the end. Still, as these things went, she had done just about everything she could to set it up properly. She had scouted the location, made the arrangements, gone over it in her head a dozen times. No battle plan ever survived first contact with the enemy, of course, but she was willing to bet she was better prepared than Aziz, who would have been informed of the specific meeting place only about the time Carruth got there.

The meeting was set for Woldenberg Riverfront Park, a twenty-acre green space right on the Mississippi River, near the French Market. There would be tourists there, even in this cold weather—there was something called "The Moonwalk," which let you hike right down to the edge of the river. You could see the big bridge from there, and the Toulouse Street Wharf. There was an old riverboat ferry moored just up the river. Very public.

New Orleans was not a good town to drive in, at least not down in the French Quarter, that part having been built long before big automobiles were the normal means of transportation. Narrow streets and a lot of traffic made for slow going, and if you had to leave in a hurry, you might find yourself in trouble. Plus there were cameras on every other corner these days—the barely controlled riot that was Mardi Gras came every year, and being able to keep an eye on things, with a filmed record to go along with that, made the local police happier.

There weren't any cameras where she was to meet Aziz, at least not any official ones. She had checked there, the day before yesterday.

The drive from the airport took a while, but she was in no hurry, and when she finally found a parking place and alighted, it was mid-afternoon. The cold wind blew off the river, which was passing wide at this point.

She carried the wrapped Walther in her gloved left hand, and kept her right hand in her Windbreaker's pocket, fingers curled around the butt of the Smith & Wesson. The fastest draw, she'd been taught, was to have the gun in your hand when trouble began. If it came to that, she'd be ready.

She spotted the white van as she headed down the path toward the river to the appointed meeting place. A man in that van with a scoped rifle would have a clear field of fire, which was what she wanted.

There was some kind of weedy smell in the air, maybe some dead fish mixed in. Not the same as you'd get at the seashore, no salt in it, but definitely not a pleasant odor. She had her hair tucked under a baseball cap, and her clothes were baggy. From a distance, she might pass for a slightly built man or maybe a teenaged boy.

Aziz was already waiting for her. He was dressed for the weather, wearing a long jacket over wool trousers, a hat with earmuffs, and leather gloves. He still looked cold.

He saw her approaching, and couldn't stop himself from glancing to his right quickly.

Might as well point that way and announce it: *Hey, my backup man is hiding right there. . . .*

She didn't bother to look. Carruth should have that covered.

Aziz glared at her, that male disdain obvious in his stare. "What have you brought?"

"See for yourself."

She handed him the package.

There was nobody else close to them. Aziz tore open the wrapping until he could see the gun.

"Ah!" he said. He smiled. Nice teeth. Even, straight, white.

He knew what it was, of course, but she pushed it a little. "You recognize this?"

"Of course. It belonged to the freedom fighter and martyr Abu Hassan. I read about the theft only yesterday." He stroked the pistol as if touching a religious icon.

"Are we to a point where you now believe we can deliver the items about which we have spoken?"

"Yes, we believe it."

Finally. How sweet to hear it, at last.

But his next words turned it all sour: "The gun, it is loaded?"

She felt her belly clench. "No."

Did he really think she was that stupid? To give a loaded gun to a fanatic who wanted something she had in the worst way? Probably he did think so.

"Ah, well, no matter." He stuck his free hand into his jacket pocket. He hadn't quite cleared his pistol when she shot him, two rounds, through her Windbreaker's pocket. He was almost close enough to touch, she didn't need to aim. Both bullets struck him in the center of the chest, and he was not wearing a vest. His eyes went wide in pain and fear, and he tried to speak, but managed only a gurgle as he felt to his knees.

She heard the sharper *crack!* of a rifle shot behind her, and looked up to see one of Aziz's ops crumple as he stepped out of the cover of the trees twenty yards away, right where Aziz had glanced earlier.

There was another rifle report a second later, but she didn't see what, if anything, that bullet had hit—she was already moving.

Crap!

Even though there wasn't anybody else close, somebody would have heard the shots, and two or three dead men sprawled in the park would draw attention soon enough, even in New Orleans.

She grabbed the Walther from where Aziz had dropped it, slipped it into her left-hand jacket pocket, and began walking quickly toward the river. The hole in her right pocket smoked a little where the muzzle blast had scorched it. Great. She'd have to lose the jacket.

She had, two days before, arranged for a small boat to be tied up, not more than a hundred meters away. It took only a minute to get to it, step in, and crank the engine. She cast off the shoreline and headed up river.

She had hoped it wouldn't come to this, but she was glad she had considered the possibility and had been prepared to deal with it.

She had never shot anybody before, and she expected to feel something other than she did—fear, regret, horror, even. What she felt was anger. The stupid, greedy son of a bitch had brought it upon himself. He would have kidnapped her and tried to use her to get the information he wanted without having to pay for it. Well, he had paid, and more than he'd planned, that was for damn sure.

Explain that to Allah, when you see him—killed by a woman?

For shame . . .

A few blocks away in a long-term lot was the other rental car she'd parked, just in case something like this happened.

She put the boat ashore—no prints because of the gloves—and walked briskly to the car. She drove away. The local cops would probably identify Aziz as a terrorist pretty quick, and figure out this was some kind of deal gone bad, but there was nothing to tie her to it. Her rental car would eventually be towed, but the ID she'd used to get it was fake, and what she looked like when she collected it was somebody in a baseball cap with dark glasses, supposedly from New Mexico.

Crap! She'd have to start over again, to find a new buyer. Doing so required caution, and would take time.

She frowned, but after a moment her frown faded. Maybe this would be to her advantage. Word might get out that she wasn't somebody you should screw around with. Sometimes these people talked to each other.

You hear what happened to Aziz? Did you hear that it was a woman who did it?

Carruth should be long gone by now—he had an escape

route figured out—and she'd talk to him once they got back to Washington.

Damn.

There was an empty FedEx box under the seat, and she put her .38 Special into that, along with the Walther, packed it tight with bubble wrap, and sealed it. She'd drop the package off at the airport and have one of Carruth's men pick it up in D.C. The Smith would have to go away, being ballistically linked to a dead man, but she had another one like it at home. The Walther? That would be tucked away safely somewhere to maybe impress the next potential buyer.

It could have gone worse. Aziz was dead, but there were more where he'd come from, and potential buyers from all kinds of places around the world. And she was still alive and kicking.

She looked at her watch. She had tickets booked on three flights leaving over the next six hours, under different names, and she had a picture ID for each. Her basic plan had been to be on the last morning flight to Atlanta, with a second leg booked from there to the D of C, and it looked as if that was going to work fine.

She had scheduled a meeting with Jay Gridley around four P.M. at her office, and that shouldn't be a problem.

Okay, so Aziz had been a setback, but it wasn't a disaster. The train was still on the tracks.

Now she needed to go and make sure Jay Gridley was in his sleeping car. . . .

14

The Club Young was dark, smoky, and packed, every table in the place occupied. Half the patrons were soldiers or sailors in uniform. A tall and willowy brunette torch singer in a black silk sheath dress stood in a spotlight on the stage, backed by a small swing band. The singer's voice was as dark and smoky as the atmosphere in the room as she sang "Mean to Me."

Her facial features bore a passing resemblance to Rachel, Jay thought. Maybe that was just him.

Save for an occasional clink from a highball glass, the place was quiet as the patrons listened to the singer.

A voluptuous blond cigarette girl in a skimpy costume, complete with black silk fishnet stockings and six-inch stiletto heels, came by and smiled at Jay. She leaned over, showing a good amount of breast cleavage, offering her tray. "See anything you want, sir?"

Jay shook his head. "No, I'm good. Thank you."

After a couple of verses, the trumpet player took a short solo with his muted horn, adding a little wah-wah effect by moving the mute in and out of the bell with one hand.

Seated next to Jay, Rachel Lewis said, "Like it?"

It was another of her scenarios, and a well-built one. You could smell the smoke, taste the liquor. "Very nice," he said.

In this milieu, Rachel had altered her appearance just a little. She had long hair, done up in what Jay had always thought of as the WWII look—smooth, flowing, the ends somehow rolled under, like a teardrop. She wore a pale brown dress with padded shoulders, and had a cigarette in an ivory holder. As far as Jay could tell, everybody in the place was smoking, save for him, and not a filter in the bunch. There was a package of CareFree cigarettes by Rachel's elbow, featuring a picture of a blonde seated on a beach in a bathing suit, looking at the crotch of a rugged fellow standing in front of her in his boxer swimsuit. There was a small box of matches on the table. The logo on the matchbox showed a hot-pink, stylized, fat letter Y, presumably from the club's name, though the logo looked somehow mildly obscene.

"So, what have you come up with?" he asked.

She took a drag from her cigarette and blew the smoke into the air. "I think I've got a line on the backbone server he hacked into for distribution."

"Really? How did you manage that? I couldn't get a fix on it."

The singer finished her song. The audience applauded, the sound of that coming in a rhythmic wave that swelled, then receded. The lights came up—still not bright, but brighter—and the band segued into Glenn Miller's "In the Mood."

A woman laughed behind Jay, a deep and almost sexual sound.

Most of crowd got up and headed for the dance floor. The walla of their voices was happy, excited, full of fun. That kind of music.

Rachel stood and held out her hand. "Come on, Jay, let's cut a rug."

He shook his head. "I'm not a dancer."

"You are in my scenario. Just let yourself go, I guarantee you'll be king of the jitterbug."

"Rachel . . ."

"Up, Jay. It don't mean a thing if you ain't got that swing."

Reluctantly, Jay got to his feet. Rachel grabbed his hand.

On the polished wood floor, Jay found that if he relaxed, he had the moves Rachel had promised—the steps, twirls, even grabbing her and shooting her between his legs, then up into the air. Her skirt flared, revealing silk stockings held up by a black garter belt.

She definitely had an eye for the little details.

A very athletic dance, this.

The tune wound up to its frenetic crescendo, then ended.

Jay smiled at Rachel, who smiled back.

The band started to play again, this time a slow one— "Stormy Weather."

Rachel smiled and raised an eyebrow at him. "One more?"

Jay shrugged. He caught her right hand in his left, and put his right hand in the small of her back, leaving about three inches of space between them.

She pressed herself against him, chest and hips, and put her head on his shoulder.

They swayed to the music.

Very nice was his first thought.

Bad idea quickly followed.

"Rachel," he began.

"Let's finish the dance, Jay, then we can get back to business."

"Okay." It was just VR, after all, right?

But it didn't feel okay. Or rather, it felt a lot more okay than it should. As he danced, he tried to think about Saji and his little boy, but that was hard, and Lewis wasn't making it any easier.

He thought about disabling the feedback again, to keep his VR body from mirroring his RW reaction, but his arms were around her, and he couldn't lift his hand just yet without breaking character.

She knew that, of course, which was undoubtedly why she had brought him out onto this dance floor.

What was she up to?

He gritted his teeth and tried to conjure up images of Saji and their son.

As they danced, Lewis allowed herself to feel Jay's body against hers. Yes, it was an illusion, courtesy of top-grade electronics and biofeedback gear; still, it was easy enough to suspend your disbelief. They could be in a nightclub in Chicago during the war years, moving now to the music made famous by Billie Holliday, who had died long before Rachel had been born. Jay here wasn't a bad-looking guy, and he was smart and as sharp as a box of fresh sewing needles. She'd always been a sucker for a bright man. Of course, she had to keep him off balance because he was dangerous to her. But it didn't have to be an unpleasant chore. What could be done in VR could eventually be done in the real world, too. . . .

She wasn't exactly dull herself. She had filled her scenario with priming elements—little devices designed to evoke a subconscious response in anybody who played it. It was an old psychological trick—give somebody a word test, making short sentences out of a jumble of five or six words, and put a theme into it by carefully choosing words in each sentence to point in a particular direction. The unconscious brain's autopilot, used to making snap choices, would fasten upon those words: bury terms like "confident," "reliant," "smart," "clever," "capable" in a session, then send the person to take a short exam? He would do better than normal.

Put the terms "dull," "stupid," "inept," "confused," and "slow" in that same kind of little quiz and send him to the test, he would do worse than normal.

Attitude, it turned out, was more important than most people knew. Affecting that attitude via the subconscious was much easier to manipulate than most people would believe. The autopilot took certain things for granted; it tended to mirror societal beliefs. Tall, good-looking, smiling people were generally viewed as more intelligent, somehow superior. Short, ugly, frowning people came across as inferior—at least subconsciously, regardless of whether people would ever admit to it if asked. Way more company CEOs were tall than short. That said a lot.

Rachel's scenario practically reeked with hints for Jay Gridley to let himself go and indulge in sensual pleasure, with Rachel as the prime focus of that pleasure. The songs being played by the band would invoke sympathy for the women singers—"Mean to Me" and "Stormy Weather." The instrumental "In the Mood"? That one was pretty obvious. The cigarette girl's hooters and offer, the package of cigarettes on the table, the overt control of the jitterbug, wherein Jay moved her as he wished, the close contact of the slow number, even the horn player moving his mute in and out of the trumpet, those were all aimed at pointing Jay down the garden path—to her bedroom door.

She smiled into his shoulder at the thought. VR sex wasn't illegal, nor grounds for divorce, unless unfaithfulness in your mind counted, and it didn't. Not legally, anyway. Of course, her intent was to befuddle Jay, and when it came down to the real world—which it would, eventually—certainly his sense of guilt would help. Happily married man with a child suddenly finds himself in an affair with a colleague? That would give him plenty more to think about so he wouldn't have a clue that Captain Rachel Lewis was the bad guy he was chasing. . . .

Jay was good at what he did, but so was she. And a man facing a bright and not-unattractive woman who was intent on having him? He was at a definite disadvantage. . . .

The music ended, and the dance stopped. She saw that her plan was working, to judge from the uncomfortable expression on Jay's face. She smiled. "Well, that was nice. So, let's get back to work, shall we?"

As they headed for their table, the swing band began playing "Smoke Gets in Your Eyes."

Indeed, it did.

Pinehurst, Georgia

Amos Jefferson Lowe invited Thorn to take a walk so the dog could stretch a little. Thorn agreed.

Amos was a big man, half a head taller and probably thirty pounds heavier than Thorn, and while there was white in his closely cropped hair, he moved like a man much younger than one in his late seventies or early eighties, which he had to be. He wore a work shirt and overalls over lace-up work boots, and there was no fat on him Thorn could see.

They started up the graveled driveway. The nearest house was probably a quarter of a mile away. The wind was cold and blowing pretty good, and Thorn felt it even through his jacket. If the cold bothered the other man, there was no sign of it.

The dog ranged back and forth, snuffling the ground, as if tracking some critter, limping a bit, but not looking unhappy about it.

Neither man said anything for a few moments. Thorn remembered walks like this with his grandfather when he'd been a boy. Sometimes they'd walk for an hour without saying anything; then the old man would stop and point at some sign on the ground: "See that? Deer tracks—doe and a fawn, see the little prints, here and there?"

The old man could spot things invisible to Thorn's eyes—and, he suspected, to most anybody else's eyes. He was tuned to the earth in ways most people never were.

Thorn smiled at the memory.

Amos raised an eyebrow.

"Just remembering my grandfather," Thorn said. "We used to do a lot of walking when I was a boy."

"He passed?"

"Yes, sir, some time back."

"You miss him."

"I do."

The older man nodded. He bent, picked up a stick. "Sheila!"

The dog turned, saw the stick. Amos tossed it—not very far—and the dog gimped off to fetch it. The old man smiled.

"So, is this my premarriage interview?"

Amos chuckled. "Marissa made her choice, and you're it. If she doesn't have enough on the ball to get something this important right by now, nothing we can say now's gonna make much difference."

Thorn nodded. "But . . . ?"

"Nope, no 'buts.' Grandma and I, we want to be able to see in you what Marissa sees. Ruth liked you the minute you stepped into the house. She feels things quickly; me, I'm a little slower—I usually have to think on it some."

The dog brought the stick back and dropped it in front of Thorn. He bent and picked it up, threw it a few feet. Sheila trotted off to fetch it again.

"Ruth's always been a quick and accurate judge of character. If she'd thought you were a threat to our little granddaughter, she'd have put poison in your biscuits."

Thorn blinked. It took a second for him to realize the old man was pulling his leg. At least he hoped that's what Amos's grin meant.

"Let me ask you something. You date many women of color?"

"No, sir."

The dog returned. Dropped the stick. Thorn picked it up and tossed it again.

"Why start now?"

Thorn felt the urge to shrug, but stifled it. It didn't seem appropriate somehow. "Usually, I found myself attracted to tall and brainy Nordic women. College professors, programmers, a doctor, once. Marissa doesn't flaunt her intelligence—but she's smarter than I am. And she's funny, and she's . . . wise, in a way I'm not. And she's gorgeous. I wouldn't much care if she were green or blue. I'm not sure what she sees in me."

The dog returned again, but she was panting as she dropped the stick at Thorn's feet. "That's enough, Sheila," Amos said. "I don't want you so tired I have to carry you up the stairs when we get home."

Thorn would have sworn the dog nodded and smiled. She left the stick, turned around, and wandered off the graveled driveway, sniffing the ground again.

"Gonna rain this afternoon," Amos observed. "Couple degrees colder, it'd be snow, but we don't get much of that down here."

Thorn nodded.

"You have a pretty good job with the government," Amos said.

"Yes, sir."

"You like it okay?"

"Most of the time. There are days when I feel like walking away."

"Every job is like that. So you can take care of our granddaughter if she decides to quit and stay home? Maybe have a baby?"

Thorn grinned.

"Am I missing something funny?"

"Marissa didn't mention that I had my own business before I went to work for Net Force?"

"I don't recall that it came up."

Thorn chuckled. "I was lucky enough to have developed some software that was popular. Sold out at the right time. If the government fires me, we, uh, won't miss any meals."

The older man nodded. "Good enough. Marissa tells us you are a fencer?"

"I train on my own, but my best moves were twenty years ago."

"Foil, épée, or saber?"

Thorn blinked again, surprised. "Mostly épée."

Amos answered Thorn's unasked question. "I expect she also told you I'm a big Shakespeare fan. Some of the roles require a little stage swordplay. I learned a bit of that over the years."

"Ah."

"Well, I don't want to overtire my old dog here, so maybe we should just head on back. Ruth'll be fixin' lunch pretty soon, and I want to tell her to make sure not to put any poison in yours."

He extended his hand. Thorn took it. Amos had a firm grip. "Welcome to the family."

"Just like that?"

"Marissa picked you, Ruth likes you."

"What about you?"

"Oh, no problem there—I knew you were okay when my dog brought you the stick. She's a better judge of character than either Ruth or I am."

15

Carruth leaned back in the first-class jet seat and sipped at his drink, ice with one of those little bottles of bourbon. He smiled. It had been a banner week for him, at least when it came to capping people. First, the two Metro cops, then those two terrorist wannabes in New Orleans. It was good to know that, when push came to shove, he still had the moves. Yeah, training on the range was all well and good, and VR was getting more and more realistic, but there was nothing quite like the real thing: There was the sudden rush of adrenaline, the pucker-factor going from zero to full. The recoil of a rifle butt against your shoulder, the smell of gunpowder, the sharp *crack!* as the bullet zipped from the barrel and broke the sound barrier, loud even past the earplugs he wore . . .

Squeeze the trigger, work the bolt, squeeze again, and the bad guys went *poof!*

He knew Lewis wouldn't count those three down on the Mississippi as a great victory—except that she had walked away alive and they hadn't—but that's why he'd been there as backup, and he'd done his job. She put two into the buyer—*bam-bam!* quick as you please—and he already had the scope dot lined up on the one who thought he was hiding a few meters away. Carruth cooked the sucker before he got his pistol into gear.

The second guy Carruth hadn't seen until he started moving, but he had a good idea of where the guy should be, if he was there, and sure enough, he was almost spot on when the guy stepped into view.

Two shots, two up, two down—couldn't do much better than that.

Three dead men on the ground and it was time to *leave*!

Lewis headed for the boat she'd set up. Either she'd make it or she wouldn't, that was *her* concern. He cranked the van's motor and took off.

He had three routes worked out, but the first one had been all he'd needed. It was as if God smiled upon him— the lights all turned green, there weren't any traffic accidents, nobody working on the roads, it couldn't have been any smoother. Some days, you got the bear, and he was happy this was one of them.

He crossed the Mississippi on the Highway 90 bridge, into Gretna, drove west, and took a dirt road to the south. He stopped at a big sludge pond near the railroad tracks— they had plenty of water down here—ponds, bayous, canals, lakes, and more.

He made sure nobody was watching him before he got the rifle out of the van.

He wasn't attached to the deer rifle. He slung the .30-06 into the pond. He got back in the van and continued west, past the St. Charles Parish Hospital, veered to the north and east on I-310 to the Airline Highway, and then back to the airport. If anybody ever found the weapon, which was unlikely, it was clean, no prints, and there was no way to trace it to him—it had been bought by one of his men at a gun show in Orange County, California, from somebody who didn't have a table but was walking around with a "for sale" sign stuck in the barrel. A cash transaction—Carruth's man didn't give a name, nor did he know the name of the man who had sold it to him. Perfect.

He'd turned the van back in, sans the magnetic sign, buried his gloves in a garbage bin, and gone to catch his flight, with two hours to spare. Slick as a spray of Break Free on a glass tabletop.

With the Winchester at the bottom of the pond, Carruth was more or less unarmed. He hadn't wanted to risk shipping his BMF revolver anywhere, so it was locked in his gun safe at his house.

He sipped the liquor. Well, he wasn't totally unarmed. He had a briefcase—one of those big, heavy, aluminum jobs, and it held two hardback books so thick he could barely close the case. He was fairly sure that the case and books would be enough to stop or at least slow down a common pistol round, enough so it wouldn't kill him if it did get through. So if some would-be hijacker tried to take over the plane, that would give him some protection when he rushed the guy. If all the guy had was a knife? Then that wasn't gonna be enough against a trained Navy SEAL swinging five kilos of metal briefcase. Carruth would pound that fool like a man driving railroad spikes.

There hadn't been a successful hijacking of a U.S. commercial jet in a while—those maniacs who'd attacked the Towers had made hijacking a dangerous business. Before, people would sit still and wait for the authorities to deal with it; now, somebody stood up and announced that he was taking over the plane? Everybody and his old granny would jump the guy—he'd be hit with everything that wasn't nailed down. If you figured you were going to get plowed into a building, then a guy with a box cutter didn't seem so scary. People survived being stabbed all the time—hitting a skyscraper at a couple hundred miles an hour and being turned into a jet-fuel fireball didn't leave any survivors.

Carruth finished his drink. He thought about getting a second one, and decided against it. He needed to stay sober, just in case. Terrible, that you had to worry about such things in the United States of America.

Well, Carruth was prepared. Nobody was taking this jet anywhere it wasn't supposed to go, not on his watch.

FBI/Net Force/Marine Corps Obstacle Course
Quantico, Virginia

There were days when Abe Kent felt like he had at nine-teen. He'd get out of bed rested, no aches and pains any-where, and if it weren't for the bathroom mirror, he could almost forget for a minute that nineteen was more than forty years behind him.

This wasn't one of those days. Normally, as part of his warm-up before he ran the obstacle course, he'd do ten or twelve chins, fifty push-ups, some crunches and stretches, to get the blood flowing and his joints limber. But a front was moving in, there was a cold and nasty drizzle falling, a little snow and a few ice pellets in the mix, and after eight chins, he knew he wasn't going to get another rep without pulling something.

He managed forty push-ups before he ran out of steam, and one set of crunches where he normally did two. After which, he was tired enough so that actually going through the course seemed to be a lot more trouble than it was worth.

The devil on his shoulder said, *Hell, Abe, you're a gen-eral now, you can delegate things. Nobody expects you to be out in the cold rain running the obstacle course like some raw recruit! You don't need to be able to beat men young enough to be your grandchildren! Bag this! Go home, take a hot shower, catch a few more winks—you earned it!*

Kent smiled. Yeah, that's how it started. Listen to that voice and pretty soon, you're sitting in front of the televi-sion most of the time, drinking beer and thinking about how tough you were in the good old days. He might fall over dead from a heart attack, but if he did, at least it was better to do it here than sitting on his butt at home.

He headed for the course.

Only a few people out here this early, in the cold and wet. One of them looked familiar, just ahead of him. . . .

"John?"

"Morning, Abe."

The two men shook hands. "I didn't know you still came out here."

"Got to," Howard said. "Too easy to turn into a couch potato, now that I'm a civilian."

"You could join a nice warm gym."

Howard laughed. "When I can come here for free? Nah. Besides, there are too many sweet young things in tight spandex at the gym my wife doesn't want me staring at. Gets hard to keep your mind on your workout. Not a problem out here with old jarheads in dirty sweats."

Kent laughed.

"I thought for a minute there you were going to turn around and leave," Howard said.

"For a minute there, I was. There are days when inertia is really hard to overcome."

"I hear that. You want me to give you a head start?"

"Oh, I don't think so. I expect an old jarhead can keep up with a fat and out-of-shape ex-Army civilian, even if I have twenty years on him."

Both men laughed.

Richmond, Virginia

"Trust me, Tommy, it couldn't have gone any better. Compared to Ruth and Amos, my parents—if they ever get back from their Canadian vacation—will be a walk in the park."

Thorn nodded. "I liked them."

"Good thing."

"So, when are we going to do this wedding?"

She shrugged. "We could do it Friday, if it was just me, but my mother will want a big church to-do. Even though I am getting long in the tooth for a white dress. I don't think she ever really expected it would happen, so that's the least I can do."

"So, you figure it'll take a couple months to set up?"

She laughed. "A couple months? Lord, even a shotgun wedding would take that long. A regular wedding takes at least a year to plan."

"You're kidding."

"You keep saying that when you know I'm not."

"What's to plan? Get a church, buy a dress, print some invitations, hire a preacher."

She laughed again. "So much to learn, so little time . . ."

16

As she drove to the meeting where she was to talk to Carruth, Lewis considered her new problem. She had started this knowing that there were some risks when dealing with people who wanted the ability to raid U.S. Army bases. Like Aziz, such men would not be above killing anybody they needed to in order to get what they wanted. She had thought to mitigate this risk going in. She had first strained possible buyers for her information through a series of blind e-drops and cutouts strung out around the world. She used a server in North Africa, piggybacked on a military communications satellite in geosynch over the Virgin Islands, and a wireless plexus in Argentina, all of these, and others, feeding their sigs back and forth among themselves before forwarding it to a generic server she kept in a rented apartment in Delaware. The server put things into a file that she could access anonymously and only via a password, and in theory nobody knew it existed save her and the domain-namers. This was a weave complex enough so that nobody was going to thread their way through it to show up on her doorstep. And if they opened the apartment door in Delaware without deactivating it, there was a block of C4 wired to a detonator that was going to reduce the server and anybody standing too close to it to little pieces, so even if they got that far, there wasn't going to be any *there* there. . . .

Some of what came her way were half-assed offers, some she was sure were law enforcement agencies from different countries, including, probably, the U.S., and a very few seemed legit.

These latter, she had separated out.

She had a highly discreet investigator working for her, and she sent him the names. Simmons had been a military intelligence op, then a contract agent for the CIA and NSA until he had been caught dealing in the black market in Syria. He apparently knew where too many bodies were to risk any public legal action, so he had been quietly cashiered out of government service and told to keep his mouth shut and a low profile, or risk being nailed using antiterrorist laws.

Being able to dig down and uncover bodies was useful to Lewis.

This was how she had wound up with Aziz, and had he not been greedy, he might have panned out.

With that buyer dead, she had to start over again. So she had gone back to the cutouts, and come up with a couple more potentials.

One of them was supposedly another Middle Easterner, the other, of all things, an Australian. Before she met anybody else, she had to make sure that they weren't cops, and that they had some references she could run down. So she sent the names to Simmons as she had before. This was the riskiest part of the whole operation, and she was very careful here.

She couldn't assume that the next potential buyer would be some kind of fundamentalist terrorist who would be impressed by the gun of a dead martyr, so it looked as if Carruth might need to make another run at an Army base. And this time, best he return with something of more substantive value than a fancy handgun.

The clock was ticking. But Simmons hadn't gotten back to her, and that was worrisome. Could be any number of valid reasons for this—but even if he didn't have anything useful for her, he was usually quick to pass that along. Whenever she had something for him, she got herself a cheap, one-time phone, sent him the number via an encrypted file, and he would get back to her the same day, or sometimes the next day.

But it had been three days since she'd heard a word from him, and this was bothersome.

The place where she was to meet Carruth was just ahead. A ratty cafe on a street that was torn up for roadwork. You had to park a block away and walk in, and it wasn't worth the effort. The food was crappy and, of course, the coffee was commercial brew that sat in the pot all day. . . .

She grinned. She and Carruth both were going to lose weight if they kept meeting at such places.

She parked her car and alighted.

Midtown Grill

"Simmons. Here's the address," Lewis said.

"Who is this guy?" Carruth asked.

"He's a former intelligence op—worked for Army Intel, JMTS, then freelanced for the CIA and NSA—now on his own. He's the man I've had running down potential buyers for our product."

Carruth nodded. "Okay. And I'm going to see him why?"

"To find out why he's not answering my e-mail and calls."

"Maybe he forgot to pay his cable bill."

"And maybe he turned into a butterfly and flew off to Central America."

Carruth looked at the address and grinned. "What do you want me to do when I find him?"

"See why he hasn't gotten back to me on the two names I sent him to check out."

"Which are?"

"You don't need to know," she said.

He laughed. "Remember when you were standing on the walk down in New Orleans and Abdul and his Ugly Brother stepped out of the trees with pistols, ready to shoot you?"

"I recall it, yes."

"Captain, we are together in this to our eyeballs and I demonstrated my loyalty by punching holes in those bad guys and killing 'em deader than black plastic. I'm not going to run off and start a business of my own here. Aside from which, if I ask this guy Simmons about the names, he might just, you know, blurt them out by accident."

She considered it for a few seconds. "All right. I take your point. One of the men is an Australian, name of Brian Stuart; the other one is another Middle Easterner, using the name Ali bin Rahman bin Fahad Al-Saud."

Carruth shook his head. "One of the princes? These guys are big on naming every man related to them, aren't they? Bin-this and bin-that."

"I expect the name is phony," she said. "No more a prince than you are."

"So I get the dope from Simmons on Brian and bin-whosit, and we're back in business, right?"

"If one of them turns out to have access to the kind of money we're talking about, we are. But I suspect they won't be as impressed with that PPK you lifted, so I'm thinking we need to hit another base and come back with something a little more useful."

"Such as?"

"Oh, I have a couple ideas. We'll meet again when you get back. Here's the new place, and the new one-time phone number." She handed him a yellow sticky-pad sheet with an address and telephone number written on it.

"Another hole-in-the-wall with bad coffee?" he said. He read the note, apparently memorized it, then wadded it up and put it into his pocket.

"Yes. Places with good coffee have customers, and we don't want the attention."

"You could always come to my apartment," he said. "I got Seattle's Best I can grind up and brew."

"Yeah, and hell could freeze over, too."

He laughed.

Cleveland Park
Washington, D.C.

This guy Simmons had an office on Connecticut Avenue, not far from the old art-deco Uptown Theater. Nice enough area, mostly low-rise commercial, and still part of Cleveland Park. The office was a brick building, the address upstairs over a storefront. Must not be doing too bad.

Carruth looked around for cameras. He didn't spot any looking right at the place he was going. If Simmons was some kind of spook, he'd probably picked a location that wouldn't get much attention.

No name on the button over the address Lewis had given him. Carruth tapped the button and waited.

No answer.

There were four other offices upstairs, and he could have leaned on those buttons until somebody buzzed him in, but he didn't want to leave any more memories than he had to.

The security door was a steel-framed job, made to look like wrought iron, with expanded metal grating filling the gaps, backed with glass. The lock would open via an electric pulse from upstairs, or with a key, and it wasn't a dead bolt, but a basic latch hitting a strike plate. Meant to keep honest people out.

Carruth had a thin and flexible piece of spring-steel a little smaller than a credit card in his wallet. He reached into his jacket pocket and pulled out his Nike wide-receiver gloves. They offered a little protection from the weather, but were still thin enough to allow you to use your hands. He could pick up a dime wearing them. No point in leaving any prints around.

He used his gloved fingertip to wipe the button clean, then worked the spring into the edge of the door.

To people passing by on the sidewalk in the cold, he'd look like he was using a key.

Using the flat spring, it took all of four seconds to slip the latch and open the door. Hell, it might as well have *been* a key. . . .

He grinned as he started up the stairs.

Simmons's door was unmarked, save for the office number—4—all the way at the end of the hall to the right. All the doors were solid, no glass, and no windows into the hall, so nobody saw him pass. There didn't seem to be a security cam in the hall.

Simmons's door was unlocked. Carruth opened the door. "Hello? Mr. Simmons?"

The smell hit him as he stepped inside. It was that sickly-sweet, something-spoiled odor that, once you'd sniffed it, you never forgot.

He didn't bother to pull his gun, but moved into the outer office, down a short hall toward a closed door. If there was a corpse that had been there long enough to stink, there wasn't gonna be a bad guy standing around watching it rot and waiting for visitors.

The inner door was also unlocked, and it opened to reveal, sure enough, a dead man lying on the floor next to a big wooden desk.

The guy was maybe fifty-five, bald, heavyset. He wore slacks and a sport coat, with a pale blue shirt open at the neck. One of his loafers had come off, revealing a pale gray sock.

There was a window behind the desk, but a set of blinds covered it.

Carruth bent down. Two, three days, probably. No obvious bullet or knife wounds. No blood.

He leaned the man's head back a bit—gone past rigor—and spotted ligature marks around the man's neck. Throttled, with a thin piece of rope or maybe wire. Not an amateur's weapon. Getting ripe in the heated building. Another day or two, the neighbors would notice big-time.

He found a wallet in the man's back pocket. It had maybe two hundred bucks in twenties, and some odd fives and ones. He also wore a nice-looking watch. So, it hadn't been a robbery.

"Hello, Mr. Simmons," he said, looking at the driver's license. Actually, there were three licenses—from D.C., Virginia, and—of all places—Oklahoma. Also a gun permit for the District—that was impressive, those weren't easy to get. Plus some very official-looking cards with photo IDs for the FBI, CIA, NSA, and Metro Police. Very interesting.

Carruth replaced the contents and slipped the wallet back into Simmons's hip pocket. When he did, he noticed a small pistol holster on the man's belt, but the gun it had contained was gone.

There was a computer terminal on the desk. He sat in the chair and touched the keyboard. The terminal was in sleep-mode, and it swirled to life.

He found the mail program and lit it. When he tried to access the in-box, it asked for a password. Carruth wasn't a computer nerd who could break into files. He looked in the desk drawers, found a box full of blank C-DVDs. He inserted one into the computer's drive. He copied the mail program and as many of the other files as would fit on the disk, ejected it, and slipped it into his pocket. Repeated the same thing three more times, copying the entire hard drive. Lewis knew how to fiddle with stuff like that, let her play with it.

He set the computer's program to "Reformat Disk," and started it. He hoped that would wipe the files so the cops wouldn't be able to get them.

He picked up the phone and touched the controls. The man had a Cable Packet Service, including call-waiting, caller ID, and forwarding. Carruth thumbed the recent-calls button, and got a list of the most recent ones. He pulled a small notebook from his pocket and copied them down. He erased them with the delete button. The cops would be able to get a record of calls from the phone company, but no point in making it any easier for them.

There were a couple of file cabinets, and he went through those, along with the desk, but other than a checkbook in the desk's center drawer, showing an account with forty thousand dollars and change in it, there wasn't anything useful he could see. Probably anything important was on the computer and password-protected.

It was tempting, but he left the checkbook where he'd found it.

He stood. Somebody had killed Mr. Simmons here, and while a man in his line of work might have made all kinds of enemies and it didn't necessarily have anything to do with Lewis and Carruth's business, making that assumption was probably not a good idea. Could have just been coincidence, but then again, maybe it wasn't. Which way of thinking would get you in the most hot water?

In the Navy, Carruth had been taught to assume the worst-case scenario and prepare for it until you had more accurate intel. If you thought there might be fifteen enemy soldiers and it turned out there were only five, well, then, that was a good kind of surprise. If you were figuring on five and there were fifteen? That could get you killed.

Whoever had garroted the late Mr. Simmons—who had been a pro and very likely armed when it had gone down—was a dangerous person or persons. And if Simmons had information in his possession that might allow the killers the slightest chance of being able to locate Captain Rachel Lewis, then that ought to be the working assumption. If they could, they would, and how best to deal with that when it happened?

Time to leave. There wasn't anything else to be gained by staying here, and much to be lost—given he was home again and carrying a gun that had killed two Metro cops.

Any more surprises like this, he would have to rethink hanging on to the piece. When this all got done, he'd have a ton of money—he could buy a matched pair and go off to hunt lions, if he wanted. Maybe he should at least hide his gun somewhere it wouldn't be found until he got rich? After all, it wasn't as if he didn't have other guns he could carry.

Well, worry about that later. First, he had to get out of here unseen.

Carruth checked the hall. Nobody around. He hurried out and down the stairs, then into the cool afternoon. He walked quickly away from the building, not so fast as to draw attention, but he didn't dawdle.

Lewis was probably not going to be happy to hear this, but better she knew it than not.

And what was it going to mean for their business?

17

Lewis had gone over the list of numbers Carruth had given her. That, plus the files he'd copied—no trouble breaking into those, Simmons had used his birthday for the password—gave whoever had killed him at least two fingers pointed vaguely in her direction. One of her one-time phones was on the list a couple times, and there was an e-mail drop.

The one-time phone she crushed under her heel and dumped into a garbage can on a street corner. The e-mail address was a spoof, and she zeroed it out. End of trail.

Maybe whoever tapped out Simmons had nothing to do with her, but it was better to be safe than sorry. There was no way to trace her from what had been in his files. The phone she'd bought for cash from a Best Buy electronics store on a busy Saturday; the e-mail addy was at a server in Hong Kong, paid for by a credit card that went no further than a post office box rented under a fake name. She wouldn't be going back to it.

But:

There was one thing. She and Simmons had met a couple times. She hadn't given him her real name, of course, but he did know what she looked like. If whoever had killed him had been looking for her—and there was no reason to believe that, but just in case—then he could have given them a description, if pressed.

If they killed Simmons to get to her? Probably he had done that much.

Of course, "a blond young woman" covered a lot of territory, and if that was all they had, they could look for a million years and never find her. But even so, it bothered her. What did it mean?

Carruth didn't even bother to sip at the coffee he'd ordered, just left it sitting on the scratched, green plastic table, going cold.

"So, is this going to be a problem for us?"

She shook her head negatively. "I don't think so. Whoever killed him, it isn't connected to us. And even if it was, there's nothing here that would lead them to us." She hoped.

Carruth nodded. "Good enough. What next?"

"We—you—hit another base."

"Won't the Army have changed all the codes and other stuff by now?"

She smiled. "I *am* the Army, remember? Gridley might think he's closed those loops, but he can't be sure, and neither can anybody else. I've got the new codes to our next target."

"Which is . . . ?"

She told him.

He smiled. "I like it. Finally something we can pick up a few bucks on. When?"

"No time like the present. How long do you need?"

"Day or two to run the scenario, get my boys up to speed. Travel to Kentucky. We can roll on it pretty quick, I'd say."

"Good. Let's do it."

After he left, she sat there watching her own coffee cool for a few minutes. She didn't like it that Simmons was dead, but he wasn't the only op who could serve. She'd find another snoop and keep checking things out. It was still on track.

Bill Curtis's Saloon
Thirteenth Street, Third District, Chestnut Valley
St. Louis, Missouri
Christmas Night 1895 C.E.

It was all about the hat, Jay knew. There were dozens of stories and versions of how it happened, scores, maybe even hundreds of versions of who did what to whom, but at the heart of it, it was the hat.

Some said it was a hat formed of human skin, made by the Devil Himself to seal the deal for the pimp Lee Shelton's soul, but from what Jay had found, largely due to the excellent scholarship of Cecil Brown, who had written a book about the whole affair, it was no more than a pale, blocked-felt, cowboy-style hat. A milk-white broad-brimmed, five-gallon Stetson . . .

Christmas Night 1895, and the Curtis Saloon was smack-dab in the middle of the St. Louis black vice district, surrounded by bars, bordellos, and billiard halls.

The place was full of cigar and pipe smoke and noise, the air thick with them, and the smell of spilled alcohol. There were men drinking or eating pickled boiled eggs, and women of less-than-sterling character offering their less-than-sterling virtue for short-term rent. While Jay didn't usually change his race in scenarios, he had done so for this visit—a face as pale as his wouldn't blend in here. Here, he was—in the terminology of these times—a Negro; and one large enough in stature to forestall casual trouble, dressed in a plain brown suit and shoes, minding his own business.

Billy Lyons and Henry Crump, two well-dressed black men, stood at the bar, among men who were of somewhat lower stripe and caste. It was a bad man's bar, mostly, and Lyons had borrowed a knife from Crump, just in case he had to take care of business. Jay knew the history: The two men had been in better establishments earlier in the evening, but they had come to Bill Curtis's to wind down, even though they knew it was dangerous.

Alcohol didn't make most men smarter, Jay also knew.

It was a cold and windy night, and Billy and Henry moved close to the stove by the bar. A ragtime band noodled in the background, playing rinky-tink piano, banjo, and guitar, a Christmas song, then something by Scott Joplin, maybe. There were occasional shouts from men shooting craps on the wooden platform in the back, and while not very crowded, the place was busy enough for a holiday when most people stayed home with their families.

Billy and Henry, already feeling little pain from earlier libations, commenced to drinking beer, talking about Christmas and the coming New Year.

Jay stood nearby, sipping at his own beer, watching the two men. He pulled his pocket watch and looked at it. Just about time . . .

Lee Sheldon, aka "Stack Lee," aka "Stagolee," arrived, and even in the dim light he was a sight to behold. He wore tailored leather shoes, "St. Louis flats," with low heels, curved toes, and tiny mirrors on the tops that reflected the light. He had gray spats, gray striped trousers, and a box-back coat over a yellow embroidered shirt with a high celluloid collar. A red vest, a gold-headed ebony walking stick, and the Stetson hat—with a picture of his favorite girl and wife, Lillie, embroidered on the hatband—completed the sartorial splendor of Stack's outfit. He was a high-rolling pimp and dressed to be seen—one of the elite "macks," as they were known locally—as well as owner of his own club, so the story went. Why he wasn't there instead of here on this night was a question never answered.

Other stories had him as a waiter, a bartender, or a cab

driver, take your pick. All agreed he was a sporting man, with plenty of folding green in his pocket, and at least four or five women in his string, including his wife.

Jay watched as Stack—so-named for a riverboat or its captain, depending on who you asked—lit a big cigar and stopped to chat with somebody nearby. Jay wasn't close enough to hear, but the story was that Stack was asking who was treating that night.

And it turned out that it was Billy Lyons who was being generous on that cold Christmas, and so Stack ambled over that way, allowing everybody to see his finery.

Being locals forever, Stack and Billy knew each other. There was one story that there was bad blood between them—that Billy's stepbrother, Charlie Brown, had killed Stack's friend Harry Wilson, and that Stack meant to take his revenge—but on that night, they stood drinking together, laughing and talking. For a while, anyhow.

Jay edged a little closer, to listen. The talk had turned to politics, and had grown heated.

"You don't know nothin' 'bout it," Stack said, shaking his head.

Billy took a pull from his drink. "I guess I know more about it than you—I was *there,* I heard the man's words from his own mouth."

"You say you did?"

"You just heard me tell you so, you ignorant son of a bitch."

Stack set his drink down and drew himself up to his full height, which wasn't that much; he was maybe five-seven or -eight. He flicked his hand out and hit Billy's hat, a derby, with a little tap.

"Call me ignorant? That fo' yo' hat," Stack said.

"That right? Well, that for *yo'* hat." Billy, a bigger man, slapped at Stack's Stetson, knocking it slightly askew on Stack's head.

Stack Lee grinned. He straightened his Stetson. Quickly, he reached up and grabbed Billy's derby, snatched it from his head. He held it in his left hand and with a sudden blow, smashed the crown in with his right, breaking the blocking. He laughed.

"You done broke the form!" Billy said.

"I believe I did." He tossed the ruined hat onto the bar. "And it's an improvement, you ax me."

"You owe me a hat. I want six bits from you!"

"Six bits? Sheeit, you could buy a rack of hats like this fo' six bits! Ain't worth a nickel."

Billy, who might have been passing drunk but not slowed from it, reached out and grabbed Stack's Stetson and pulled it off. "Well, I reckon we trade, then."

"Gimme back my hat," Stack said.

"Nossuh, I ain't gonna, till you give *me* my six bits!"

"You will give me my hat back, or I will blow out your fuckin' brains!"

"That's what you say."

Jay watched the next part carefully. It was a lesson in escalation of violence—and why drinking and arguing in a bad man's bar was not a good idea.

Stack pulled a blue-steel Smith & Wesson .44 revolver from his coat pocket and clouted Billy Lyons upside the head with it.

Billy didn't speak as he bounced off the bar and came back glaring at Stack. He hadn't been hit that hard, but certainly it was hard enough to both stun and piss him off.

Things got real quiet in the saloon.

"You give me my hat *now,* motherfucker, or I will shoot you!"

Lyons, still holding the hat in his left hand, jammed his right hand into his pocket, where, Jay knew, he had the borrowed knife.

He said, "You cockeyed son of a bitch, I'm gon' make you kill me!"

There was a general stampede for the door as most of the two dozen patrons decided at that moment they had pressing business elsewhere. Men did pull guns in that part of town frequently and they did go off. That Christmas Day, there would be at least four or five other shootings in bars, poolrooms, and whorehouses within a couple of miles. Some of the shooters weren't very good at it, and innocent bystanders had been known to collect bullets more than once. Bad enough to be killed for something you did; worse to be killed by a stray bullet by accident. Dead, either way.

Stack took three steps backward and pointed the gun at Billy. Jay stayed where he was.

Stack shot Billy. Just the one time, in the abdomen. The noise was very loud in the saloon, and the gray smoke that belched to join that of the tobacco had that unmistakable gunpowder stink.

Billy Lyons fell back against the bar, lurched to one side, still clutching Stack's Stetson.

Nobody said anything. The few patrons and bartenders still there stood frozen. Nobody wanted to move and become a target.

Billy sagged against the bar, and dropped the hat. Stack stepped up to him. "I told you. You give me back my hat!" And with that, he bent down, retrieved the Stetson, and put it on.

Lyons slid lower. "You done killed me," he said.

"You took my hat. It's on you."

With that, Stack put his gun away and walked out.

Strolled out, in no hurry at all.

Billy, Jay knew, would linger on for a time. They would take him to the infirmary, and later to a hospital, where he would pass away at about four in the morning. Not a testament to his intelligence. What kind of man refuses to give a swiped hat back to its owner when staring down the barrel of a gun?

Well, the kind soon to be a dead man . . .

Stack, Jay knew, went to one of his houses—he had a couple—reloaded his .44 and stuck it in a drawer and, apparently unconcerned, went to bed. That was where the local police found both Stack and his gun at about three A.M., an hour or so before Billy Lyons died.

That was the true story of how Stagger Lee shot Billy.

No gambling late, Lyons didn't win all Stack's money,

and while Lyons did have three children by a local woman, he wasn't married to her or anybody else, so most of the versions of the songs that came later got it wrong. It was in St. Louis, not Memphis, nor Chicago, nor New Orleans. And how Stack Lee Shelton became any kind of hero after that was a puzzle to Jay. Cold-blooded murder over a hat didn't seem like the stuff of heroic legend to Jay.

Stack Lee was tried twice for the crime. The first trial ended in a hung jury, with Stack's white lawyer arguing self-defense, due to the knife in Billy Lyons's pocket. But the lawyer, an alcoholic, died shortly thereafter following a drinking binge, and Stack's next attorney apparently wasn't as good as his first. The second trial, he was convicted, and sentenced to twenty-five years. After a brief parole, he was incarcerated again, and died in the Missouri State Prison Hospital, on March 11, 1912, of tuberculosis.

One of the most accurate of the songs that came from the Missouri riverboat roustabouts around the end of the nineteenth century had a final verse that Jay liked:

> If you evah in St. Louis
> And you goes to the Curtis Club
> Well, every step you walk in
> You walk in Billy Lyons's blood
> Talkin' 'bout a dead man
> Kilt by mean ole Stagolee . . .

Jay watched the bartenders and bystanders haul Billy Lyons out of the club. What had he learned here? Well, not as much as he'd hoped, but at least it had been interesting. And maybe if he ever got tired of working for Net Force, he could go into the entertainment biz. He could tell and show a pretty good story. There was always a market for scenario-builders of his caliber.

Shoot, maybe even *Hollywood* . . .

18

It had been going so well, Carruth thought. Done and on the way out, and then, out of nowhere, that X-factor appeared, and royally screwed it all up. Some guy with insomnia or having to walk out a cramp or sneak a smoke, whatever, and all of a sudden he's yelling and lights are coming on. . . .

Carruth had shut him up, but the cure—a round from his BMF revolver—was worse than the disease. He hadn't thought, he had just pulled the piece and cooked, almost instinctively.

The gun was like a bomb going off, and anybody who was a light sleeper certainly sat up in bed when he heard that honker's roar.

Now, as their truck careened around an S-curve two miles away from the base, a Hummer full of MPs chasing it, Carruth realized they were in deep trouble. Oh, they might outrun the MPs, but there was such a thing as radio, and when the Army got its act together, they would start calling for help. Yeah, they wanted to take care of their own business, but if Carruth and his men got away, their heads were gonna roll, and that was more important.

A roadblock of state cops sure wasn't going to be helpful to Carruth's situation.

Lying in the back of the truck, Stark wheezed around the M-16 round that was probably lodged in one of his lungs. Dexter had slapped a pressure patch on the hole to stop the bubbling, and hit Stark with a syringe of morphine to ease his pain, but his chances weren't good. Being bumped and thumped around in the back of a truck rolling at eighty down the highway wasn't helping the wounded man any.

To Hill, Carruth said, "Break one out."

He was talking about the toys they had just swiped, four M-47 wire-guided, semiautomatic missile launchers, with rockets. Called the Dragon, the M-47, aka the FGM-77, was a portable antivehicle weapon from McDonnell-Douglas consisting of a launcher, missile, and wire-guidance system. Pretty much obsolete and on the books as surplus, having been replaced by the FGM-148 wireless Javelin, there were still a bunch of them in military armories and they still worked just fine. The Dragon was simple to use: Set the crosshairs on the target and squeeze the trigger. As long as you kept the sight steady, that's where the rocket would hit. Good for twelve, fifteen hundred meters, and able to pierce 400 mm of armor, it was a great tank-buster.

"We can't shoot it in here, Boss," Hill said. "The backwash will scour the inside of the truck down to the metal and roast us all."

True. The old system didn't have a low-gee, soft-launch motor and wasn't IR-guided like the newer Javelins, which were fire-and-forget. You could reload one of those instantly from inside a house or truck, you didn't have to wait and use the guidance wire. "I know that. Get it ready. Drop a couple grenades to back 'em off some and next time we round a curve, we'll slow it down enough for me to bail out."

"That's crazy," Hill said.

"Better than spending the rest of your life in Leavenworth—or winding up on a slab."

Hill nodded. He pulled an M-61 fragger, olive green with the yellow stripe up top, yanked the pin, waited a second, and underhanded it out through the rear. The grenade was an antipersonnel weapon, it wasn't designed to stop vehicles, but it would make a big noise and flash and maybe pepper the chaser with a bit of shrapnel. Slow them down a hair.

The grenade bounced on the road—Carruth saw the spark where it hit the pavement—and shortly thereafter blew up.

The headlights of the Hummer dipped as they hit the brakes.

Stateside Hummers weren't armored well, if at all. A grenade could punch holes in the sucker and maybe kill a rider. They would know that better than anybody.

"Curve coming up, Boss. We have a couple hundred meters."

"Slow it down once you are around it. Find me a soft spot!"

Carruth grabbed the Dragon. The package weighed twenty, twenty-two kilos or so. He hoped he wouldn't drop it, or have it fall apart when he hit the ground.

Hoped *he* wouldn't fall apart, either.

Hill threw another grenade, this one timed to go off in the air.

The truck slowed. Carruth bailed, hit the ground next to the road, tumbled, rolled, came up, fell again, the wind knocked out of him. Man!

The truck sped up.

Carruth crabbed further away from the road, then dropped prone.

The headlights of the Hummer swept around the curve. The vehicle roared past. A soldier leaned out of the passenger window, aiming his M-16 at the truck ahead of them.

Carruth sat up, lit the electronics, lined the crosshairs of the sight on the rear of the Hummer. It was a hundred yards away. Too close, he didn't want to be eating shrapnel. . . .

Two hundred yards . . . two-fifty . . .

He squeezed off the round. There was a big *whoosh!* as the rocket's exhaust blew out behind him. The rocket sped away. Top speed was only a couple hundred meters per second, and it would take a little while to get there, keep the sights on the target, keep them lined up. . . .

The rocket hit the back of the Hummer. The rocket and the Hummer went up together, a terrible flash, and the noise washed over him a second later. . . .

It seemed like a long time before the truck came back to collect him, but it couldn't have been more than a minute or two. They drove past the burning remains of the Hummer, and the soldiers who had manned it.

"Sorry," Carruth said as they went by.

"Stark's dead," somebody said.

Carruth nodded. "We'll have to ditch the truck, fast. Get to the exchange point."

The exchange point was behind an old gas station; there were two pickup trucks waiting. They piled out of the bigger truck, loaded the Dragons into them, covered them with tarps.

Carruth siphoned a couple gallons of gas out of the big truck's tank and soaked Stark's body and the inside of the vehicle pretty good. He climbed into one of the pickups, leaned out, and lit a flare. As they drove past the big truck he tossed the flare. There was no ID in the vehicle, nothing to tie Stark to them, and by the time anybody got there, he'd be a crispy critter.

"Go!"

The two smaller trucks peeled out.

The big truck erupted into an orange fireball as the gasoline caught.

"Adios, amigo," Carruth said. He saluted the outside rearview mirror. At least they gave Stark a Viking funeral, sort of.

The light from the burning truck was visible for a long way behind them as they drove off.

It was a night to burn stuff up, for sure.

Lewis wasn't gonna be happy about this.

The Pentagon
Washington, D.C.

This time, General Hadden had Thorn come to his office. And he wasn't a man to beat around the bush.

"I'm not happy with your unit's progress on this, Thorn. Last night, somebody stole four surplus rocket launchers from one of my bases and killed some of my soldiers—we lost six men when they cooked a vehicle full of MPs!"

"I'm sorry. We've got the best people in the world working on it as fast as they can go. It doesn't get any better than that."

"So you say, but I'm not seeing results and I've got a body count!"

"With all due respect, sir, we're not making burgers and fries here. Sometimes you don't get it your way. We're dealing with a bad guy who is clever and who doesn't want to get caught. Our people are on his trail, they are making progress, that's how it works."

Hadden said, "There is always something that can make things go faster—the trick is to figure out what. Maybe your computer geeks need some more motivation. Some . . . direct supervision. From what I'm able to tell, you give them something and turn them loose—you aren't there keeping their noses to the grindstone."

Thorn shook his head. "Sir, I came to this job by way of the computer industry. I worked with 'computer geeks' all the time. Hell, sir, I was one myself. They deal well with time pressure, most of them, but standing over them and micromanaging their actions is worse than trying to herd cats. The best players here are like artists; you lean on them, they will stop what they are doing and cross their arms. This isn't paint-by-numbers."

"I'm not talking about a guy with a bullwhip, Thorn, I'm talking about maybe giving you an . . . assistant. An efficiency expert, office manager, somebody who might be able to make things run a little smoother."

Thorn laughed.

"I'm not used to people laughing at my ideas, son."

"You aren't used to dealing with this kind of civilian, General. You can't fool my people into thinking I'm still running things if you send some hard-ass in to whip them into shape. They are smart enough to know I wouldn't hire somebody like that. If one shows up, they'll know who sent him, and they will know why. Any of our top operatives could quit this afternoon and have a better job lined up by supper time—more money, more perks, no direct supervision at all, and they could work from home if they wanted. You might be able to draft them and keep them, but without their fullest cooperation, you won't ever get what you want from them."

He paused, maintaining eye contact with Hadden. Then he added, "And if you want to fire me, sir, that's fine, too. I'll have my desk cleared out this afternoon."

"Nobody is firing you." Thorn heard the unspoken "yet."

"Fine. Then as long as my name is on the door, nobody is sending me an assistant I don't want or need. My people will get this job done as soon as it is humanly possible. They won't go any slower and they can't go any faster— you standing on the sidelines yelling 'Hurry, hurry!' at guys running full out isn't going to help."

The Chairman of the Joint Chiefs was at the beck and call of a civilian, the President of the United States, but Thorn guessed he wasn't used to hearing lip from anybody less than that. Thorn could see it didn't set well.

"Sir, it's like sifting a beach, looking for a particular grain of sand. Our guys will know it when they get to it, but they can't just walk out into the dunes and pick that one grain up and say, 'Aha!' "

Hadden didn't say anything.

Thorn had dealt with people like him before—CEOs of major corporations tended to be control freaks; that was part of how they got to the top, by attending to all the details. And the United States military was as major as it got. Thorn said, "I understand you are the man in the hot seat, General, and that you are responsible for all kinds of things about which I don't have a clue. But this is what we do. Once you set the dogs loose, you have to wait until they get the scent and run your game to ground."

"I don't like waiting."

"No, sir, I understand, I don't either. You don't have to like it, but you need to understand it. This is how it is done."

Hadden chewed on that for a moment. "All right. But you put a bug in your man's ear and make damn sure he is making all due speed."

"Yes, sir."

But Thorn wouldn't say anything to Jay. The general believed that a little bit of time pressure would help keep people on their toes; feeling as if somebody was looking over your shoulder. The general was wrong. With these people, at any rate, that would just make things worse.

As Thorn was leaving the Pentagon, walking to where his car and driver waited, he saw Marissa angling across the walk toward him.

"Why, hey, Tommy, fancy meeting you here."

He didn't think for a second that it was a coincidence. "Are you following me?"

"Of course. You didn't think this was a *coincidence,* did you?"

He smiled. "Why?"

"Well, sometimes you are pretty dense, so you might have thought I just happened to be in the area—"

"No, Marissa. Why are you following me?"

"Just concerned about you. Worried you might have been in there telling the Chairman of the JCOS to go play with himself."

"Close. But he didn't fire me and I didn't quit."

"That's good. You're learning patience, I like that. Truth is, I have something for you, in my capacity as CIA liaison to Net Force— for whatever that is worth these days."

He raised an eyebrow.

"That break-in, the one where they got the M-47 Dragon launcher and rockets?"

"The one they used to wipe out the MPs chasing them?"

"Yeah, that one. Well, it turns out we got one of their guys. He was killed by an M-16 round. They tried to burn the body in the truck they used, but it was recovered, and an ID made; dental records confirmed it."

"That's great."

"For you, maybe. Turns out he was one of ours—a CIA asset."

"No shit?"

"Plenty of that, but, yeah. A contract man, not a direct employee. Name was Stark. Ex-military—he was a Ranger—then he got into mercenary work in Congo, eventually wound up knocking around in Iraq, working private security. Apparently the local station used him for gathering intel—he spoke some Arabic and a little Kurdish. We lost track of him a couple years back. According to his passport, he's still in the Middle East."

"If you found his body in the back of a truck in Kentucky, then I'm guessing maybe he was using a different passport," Thorn said.

"Give the man a cigar. Anyway, I'm having the information couriered to your people—known associates, relatives, his old unit, like that. Maybe Gridley can find something that State missed."

"I hope so. Those rocket launchers they stole—how easy would it be to take down a passenger jet with one?"

"Well, they are outdated, there are better ones now, but—as easy as pointing your finger and going 'bang!' If they can get within half a mile of a target like, say, the White House? They might be able to put a rocket through the President's window."

"That's what Hadden is really afraid of," Thorn said.

"Sure. And he's right to be. Bulletproof glass won't stop an armor-piercing antitank rocket. It'll go through the wall of a brick building like a hot knife through butter."

Thorn nodded. "You need a ride?"

"Got one. Call me when you get off work."

"Yes, ma'am."

As he headed to his car, Thorn considered the new intelligence. He could understand how General Hadden was worried. These people seemed to be able to penetrate the Army's bases at will, and this last episode gave them weapons that could do a lot of damage.

What might they try and collect next time?

Maybe he did need to at least mention this to Jay Gridley. . . .

19

Jay Gridley, dressed only in a loincloth with a sheath knife strapped to his waist, swung through the trees on a thick and flexible vine. As the hot jungle air rushed past him, he did the yell:

"Uhhh-ahhh-uhhh-ahhh-uhhh-ahhh-uhhh!"

He grinned. He had gotten pretty good at the ape-man's attention-getting cry. He had watched a lot of Tarzan movies growing up, and he had practiced the yell made famous by Johnny Weissmuller. Yeah, there had been other Tarzan actors, before and after, some good, some terrible, but as far as Jay was concerned, there was only one Tarzan—just as there was only one James Bond, Sean Connery. . . .

He reached a fat tree limb at the end of his swing and let go of the vine. He thought about doing the yell again, but decided that wasn't necessary. The denizens of the jungle knew that Jay of the Apes was here, no question about that.

As he did for most his scenarios, Jay had blended fact with fiction into what he thought was a seamless whole. The yell, for instance. There were several stories on the genesis of it. Weissmuller's version had it that he had come up with the cry based on being able to yodel as a boy. Pure fiction, that. Johnny Sheffield, who played "Boy" starting in 1939, remembered that a guy from the sound department hit a note on a piano and taped his voice, then fiddled with it. The truth was, the cry—the original MGM version—had been put together by Douglas Shearer, a technician who taped a shout, probably Weissmuller's, though the verified identity was forever lost to anonymity, enhanced it using the crude electronics of the day—this was, after all, in the 1940s—spliced it, and then ran it backward. Since the second half of the yell was the reverse of the first part—like a wordless palindrome—it sounded the same from either direction.

Later, when the movies moved from MGM to RKO, Weissmuller did develop his own yell and actually did it on-screen. It didn't sound the same, and although some preferred it to the original, Jay had always liked the MGM version. He got pretty good at, well, aping it—if you were going to swing through the trees, you had to sound right. . . .

But enough about that, Jay. There were evil hunters in the bush, and he needed to track them down and find out exactly where they were headed. He grabbed another vine, conveniently hanging there, and leaped into the air.

He wondered who had put all those vines in exactly the right spot. Did Cheetah get up every morning and go rig them? It would sure be bad if the ape-man landed on a branch and leaped into space and somebody had forgotten to leave a vine there for him. . . .

Oh, why not, he could do the yell one more time:

"Uhhh-ahhh-uhhh-ahhh-uhhh-ahhh-uhhh . . . !"

He was having way too much fun here. . . .

In due course, Jay achieved the jungle floor again. The spongy humus felt good under his bare feet. The evil hunters' camp was not far, and he slipped through the trees with a practiced stealth.

One of the elements of his scenario was a lack of mosquitoes.

He'd always wondered about that—either feral junglemen generally had a great natural chemical resistance to the things, or they would have looked like they had some kind of pox all the time, being bitten constantly. Jay also allowed some large, constrictor-type snakes, but didn't populate the bush with itty-bitty poisonous ones. Stepping on an asp barefooted while slinking through the woods seemed like a good way to guarantee a bad afternoon:

"Uhhh-ahhh-uhhh—oh, crap, I'm snakebit—!"

Still, it was at least an approximation of the movie version of the jungle.

There was a huge boablike tree near the hunters' camp, and Jay shinnied up it easily, perching on a broad branch that was three times his height above the ground. It was dusk and getting dark fast—night fell quickly in the tropics—and the hunters were gathered around a large fire, their native bearers hunched around a couple of smaller fires, roasting critters of some kind. In the gathering evening, Simba roared, and Jay was pleased to see the hunters and bearers tense against the lion's cry. Although it was the female lion who did most of the hunting, the big-maned male was most impressive-looking and he did like to talk loudly.

In the twenty-first century, sitting on a big tree branch in the gathering night wouldn't be much protection: There were infrared glasses, starlight scopes, heat detectors, FLIR, all kinds of ways to see a mostly naked man in a tree even in pitch darkness. But in the generic 1940s such toys weren't available—and nobody thought to look up. That seemed fair to Jay, given that all he had were his wits and a knife, whereas the hunters had pistols, rifles, shotguns, and bearers to haul the hardware around.

The voices of the party—there were five of them—drifted up to Jay's hiding place:

"And I'm telling you, I don't believe in native curses." That was from Stone, the leader. He was the most venal of them—just as soon shoot you as look at you, and he would do anything to get to the treasure. He had a pencil-thin moustache, and would be considered devilishly handsome in certain low circles.

"Yeah, but our bearers do." That was Mackey, and his voice came out as a whine. He was mostly a coward, but he'd shoot you in the back if he had a chance. "Who is going to help us carry out all the treasure if the bearers melt away into the jungle?"

"We can all haul our own shares," Stone said. "Or you can turn around and head back to Boombahbah now, if you are so worried."

"Gentlemen, this isn't getting us anywhere." That was the Professor. He was the oldest, and most educated, of the lot. Gray-haired and -bearded, he was here for science, but he had allowed himself to be co-opted by the others. Not wise in the ways of the world, when it all came down the Professor would be stunned to find out how evil the men he traveled with actually were.

"The Professor is right." That was Armstrong, the semi-good egg. A decent chap, as the Brits would say, and here primarily because of Josephine, the Professor's daughter, who was beautiful and a bit on the wimpy side to be running around in the jungle in her khaki skirt and blouse.

"I keep thinking about that poor boy who was eaten by the crocodile." And that was Jo, who really should be at home sewing or baking cookies or some such. The jungle was no place for a woman such as she. . . .

There was a shrug-it-off walla: "Yeah, too bad. Croc. Uh huh."

In those old movies, the white men's attitude toward the native bearers was something approximating who-gives-a-damn.

In the course of these things, only Jo was destined to make it out of the jungle alive, and then only with Jay's help. They had seen lions and rhinos and crocs and gorillas and elephants, and would soon be meeting some pointy-teethed cannibals whose sole reason for existing seemed to be to guard the fabled Jewels of Alabara and to gobble up would-be thieves.

The native bearers, actually much smarter than the white hunters about such matters, had already figured out which way the wind was blowing out there in the dangerous woods, and would indeed scamper as soon as the hunters went to sleep.

Once they reached the cave, Mackey would get greedy trying to fill his pockets with treasure, and wind up sinking in quicksand. Armstrong would step in front of Jo and catch a thrown spear in the liver for his trouble. The Professor would go next, courtesy of a blowgun dart. Stone would empty his revolver into the charging cannibals, and last be seen quaking in a closing circle of the lean and hungry locals moving in for dinner. And Jo would be rescued by Jay of the Jungle, as the roof of the cave collapsed, burying the hidden treasure forever.

Jo would learn to like tree houses, chimpanzees, and swimming in the pool naked with Jay, only it would never get that far.

Jay smiled. It was all so . . . simple. Ah, those were the days, when nobody asked the hard questions, and the bad guys got their just deserts. . . .

What Jay was looking for was a link from the dead terrorist to his live friends. A hoard of jewels was as good a metaphor as any.

How had such a king's ransom of diamonds, rubies, emeralds, and assorted gold chalices and the like come to be in a mountain cave in the middle of the unnamed African country's deepest, darkest jungle? Bother that. There never had been any civilization here higher than daub-and-wattle huts and subsistence natives—the Aztecs and Mayans had been in South America. The gems were all polished and set, requiring expert jewelers and gold workers, none of which had ever existed here. And why would people capable of producing such a hoard of price-

less baubles haul it fifty miles through the deepest, darkest, animal-infested, malarial jungle to stash it in a cave
anyhow?

Because the screenwriter willed it so, Jay knew. No
other real reason, despite whatever throwaways the writer
would toss off about ancient civilizations and other such
rot. Jay was just using the setup, he hadn't created it. . . .

Jay grinned. Well, realism wasn't exactly primary in a
scenario wherein he swung through the trees yodeling,
knocking down bad guys, and rescuing fair damsels. . . .

But back to the conversation. Jay was here to learn
something, and eventually it would come out. Where exactly was the cave? He didn't know that, but if he stayed
with this group long enough, he would.

As the five sat around the fire, front-lit by the orange
glow, with fitful sparks flying into the darkness, Jay of the
Jungle sat on his branch, master of it all, listening.

In the night some unseen creature went, "Ooh-wow!
Ooh-wow! Ooh-wow!"

Nice touch that, if he did say so himself . . .

"Jay?"

It took him a second to track. Here was a voice that
didn't belong—

Thorn. One of two people with overrides to reach into
Jay's VR world.

He would have to get back to the evil hunters later. If
the boss was calling and willing to interrupt Jay while he
was in VR? That meant it had to be important.

"End scenario," Jay said.

The jungle faded away, leaving Jay in his office, wired
in his suit.

Thorn stood in the doorway.

"'Sup, Boss?"

Thorn said, "I just had a wonderful discussion with
General Hadden," he began.

"Uh oh."

"Yeah, you got that part right . . ."

20

Near Mare Ingenii
Luna

The FBI and military intelligence had ops chasing information on the dead terrorist, too, and after talking to Thorn, Jay decided that his time might be better spent working on things they couldn't find as well as he could. So after Thorn left, Jay bagged the jungle-man scenario and flew off to the other side of the Moon.

From the lip of the crater where he stood, Jay had a good view of the alien base. For all that it was the "dark" side of Luna, there was a good amount of light—unnatural light, to be sure, but still. The terrain was rocky here, just north of Mare Ingenii—the Sea of Cleverness, which seemed an appropriate location.

He was at one of the final levels of the bug game. And it was stumping him—he couldn't figure out which military base it corresponded to in the RW.

He jumped, falling down the wall of the crater. Gravity was only 0.165 that of Earth, but there was inertia, so he used his braking rockets to slow his descent even more. He floated downward like a broad leaf.

The VR was gorgeous. Dynamic lighting and particle effects added to the visuals, making him feel that he was really *here*. The stark lighting and eerie silence combined with the very realistic alien base to give him the creeps. Smooth, powdery dust flew from his boots as he bounded down the steep slope, ghosting into the vacuum and back down in slow motion.

He wasn't live in this mission—the goal here was to evaluate the base and see if he could find out what his team had missed. So the game was frozen as he roamed around the set.

He trotted toward the base, kicking up more slo-mo dust.

Good thing this isn't *real-time, or they'd see me coming for sure.*

The base was roughly hexagonal, the most unusual layout he'd seen yet. It was a deep blue color, and slightly translucent, as if made from huge sapphire crystals. There were alien-sized air locks on all six sides, with larger, vehicle-sized locks on three walls.

The walls had a monumental look, like something built in ancient Sumeria or Babylon. He almost expected to see huge bull-gods emblazoned on the wall, or ziggurats peeking up from inside.

Some memory nagged at the back of his mind. As if he'd seen this before—something like it, but not this, exactly.

He hit a button on his space suit and was propelled upward by a small rocket on his backpack. The wall was well-defined VR, but not quite as sharp as the rest of the scenario. The crystalline texture seemed to have been overlaid on somewhat older code. It wasn't as . . . integrated as the rest of the scene.

He reached the top of the wall and looked at the roofline.

Here was a sharper, more defined VR—a herringbone of giant crystals.

The roof is newer.

Jay paused the scenario and shifted frame of reference, which grew larger as the base shrank to the size of a coffee table.

"Remove newer base sections as defined by these parameters," he said to the analysis program. He rattled off some code.

The base shimmered for a moment, and then it reformed, still six-sided, but now looking more like an ancient walled city, without a roof.

He *had* seen this before. But—where?

Jay paused the scenario and exited to personal cyberspace. He was in a wood-paneled hallway with leather-wrapped doors leading off it. Here was the Game Room, the repository of games he had gathered over twenty years, going back to when he was a kid. Each door had a brass plate with a year engraved on it.

When had he seen it? What year had it been?

A few VR glove motions later, the walls of the corridor morphed outward, expanding into a cavernous space. Acres of blond oak floor stretched out toward art exhibits, each representing a favorite video game he'd played.

Here, a Rodin-like pose by Gordon Fremaux from *Half-Life 4*. There, a model of the Ghost Attack Craft from *Halo*. Over on the wall opposite was an oil painting from the tenth level of *Goldeneye*—the updated Nintendo-21 version.

None of these, of course. But he was sure it was this way.

He reached the section of VR games made up of realistic dioramas.

Past the *Doom 5* exhibit he saw a huge building on top of a hill, a great walled city from the Bronze Age, complete with winged bulls.

The city layout wasn't hexagonal, but that would have been easy to change with a few lines of code. What was important was that, aside from the shape and the new overlays, this was the same basic structure.

Jay read the card posted on the wall of the exhibit.

Siege of Troy—Student MPO, v1, MIT. The date—day, month, and year—were there. A couple years after he'd graduated.

He remembered it. VR games had been fairly new, and

someone had written a massive multiplayer on-line version of a game that had hundreds of players attacking the ancient city of Troy.

A buddy had told him about it, so he'd gone to see it via VR. The experiment had turned into several weeks of multiple-player gaming, culminating in the destruction of the ancient city. It was a beautiful, thoughtful, complex scenario. Jay had been impressed at the time. It was still impressive. Helen, Paris, Achilles, Ajax, the gods . . .

He VR-shifted and was inside the game again.

No doubt about it—same wall structure, same gateways.

The purpose of all the other bug-game levels had been to break into real-world bases, but something was not right here. What was he missing?

"Topographic scan to crater walls, overlay and search for Terran base matches."

An aural progress bar played—this one the sound of a locomotive chugging closer and closer before Dopplering away. When it was finished, a steam whistle blew. Maybe this wasn't so much about a real base as it was about something else?

"One match found." His generic, non-scenario-specific programs usually had a sexy, sultry female voice. This one was no different.

Jay tapped a space near where the steam whistle had sounded and a blue globe appeared in front of him. It spun and rotated. He triggered a flyby mode, and suddenly he was scaled to human size over the globe, flying across it, heading toward where the program had found a match.

There.

He was moving past the northern tip of South America to the Caribbean. Now he was heading toward the water.

He went along with the sim and found himself underwater, looking at a huge submerged base, domed in some sections, more like tin cans in another. A nuclear submarine was docked at the base.

He had his answer. This was an Army VR construct—it

wasn't real. Some kind of practice run, to get the topographic stuff right. A test pattern.

Jay grinned. At least that part of the problem was solved.

So, either somebody who had access to it had swiped the game data from MIT, or maybe whoever had built Troy, the game, was the person who used it as a basis for the bug-war scenario. Either way, it was a big clue. It gave Jay a place to start filtering.

You can run, but you can't hide.

The Fretboard
Washington, D.C.

Kent wiped his guitar down with the black silk and put it into the case. Jen put her instrument away.

He took a deep breath. "You, uh, want to get some supper?"

She stopped latching the case for a second, glanced over at him.

"Supper?"

"Yes. Food. Dinner. At a restaurant."

She didn't say anything.

He said, "Help me out here. I haven't done this in a long time."

"You haven't had food in a long time?"

He laughed.

"Sure. I'd like that," she said. "Maybe we should leave the guitars locked up here? Safer than in the car."

"Sure. You know any good places locally?"

"A couple."

"You want to drive or give directions?"

"I'll drive."

The night was chilly as they walked toward her car. She said, "So, Abe, when was the last time you asked a woman out?"

He thought about it for a moment. "Four, five years ago?"

"Really?"

"Yes, ma'am."

She shook her head. "Wow."

"Better than that—she turned me down."

Jen laughed.

"I won't keep you out late," he said. "Wouldn't want your cat to get hungry."

"Don't worry about the cat," she said. "She's got an on-demand feeder in the kitchen. She won't starve."

He smiled. So far, so good . . .

She drove them to a little Italian place maybe a mile away from the music store. Dino's was one of those checkered-tablecloths, candles-in-wine-bottles kind of cafes, ten tables, most of them full. The guy at the front, a good-looking dark-haired kid of maybe twenty, smiled at Jen when he saw her come in. "Ah, Miss Jennifer, how are you this night?"

"Fine, Gino. Got room for two?"

"We do." He collected a couple of menus and led them to a small table in a dark corner. "Pasta with clam sauce is the special tonight. Enjoy."

Before they could do more than sit, a busboy brought glasses of water, a basket of garlic bread, and a bottle of red wine with two glasses.

Kent noted the unasked-for wine as he picked up the menu. "What's good?"

"Pick anything—never had a bad meal here. I come in once or twice a week. Gino's father is the cook, his mother the cashier, and there are a couple of sisters who work here."

The waitress, a young woman who was indeed obviously related to Gino, arrived. "Good evening, Miss Jen."

"Hey, Maria. This is General Abe Kent, one of my students."

The young woman smiled at Kent. "Ah, welcome to Dino's, *Generale*."

Jen ordered the special, and Abe asked for spaghetti with meat sauce. After Maria left, he took a bite of the bread as Jen poured them each a glass of the house red.

Both the bread and wine were excellent. "How did you know I was a general?"

"I have a computer and access to the Internet," she said. "I looked you up."

"Ah."

"Ah?"

"Well, I looked you up, too. You never mentioned that you had a couple of music CDs out."

"It's been a couple years since I did one of those. Old glory."

"I enjoyed hearing them. I knew you played well, but those were very nicely done."

She shrugged. "I'm no Ana Vidovic," she said. "If you get a chance to hear her Prelude to Bach's Fourth Lute Suite? Best version out there in the last twenty years, for my money, even if it is a little showpiece fast. But now and then, I have my moments."

She sipped at her wine and looked at him over the rim. The candlelight sparkled in her eyes. "So, we have checked each other out."

"So it seems."

"To what end, General Kent?"

"Well, right now, dinner."

She smiled, large and lazy. "And after dinner? Would you like to come back to my place?"

He paused and took a slow sip of his wine. He had been out of this game for a long, long time.

"Yes, ma'am, I would be honored."

She smiled at him again.

They drank more wine.

Washington, D.C.

Saji was holding the baby on her lap when Jay got home, rocking him in the creaking wooden chair. It had been a long day, and the traffic had been horrendous. The President had gone to some kind of function and they had shut down so many streets that it had taken Jay an hour and a half to drive home. He was really going to have to start doing more web-commuting. As soon as he could get out of having to do RT visits to the damned Pentagon . . .

"Hey, babe," he said.

"Hi."

"You okay? You look tired."

"No, I'm fine." There was a long pause. "You got a call a few minutes ago, from a Captain Rachel Lewis."

Jay felt his stomach clutch. Why was she calling him at home?

"She wants you to call her back as soon as possible. She said it was important."

"Yeah, sure." If it was so important, why hadn't she called him on his virgil? She had the number. Jay's belly tightened even more. Why did he feel guilty? He hadn't *done* anything!

He shrugged. "She's the Army computer guy I told you about."

"Funny, you didn't mention she was a gorgeous blond female guy."

Made the call on-cam, too. Damn.

"Not my type. I hardly noticed."

"Uh huh."

Jay went over and gave Saji a kiss, then stroked Mark's young head. He loved to touch that silky fine baby hair.

"You're funny," he said. And: "I love you."

He moved to the house phone on the table next to the couch and brought up the number from the caller ID. The call went through, and Rachel answered. She had her phone's cam lit, and apparently she had just stepped out of the shower—her hair was wet, and she had a towel wrapped around her, covering her from the breasts down.

"Jay."

"Captain Lewis."

"Captain Lewis? Oh, come on, Jay, we are way past that!" She laughed and shook her head.

He should have made this call from his office, he suddenly realized. While the phone's viewscreen wasn't angled so Saji could see it from where she sat rocking the baby, she wasn't deaf.

"What's up?"

"I came across a piece of material, regarding the game. It looks as if somebody posted something on a university board a few years back, using similar tropes."

"Yeah, I found that, too," Jay said. "Joint MIT/CIT files, a couple years after I graduated. But it was posted anonymously and when I tried to backwalk it, I hit a dead end."

"Me, too. But I found a link embedded in the software. Not in the credits, but in a line of code. An old URL. Long gone, but I got a copy of it from Antique Pages—we should check it out. Might mean something."

"Great work." Jay felt a sudden stab of . . . something. Irritation? That she had found something he'd missed? Well, he didn't have time to run down every line of code in an old game, even if it was similar to the bug game. Probably it didn't mean anything anyhow.

"We should get together and compare notes," she said. She leaned back in her chair.

The towel wrapped around her chest came undone and all of a sudden Jay found himself looking at Rachel's bare breasts.

Quite a spectacular view, pebbled and erect nipples and all.

Jesus Holy Christ!

It seemed to take a long time for her to collect the towel and wrap it back into place. "Oops," she said. "Sorry about that." She smiled. "Call me later, we'll set up a meeting to go check out the page."

After he discommed, Jay had trouble looking over at Saji.

"Everything okay?" she asked.

"Yeah, fine. Here, let me take the boy. I've missed him."

Jay walked over to where Saji sat and lifted his son up to face level. "How's the world's best baby doing today?"

His son grinned at him, and chortled.

Jay smiled back. He had a beautiful, brilliant, loving wife and a gorgeous, happy baby. He didn't need anything else. Certainly not anything that might cause any strain in his family life. No, sir.

But—Lewis was a smart and not-hard-to-look-at woman who obviously didn't think Jay was all that hideous himself. It was flattering, to have a sharp and good-looking woman flirting with you. As long as you didn't follow up on that, no harm and no foul, right?

Why, then, was his mouth so dry? Was it because that quick flash of Rachel's breasts matched exactly the VR view of them he had seen when first they'd met? Right down to the little red mole next to the left nipple?

"Hey, sweet boy," Jay said, putting his son's face over his shoulder. "What say Daddy takes you for a little walk, hey?"

Yeah. Out in the nice, cool air, where Jay himself could let some of the heat in his face escape . . .

Lewis smiled as she broke the connection with Gridley. It had taken him long enough to return her call. She'd been sitting around in her apartment for almost two hours in a damp towel, going into the shower every thirty or forty minutes to re-wet her hair, so she'd look as if she had just stepped out to answer the phone. Not the most comfortable way to spend the evening, but effective for what she intended.

The flash of her boobs had been easy enough, the towel was rigged to fall if she inhaled deeply, and the look on Jay's face as his eyes went wide was priceless. The seduction of Mr. Gridley was coming along nicely. Calling him at home and talking to his wife was part and parcel of it. The little mother and child, stuck at home, waiting for Daddy, bored, maybe, or just a tad jealous of his mobility? If it made Jay's wife a little frosty toward him? So much the better.

The business with the college game was, she thought, very clever. She had written it, of course, and it was too good not to reuse—it couldn't be traced to her. But the URL buried in the code? She'd done that last week. She'd expected he would find the old game on his own, and if he hadn't, she would have pointed it out to him. Posting a revision and ex-post-facto-ing it would have been tricky, save that while she had been at school, she had managed to leave herself a back door in the school's operating software. And it had been a brilliant piece of work, because she had allowed for updates in the OS and server, and rigged telltales to let her know when such things happened. It wasn't so much a worm or a virus or even a Trojan horse, but a kind of one-time VR cookie that allowed her to access the upgrades as they came along, keeping her back door current. She would rebuild the cookie each time she updated her password, and was thus able to keep a line into the college's system. From her hidden server, which nobody would be able to find, even if they thought to look. And anybody looking for problems from a hacker likely wouldn't spot it, because it didn't *do* anything they might be checking on—didn't steal space, didn't corrupt anything, didn't replicate itself or screw with e-mail. It just sat there, waiting for a change in the OS, and then it called to tell her. A one-shot deal, and almost impossible to catch unless you were looking right at it when it happened.

Her giving it to Jay before he found it would have been a nice touch, but even so, finding a bit in it that he'd supposedly missed was just as good. The date was locked into the system, no way to tell it had been posted years after it was supposed to have been.

She laughed. It was good to be the Queen.

She stood, and went to get dressed. There were other fish to fry. She had to talk to Carruth again, and there was also the matter of the new operative she'd found to verify background information on possible buyers. She needed to test the guy, to make sure he was providing her with le-gitimate information. She'd give him something to run down that she already knew about, and see how well his answer tallied with hers. If he came up gold, that would be great.

So there had been a couple of setbacks; that was to be expected. By and large, things were going along just fine.

21

Washington, D.C.

"Wow," Kent said.

"I take that as a compliment," Jen said.

They were lying side by side in her bed. Almiron, the cat—named, Kent had been told, for a famous woman classical guitarist who had been born in Argentina in 1914—lay sleeping next to his feet.

"Yes, ma'am, please do."

Jen propped herself up on one elbow and smiled at him. "So, what took you so long to ask me out, Abe? You couldn't tell that I found you attractive after that first lesson?"

"Well, no. I'm a little slow about such things."

She laughed. "Better late than never."

"Yes, ma'am . . ."

It was amazing how relaxed he was with her. Well, okay, at the moment being relaxed might not be so amazing, but . . . overall . . .

"In case you think I do this with all the boys, let me disabuse you of that notion. You're the first man I've invited home for, well, for longer than I care to remember."

"I'm honored."

"You should be."

"Why me?"

"Well, don't take it the wrong way, but you're like an old pair of shoes I suddenly found in my closet. They fit, they are comfortable, they don't look too bad."

He laughed. "You should do stand-up comedy."

"Why? Don't you think I'm better lying down?"

"Yes, ma'am, no question."

She laughed, and he was happy to have caused it.

New York City
East Coast Fencing Championships

"Jamal's pretty good, isn't he?" Marissa asked.

Thorn nodded. "He's getting there."

They'd come by to offer their support in today's match. This was the last day of the Sectionals competition—one step below the Nationals—and Jamal was in the title bout. He'd just scored a touch that put him ahead of his opponent. If he scored the next point, he'd win; if he lost the next point, the score would be at *la belle* and they would likely be fencing for a while, since in this format you had to win by at least two touches.

The air was cool in the large gym. The bleachers had been retracted to provide space for more pistes, so all the spectators were standing off to one side, watching. It was a very quiet crowd, murmuring softly about that last touch. . . .

The director positioned the fencers on the guard lines, asked if they were ready, and when they both indicated they were, said, *"Allez!"*

Match point.

The crowd fell silent.

Jamal's opponent, Michael Sorenson, was the favorite. He was twenty-two years old, a former national champion, and everyone had expected him to walk away with the match. The fact that Jamal was giving him a run for his money—indeed, was a touch away from victory—had created quite a buzz.

"I can't watch," Marissa said, clutching his arm. "Tell me what happens, Tommy."

Thorn smiled. She was pulling his leg. If anything, he was more nervous than she was . . . and she knew it.

Jamal was on their left, which was unfortunate. He was a right-handed fencer, so they had a good look at his back, but couldn't see him as well as they would have liked. That was too bad, but it's how it was. The fencers came to the strip in the order they were called, and the spectators were confined to a specific spot.

Thorn didn't mind, though. He could see all that he needed to see.

Sorenson was pressing the attack.

For a time, the only sounds were the sussing of the fencers' shoes sliding along the copper piste, the *tick-tack* of the blades working against each other, and the occasional grunt or cry from one fencer or the other.

Sorenson kept pressing, and Jamal kept retreating, giving ground reluctantly, but giving it up step by step.

"He's gettin' awfully close to the end line, isn't he, Tommy?"

Thorn nodded.

"And he'll lose a touch if he goes off the end with both feet, won't he?"

"He won't," Thorn said.

But Jamal was getting awfully close. His back foot had already crossed over the line, and Thorn suspected that Sorenson was setting him up for a particular feint. He figured there was a good chance that Sorenson was going to drive a hard attack, probably high-line, then suddenly drop off into a darting thrust at Jamal's lead foot.

The reflexive counter to that was to draw the front foot back and counter with a thrust to the opponent's mask.

The problem was that, if Sorenson timed it correctly, Jamal could actually win and lose at the same time. If his front foot drew back and touched down beyond the end line even a fraction of a second before his point struck Sorenson's mask, the director would award the touch to Sorenson, not to Jamal, and the match would be tied again.

"Watch," Thorn said. "Tell me what you see."

"With them down at that end of the strip, about all I can see is Sorenson's back."

"Can you see Jamal's face?"

"Through the mask, sure."

"Watch his eyes."

Jamal's defense had stiffened. Sorenson was pressing, pressing, but Jamal resisted, halfway over the end line.

Back and forth the blades. Attack, parry, riposte, parry, remise, parry, press.

Inside himself, Thorn went still. This was the hardest part of coaching. For that matter, it was the hardest part of spectating, being reduced to an observer. It had been a very long time since he had fenced competitively, but every time he watched a bout a part of him longed to be out there.

"Here it comes," he whispered.

Jamal had overparried Sorenson's last attack, leaving his own blade a little higher than he should have. Sorenson reacted immediately, stepping forward and starting a compound attack that began with Jamal's right wrist, feinted to the outside of his right elbow, then circled over his arm to come in toward his shoulder. As Jamal worked to close out that line, Sorenson's point dropped suddenly, streaking toward Jamal's front toe.

Beside him, Thorn heard Marissa gasp.

He smiled.

On the strip, Sorenson had dropped into a crouch, trying to buy an extra moment or two before Jamal's counter could hit his mask. So the feint toward Jamal's toe hadn't been a feint after all. Sorenson was trying to score a touch, or to drive Jamal off the end of the strip.

But Jamal wasn't reacting as anyone had expected. As soon as Sorenson's point started its dip—later, Thorn even heard some of the audience say it looked like he started moving a bare instant *before* Sorenson's attack, which made Thorn smile—Jamal had leaped, but he hadn't gone backward. He had jumped up, tucking his right foot under him and dropping his own point directly on top of Sorenson's mask.

Touché.

And match point.

The director called halt and awarded the touch, but it was all a formality. Jamal had won.

"How'd he do that, Tommy?" Marissa asked.

Thorn smiled again. "Tell me what you saw."

"His eyes, you mean? Well, it's hard to see through that mesh, but they looked different. Unfocused, I guess, but more so than usual, if you know what I mean."

Thorn nodded. "What else?"

She paused, thinking, then said, "The oddest thing was his face. I mean, I've seen Jamal fence a few times, and it always seems that he's grinning, or gritting his teeth, or biting his lip, or something, you know? But this time, there at the end of the bout, it was like his face lost all expression." She looked at him. "Why, Tommy? Does that mean something?"

Thorn smiled. "It means he's getting there."

They went over to join the small crowd gathered around Jamal.

"Great bout, Jamal," Thorn said, shaking his hand.

Jamal grinned. "Thanks," he said.

"Yeah, amazing." Marissa shook his hand, too.

They started walking away, away from the others and toward where Jamal had his gear.

"Tell me, though," Marissa said when they had gained some space. "What happened with that last touch? It looked almost as though you knew what he was going to do before he did it, but that can't be right, can it? Tommy always says—"

"Anticipation will get you killed," Jamal finished, grinning again. Then his smile faded. "Honestly, Marissa, I don't really know what happened. I could feel him pressing, and I knew he was setting me up for something, and of course I knew I was out of room, and then, I don't know. It's like I found myself three feet up in the air, my point coming down on his mask, without really knowing how I got there." He shrugged, looking slightly embarrassed, and darted a glance at Thorn.

Thorn nodded. "It's like your counter just happened."

Jamal's eyes grew bigger. He nodded. "Exactly," he said. "Like it wasn't me doing it."

"Excellent," Thorn said. "And congratulations."

They were already calling people over for the medal ceremony. "Go get 'em," Thorn said.

Jamal grinned again and darted off.

"Tommy?" Marissa said. There was an edge to her voice, a tell-me-now-or-you'll-be-sorry note.

Thorn chuckled. "It's called 'no-mind,' and it's not a Western thing at all. But it's a very good thing. Being one with the moment, so that the blade itself seems to react, not the fencer, and the parries and attacks throw themselves. It extends further, to where the touch happens before the move, and the bout is over before it begins, but I think we'll save that conversation for another time."

She looked at him, frowning. "Why?"

He grinned. " 'Cuz I want to see Jamal get his medal."

The Great Desert Waste
North Africa

One of the things Lewis had learned about men over the years was that the surest way to catch them was to use multiple baits. Some men liked to be thought physically attractive; some preferred to be admired for their minds, or personalities, or their senses of humor. Some wanted you to be impressed with their ability to make money—or to wield power. A man who might laugh out loud if you called him a "hunk" or a "stud" might also preen like a peacock if you flattered his intelligence or his compassion.

With a man like Jay, you wanted to hit him on at least two fronts. The first and most important bait, Lewis figured, was to be a fan of smokin' Jay, the computer whiz. That was easy enough to do—he *was* good, as good as any, and better than most, so it didn't take much acting on her part to admire his moves and knowledge.

But computer geeks tended to be insecure about things on the physical plane, and letting it be known that he was attractive on a male-female basis was the second prong of the attack. She knew he was a normal heterosexual man— he had a wife and child—and she was making it apparent that she would like to roll around with him and break furniture, doing some things he probably wouldn't be able to do at home with the baby sleeping in the next room.

He had to be at least curious and flattered.

Given her choice, she would be running a custom-made-to-attract-Jay-Gridley scenario, full of subconscious prods to get Jay's hormones stirred so she could take advantage of them, like that club in WWII Chicago. But Jay had been fairly adamant that she join *his* VR creation this time, which meant that he was nervous about hers, which was good. Keeping him off balance was where she wanted to be.

She smiled as she walked along behind Jay. He had them walking in a classic desert, dressed in Bedouin-style white robes and sandals, with high-tech snake sticks, moving along a trail passing tall sand dunes dotted with bits of scraggly grasses. She had a cowl over her head and a scarf over most of her face. In fact, save for her eyes and forehead and hands, she was completely covered, and that was worth another smile.

Her staff was not the crook'd wood of a sheepherder, though, but aluminum or titanium, expandable, with a wrist loop and a spongy, padded grip. The bottom end was sharp and pointed, with a round concave metal disk "basket" a few inches up, to offer more support in snow or, in this case, sand. There was a button under a flip-up cap on the staff's butt, and if you pressed it and grounded the tip, it would charge the basket with enough low-amp voltage to send a serpent on his slithery way if it was anywhere close to the critter. If that didn't work, you could stab the crawler with the point itself, or just bash him with the staff like a club.

And if need be, the point was sharp and heavy enough to seriously deter a human who might want your wallet or virtue.

She wondered how Jay would react if she goosed him in the rear end with the sharp point.

She laughed at the thought.

Jay turned to look at her, all Lawrence of Arabia in his robe and that Arab headgear—what did they call those scarves? *Kaffiyeh*? Yeah, that was it. Held in place by a piece of goat hair or some such, called . . . an . . . *agal*? Something like that.

"Sorry," she said. "I just remembered an old joke."

Jay looked at her with the question in his eyes, but she didn't follow up on it.

Finally, he said, "The URL and page ought to be around that next big dune."

This was the piece she had gone back into her old game to plant for Jay to find, and it was a red herring; there wasn't anything there that was going to help Jay locate anything useful. But there were a couple of things that would, on the face of it, look as if they might be worth chasing down. If Jay was chasing a false trail, that would be good. Eventually, he'd figure out it went nowhere, but "eventually" could be more than long enough.

They rounded the sloping dune. A warm little sirocco wind dusted them with fine-grained sand from the twenty-meter-tall hill.

An oasis lay three or four hundred meters ahead—a splotch of green, with desert grasses and palm and olive trees bordering a water hole. Of course. What else would there be out here?

A horned viper crossed the path ten meters ahead, sidewinding in a pattern like a letter S. Looking, she didn't doubt, for shade, and good luck with that, snake.

It was hot out here, and while she knew the pale robes she wore were ideal for such a climate, keeping the sun off and her body's moisture in, if were it up to her she'd be slathered in #30 sunblock and naked. Of course, if Jay turned around and saw that, he'd probably have a heart attack.

Between the shade and the water, the oasis was twenty degrees cooler, probably eighty F. instead of a hundred. Even though it was Jay's metaphor, she knew what he was looking for, and she could easily spot the "clues" that were hidden here.

Jay said, "I saw something up in that palm tree," he said. "I'm gonna go check it out."

"I'm going to splash some water on my feet," she said. "I'll scope the water hole."

"I'll meet you there," he said.

Lewis slipped her sandals off at the sandy edge of the water hole, which was actually a fair-size pond, fed, no doubt, by an underground spring. The water was cool and fairly clear. In RW, it would probably be scummy and full of bacteria that would make it pea-green, but here it was like it had just come from the tap.

She padded down the shallow slope of wet sand, raising the hem of her robe with her hands. She waded into the water until it was halfway up her thighs, with the robe bunched around her hips.

Jay hadn't bothered with underwear, which was good.

She stood there for a few moments until she heard Jay coming through the dark bushes toward the water. She turned around and gave him a quick glimpse beneath her robe. As he already knew from her beach scenario, she was a natural blonde, and a reminder would be good. . . .

She waded to the shore, lowering her robe slowly as she ascended the gentle slope.

He watched her most attentively.

"See anything?" she asked. Butter wouldn't have melted in her mouth, her voice was so cool and sweet. *Other than the doorway to sensual bliss, I mean?*

It was as if he was afraid his voice would crack. He wordlessly held out his hand. Upon it was a small electronic device, about the size of a book of matches. She knew what it was, of course, since she had put it here.

"Looks like some kind of signal generator," she said.

Jay finally found his tongue. "Narrowcaster," he said. "Probably set to send a slimbeam radio or LOS pulse. We need to see if we can figure out where it was sending its signal."

She needed to give him another victory. She said, "It seems awfully small."

"You're right. Probably there's a camouflaged parabolic dish here somewhere," he said. "This thing is too weak to have much push. The dish will boost and relay the sig. Find that, and we can figure out which direction to head in."

She nodded. "You're really good at this, Jay. A lot better than I am."

"You found this page," he said.

"You would have when you got around to looking."

He nodded. That was true enough, she knew. Of course, he wouldn't have known he was *supposed* to find it because she had put it here for him to find.

Lewis knew she didn't need to be entirely stupid here. Really bright men were often attracted to smart women, especially if the men were confident in their fields of expertise. That she was also competent at what Jay did was a plus—by being so, she could understand how really impressive he was, and he'd know that. Just as a good amateur basketball player could appreciate a real expert's skill better than somebody who couldn't play at all, her being able to run with him at least part of the way was good. Everybody liked an appreciative audience. Impressing the rubes was one thing; impressing other experts in your field was something better. And everything Jay Gridley did from here on out was going to impress the hell out of her. *Oh, Jay. You're so smart. And so good-looking, too . . .*

"Let's see if we can find the dish," he said.

"Where do you want me to look?" she asked. Let him be the director. *Anything you want me to do, Jay, just say the word. Anything at all . . .*

"Check the bushes on the left, over that way. I'll go to the right."

"You're the man," she said.

She knew the dish Jay was looking for was to the left, but she also knew she was going to miss it on her search, leaving it to Jay to come and find and point it out to her. Another victory for which she could admire him. *You're so smart, Jay. So adept. I bet you're good in bed, too, huh? Wanna show me how good?*

She grinned to herself. *Come into my parlor, said the spider to the fly.*

It was just a matter of time. A small push, and he would fall, and she would be under him when he came down. She was going to enjoy it, and on more than one level, too.

22

Somebody was following Carruth.

He hadn't gotten a good look at the guy, only the car he was driving, and while it might be paranoia, Carruth didn't think it was. There was a late-model American something-or-other back there, one of those boxy little sedans that looked like everything else produced in the U.S. in the last ten years, with some stupid, made-up name—a Springa or Freemele, something like that. Chevy, Ford, Dodge? It didn't matter.

Carruth was on his way back from the Safeway, where he'd picked up staples. He wasn't much of a cook, but there were times when he didn't feel like going out to eat, so he kept the freezer stocked with stuff he could microwave—burritos and pocket sandwiches and chicken strips, like that. Low-fat, most of it. Plus cereal and milk and coffee and beer. And fruit, lots of apples and bananas and oranges and pears and grapes. Too much junk food, you got fat, and you needed fresh produce to oil the works. Fruit was good.

So, every couple of weeks he'd make a run, fill a basket up with stuff, and he'd be good for a while.

As he'd left his home and walked out to his car, heading to the supermarket, he'd seen the little gray nothingmobile, one of four or five cars that went by as he cheeped his car's locks. He hadn't paid any real attention to it, no reason to do so. It was on the radar, but low priority.

The market was six blocks away from his house, and halfway there, he caught a glimpse of the same car in his rearview mirror.

Still no alarms—there were a million automobiles like it on the road. But when you were in a business where what you were doing was either iffy or outright illegal, you had to pay more attention to things. He couldn't ever forget those two cops, what a screwup that had been.

He'd hit the grocery store, loaded his purchases into the car, and cranked it up. And as he left the lot, he saw the gray car pull out behind him. Couldn't read the plates, but they were local, he could see that much.

Third time was the charm.

Could be it was just his imagination, but he couldn't take that chance. He turned at the first intersection he came to. Not going home just yet . . .

After he had gotten out of the Navy, Carruth had figured he would be a merc, a soldier of fortune, working for whoever had the money to pay him. He'd done a little of that, in a couple places—North Africa, South America. He'd drifted into civilian security for a company in Iraq and Iran—that paid real well—which is where he'd hooked up with some of the team he was running now. On one of the civilian gigs, he'd worked with an ex-spook by the name of Dormer. Or maybe he wasn't ex. You never could tell with those guys, they'd climb a tree to tell a lie rather than stand on the ground and tell the truth. But Dormer was an old guy who knew his stuff, and when things were slack, which was most of the time, he'd teach Carruth little bits and pieces of spycraft.

Dormer was about sixty, and as average-looking as you

could get—medium height and weight, and in-country he wore a moustache and dyed it and his hair black so that with his tan he could pretty much pass for a local. He spoke the language, dressed like most men on the street, and Carruth had once watched him walk into a crowd and just vanish, as if he had turned invisible.

Dormer showed him the ropes, including drops, how to tail somebody without being seen—and how to spot a tail without letting him know you'd made him.

"Thing about being followed," Dormer had said, "is that it's easy to check if all you want to do is know if you're being tailed. The trick is to do it so the guy on your ass doesn't know you've spotted him."

"Why is that?"

"Because, my large ex-SEAL friend, if the guy thinks he's burned, he'll drop off and they will replace him with somebody else. Better the tail you know than the tail you don't."

Carruth had nodded. Yeah, he could see that.

"So you think the guy half a block back is on you, doesn't matter if he's on foot or in a car, you don't turn around and stare at him. You're driving, you don't slam on your brakes and pull over, making him pass. You don't run a red light and wait to see if he runs it after you. You don't do *any*thing that makes it look as if you have a clue. You want him to think you are blind, deaf, and stupid."

"What *do* you do?"

The older man had grinned. "Listen and learn, son. . . ."

Dormer had disappeared for real a couple months after that conversation. Gone into the desert in a van with some guys heading south to haul something illegal to an Iraqi port city, and far as Carruth could tell, nobody had ever seen any of them again. Probably he was bleached bones in the desert sands, though Carruth kinda liked to think the old spook was still out there somewhere, wheeling and dealing.

Driving through the streets of the District, Carruth remembered the lesson. He wasn't going to go directly home. He had a little stop to make first, and it had to be in the right location.

He drove for a few blocks, turned left, went another half mile, then turned right. He didn't hurry, and while he made enough turns so that it would have to be an unbelievably big coincidence for anybody to accidentally stay with him, he was heading for a particular place and making reasonable efforts to get there via a reasonable route.

There was a cutlery shop Carruth went to sometimes to check out the knives, those being basic tools of his trade. He usually carried a tactical folder, and sometimes a little push-dagger disguised as a belt buckle, or even a neck-knife that hung on a thong around his neck and was hidden under his shirt. In the field, he always had a good-sized sheath knife—he was partial to the tanto design, though he also liked a basic Finnish pukka.

The thing about the knife store was, it was on a street that looped around and had but one way in or out from the main road. If it was a letter P, the shop would be on the right just before you got to the top of the loop.

When Dormer had first shown him the trick, Carruth thought he had it nailed. Take the tail down a dead-end street, and when he followed you, you had him, right?

"No," Dormer had said. "Most dead-end streets are marked these days. They have signs that say, 'Dead End,' or, 'No Outlet.' Guy following you knows what he's doing, he won't pull in after you, he'll set up where he can see the only way in or out and wait for you to come back."

"Ah."

"If he absolutely needs to know where you went on that road and who you saw or talked to? He can park and hoof it, or risk pulling in a ways. A good tail won't try it if he thinks you might see him. He'll have binoculars and a camera, he can probably spot you if you get out of your car, and he can go back later and figure out who you went to visit. He knows you have to come back out the way you went in, so all he has to do is wait where he can see that intersection, since he'll know you can't drive out the other end."

"Right."

"So, you lead him into a district that isn't a dead end, but has only one way out, and you make sure when you leave, *you* can see the intersection."

Dormer had paused, then added, "Now, this still might be a coincidence—guy happened to have business in that same neighborhood. But if you take a long and roundabout way getting there, that's not likely."

Carruth smiled, remembering the old man's lessons.

The visit to the knife shop was short—he didn't really need a new knife, though he did look at a couple titanium-scaled folders from Cutter's Knife and Tool—the Bengal Karambit was really nice and not too spendy. Had a frame-lock and a nice heft. Some knife gurus didn't have much use for the little hook-blade shape, but they didn't know how well it could be made to work in the hands of an expert. Use the thing right, the guy giving you grief wouldn't know you even had the sucker until you bit him with it. He could bleed out on the way to the hospital, if you cut the right spot, and Carruth had practiced cutting the right spots more than a little.

He thought about it, but decided to wait until next time.

When he got back into his car, he didn't see the gray sedan. He pulled around the loop and sped up a little, not much, and back to the straight line to the intersection. He pulled out, turned right, and drove somewhat slower.

It was maybe fifteen seconds later that the guy following him reached the intersection. Same gray car.

Carruth felt a cold rush in his belly as he saw the tail.

So. Somebody *was* following him. That didn't make any sense.

Who?

And—why?

He slowed down enough to be able to read the license plate on the tail. He pulled a pen from his shirt pocket and wrote the plate number down on the back of his hand.

He needed to tell Lewis about this. Might be it was her having him shadowed. He couldn't imagine why, but stranger things had happened. And if it wasn't her, she needed to know about it. Other than their business, and those two dead cops, there wasn't any reason anybody should be following him.

He didn't think it was the cops. If they suspected he was the guy who had killed two of their own, they'd have come down on him like an imploded casino. And it wouldn't be just one guy tailing him. They'd have his toilet wired for sound and they'd be on him like ugly on an ape. Lewis had access to computer stuff; she could maybe do something with the license plate.

He pulled the throwaway phone from his belt and thumbed in the number for Lewis's one-time cell.

Pentagon Annex
Washington, D.C.

As Lewis sifted through the mounds of information—here in her VR scenario represented as dirt and crushed ore from a gold mine, being washed through a huge strainer—she came across a fist-sized nugget. She looked at it.

The "nugget" popped open and a voice started talking from inside it. She listened for thirty seconds or so. . . .

Oh, crap!

"End scenario," she said.

In her office, she took several deep breaths, to calm her racing heart. The information was ugly—and in more ways than one.

Carruth's call about the shadow had been bad enough when she hadn't known anything about who it might be. Now it was a real can of worms.

Her new op had run the plates on the car. Fortunately, the driver had been dumb enough or confident enough not to swipe a clean plate or use a rental car. Her op figured out who he was, and then a connection that was surprising—and dangerous.

It had been a surprise. Even if she'd suspected, and if

she'd had to guess between the two trying to talk to her, she'd have picked Ali bin Rahman bin Fahad Al-Saud. She'd have been dead wrong, too. No, it was Brian Stuart, the "Australian."

She shook her head at the stupidity of her mistake. Could have been worse, but fortunately, Carruth had spotted the tail, and she *had* checked it out.

They were also getting into dangerous territory with her new hired op—information that she didn't want him to have might come up, and if it did, then eventually he was going to have to go to that great detective agency in the sky. At this point, one more death wouldn't make things any worse, and they had to start covering their asses now. She hadn't set out on this path with the intention of killing people, but that's how things went. Then you had to deal with it.

Next to the surprise about the "Australian" was the general crappiness of the situation itself. "Brian Stuart" was not a viable buyer for her data. His real name was Yusuf bin Abdulla Al-Thani, a Qatarian? Qatarite?— whatever, he was from Qatar—and, if her investigator could be believed, was the older brother of a man named Mohammed bin Abdulla Al-Thani. Which hadn't meant anything to her, until her op had passed along that Mohammed, who had recently left the land of the living to join Allah in Paradise, had used the alias "Mishari Aziz." Like his brother, Aziz/Al-Thani had been a terrorist of some note.

Him she knew, because she had shot him dead in a park in New Orleans when he had gone for a gun in his pocket.

Shit, shit, *shit*—!

The Al-Thani brothers were Tamim Arabs, and distantly related to the rulers of Qatar, if no longer included in polite family company because of their most radical beliefs. Not the most reliable of customers, terrorists.

It was pretty obvious why Yusuf/Brian was looking for her. She'd killed his brother and he was understandably pissed off about it. But that he had gotten as far as he had bothered her no end. How far was that? She was pretty sure that Yusuf and a friend or two had somehow backtracked their way to Simmons, her former sub-rosa investigator, and killed him, trying to find her. Unless Simmons had an old enemy who'd happened to find him, that was the only thing that made sense.

How?

It didn't really matter how the tiger got into your house until after you got rid of it, but she was curious nonetheless.

She didn't know how much they had gotten out of Simmons, but they probably would have determined that she was a woman. If the two men killed with Aziz/Al-Thani down on the river in New Orleans hadn't been the same two who'd followed her to a mall in Florida after their first meeting, then it was likely that big brother Yusuf had a better description of her than that she was just a young, blond woman.

Of course, knowing what she looked like was not the same as knowing who she was, and it was a big country. Still, it was a rock in the road and she didn't want to hit it. . . .

How ever had they found Carruth? It didn't seem possible. And yet, according to her op, the car belonged to a shell company that was run by Al-Thani, and what were the chances of *that* being a coincidence? That somebody was following her guy and that the somebody was connected to the man she'd iced in New Orleans?

Shrugging that off wasn't going to happen.

This was bad. Having a terrorist actively looking for you to exact revenge for killing his little brother? It would certainly throw a big bag of sand into the gears if he showed up. Not to mention into her personal life.

So, what was she going to do about it?

He might not have a clue as to her identity. Simmons hadn't, and no way to directly connect to her. But that Yusuf Al-Thani had gotten this far already meant he had damned good resources—either Simmons had screwed up, or not, and if not, how Al-Thani had wound up on *his* doorstep was troublesome in the extreme.

Simmons maybe stepped on somebody's telltale while checking out Aziz? Possible.

But even so, Simmons hadn't known who Carruth was.

And yet, there Yusuf was—him or one of his people, dogging Carruth.

She scanned the rest of the file the new op had sent. Well, at least she knew who he was now, and what he looked like. Might not do her much good if he was waiting in her bedroom with a big sidekick and weapons when she got home one dark night, but it was something.

She thought about it. Once you started down the violent road, it was hard to step off it; she *had* killed the man's brother, and there wasn't any way to downplay that if he ever did find her.

He went for his gun first! probably wasn't going to make much difference to an enraged and murderous brother.

So. What was the best way to protect herself? She didn't want to spend the rest of her life looking over her shoulder for some fanatic bearing the sword of retribution, looking to lop her head off.

She dug out her current one-time phone and manually tapped in the number for Carruth's current one-time.

"Yeah?"

"I found that information you requested. Meet me at the place, tonight, seven P.M."

"Copy."

She discommed. Shut off the phone and stuck it into her purse. She'd lose it after she left work, and pick up a new one at home. She had a dozen of them, all identical. The guards never checked the numbers, only to see if it was a real phone, which it was.

Carruth had his uses, and this would be right up his alley.

Dark Horse Restaurant
Richardson, Maryland

"You're shittin' me," Carruth said.

"Would that I were."

He shook his head. "Damned ragheads are thicker than

fleas on a camel in this deal, ain't they? How'd they find *me*?"

She said, "I don't have any idea."

He shrugged that off. "So, what's the plan?"

"We set up a meeting with 'Brian.' You and some of your men will be there and when he shows up—probably with some of his men—you erase them."

He nodded. That was the best way. Bastard couldn't come back to backstab you if you cut him into enough pieces. How had they found him, though? He'd like to know, but if they weren't around, it didn't matter. "I can do that. They'll be looking for trouble, though."

"Set it up somewhere they'll have to drive to, a long way from anything. Somewhere with one way in or out. You get there and prepare before we even tell them where. If they come armed and alert—which, you're right, they will, of course—your troops still have the advantage."

"They could bring a whole van full of shooters. I would, if I was them. It could get real gory."

"You didn't throw away the rest of those Dragons, did you?"

He grinned. "No, ma'am."

"Find a place you like, reconnoiter, figure out what you need, let me know. But we have to do this soon. I don't want this guy and his friends showing up for supper some night at my house."

Carruth was not exactly thrilled to know that they'd found him, either. "Me, neither. I hear you."

23

"Mr. Gridley?"

Jay stared at the image on his phone's screen. "My number. Who else?"

"Doyle Samuels, FBI. I have some information for you."

"Fire away."

"As you are no doubt aware, we are conducting a joint investigation with Army Intelligence in regards to your agency's investigation into the Army base break-ins."

"Yeah?"

"This is in regard to Private First Class Jerome Jordan, who was one of the soldiers killed during the terrorists' raid on Fort Thomas Braverman."

"Right?"

"Private Jordan was the first man shot by the perpetrators. This was on the base itself. Before the destruction of the Hummer and its occupants."

Jay stifled a sigh. *Why couldn't these feebs ever just get to the point?*

"Uh huh."

"FBI Ballistics has determined that Jordan was killed by a single round from a handgun, and that the caliber of the slug was a variation of the .500 Maximum." The agent let that hang for a second, as if it was supposed to mean something to Jay—which it did not.

"And . . . ?"

"This is an unusual caliber for a side arm. As large as legally allowed to be made in the U.S."

"Agent Samuels, I don't know from guns, I'm a computer guy. Are we getting to a point here any time soon?"

"It turns out that the rifling on the round matches that of the bullets that were used in a recent shooting in the District in which two Metro officers were killed."

"Wow." He'd sure heard about that.

"It further turns out that the particular kind of bullet used, a .510 GNR, is custom-made in small numbers for a discriminating user group, as are the guns that will shoot it, and we have begun to gather the information on those. Given that Net Force's computer capabilities are better than most, it might be that you can help us find the gun for which we are looking."

"Oh, yeah, you bet," Jay said, suddenly very interested indeed.

"I'll have the file uploaded to your secure address."

"Yes, sir, you do that. And thank you."

"You will keep us posted?"

"As soon as I have something, you'll get it."

"Pleasure doing business with you, Mr. Gridley."

"Likewise."

Jay grinned as he discommed. This was a break. He had access to the Super-Cray, as much time as he wanted. He knew people who would cheerfully kill their grandmothers to be able to do that, and that was understandable—Super-Cray access was worth gem-quality diamonds. If he could come up with a proper parameter set, he could strain down to the quantum level—and if the information was out there, he could find it.

He *would* find it.

He grinned again, then waved his hand over the control and waited for the file to finish downloading.

Come on, come on—!

Galactic Science Fiction Convention
Phoenix, Arizona
Labor Day Weekend

The scenario was in the dealer's room.

Such a place was passing weird, even for VR. There were thousands of people in the huge room, a convention center space across the street from a big chain hotel in Phoenix, Arizona. There were hundreds of tables stacked with moldy, old pulp magazines, sci-fi videos, and all manner of science-fiction and fantasy impedimenta, from toy ray guns that flashed lights and made electronic cheeps and chirps, to movie posters, to real swords based on those used by Conan the Barbarian and the Highlander.

It was a zoo. Noisy, packed, and very colorful. Must be a thousand people in the place milling back and forth.

Every third or fourth person in the place was dressed in some kind of science-fiction or fantasy costume—there were Darth Vaders, Captain Kirks and Mr. Spocks, Klingons, fairies, druids, Batmen, Supermen, purple aliens, and Luke Skywalkers. There were Princess Leias, in white robes and hair buns, and girls in tiny fur bikinis—some of whom looked great, some of whom looked like they—and anybody who had to look at them—would all be better served if, instead of bikinis, they had been wearing shrouds. . . .

At one point, what appeared to be the entire cast of the *Rocky Horror Picture Show* trooped past.

Jay shook his head. He'd read the stuff as a kid, but never really gotten into the fandom thing, though he had gone to a Worldcon once, just to see, and this was exactly what it had looked like in RW: a giant, multispecies party. . . .

Somewhere in this mob was a guy in a costume of an alien cowboy with a big six-shooter strapped on his hip, virtually speaking, anyhow. According to Jay's Super-Cray search, this was the guy the feds were looking for, the guy who had bought the gun used to kill two Metro cops and at least one and probably a bunch of Army guys.

He hoped it didn't turn out to be the dead and burned-up terrorist they'd found, Stark. That wasn't going to do him any good.

Whatever.

Jay had come to one possibility he liked, a guy who had given his address as being in Alexandria, and that had turned out to be fake. Well, there *was* a guy with that name living there, only he was five-foot-two, a hundred and fifteen pounds, eighty years old, *and* in a wheelchair, and hadn't bought any custom-made revolvers costing almost three thousand dollars. If he shot such a sucker, it would probably break both his wrists. Somebody had swiped his ID to get past the NICS registration. So, whoever did that might not be their man, but it was the best clue they had gotten so far. The guy might not be a computer player, but like any other person living in civilization these days, he left an electronic trail. His was faint, but Jay was on it.

He was in here somewhere. All Jay had to do was find him and, in this scenario, get him out of his costume and see who he really was. Then he'd pass that along to folks who could go and fetch him, and that would be that. Once the authorities had one of the terrorists in hand, they could probably convince him to give up the others.

Of course, with the mass of humanity milling around, and the hundreds of costumes in evidence, it might not be so easy to find the guy here. . . .

A very stout man wearing the costume of a Klingon warrior bumped into Jay, jolting him. "Watch where you step, *p'tahk* human!"

"Sorry," Jay said.

"Qui'yah!"

For just a second, Jay considered manifesting a blaster and turning this clown into a pile of smoking ash. He didn't recognize the words in what he assumed was Kling-on, but he knew an insult when he heard it.

Then again, why bother? Everybody had to be some-where, and if it made this guy, who was probably a file clerk or an accountant, feel better to spend a couple hours getting into costume as a Star Trek alien to wander around a media convention spouting a made-up language, so what? It was a harmless fantasy, and better than a lot of ways he could be getting into trouble. At least he wasn't out on the street mugging old ladies or selling crack.

Jay was all for whatever floated your boat, as long as you didn't hurt anybody when you did it.

Jay raised his right hand and split his fingers into the Vulcan V-sign that Spock used to do on the Trek television show. "Live long and prosper, Warrior."

The ersatz Klingon sneered, but moved off.

Cowboy, cowboy, where was the space cowboy?

Jay wound his way past a display of toy rockets and space ships, then a table stacked with lurid magazines fea-turing busty women in what looked like brass bikinis, be-ing menaced by tentacled monsters. A television monitor flickered with an old black-and-white serial showing Flash Gordon in front of the Emperor Ming. The music sounded familiar. Was that Liszt's Prelude?

He glanced up from the TV and caught a glimpse of a white hat ahead. Definitely a Stetson-style cowboy hat.

He smiled as he recalled the Stagolee scenario. All about the *hat* . . .

Jay tried to worm his way closer, but the crowd was thick here. He stepped on an alien's foot, and was rewarded with a curse that was very much human. He brushed past a guy with a head shaved bald, save for a topknot, with green makeup on his face and hands, and long fingernails. He was holding hands with a drop-dead-gorgeous blond woman in purple spandex and leather boots, with a blaster on a hip belt.

Jay nearly stepped on somebody down on all fours, dressed up like some kind of four-legged alien critter and following the happy couple. The creature snarked at him, halfway between a bark and a moan.

Lord.

He looked up, but he'd lost sight of the hat.

Damn!

A very tall man dressed as an Amazon woman, complete with a wig, a spear, and what looked like a fiberglass copy of a bronze breastplate over huge fake hooters, stood in front of a table stacked with tapes from 1950s Saturday morning television shows, like *Howdy Doody*. The Amazon was six-four, if he was an inch. Somebody that tall would have a good view. "Excuse me, I'm looking for a cowboy," Jay said.

"Honey, aren't we all?" the faux-Amazon said. "Her" voice was as dark brown as L-O-L-A Lola's, and closer to Darth Vader's than any woman Jay had ever heard. She could sing the bass parts in opera, easy.

After a fruitless fifteen minutes of searching, which included at one point hopping up on a bare table to see better, Jay gave up, at least for now. The cowboy with his six-gun was here at the convention somewhere, but he seemed to have left the room.

Maybe he had gone across the street? There were all kinds of programs scheduled at the hotel.

Jay headed for the door. As he worked his way through the stream of humanity, real and fake, he thought it was kinda fun, actually, though he wondered what a straight person who happened into this scene would think upon seeing people dressed up in such outlandish costumes.

Probably think they were all nutty as fruitcakes.

Oh, well. Reality was almost always stranger than fiction.

Jay headed out into the hot afternoon. Jeez, it was like an oven! Like being hit in the face with a board. Dry heat or not, when you went from seventy and AC to maybe a hundred and ten, that was hot. A wonder people weren't passing out in the street.

The hotel was just across the street. Jay started walking.

Was that somebody wearing a cowboy hat, just heading into the building?

Heedless of the heat, Jay ran.

24

Carruth picked a place he'd been to back when he'd been in the Navy. He and a bunch of buddies had gone camping, hiking into the woods in Virginia, and they'd passed this old falling-down barn way the hell out and gone in the country, down a gravel road. The farmhouse that had been there was gone, burned down, except for a chimney mostly covered with kudzu.

There were other farms around, but nobody within a mile or two of the old place.

He took Dexter, Hill, and Russell. They spent a couple hours checking things out—nobody had been down the gravel road as far as the barn lately; there might have been some hunters or cold-weather campers using the road, but no fresh tracks.

One they had the lay of the land, they turned to tactics. A couple shaped-charge shot-canisters were set up next to the road in trees, devices that could be triggered by a re- mote, right at eye level for a guy driving a car or van.

Those would serve as backup. Nasty little things, they were essentially explosives packed heavy inside a fan-shaped tube that was welded shut on one end. The explosives were laced with little steel ball bearings. When the thing went *blam!* anything in front of the blunderbuss-bell would get blasted hard. It would turn the driver of a car within ten meters into bloody hash, window down or up, and with a pair of them, one on both sides of the narrow road, any passengers would be likewise chewed to ratburger PDQ.

Other than that, they didn't need anything fancy. They had the ground. Carruth knew that Keep-It-Simple-Stupid was the best way. It might not always work every time, but KISS kept you from screwing up more often than not.

There were plenty of trees and scrub brush around the barn. Nobody would be inside the place—the wood was so rotten it might collapse from a big sneeze. They'd come in two cars—one would be the decoy, set up where it was easy to see, the other well hidden. They'd wear gillie-suits, and when the bad guys showed up, they'd do it by the numbers. Wham, bam, thank you, ma'am . . .

He opened his cell phone. NO SIGNAL, it said. Good.

"Okay, boys, rendezvous at my place tomorrow morning, 0600. I'll bring the hardware. Get some sleep, I want fresh eyes and trigger fingers, come the dawn."

The other three nodded.

They had the decoy car set up—one that Hill swiped and switched plates on—and they were well hidden in the woods. Hill and Russell had overlapping fields of fire, using M-16s, though if it went the way they figured, they would only need those for mop-up.

They were in place and ready an hour before Lewis made the call to Al-Thani. The meeting was set for four hours after that, but it would only take maybe half that long for Al-Thani to drive there, assuming he was in or around the District, and if Carruth had been him, he would have pushed that to make it even sooner. But ninety minutes was way more time than they needed, since they were ready to rock now. . . .

Carruth had the Dragon, and the plan was simple. As soon as Al-Thani and his troops arrived, he would put a rocket through the windshield of whatever vehicle they were in and cook 'em. Bye-bye, boys.

If anybody survived that and managed to get out of the car alive, Hill and Russell would chop them down with automatic-weapons fire, and the dance would be over.

It would be a bit noisy, but by the time anybody got curious and came to see what all the thunder had been about, Carruth and his troops would be long gone.

They just might be smart enough to have a second car following, and if so, the shrapnel exploders would spray that sucker with hard sleet and Dexter would run a couple magazines of ammo after it, with Hill coming to add his fire as soon as they were done here.

It didn't get much simpler than that. See the bad guys, cook the bad guys, and see ya, boys—we're outta here. . . .

The four of them wore short-range, low-power LOSIR headsets that wouldn't carry for more than a klick, and any changes that were necessary could be conveyed instantly. Carruth was wired, feeling speedy from the adrenaline rushing in his body. That's how it always went when you were getting ready for war. Everything tuned up to full alert and hammers circulated in your blood . . .

It was forty-five minutes later when things stopped going according to plan.

It was Dexter who heard it first. They all wore shooters' earplugs, designed to stop loud noises and to amplify normal sounds, but Dexter had always been able to hear a mouse twitch in the next room.

"Incoming helicopter," Dexter said.

After a second, Carruth heard it, too. Well, damn!

He didn't believe for a second it was a coincidence.

Crap. He hadn't figured they'd be that well equipped.

He went over the terrain in his mental map. The nearest clearing big enough to land a chopper was three hundred meters to the south. They'd put the bird down there; the troops would alight and try to ghost through the woods, to set up on the barn. Once they hit the ground and spread out, that would be bad—Carruth and his men might well be outnumbered and the advantage of surprise would only go so far. They needed the targets in a bunch.

"Go, go, the clearing to the south!" Carruth ordered.

It was a bitch running in a gillie-suit, all that crap flapping in the breeze, and the Dragon was heavy enough to start him breathing fast after a hundred meters, but the sound of the chopper was getting louder. Walking wasn't going to get it done.

It seemed to take forever, but they reached the edge of the clearing while the chopper was still a couple hundred meters up. Looked like a Sikorsky S-series to Carruth, a 76 or maybe the S-76A. Those would hold six or eight passengers and two pilots comfortably, with gear, but you could stuff as many as a dozen people into one and still get it into the air. Even if the pilot stayed with the craft, that could mean as many as ten or eleven pairs of boots on the ground, and that was way too many against their quad.

"Fan out," Carruth ordered. "Don't nobody get behind me."

Somebody laughed.

Carruth sat, perched the rocket launcher on his shoulder, and lined it up on the gently settling helicopter.

There came the big *whoosh!* of exhaust back-blast blowing leaves and bushes apart behind him, and the missile zipped away.

The pilot must have seen the flash or the back-blast and recognized it; he tried to turn and power up, but it was too late. Carruth kept the crosshairs on the craft's body amidships, and almost instantly the rocket lanced into the copter and blew up, making a hellacious noise that his earplugs cut out. Mostly cut out, anyhow.

The main rotor ripped loose from the impact. The tail rotor then spun the bastard like a top as the Sikorsky dropped like a brick soaked in flaming fuel—which is what it had become.

From two hundred meters, it wasn't likely anybody was

going to survive the impact, but Hill and Russell tracked it to the ground. When it hit, it rocked Carruth like an earthquake. Fiery gas spewed in all directions, arcing sheets of flame up and out in a ragged circle as the frame crunched and collapsed in on itself.

Hill and Russell ran toward it, but couldn't get any closer than twenty meters because of the intense heat. Carruth could see their suits stirring under the force of the radiant heat.

If you couldn't get any closer than that, then anybody *in* there was already quick-barbecued by now, Carruth knew. If the fall hadn't killed them, the fire sure had.

Thick, roiling, black smoke erupted into the clear sky in a great cloud, and even if there was a car coming later for backup in an hour or so, Carruth and his men sure as hell weren't going to be here to see it. This much smoke in the woods was a bad thing, and the locals would be heading this way to check it out in a hurry. Which meant Carruth and his troops needed to be leaving for the car *right this minute*.

Carruth triggered his LOSIR transmitter.

"Dex, grab the explosives, crank up the decoy car, and head out. Rest of us'll take the primary vehicle. Don't stop until you get to the rendezvous."

"Copy."

"Let's go, boys. We're gonna have company if we stick around here."

They ran for the hidden van.

The FAA would show up sooner rather than later, too, and it wouldn't take them long to figure out that a helicopter full of armed guys hadn't fallen out of the sky due to pilot error. Well, except that he was stupid enough to be flying out here where Carruth was with his rocket launcher.

Wouldn't take the feds long to figure out what had done the trick, either; he didn't have time to clean up, they had to cut and run. If they found pieces of the rocket, and they would, there was the wire stretched out right there, it'd be like a fingerprint, so they'd know it was from a Dragon, and it wouldn't take a big brain to figure out where *that* had come from, either.

Who had gotten shot down and why? That might be harder, but probably they'd figure out the dead guys were on some list. Maybe one terrorist faction was going after another, and let Homeland Security try and sort through *that*.

Not that it mattered. Carruth and the boys wouldn't be here.

Lewis probably wasn't gonna be too thrilled about this, either. Chances were, the head honcho had been in the chopper—the backup car, if there was one, wouldn't have been the way for the boss to travel. Carruth couldn't be positive—maybe the guy was afraid of flying or something—but probably he was in the copter, which was mostly melted into slag by now and anybody inside it would be a crispy critter. No way they were gonna be able to stick around and get IDs, though. He mentally shrugged. It was what it was. You did the best you could with what you had. Anything else, fuck it. . . .

25

"Boss?"

Thorn looked up and saw Jay in the doorway. "Jay. What can I do for you?"

"I just got an urgent priority report from Homeland Security and the FAA—probably a copy heading into your in-box right now. A helicopter blew up and fell out of the sky over in Nowhere, Virginia. Killed nine people."

"Oh, Lord."

"It gets better. The guys in the copter were hauling enough guns and ammo to start a small war. M-16s, AK-47s, and hand grenades, at the least. HS has ID'd a few of them, and those were on the don't-let-'em-in-the-country-and-shoot-'em-if-you-see-'em list."

"Terrorists?"

" 'Suspected' is what HS says officially. Off the record, though, they absolutely were terrorists of the worst kind. A couple are from Qatar, one from Iran. They traced the pilot. He was a Saudi, no IDs on the others yet. The bird was a rental."

Thorn shook his head.

"Here's where we come in—the FAA guys said the copter was brought down by a rocket, and that it came from an FGM-77 Dragon. They found some kind of wire and bits of the rocket that confirm it."

"As in the same kind that was stolen in the raid in Kentucky."

"Oh, yeah. As in *exactly* the same kind. Odd coincidence, huh?"

"I'm sure." Thorn frowned. "So, why is whoever stole the launchers using them to shoot down armed terrorists?"

"Got me. Patriots, maybe. Or maybe they are bucking for jobs in Homeland Security?"

A chime on Thorn's computer alerted him to an incoming priority message. Thorn waved his hand, and a security-encoded text appeared, repeating what Jay had just told him.

"How did you get this before I did?"

"Friends in low places."

Thorn sighed. "You will see what you can find out about this, won't you?"

"In my copious spare time, sure."

"Thanks, Jay."

"No problem, Boss."

But after he was gone, Thorn sat there thinking about it. It was a problem. That the missile had been used against the bad guys was good, but they still had two left, and the next one could just as easily be shot in another direction. Or not. He wanted to run these thieves down and make sure they didn't get another shot off in *any* direction. . . .

His assistant said, "General Hadden is on the phone."

"Of course he is," Thorn said. He shook his head and reached for the receiver.

* * *

Tex's Truck Stop and Grill
Alexandria, Virginia

Lewis listened to the story without interrupting. At the end of it, she nodded. "Couldn't be helped. Even if you'd known they had a chartered helicopter, you would have still had to take it out. Bringing the rocket launcher was smart."

Somebody fed money into a jukebox by the pool tables. A country and western song started playing in the background. A twangy-voiced woman singing something about a lyin', cheatin' man.

Ain't they all, honey?

Carruth nodded. "I'm guessing our boy was on it, and unless he melted down to butter during the fire, they'll eventually get around to identifying him."

"Already have," Lewis said. "And he *was* killed in the fire. Good news for us. He doesn't appear to have any more blood kin in the terrorist business, so maybe we are done with that."

"Must be nice to have access to all that," he said.

"It is. And to have them giving it to you because you are helping protect them from yourself? That's even better."

"You hate the Army, don'tcha?"

She blinked at him. "Why do you say that?"

"I'm maybe not the brightest bulb on the string, Captain, but I'm not completely stupid. I *can* hear. It comes out every time you talk about the service, there's a nasty edge in your tone. Contempt."

She didn't speak to that. It wasn't supposed to show, though. If Carruth here could see that—and he wasn't exactly a candidate for Mr. Sensitive—then somebody else could. She would have to work on that. It wouldn't do at all for people on the inside to be looking at her squinty-eyed. Certainly not Mr. Jay Gridley.

"So, now what?" he said.

"We're back to one decent buyer. If he's legit, we talk deal. If he pans out, we're done. If not, we keep trolling the waters."

"Think ole Benny is gonna want another token of our ability to deliver?"

She shrugged. "Maybe. Whatever it takes. I'll call you as soon as I have something."

"Yes, ma'am. You do that."

After she was gone, Carruth ordered a beer and listened to the jukebox. He liked country music, and a truck-stop bar was as good a place as any to have a beer. Truckers and cowboys, though most of the guys in Western gear here would be all hat and no cattle. There might be a few real ranchers who dropped by—they still had farms and ranches in this part of the world. Carruth had grown up in cattle country, at least partially, outside of Denver, and he had some good memories of that time. First girl, first woman, first beer, first bar fight, all as a teenager. One of the reasons he went into the Navy had to do with the last of those bar fights, in which a loudmouth asshole had bought himself a week in the local hospital when he pissed Carruth off. The judge, an ex-Marine, thought that the service was a good place for boys who liked to mix it up, and Carruth agreed with him—given the other choice, which had been doing a few months working on a road crew out of the local jail.

So he joined the Navy, found he had a talent for warfare, and was accepted into SEAL training, where he did real good. He'd always been a swimmer, no fear of the water, and the physical stuff was challenging, but something he liked doing. He was big, strong, got the training, and no-body messed with him. There were a lot worse ways to get by in life.

He sipped at the bottle of beer. Of course, there came a time when he and the Navy found themselves at odds and he had more or less been told to leave under his own steam or be tossed out, but he had learned a trade, and he'd done okay since. This deal with Lewis would be his ticket to freedom. He could travel, live high, enjoy his life, work or not as he felt like. There was risk—but, hell, all life was risk. You could get caught in an earthquake, be hit head-on by a drunk driver, or have a heart attack—you never knew when your number was gonna be up, and Carruth figured that it was best to live life to the hilt before God tapped you out.

He finished his beer. At the pool table closest, a couple guys in baseball caps wrangled over something. Time was, he'd have moseyed over that way and looked to put himself in the middle of whatever was going on, and maybe got into kicking some ass. He couldn't risk that now. There was too much riding on him staying out of trouble. Time to pack it up and go home. That mess with the Metro cops? That had sobered him. The big gun under his jacket was worth his neck just being on his hip—

A sudden thought ghosted through his head, and it went by so fast he almost couldn't snag it. The gun, something about the gun . . .

Holy shit! The Army *guy!*

Carruth sat there stunned, unable to move, held in his chair by the realization. *How could he have missed it? His brain was turning to Jell-O!*

Well, yeah, okay, blowing up the Humvee full of soldiers a few minutes later had kind of taken over the memory of that night, the first guy he'd tapped had faded, but still. Stupid!

He dropped a ten on the table to pay for his beer, stood, and headed for his car. He had to hide the big revolver. The cops all talked to each other these days—feds, NCIC, everybody—and sooner or later, somebody was gonna notice that the ballistics on the BMF slug that nailed the Army guy in Kentucky matched those on the bullets that hammered the D.C. Metro cops. It might not happen soon, but it would eventually. Now he had three dead guys notched on the big honker, and a line between them. It wasn't as if it had his name on it or anything, but Jesus, carrying it around really wasn't smart. If he had to shoot somebody else, they would start triangulating in on him. They already had too much information; he ought not give 'em any more.

He didn't have to destroy it. He could get down in the

crawl space under his house, wrap the piece in a plastic bag, stick it under the moisture shield. Nobody would find it there by accident, and if they found it on purpose, he was screwed anyhow.

He should have done it as soon as he had capped the Metro cops, he knew that. He just hadn't *wanted* to—he really liked the BMF, liked carrying it, liked how it made him feel. It was a man's gun.

But if he wasn't the brightest bulb on the string, he also wasn't the dimmest one, and he needed to get his act together. He had a SIG, an S&W, he could use one of those, and they were enough gun for soft targets like people. When it was all done and he had money coming out the wazoo, he'd buy another honker or two, and maybe move someplace where it was legal to carry, get a license, and never have to worry about it again. Yeah. That was the way to go.

He headed for his car. If he could get home without being pulled over by a state trooper, he'd be fine. And he was gonna drive real careful. . . .

Graham Land, the Weddell Sea
Antarctica

High over the ice, Jay Gridley considered the geekiness of programmers. He'd long known that while people in most professions tended to enjoy in-jokes, programmers in general tended to take it to the extreme.

Like this VR, for instance. It wasn't his, but somebody had put a lot of thought into it. A lot of silly thought . . .

Down below, thousands of Adelie penguins waddled about, moving little chunks of ice from a huge white pyramid in the middle of their rookery. Adelie penguins were the ones most associated with the classic "tuxedo" look— black and white with the white ring around their eyes.

What Jay was really doing was looking at a huge records database at MIT. He'd come to see if he could check the data logs from the Troy game. Those records had naturally been stored and archived—put "on ice," so to speak.

Ice tended by penguins. Geek joke one.

Men dressed as arctic explorers stood in a huge queue in front of several desks, each one manned by an identical green-garbed figure with black question marks stenciled onto his fur costume. The explorers were actually information requests—from a variety of sources—and the green figures were the processors that directed searches via penguin to the ice cathedral.

The guys behind the desks were out of the old Batman TV show.

The Riddlers and the Penguins. Joke two.

But flacking the metaphor even further was that each of the portly penguins much resembled "Tux," the famous penguin mascot of the Linux operating system.

Said mascot had been named not due to its appearance, but due to the fact that a man named Linus Torvald had written the key kernel of the OS—itself based on another operating system called Unix. The name for the penguin had apparently come from *T*orvald *Uni*x. Which were injokes three, or four, depending on how you looked at things.

And the final self-referencing gag in this scenario—at least the last one that Jay saw—was that the VR scenario was actually being run on a cluster of Linux-based systems.

It was a little over the top, but he understood it. If you can't have fun, why bother?

In his current guise, Jay was a Skua gull, one of the natural predators of Adelie penguins, the eggs and young ones anyhow. He flapped his wings and soared slightly higher, watching the queue below.

He didn't much care for nonhuman VR avatars, but this scenario required it. The security on the database was extensive. On the other hand, there were always weaknesses.

In this case, the programmer had wanted to keep the scenario realistic. It would have been more secure to restrict the VR avatars to just the penguins, riddlers, and requesters. But the programmer had been fixed on keeping the scenario more realistic, which meant a few Skua gulls flying overhead, leopard seals in the water, whales, the works.

Which had left Jay a way in.

So here we was, having dropped his request for information on the back of one of the explorers below—in the usual gull way. When said explorer reached the riddler desks, he'd include Jay's request with his own.

My piggybacked request. If his gull avatar could have grinned, it would have. Instead he let out a *craw*.

Within the scenario the request wouldn't be checked. But when the penguin brought the information back, it would be checked before being given back to the explorer.

So Jay had to grab it from the penguin before it got there.

He looked again. His explorer was at the request desk.

The man made the request, and Jay watched as the riddler handed a slip of colored paper to a nearby penguin attendant. The penguin walked away from the desk and toward the giant ice pyramid.

Jay glided along, letting out gull cries as seemed appropriate.

The penguin made its way to one of the pyramid entrances and disappeared inside. Now all Jay had to do was wait for the penguin to come back.

There were thousands of penguins here, and they all looked alike. How was he going to know when his came back out?

The request paper. The VR resolution was sharp enough that he could see the coded order number.

Penguins waddled back and forth, in and out of the pyramid, through the entrance, which was about halfway up. The steps up the side were incredibly shallow, made for the tiny strides the penguins took, which meant the pyramid was much wider than it was tall.

Jay took his time, soaring up and down the walkway,

tracking each penguin that came out, dialing his vision in to check the order numbers.

There.

There was his tuxedoed bird.

Skua gulls were the natural predators of Adelie penguins, but they tended to only attack young or old and sickly ones—healthy adults were not usually on the menu.

So while the sight of a diving gull might not stand out in the scenario, seeing one dive on a full-grown healthy penguin would probably set off some kind of alarm.

Then again, once he had his data he could drop out of the scenario. He just had to get it and boogie.

Jay dove.

Some avian sense warned the little waddler. It tilted its head to the side and saw him coming. The penguin leaped over the edge of the walkway and belly-first onto the icy pyramid, using its stomach like a sled.

Jay tightened his wings and increased his speed.

Almost there . . .

The penguin shot up a short incline and then was airborne.

What?

Penguins couldn't fly—!

And this one didn't either—it coasted briefly before falling and splashing into the water below.

Damn!

Jay dove into the water, morphing from Skua gull to leopard seal as he hit.

If the penguin had seemed fast on land when it was sledding, it was like a rocket now, little wings flipping out, propelling it like some kind of formal-wear torpedo.

Jay focused on his seal body.

They swam around submerged pieces of ice, through silvery schools of fish, faster and faster.

Jay realized that he wasn't going to catch it.

Well, hell. How did leopard seals get by without starving?

Wait a second—something he'd read about cautious

penguins—how they didn't want to jump into the water and risk being eaten. But . . .

Jay slowed and let the penguin swim on ahead.

Most successful attacks happened when the penguins were least cautious—coming *back* onto land.

Jay circled back, went up for a fresh breath, then sank and hid behind a chunk of iceberg. He waited with a predator's patience.

Thinking he had outrun his attacker, Tux eventually made a big loop and headed back to shore. Jay spotted him a couple minutes later—fortunately, the paper was waterproof, the number still visible. It was his, all right.

Jay waited until the penguin was almost to the ice before he made his move.

Compared to the earlier chase, it was easy. He pounced and grabbled the little bird with his seal teeth.

Gotcha, Opus!

Unfortunately, after all that, catching Tux didn't do him any good. The bird turned out to be hollow—a simulacrum. Not a real data carrier, but a fake. It took Jay all of two seconds to determine that it wasn't a penguin at all—it was a mouthful of red herring.

Damn!

The guy who had built the Troy scenario was good. Too good. Why would he have done this? Unless he had known he was going to use the game for nefarious purposes that far in advance? That was a hell of a long-range plan. Who had that kind of patience? That kind of forethought? That he would leave false clues *years* in advance?

Jay shook his head.

Something was not right about this. What? And how to find it?

26

Abe Kent looked at General Roger Ellis. Roger was a couple years younger, but his hair had gone white, he'd picked up a few more pounds around the middle, and he looked ten years older. Being in command of the Marines' Special Project section at the Pentagon was apparently more than a little stressful.

"New desk?"

"Yes. Made out of pecan." With his Southern twang, he pronounced the last word "puh-kahn," not "pee-can," and had always insisted that his version was correct. A pee-can, he liked to say, was a toilet. . . .

Kent agreed with him—he'd spent time in Louisiana as a boy, and "puh-kahn" was how they said it down there, too.

Roger leaned back in his chair, which creaked a little. "You know the shit has hit the fan big-time over these Army base break-ins." It was not a question.

"Yes, sir, I got that impression."

"General Hadden is having fits over this. The only good thing about it is that the terrorists have confined themselves to the Army and not bothered the Navy, Air Force, or the Corps."

Kent knew this was going somewhere, but since Roger was his boss and had two stars to his one, he wasn't going to try and hurry him along. Ellis would get to it.

"The thing is, the Chairman of the Joint Chiefs is responsible for 'em all, and he is, as I'm sure you realized, highly perturbed even if it is just the Army. He was big on getting all the high-tech stuff on-line, and this is making him look bad."

Kent nodded. "I hear you."

"Maybe you can help."

Kent said, "I don't see how. I'd be more than happy to lead a team of my troops to hunt these guys down and slap them into a collective coma, but I wouldn't know where to start looking."

"Neither does anybody else. But you're connected directly to the people who are most likely to find out."

Kent nodded, but said, "Not exactly my area of expertise, Roger."

"I know that."

"And it's not like I can march into the computer geek's office and order him to hurry up, find the bad guys. He's not one of mine."

Ellis rubbed at his eyes with one hand and nodded. "I know that, too. But when the big dog barks, the puppies sit up and take notice. Hadden wants something done and he wants it done yesterday, and you don't just tell the man to piss off and die."

Kent grinned at that thought. "Be guarding a warehouse of rancid seal blubber up above the Arctic Circle the rest of your career, if you did."

"If you were lucky. The thing is, the way I heard it, that's what your immediate supervisor Mister—ah, I mean *General*—Thorn did. Not in so many words, but pretty much that's what he meant."

"Man's got balls, got to give him that."

"So do we, and I'd like to keep mine, thank you very much. I know and you know there's nothing you can do to hurry things along, but I will now be able to report to General Hadden that I have leaned on you. If there is anything you can think of, anything at all that will be part of the solution, I want you to effect it at the earliest."

Kent nodded. "I understand." And he did. He had been in the service of his country for a long time, and he knew how the chain of command worked—or, sometimes, didn't work. He knew he couldn't do anything substantial. Ellis and Hadden both knew *they* couldn't, either, but that didn't stop the effort down the line. Sometimes, the pressure added some incentive. It wouldn't here, since the man running the search on the computer end, Jay Gridley, wasn't really amenable to that kind of impetus. Push him too hard, he'd give you the finger and walk away, because he could. Even if they could draft him and keep his ass in the chair, they couldn't compel his best effort, and with a man like Gridley, he could look like he was working his tail off 24/7 and be doing exactly nothing useful. How would anybody outside know? It would take somebody as good as he was to keep tabs on him, and the truth was, they didn't *have* anybody as good as he was. He knew, they knew, and that was how that song went.

Kent smiled again at the idea of a musical metaphor. It reminded him of his date with Jen. Now that had been a major event. Neither one of them was a dewy-eyed adolescent, and although the magic had certainly been there for him, there was a certain no-nonsense air about her that came from experience. She liked him, he liked her, and the dinner had progressed to something he hadn't really expected—certainly not on a first date.

It had been a long, long time for him before that.

Did anybody even use that term anymore? Dating?

"Abe?"

He pulled his attention back to Ellis. "Sir. Sorry. I was wool-gathering."

"Yeah, well, go home, take a nap. If you can light a fire under anybody, even a tiny one, it would help."

"I'll do what I can. Either way, I'm sure the eventual result will come back up the chain." Which meant at the least he could probably get Gridley to confirm that some impetus had come from Ellis's office to speed him along, and that datum would eventually find its way to Hadden's desk. It wouldn't mean an awful lot, but every little bit helped.

Ellis gave him a tired smile. "I appreciate it."

As Kent left, following the Marine sergeant escort toward the exit, he considered the best way to approach Gridley. Straight on, he decided. Drop by his office, lay it out that Thorn's boss had leaned on Thorn, then on him, and allow as how he knew it wouldn't make Gridley go any faster than the flat-out speed at which he was already going, but that this was how the military mind worked. Gridley wouldn't get his jockey shorts in a wad about it, if Kent presented it that way.

He wasn't too worried about it; besides, he had a guitar lesson this evening, and however that turned out, given his new connection with Jen, it was going to be much more interesting than the rest of his day.

When they reached the exit, the sergeant said, "Congratulations on your promotion, General Kent."

"Thank you, son."

He still hadn't gotten used to that rank, but he didn't mind hearing his name with it attached.

"Semper fi, sir."

"Always, Sergeant. Always."

The escort gave him a crisp and perfect salute, and Kent returned it with one almost as good. He gave the man his ID badge and exited the building.

Outside, the day was cool, but sunny. It felt almost like an early spring day. Of course, this was Washington, D.C. If you didn't like the weather, all you had to do was wait—it would change soon enough.

* * *

Lewis General Hospital
Maternity Floor
Washington, D.C.

When Jay logged into Lewis's scenario, he was surprised to find himself walking down the hall of a hospital. It was a well-built visualization—there was that too-clean antiseptic smell, and that soft echo-stopping sound of carpeted floors and thick walls. Jay looked around, saw mothers walking with tiny babies, or in wheelchairs, holding infants on their laps. The maternity floor.

He saw Lewis up ahead, standing with her arms crossed, staring through a wall of glass into a large room marked NURSERY.

Jay approached, not speaking.

"Well-baby nursery," Lewis said.

There were rows of plastic cribs with babies in them, all kinds, and it made Jay smile to see them. He remembered going to see his son in just such a place.

Not looking at him, Lewis said, "The road partially taken."

Jay didn't say anything.

"I was engaged once. My fiancé and I got started a little early on our family. I got pregnant, and we decided to wait until after the baby was born before we had the wedding."

She kept watching the infants behind the glass.

"Sean was a seven-pound, healthy, pink boy. Or so we thought."

Jay blinked. She had never mentioned having a child before.

"He had a rare condition, he was born with an aneurysm. A congenital defect. His aorta just . . . burst when he was two days old. He died in a few minutes. Right in the RW version of there."

Jay was stunned by this news. "I'm so sorry."

She shrugged. "Wasn't anything that could be done. No way to tell until it was too late. Well. I found out later that this had happened several times in my fiancé's family—apparently it was a genetic thing. One baby in four or five had it."

"How awful."

"What was awful was that the son of a bitch didn't *tell* me about it. If I had known, I never would have allowed myself to become pregnant—I wouldn't have risked my baby's life with those kinds of odds."

Jay stared at the floor.

"I come here from time to time," she said. She looked grave for a second. Then she gave him a sad smile. "Well. No point in us standing here being morose. It was a long time ago. I can't change it."

Jay nodded. The thought of his little boy dying was beyond painful. His own experience when the baby had developed pneumonia and had to be rushed to the hospital would be with him until, he was sure, he died, even if he lived to be a hundred. He had thought he was smart and powerful—that incident had made him realize just how helpless he was when it came to such things. He couldn't imagine how Rachel Lewis must feel. How terrible it must be. . . .

"So, what is the scenario you have on tap for us today?"

Distracted by his own thoughts, Jay said, "Uh, well, I thought we might take a run at the cowboy."

"Cowboy?"

"Um, yeah, I didn't have a chance to tell you about that yet. FBI came up with a ballistics match. The gun that killed the G.I. on the Kentucky base is the same one that was used to kill two Metro cops. A great big piece, shoots elephant-stopper bullets. There aren't that many of them around, and I think I've got it narrowed down to the right guy."

She looked surprised. "Really? That—that's great."

"Maybe. It might be a dead end—might be that the terrorist they found in the burning truck after Kentucky, Stark, is the guy who bought the gun, but it's a place to start. The cowboy image is one I came up with once I got it winnowed."

"Let's go find him," she said. "Lead on. The scenario is yours."

Jay nodded.

Galactic Science Fiction Convention
Art Show
Phoenix, Arizona

Lewis was furious. The stupid son of a bitch Carruth had shot two Metro policemen and never said squat about it— she could understand that, because she would have dumped his ass in a hurry had she known that. But he had kept the fucking gun he used to do it, and shot somebody else! And between the FBI and Gridley, they were about to run the bastard down.

This was bad.

She didn't know how stand-up Carruth would be if they pulled him in for murder. The District didn't have the death penalty, though life without parole wasn't a walk in the park. Kentucky still fried people, though, and if they caught Carruth, he'd have to answer for the soldier killed on the base there as well as the ones in the chase car he'd blown up, and it would be in a civilian court, not the Army's. She couldn't remember if they used lethal injection or the electric chair down there. Not that it would matter much.

If he knew he was going to be sent to ride ole Sparky or dance with the Needle, would Carruth give her up to save himself?

Maybe not, but she couldn't take that chance.

Carruth was, all of a sudden, a liability. Maybe a fatal one. She couldn't let the authorities get to him.

And she definitely couldn't let Jay here find him.

How lucky was it that he had come to her with this instead of nailing it on his own? It was his construct, but she had some control, since she was allowed into it. If she had to, she would use it.

Next to her, Jay said, "I could get you a costume, if you want."

"I'll pass. What are we looking for?"

Jay always like to have his basic research clean, so the displays in the sci-fi art show were taken from the real thing. He had also learned that true fans hated the term "sci-fi," too, but that was too bad, 'cuz that's what people in the real world called it.

Pieces ranged from pencil drawings to oil paintings to sculptures, some of the last kinetic or motorized. Much of it was first-class and professional work—book covers, trading cards, game or magazine illustrations. There was what appeared to be the skeleton of a gargoyle, cast in plaster or some kind of plastic that looked like old bone, and from what Jay could tell it certainly looked as if it could have been real. Next to that crouched a giant robotic frog that was amazing.

He saw Rachel taking it all in, and while she didn't laugh or sneer, he didn't get the impression she was all that hot on the scenario. She looked distracted. Probably remembering her baby son. He was still thinking about her revelation. So sad. It made him want to put his arm around her and comfort her. At the least.

But—they had work to do.

They cruised through the art show.

Jay saw an oil painting of a centaur with glowing red eyes that looked so creepy Jay couldn't imagine living in the same house with it—those eyes did seem to watch every move you made. He stood next to the painting and watched people as they came upon it, and that was interesting in itself.

If it bothered Rachel, it didn't show.

There was a quarter-size bronze sculpture of a gorgeous black woman in spandex who had some kind of high-tech guns mounted on the backs of her hands, the barrels extending in a line with her index fingers. It was a beautiful piece of work, and the ten-thousand-dollar price reflected that.

There were some funny drawings—covers for Stephen

King books that he never wrote, with titles like *Big Hairy Monsters!* or *Huge Yellow Fangs!*

There were altogether too many unicorns and cute fantasy animals—tigers with butterfly wings, winged horses, even flying dogs—and a whole bunch of badly rendered fairies, sprites, Hobbits, and characters from *Star Trek* and *Star Wars*, some of them sans clothes. Some of the artists had great imaginations and talent, and some were obviously not folks you'd want to find yourself trapped with in close quarters. . . .

Some of the paintings, collages, assemblages, and sculptures were, in Jay's view, flat-out, turn-away-and-make-a-face *ugly.*

What was amazing about many of these awful artworks was the bid-lists under them, with ten or twelve names and escalating offers.

Rachel did notice this and remarked on it: "Somebody would pay two thousand dollars in real money for *that*?"

Jay laughed. Apparently, it was true: Beauty was in the eye of the beholder. If he'd had time, Jay would have checked out the faces that matched the names of the bidders on some of the more hideous pictures. . . .

But not now. Now, he had spotted his quarry—at least he thought so. A tall man with red makeup, but dressed in neo-cowboy clothes—kind of a futuristic version—and with a big, low-slung holstered gun strapped to his hip. The gun had a multicolored ribbon tied around it and the holster—a "peace bond," Jay had been told. The convention runners frowned on the idea of fans waving guns, knives, or swords around—and the hotel staff *really* didn't like it. What better setup for a robbery? A bunch of armed people wearing disguises? You could just walk up to the front desk, point a gun at the clerk, and rob the place, and nobody'd have a clue who you were. Jay could imagine the interview with the local police:

"Yes, sir, it was a Wookiee, all right. Yeah, he just harned and growled and said, 'Give me the credits or die,

Earthman!' What was I gonna do? How would that look in the paper, if I got shot and killed by Chewbacca?"

"That's him, I think," he told Rachel.

"He's wearing a gun in here?"

Jay explain the convention policy about such things. "Yeah, if you wear a costume featuring a weapon, you have to keep it holstered or sheathed, or whatever, and the ribbon is attached to do that."

"Like that will keep it safe?"

Jay shrugged. "If you get spotted in the halls or elevators twirling your blaster or carving the air with your enchanted sword, Security will kick your ass out, and good luck catching a cab dressed like the Crab Man from Mars. . . ."

She nodded, but didn't smile.

Right now, convention security and social mores weren't Jay's worry. The Red Rider was just ahead, and he needed to stay with him until he found out where he was staying and under what name.

"Stay loose," he said. "Let's see where he goes."

They were doing fine. The guy was heading for the door, when all of a sudden the scenario crashed, a full whiteout.

What the hell—?

The Pentagon
Washington, D.C.

They came out of VR, and Lewis said, "What happened?"

"Damned if I know. Software glitch, maybe."

"You want to go back in?"

Jay shook his head. "No. I have a meeting with my boss at HQ this afternoon, I need to get back." He started to strip off his gear. His neck was tight. He did a head-roll to loosen it, rubbed at the back of his neck with one hand.

"You okay?"

"Yeah. Too much chair time."

"Here." She stood, walked over behind him. "I know just the thing. Lean forward a little."

Jay blinked, but did what she said.

She stood behind his chair and dug her thumbs into the base of his skull, started kneading. It felt great.

"Wow," he said, "that's good."

"Had a friend once who was a masseuse. She showed me how to work the trigger points." She put her left hand on his forehead and supported the weight of his head while she continued to work the back of his neck, using her thumb and fingertips.

Oh, man, that felt good. . . . If she moved her left hand, his head was gonna fall right off. . . .

"Better?"

"Oh, yeah."

"Okay, turn a little to your right and lean back."

He did—and found his head pillowed against her firm breasts. She must be in a squat behind him. She began to rub his forehead with both hands, pressing his head into her bosom harder.

He couldn't help himself. He moaned.

"Like that, huh?"

Of a moment, Jay knew that if he were to turn his head around and put his face into her boobs, she wouldn't mind in the least. That she would join him in the chair, and that the massage would turn into something else entirely. . . .

Jesus!

He leaned away. "Much as I'd like to spend the rest of the day doing this, I really do have to get back to HQ."

"That's all right," she said. "We can finish another time." She smiled.

No question about it. She was letting him know she was available.

How did he feel about that?

Thrilled. Scared. Excited.

And guilty . . .

27

Kent toweled himself off as he stepped from the shower. He was about done when he heard the music coming from the bedroom. He smiled, wrapped the towel around his waist, and headed that way.

Sitting naked on the edge of her bed, Jen played a guitar he hadn't seen before. She had some kind of leather-strap thing with suction cups on it stuck to the side of the instrument, propped on her bare left leg.

Nude with guitar. A beautiful sight.

She was playing Nelson Riddle's theme for the television show *Route 66*.

The original music had been a full orchestral thing and a single guitar couldn't address it that way, of course, but what she played was lovely. It brought back a lot of old memories. He remembered the show from when he'd been a little boy—it was about two young men, Tod and Buz, who knocked around the country in a red Corvette convertible, having adventures along the old Route 66. Today, much of that road was Interstate highway, but back in the late fifties and early sixties, when the show ran, it was mostly two-lane, undivided, untamed.

Kent leaned against the wall and listened as Jen played. It might not have been composed for a classical guitar, but it sounded great the way she did it.

When she was finished, she smiled at him.

"Wonderful. But you can't possibly remember the old television series," he said, "because I barely do and I'm ten years older than you."

She shook her head. "Before my time, except in reruns on the Nostalgia Channel. I saw an episode once—it was silly, but I did like the music, so I transcribed it for this."

"I watched the show when I was a boy, eight or nine, I think. Martin Milner, George Maharis, driving their 'Vette through the little towns, looking for a place where they could belong. The world was a simpler place, back then."

"Better, you think?"

"Not necessarily, especially if you were black or a woman or had polio. Or if your father or uncle or brother was on the ground in Korea. But in some small ways, yeah. I can recall going on a couple of trips with my folks when I was little, along the old Route 66. Main Street, U.S.A., it went right through the heartland, mostly between Chicago and L.A. I remember gas stations and truck stops and ratty motels where my father would stop. Made the run in an old woody station wagon once. I drank Coke out of little bottles. I remember the hot sun beating down in Oklahoma, Texas, New Mexico. Eating bologna sandwiches with mustard on white bread my mother made. Most of the route was upgraded years ago, a lot of it is I-40 now, I think. Now, the only place you see that kind of stuff is in museums. . . ."

He allowed the memory to fade. He looked at her. "New guitar?"

"No, an old one. From Romania, called a Troubador. Spruce top, maple sides and back. I got it off the Internet a few years back for a knock-around. It was cheap, I didn't have to worry about it if it got damaged or swiped. Put new tuners on it, and it turned out to have a really good sound for the couple hundred bucks I paid for it."

"What's the little leather doohickey on the side?"

"Called a Neck-Up. Some longtime players eventually develop nerve or muscle problems with one foot propped on a stool, so somebody came up with this. Keeps the neck at the right angle so you can sit without your leg being cocked up. I use it sometimes when I'm somewhere a foot-stool doesn't work well." She waved at the bed.

He didn't say anything to that. He just stood there, smiling.

She was just full of surprises.

After a moment she looked up at him, saw the expression on his face, and her own grew serious. Gently, she laid the guitar aside, then turned back to him once more.

"Come on back to bed, Abe," she said, her voice soft and throaty.

He dropped the towel and his memories and did so. Yesterday was great, he'd had a full life and a lot of wonderful times to look back on, but he would not trade this—this woman, this moment, this here and now—for any of them.

Pamela Robb Art Gallery
Washington, D.C.

After dinner, Marissa directed Thorn's driver to take them to a street address a couple miles away from the restaurant.

Thorn said, "Where are we going again?"

She said, "We're going to the Robb Art Gallery to see the Byers show."

Thorn said, "Who?"

She smiled. "Do you ever read a paper, Tommy? Watch the news? Mike Byers, he works in glass. Stained, etched, fused—and the fused stuff is where he shines. After thirty years at it, he was 'discovered' a couple years ago and is now the hottest artist in the medium since Dale Chihuly."

"Who?"

"You're pulling my leg, aren't you?"

Actually, he was—he'd seen Chihuly's fantastic glass sculptures. Though, he recalled, those were collaborations, Chihuly had been the director and motivating force behind them.

He smiled at her. "A little."

She shook her head, raising her eyes heavenward. "The man made a joke. Not a great joke, but nonetheless, it's progress."

The Pamela Robb Gallery was a place of tall, vaulted ceilings and lots of windows arranged and angled to offer sunlight to the pale walls. It being night and dark out, they had to make do with artificial light, but care had been taken in the selection and placing of that, too. There were a fair number of people milling about inside, but the place was laid out in such a way that it didn't feel crowded when you went to view the art. Some of it was hung on the walls, some propped up on easels.

Thorn wasn't an art expert by any means—but he found that the abstract glasswork was more emotionally evocative than he would have expected. A lot of it was black glass, geometric shapes with different-colored overlays. Some of them had pieces of copper or bronze mixed in with them. One in particular that caught his eye was called "Fuhoni-te," three black squares set slightly apart, with a vein of red and one of blue running through them. There was another one called "Seeking a Lower Orbit," of glass and copper. There was one named "Thebes," another named "In the Dream Time," a "Timebinder," and one called "Death in Somalia." Colorful names, for sure. His favorite title was "The Physiology of the Eleventh Dimensional Cloned Feline."

Many of them were small—he remarked on this to Marissa.

"These things have to be fired in a kiln, between thirteen hundred and fifteen hundred degrees. Bigger is harder to work with, and needs a larger kiln. Most of his early stuff was small. Once he got the feel for it, he started stretching."

"How do you know all this?"

"If you'd looked as we came in, you'd have seen it printed out on a card by the door."

"Oh."

They came to a larger panel, one that looked almost like slightly misshapen piano keys, with eighteen segments that were skinny, narrow not-quite-rectangles, all done in different iridescent hues, with black spaces between them and three thin lines of black across the bases. The second-to-last shape on the right had a small red dot of glass on the bottom. The whole thing looked to be sixteen, eighteen inches wide, two-and-a-half, three inches tall, framed and matted so that the entire piece was maybe a foot by two feet.

"I like this one a lot," Thorn said. "Called 'Chromatic Sequence.'"

Marissa looked at the price tag. "Six thousand dollars," she said. "But it's already sold."

"Too bad. I could see that hanging over our fireplace."

"We have a fireplace?"

"If you want one."

She shook her head.

He reached into his jacket pocket and took out the velvet-covered box. "Oh, I almost forgot. Here."

She knew it was jewelry—the size and shape of the box was a giveaway—and she almost certainly knew it was an engagement ring. But she didn't know. . . .

She opened the box. "Oh, wow!"

The ring was simple, a fairly plain band of yellow gold, with a diamond-cut emerald inset into it. He'd had it made by a jeweler in Amsterdam and couriered to him when it was done.

"How did you know?"

"I asked your grandmother."

She slipped the ring onto her finger. "Perfect fit. You never asked my size."

"Grandma Ruth has your high school ring in a box at her house. She says you haven't gotten any fatter since then."

Tears welled in her eyes. "Thank you, Tommy. It's gorgeous."

"Not as gorgeous as you."

She hugged him.

Life felt pretty good at that moment.

Washington, D.C.

Carruth had a pretty good gun safe, a five-hundred-pound Liberty, that would hold a dozen long guns and twice that many handguns, though he didn't have that many on hand. The safe would protect his hardware from bad guys, mostly, but if somebody kicked in the door with a search warrant, that would be the first place they'd want to look. They'd be able to get it open sooner or later, so putting the BMF there wouldn't help. If he was going to keep it, it had to hide somewhere else.

The problem was, cops had seen just about every kind of hiding place there was in a house—toilet tanks, the freezer, under the fridge. Dope fiends apparently got very clever about their stashes—hung down inside walls behind light-switch plates or electrical outlets, inside fake cans of Ajax or hollowed-out books. Cops would move furniture, look behind drawers, under loose floorboards, inside stereo speakers or television cabinets. The only way to hide something as big as the BMF in a house would be to put it somewhere nobody would ever think to look, and that wasn't likely with detectives who'd been on the job for ten or fifteen years. They had seen just about every place. He was still thinking about a spot they wouldn't look—under the safe? outside, up in a tree?—when the latest throwaway cell phone chirped.

"Yeah?"

"We need to meet. At the new place. Tomorrow, six A.M."

"Trouble?"

"Just be there."

Well, wasn't that just dandy? What this time? Another terrorist?

For now, he stuck the gun back into the safe. He'd figure out a hiding place later.

Jane's Pottery Shop and Cafe
Washington, D.C.

"You outdid yourself this time," Carruth said. "Coffee tastes like it was made out of old cigarette butts."

She waved that off. She didn't want to tell him that Jay was hot on his trail, but she allowed as how Gridley had something, only he hadn't shared it with her, and it sounded big, to see what Carruth would say. Give him a chance to come clean. Not, at this point, that it would really matter, but just to see.

He didn't bite. He said, "So if this clown is such a linchpin at Net Force and the whole place revolves around him, why don't I just put one behind his ear and let's get rid of the problem?"

Lewis shook her head. "Once upon a time that might have worked, but not anymore. Apparently, Mr. Gridley used to play his cards pretty close to his vest and something like that happened—a guy Net Force was chasing ran Gridley off the road and shot him. He was in the hospital unconscious for a time and there was some doubt he was going to make it. He had vital data locked up in his head nobody could get to. After that, he started backing up his files and leaving them where his boss could get to them. Take him out, they don't lose any of Gridley's input— somebody else picks up the ball and runs with it. Maybe not quite as fast, but eliminating him doesn't help us much."

"And you don't know what he's got?"

"Only that he thinks it is going to break this open."

"Can you get him to tell you?"

"I'm working on it."

She was still hoping to maneuver Jay into her bed. And once she did, she'd make that knowledge public, and that would take Jay out of the action. He would be so busy running around trying to save his marriage that work would be the last thing on his mind.

That her last try hadn't quite done the trick was irritating, but it was still an option. Real pheromones and a warm and willing body were still better than anything anybody had come up with in VR. He wanted her, she was sure of that, she could feel it, and she had primed his pump about as well as she could. She'd have to see if she could get it going soon.

She also didn't bring it up that it was Carruth who was going to get killed. Stupid son of a bitch, she still couldn't believe it. It was just a matter of setting it up and doing it, and soon. Next meeting, or the one after that, they'd meet somewhere nobody would be around. She'd come up with a good reason, and then Carruth here was going to become a major fall guy. They'd find him, and maybe that enormous gun he'd used, something to tie him to it. He was a dead man walking, he just didn't know it yet.

Carruth nodded. "Okay. You're the boss. But why tell me if you don't want him erased? You're the computer girl. You didn't need a sit-down for that."

"That's not the reason. I've got another buyer interested," she said. "A new player." A lie, but how would he know? "He wants a demonstration, so we need one last raid."

"What's he want? A fucking tank?"

"No. He wants a colonel."

"Say what?"

"He wants us to kidnap a bird colonel and turn him over."

"Why?"

"What do you care? We deliver the guy, we have a deal."

"Dead or alive?"

"Alive. Apparently, he has a history with the guy and wants to speak harshly to him."

Carruth shook his head. "This is gettin' old, Lewis."

"Almost over," she said. She wanted to smile, but kept her face as expressionless as she could.

"Details?"

"I'll get those to you next meeting. I still have some codes to collect, plus some background information on the target. Here's the new meeting place. I'll call with the day and time."

She handed him the sticky note. He glanced at it. "Vickers Crossing? Where is that?"

"In the country. The GPS coordinates are there at the bottom."

"More crappy coffee. Great."

Not this time, Carruth. No coffee, because the little country store in question was closed. Nobody would be there except them.

And only one of them was going to be leaving under her own power when that meeting was over.

Too bad it had come to this. It was going to make the rest of the project a bastard—she'd need new muscle, another shooter, and that would be tricky—though with new guys, she wouldn't be so forthcoming. She'd learned that lesson, at least. There were a couple candidates, mercs she had lined up second and third before she'd hired Carruth. Hire a couple, pay them a flat fee, don't tell them any more than they had to know.

She watched Carruth leave. Too bad. But better him than her.

28

Confederation Prison
"The Cage"
The Planet Omega

Jay hadn't figured out why his sci-fi convention scenario
had crashed, but he didn't have time to sit down and debug
the software—it wasn't as if he didn't have other things on
his plate. He'd get back to it later, or maybe he'd just
crank up something totally different and bag the convention imagery.

Sometimes, half the fun in finding information was in
coming up with a new scenario for VR. Jay had to admit
that he did more of that than was absolutely necessary, but
he figured, if he couldn't have fun, why bother? Any hack
could use off-the-shelf software and filters—Jay liked to
think of himself as at least a good craftsman, if not an
artist. . . .

So it was that to hunt down a connection for the dead
terrorist Stark, he had spent a couple hours building a scenario. Sure, it was easier to do these days, because a lot of
the construction material was prepackaged, but that was

kind of like buying a steak at the store instead of going out and hunting down your own cow. He had no problem with taking that shortcut; after all, it was the way you cooked the meat that made the difference. The proof was in the meal—nobody cared if you'd butchered the beef yourself or had somebody else do it.

Over the years, Jay had VR'd to many corners of the world, from Africa to Java, from Japan to Australia, China to Canada, you name it. Not only in the present, but throughout history. And he had built more than a few fantasy scenarios—and not just here on Earth. The solar system, the galaxy, the universe—shoot, the next universe over—Jay had explored all kinds of territory, real and imagined. Sometimes, the trick was more about how to keep it interesting than it was to find what he was after. That was part of the challenge.

This time, he had come up with one he thought was a hoot: He had gone to the planet Omega, in a stellar system far, far away, to the galaxy's toughest prison. Ordinarily, this was a one-way ticket. Nobody was paroled, all the sentences were for life, and nobody had ever escaped—not and lived to tell of it.

While Richard Lovelace had it that stone walls did not a prison make, nor iron bars a cage, a joint with fifteen-meter-high walls painted with slick-ex too slippery to allow a fly to land, armed guards who'd just as soon shoot you as look at you, and set smack-dab in the middle of a pestilent, tropical swamp full of quicksand pits and man-eating critters that flew, ran, crawled, or slithered all over looking for a two-legged meal? Those made for a pretty good cage. Even if you *could* get out, the nearest port was a thousand kilometers away—how would you get there?

Jay, in his guise as a notorious drug smuggler sentenced to The Cage, as it was known, had arrived, beaten the crap out of the bully who had been sent to test him, and integrated himself into the population.

Stark was dead in this reality, too, but he'd been in the prison a while, and there were people who had known him. Jay needed to find them and get them to tell all. Which meant running down e-mails or postings or URLs or newsfeeds where somebody had mentioned Stark. At least enough so he could make a connection between Stark and whoever else might have been on the raids at the Army bases. Every new lead he found would need to be checked out.

He thought about calling Rachel and inviting her into his hunt, but since she was military and restricted to using their systems on this project, that would mean he'd have to go to the Pentagon and set it up there, and at the moment, the only place he wanted to deal with Rachel was in VR, not the Real World. Not that he was repelled by her, no, that was the problem. She was altogether too attractive. It was way too easy for him to visualize her with her hair spread out on a pillow. Something he had certainly thought about.

He wanted her, and he knew he wanted her, but he didn't *want* to want her. He was married—happily—and in love with his wife. This thing with Rachel—no, it wasn't a thing, not yet, and it wasn't ever going to be. This would-be thing with Rachel was a temptation, a distraction, a fantasy—albeit a very pleasant fantasy. But no way was he going to let it be more than that.

Fortunately, they couldn't hang you for thinking—not yet anyhow.

But she had rubbed his neck. And it had felt really good. . . .

Bag that, Jay—get back to work.

Jay drifted across the exercise area, looking at the yard monsters lifting weights. The temperature out here was well above body heat. Some of the iron-pumpers had arms as big around as Jay's head, and looked as if they could pick themselves and all the weights on the bench next to them up with one hand. Jay was here to find information on a guy who'd lived in the same barracks as Stark when they'd gone through basic training. His contact-metaphor, whose name here was "Jethro," wasn't a weight lifter, but a boxer who was working the heavy bag.

High-tech as the prison was here in the future, there were still some old-style technologies extant, and a stuffed bag hung from a steel frame was among them.

Jethro was muscular in the way of a heavyweight boxer, and he wore bag gloves and shorts and boxing shoes. Here in the sticky heat, sweat beaded and ran down his torso to stain the waistband of his shorts, and more perspiration ran in rivulets along his legs to soak his socks. He had a few interesting scars on his body, along with a few tattoos. He hammered the bag, chuffing and breathing hard, grunting with effort. Jab, jab, cross. Jab, cross, hook! Overhand, jab, uppercut . . .

Jay stood by, not speaking, watching Jethro work. And maybe patting himself on the back a little at how good his sensory details were.

After a few minutes, the man paused to drink something colored a phosphorescent orange from a plastic bottle, and to wipe his face with a towel.

"What?" he said.

"We had a friend in common."

"Yeah? Who?"

"Stark."

Jethro shook his head. "Stark didn't have any friends."

"It was more of a work arrangement," Jay said.

"So?"

"So I need to know something he knew."

"Too bad. Why would I care?"

"I cut a deal with somebody. I find out this information he knew and pass it along."

"And this buys you what?"

Here Jay had but one thing of any real value to sell. Everybody here was a lifer. The only way to leave The Cage was to die, get recycled, and flushed through narrow sewage pipes into the swamp. Hardly a glorious exit.

"A way out."

"Sheeit."

Jay shrugged.

Jethro wiped at his face again. "How?"

"A door is going to be left unlocked, a guard will be looking the other way. I'll have a weapon. Not much chance I'll survive the run to Port Tau, but at least it's a shot. Better to die on my feet free and running than in here."

Jethro considered that. "Say I buy this. How long is that door going to be unlocked? How long is the guard gonna be blind?"

Jay shrugged. "Could be long enough for two guys to pass."

The boxer shook his head. "You know that's how Stark got it? He was trying to run, got a needler bolt in the back."

"I heard."

"Been a while since Stark and I were tight."

"I just got here," Jay said. "More likely you can talk to people than I can."

"What do I have to pay them with?"

"Two, three fast guys can run through an open door as quick as one, if they hurry."

Jethro considered it. Nodded. "I can maybe talk to a couple people. Of course, if this is bunta-crap, you're a dead man."

"Of course. Whaddya got to lose?"

"That's the prongin' truth." Jethro hung the towel over a steel strut, stepped back up to the bag. Hit it with a short right, hard. "I'll find you if I get something."

"I ain't goin' anywhere," Jay said. "For a while, anyway."

Jethro smiled at that one.

Partin's Country Store
Near Damascus, Maryland

Lewis had picked the little country store because it had recently closed. She had happened across the place while out driving one day, feeling too cooped up after a long VR session and needing to move. The store was for sale, and there was a sign up over the front window saying so. Who owned it? Why had they shut it down? Where were they now? Those things didn't really matter.

The place was not exactly the middle of nowhere—the sun didn't come up between it and town—but it was an hour and some away from the District, half a mile from any other building, and the closest of those was a farmhouse off the road and mostly screened by trees. If she could get in and out fast, there wouldn't be a problem. She rented a car, switched license plates with a vehicle parked in the back of an apartment complex that was the same make and model, and wore her standard disguise—baseball cap with her hair tucked under, sunglasses, dark T-shirt, jeans, running shoes, and a Windbreaker. Plus she had a new revolver, another S&W Chief .38 Special.

She didn't want to be parked out in the boondocks long enough for anybody driving past to take notice. Her intent was to arrive five minutes before the meeting time, pull in, and wait for Carruth. As soon as he showed up, she would put two into his head before he could get out of the car. She hoped he had that big handgun with him, but if not, she would make sure there was something in the car to lead the state troopers who worked the case to his house. He'd rented that under a phony name, and she didn't know if his driver's license matched the address or not, but a wadded-up piece of paper with the street number and name on it dropped onto the floor would be enough, and they'd find it. They tended to search the cars of murdered folks very carefully. If Carruth still had the cop-killing gun, it would be on his hip, in the car, or stashed at his home somewhere.

She was tempted to run past his house and make sure there wasn't anything she didn't want the cops to find, but she didn't think there would be. Carruth was pretty good about stuff like that.

Well, that's what you thought about him before you found out about the two cops and that goddamned gun. . . .

So she drove slowly and carefully, and got to Partin's Country Market four minutes before the appointed time.

The sun was shining and it was cool, maybe forty degrees or so. Bracing . . .

Carruth arrived three minutes later.

She had been breathing slowly and deeply, but even so, her belly was roiling and her heart pumping faster than normal. It wasn't every day you cold-bloodedly shot somebody to death. That thing in New Orleans hadn't been planned, it had just happened, and yeah, she had been prepared, but she had not really expected, nor wanted, it to go down that way.

This was different. She was gonna smile at Carruth, a guy she had worked with for months, and knew, and then punch holes in his skull, *bam-bam*. Yeah, it had to be done, but still, it made for a dry mouth and fluttery bowels. She took a deep breath. *Get to it, sister.*

As she stepped out of her rented car, she looked up to see a state police patrol cruiser coming along the country road. And slowing down.

She went cold, but let none of her reactions show.

Unless she was willing to kill a state cop, Carruth was going to live to see another day.

She considered it.

Carruth was armed and he was good with a gun. She didn't know how good the trooper might be. If she pulled her piece and blasted Carruth, the cop might be a danger before she could do him. Carruth certainly would be if she shot the cop first, though he would hesitate, trying to figure what she was doing, and she could nail him while he was trying to work it out. . . .

No. She didn't need any complications—somebody might spot the dead police officer before she was out of range, and they would certainly throw up roadblocks every which way. Maybe he had already called in their license plates. Dead police officers were a major glitch, to be avoided if at all possible. She could screw up Jay Gridley's search for a little while longer, and take care of Carruth later.

"Follow my lead," she said to Carruth as the trooper

pulled into the lot. "We're thinking about buying this place," she said.

The gravel crunched under the trooper's tires. The cop eased closer and rolled his window down. "You folks okay?"

Carruth stepped of his car with a notepad. He looked at the for-sale sign and began writing on the pad. He smiled at the trooper and raised a hand in greeting.

"Yes, sir," Lewis said. "My friend and I came out to look at the store. We heard it was for sale."

"You live around here?"

"No, in the District. But we're tired of the city," she said. "And we're thinking maybe about getting married and starting a business away from all the noise and traffic."

The cop, who was maybe twenty-five, smiled. "Really nice country."

"It is. We figured we'd get the Realtor's number and see if we can set up a meeting."

She smiled at the trooper, who grinned back. "Shame you had to come in two cars."

Cops never just took anything at face value, the good ones. She leaned down closer to the cop. "My friend and I, we're, uh, married to . . . other people right now. We're going to, uh, take care of that, but we kind of don't want to be seen together just yet."

"Ah. I understand."

She nodded. Give them a story they like, they'll buy it.

"Well, you all have a nice day."

Carruth turned and ambled over to where Lewis stood. He put his arm around her and smiled at the trooper. Pressed the tips of his fingers against her breast so the cop could see that.

The trooper pulled out of the lot and drove slowly away.

"Bet he turns into a driveway a mile down the road and waits to see what we are going to do," Carruth said.

"If you don't get your hand off my boob, he's going to see me kick you in the balls."

Carruth laughed. He moved his hand away. "I had to help sell it, didn't I?"

"We need to leave," she said.

"Why? We can talk for a couple minutes, walk around the place. Even if the cop can see us, it's not like we're trying to break into the place. We can hold hands, make out, give him something to tell the boys back at the station." He grinned.

"Forget it."

She hadn't planned on having to lay out another base incursion, since she'd expected he'd be dead by now. She didn't have anything to tell him. A mistake. "No, we'll do it later. I'll call and set it up."

"Why'd you want to meet way the hell out here anyway?"

"I wanted a quiet drive in the country. What do you care?"

He shrugged. "I don't. *My* last trip to the country involved shooting down a helicopter full of armed dweebos—not a real peaceful memory."

"Go. I'll call."

He shrugged again and ambled to his car.

Well—damn. This certainly hadn't gone the way she'd visualized it. A reminder that RW was messier than VR. She needed to keep that in mind. If that trooper had chosen to play it differently, maybe been in a bad mood and needing to feel powerful, if he'd wanted to see ID, maybe decided he needed to pat them down, it would have really been a bad scene. She supposed she ought to consider herself lucky it hadn't gone that way. Carruth killing cops was why they were here—they didn't need another dead one calling attention their way.

She climbed back into her car and started the engine.

As she did, she had a sudden inspiration. A way to get rid of Carruth without doing it herself. She smiled. It was perfect. She should have thought of it before.

Better late than never.

29

Thorn sat at the head of the conference table, with Jay Gridley and Abe Kent sitting across from each other to his left and right. Thorn said, "All right, Jay, if you'll update us, please?"

Jay nodded. "Not a whole lot new. Most of what I've been chasing has run to dead ends. I haven't been able to chase the game-maker down."

He paused, taking a moment to make eye contact with General Kent as well. "There are two lines of inquiry that I can see might still pay off, though there is a possibility they lead to the same place. First, there's the gun that killed the Army guy and the Metro cops. I've narrowed down the possibilities to one good one, but I haven't been able to pin it to the wall yet. The gun was bought under a phony name and ID and I'm working on that."

Thorn nodded. "Go on."

"Second, there's the dead terrorist found in the burning truck down in Kentucky. We have an ID on him, including his name and CV. He was a Special Forces guy, an Army Ranger, by the name of Dallas R. Stark. He was doing soldier-of-fortune and security work in the Middle East two years ago when State lost track of him. I am running down his old military unit, guys he worked with in the Middle East, family and childhood friends, all the usual stuff. Since we know he was using a phony passport, otherwise he couldn't have gotten back into the U.S., it could be that he was the guy who bought the gun and shot people with it. That wouldn't be real helpful. If I can pin the Alien Cowboy—sorry, that's a characterization from my search-scenario—I should be able to figure it out. If he matches Stark, then that line ends. If he doesn't, we have another player. Stark has been somewhere for the last two years, and since he wasn't alone when the terrorists hit Braverman, if we can link him to anybody in that group, that'll be good."

Thorn nodded again. "Anything else?"

"Not really. I've been working with Captain Lewis at the Pentagon, but most of what we've done has been eliminating stuff, not coming up with any arrows pointing in the right direction. She's pretty sharp, though. She spotted some things before I did."

"General?"

Kent smiled. "I don't know enough to ask intelligent questions. General Ellis has indicated that General Hadden is about to blow a gasket and I'm supposed to hurry things up, but since Jay is already going as fast as anybody can go, me saying, 'Go faster!' ain't gonna help." He nodded at Jay, then added, "Although, when you do catch these guys, it would be to my benefit and General Ellis's if you allowed in a report somewhere as how our urging somehow expedited the process, even though we all know it didn't."

Jay grinned at that. "I can do that."

"Thanks, Jay," Kent said.

Thorn looked around at the small meeting. "Okay, gentlemen," he said, "I think that's it for now."

Kent and Jay left.

Thorn leaned back in his chair. Working for the military had one big advantage—you weren't running around all over the place trying to stomp out little fires. This was their priority, and it wasn't going to be diluted by having to attend to other things until it got resolved. Nobody at Net Force was going to be hunting down Internet scam artists or porno-sellers, or people breaking into banks—those were somebody else's problems now. On the one hand, that was good. But on the other hand . . .

Eventually, the organization of Net Force would have to change. How necessary was the staff they had if their workload was dramatically decreased? What was the need of a military unit of what was now Marines for domestic problems? As National Guard, Net Force's military had been at least semilegal; as Marines, that got a bit more iffy, even under the relaxed antiterrorism statutes of Homeland Security. A unit of Marines charging across a mall parking lot to kick in a door? That wasn't going to play well on the evening news—the idea of a strong military operating at home hadn't been high on the Founding Fathers' list of things that were good for the country. The Marines were supposed to go to foreign shores to clear the roads for the Army to follow, and, if need be, help defend the U.S. from invaders, but when was the last time the U.S. had been invaded? 1812? Or did the Alamo count, even though Texas wasn't a state for another eight or nine years?

What Thorn foresaw was a dismantling of Net Force as a separate unit, with the pieces being mainstreamed into other commands. Some of his people would stick around, some would not. In his case, probably not. There wasn't a lot for him to do with all the generals around him. The DoD ground slow, but fine, and how much longer would there be a Net Force as such?

Not long, Thorn figured. He'd have to quit or be fired, and while it didn't really make any difference on one level, he'd rather leave the party before they kicked him out. . . .

Well, he had taken on the job, and done it as best he could. He had served his country, given something back, but he didn't need the work. Maybe it was time for him to smile and walk away. Marry Marissa, go and play for a while. Travel, see the world, get to know the woman he loved.

There were certainly worse ways to spend your time.

The Fretboard
Washington, D.C.

As Kent started to uncase his guitar, flipping latches open, he glanced at Jen. "What's the problem?" he said.

Jen looked up at him. "How do you know I have a problem?"

"Nothing specific. It's like there's a . . . darkness around you." He shrugged.

She played a series of arpeggios up the neck of the guitar, and they sounded somehow sad to him. "Minor chords," she said. "For when your mood is low."

Kent didn't say anything. One thing he had learned from being married was that there were times to speak and times to keep his mouth shut. If she was going to tell him what was bothering her, she would—pushing it wouldn't help.

She stopped playing. "An old enemy of mine died recently," she said.

He kept silent. Enemy? Jen? That didn't seem likely.

"When I was a girl, in junior high, I was a geek— already learning how to play classical guitar, no interest in pop music. Probably a good reason for that—this was the late seventies, when disco was still hot—'Stayin' Alive,' 'Saturday Night Fever,' like that. The only pop song I learned was Randy Newman's 'Short People,' and that's because my best friend at the time was just pushing five feet tall."

Kent smiled.

"People would see me sitting in a empty classroom practicing, and they'd ask me to play 'Dust in the Wind,' or

'How Deep Is Your Love,' and I had no interest in any of that. 'Romanza'? Sure. I'd even try 'Canon in D,' though technically you can't do it on one guitar by yourself. And anything by Bach I could manage. But if you wanted Barry Gibb, I was not your girl, thank you very much."

Her hand moved lightly on the strings but didn't make a sound. "It was kind of lonely, not being part of any of the cliques, but that's where I was. Then I met another classical music fan one day, a girl my age, and since we were the only two people we knew at the school who even liked the stuff, much less played it—she was a cellist—there wasn't any way we weren't gonna be friends."

He waited.

She looked at him. "Elizabeth Ann Braun. She wore braces, her hair in pigtails, and was a short, skinny little thing who never got any taller. We hung out, we played music, we discussed boys, with whom we had almost no experience. We did our homework together. Her mother was divorced, she'd never known her father, and she was half again as geeky as I was. Beth liked poetry—she had memorized 'The Raven' and used to go down the halls at school reciting it aloud, giving everybody who looked at her the evil eye."

He smiled.

She smiled, too. "Those were good days. We gloried in our dweebness—we felt superior to all the mundane jocks and big-hair girls all trying to look like Farrah Fawcett. We thought they were all wasted space. Fourteen-year-old girls with superiority complexes, and we were our own clique, just the two of us, we lived in each other's pockets, finished each other's sentences, even had our periods together. Friends to our cores."

Kent nodded but stayed silent. She was on a roll and he didn't need to oil the machine.

"We stayed that way through junior high, high school, and the first few months of college. Then she got into a yelling match with a music professor who wouldn't let her take an advanced class she wanted to take without a re quired course. Pissed her off so bad she quit school. She had a full-ride music scholarship—it was a state school—but she just . . . left. And to complete shooting herself in the foot, she joined the Army. Didn't tell me until after she had done it."

He chuckled. "Yeah, that military is the lowest job on the totem pole, all right. Below the guy who cleans out Porta Potties."

Jen laughed. "No offense. It just wasn't for Beth."

"No offense taken. What happened?"

"She hated it. Really hated it. Discipline was not her thing. So she just . . . left. The Army doesn't much care for that, once you sign on, apparently."

"No. They don't."

"She came home, hid out in my apartment, sneaked back and forth to her mother's. Eventually, the FBI came looking for her. Apparently, desertion is a federal offense."

"Yep."

"Scared the hell out of me when the FBI agents showed up on my doorstep one day. They rattled me good—threatened me with dire things if they found out I knew where Beth was, or was helping her. Really scared me because, at that moment, she was hiding in my bathroom, not twenty feet away."

"The weed of crime bears bitter fruit," he said.

"What?"

"Sorry. That's what the Shadow used to say on the radio."

"Yeah, well, it was bitter enough I didn't like the taste of it. I told Beth she needed to get this straightened out, that I certainly wasn't planning on spending any quality time in a federal pen for helping her."

"Prudent."

"I thought so. Beth saw it as a kind of betrayal. We were friends, I should be willing to put myself on the line for her, even though she had done something stupid to get herself in trouble in the first place. We had words."

"Ah."

Jen nodded to herself, lost in the memory. "Yeah. The

thing was, I had blossomed a bit by the time I got to college. Filled out a little, found there were other music geeks, some of them boys, a whole department full of them. I had acquired a boyfriend. My first love."

"I'm jealous."

"Harold was tall, reedy, very talented as a pianist, and, I thought, in love with me. We had discussed engagement, marriage, blending our music careers together, the whole nine yards."

"But it didn't work out," he said.

"No. Beth was really upset with me for not being more supportive. She had also ripened some, and while she never got taller, she had developed some curves and learned how to use them."

Kent could see where this was going, but he said nothing, letting her tell it in her own way.

"So my best friend seduced my boyfriend and convinced him to run away with her. He left me a note:

" 'Jenny, I'm sorry, but Beth and I are leaving together. She needs our support and since she can't get it here, we think it best that we go. Love, Harold.' "

"Ow."

"Oh, yeah, big-time 'ow.' I'd never had a boyfriend before and had never been dumped, much less for my best girlfriend. I fell apart. Had no clue how to handle things. Dropped out of school, went home to Mama, and spent a month locked in my room crying. I lost twenty pounds. Never even touched my guitar the whole time."

Her hand moved again, still silent on the strings. "Eventually the tears dried up, I started playing again, and picked back up at school, but it was a pretty miserable time for me."

"I can understand that." He could see she was upset by the memory, even now.

"Beth used Harold to support her just long enough to find a better ride. She dumped Harold, and married a well-to-do lawyer.

"Harold eventually got a music degree and went to

teach somewhere out west—Colorado or Wyoming, like that. He called me a couple times. I hung up on him." She smiled, but it was a sad, twisted thing. "Beth's husband was apparently a pretty good attorney. He worked a deal with the Army, and she was discharged dishonorably, but didn't have to serve any time. A few months later, she called me. She was living a hundred miles or so away. Said she was sorry about what she had done, wanted to make amends, patch things up, get back to being friends."

Kent shook his head.

"Yeah, that's what I felt. But I was sweet. Butter wouldn't melt in my mouth. 'Sure, okay. Give me your number and address. I'll call you.'"

"But . . . ?"

"The Devil would have been ice-skating in Hell before I ever called her. She tried again a few times, eventually gave it up."

"You never forgave her."

"Some crimes earn you a life sentence," she said. "But I kind of got past the bitterness. We weren't going to be friends, but eventually I was able to get up in the morning without wishing she'd be hit by a train. I kept a loose kind of track, through mutual family and acquaintances. She had a hard life. Divorced and married three times, four kids, two of whom got into drugs and wound up in jail. Her last husband was a long-haul truck driver. She gave up the cello, drank too much, smoked too much, and got fat." She paused, her eyes far away.

"One day last month, Beth apparently went out to collect the newspaper, and she had a heart attack and fell over dead in her driveway. Same age as I am."

Nothing for him to say to that.

"It's kind of hard to believe," she said. "She'd been dead three weeks before I heard. I somehow thought I'd sense it if that happened, though I didn't expect it to happen for a long time. She was my best friend, then my worst enemy, and then just . . . not much of anything to me. She was a huge part of my growing up. My best memories of that age include her; also my worst memories. I still can't quite wrap my mind around the idea that she's dead. I mean, we never wiped the slate clean, and on some level I always hoped she would realize how badly she had behaved, and would have come and fallen on her knees and admitted it and begged forgiveness."

"Would you have forgiven her?"

"I don't know. I would have liked to have the choice, though."

He nodded again. He understood.

She sighed. "You know why I told you this story?"

He shook his head.

"So you'll know I'm not an altogether nice person before we get too far down the road. I held that grudge for a long time. I wasn't a cosmic, realized being who could look at my friend's youthful mistakes and just let it go. Eighteen-year-olds aren't that mature, I wouldn't want to be judged at that age, but I was angry and I stayed angry, and even now I can get pissed off all over again if I think about it too long."

He smiled. "What—you're human like the rest of us? For shame."

She laughed. "Yeah, I know you had me up on this goddess pedestal and all."

He took his guitar out of the case and looked at her. "Remind me to tell you the story about my brother's daughter some time. She married a guy who was a Christian Scientist, she converted, and she later died of breast cancer. At her funeral, I heard him say that it was Susie's own fault she died—her faith wasn't strong enough. If he hadn't been the father of their five-year-old child, I think I might have killed him."

She shook her head. "Couple of fine old retreads, aren't we?"

"Take it slow and you can drive a long way on retreads," he said.

30

Desolation Swamp
The Planet Omega

Jay had paid off, and now there were four of them outside the prison and on the run. Jethro, who had already given him all he knew; a giant of a man named Gauss; and a grizzled old guy who called himself Reef.

Five hundred meters away from the walls, Jethro stepped into the maw of a flesh-eating plant and was gobbled down in this slow-motion peristaltic spasm that took a while, though the plant apparently injected him with some kind of narcotic so that he was smiling as it ate him. Jay had a handgun, a blaster that fired a charged-particle beam, and he'd started to cut loose on the plant, but Reef said, "Don't! The guards'll spot the beam on their sensors this close! Jethro's already dead anyhow, no point in shooting."

So Jay, Gauss, and Reef kept running. They wanted to be deep in the swamp before the guards came looking for them.

If they could stay alive for a while—and Jay would make sure of that as best he could—he should get something from the two escapees that might be useful.

A thunderstorm rolled in from somewhere, fast, and lightning and thunder flashed and boomed as a rain so heavy it turned the world into watery grass fell.

"Don't step on anything red or blue," Reef said. "Or round," he added.

Given how hard it was to see anything, much less colors or shapes in the deluge, Jay was trusting to mostly blind luck about that.

After fifteen minutes, the rain stopped, as suddenly as it had come, and the sun burst out and started cooking the water away. They splashed through puddles, avoiding red, blue, and round.

"There's a caldera that way," Reef said, "Hot springs. That'll throw off the guards' IR scanners. They won't put anybody on the ground there, it'll be skimmers above the treetops. If we can make that before they come looking, we'll have a chance."

"How do you know this?"

"I been in the Cage for thirty-three years—what there is to hear, I heard five times already."

"Lead on, then."

"I don't suppose you want to give me the blaster, since I'll be in front?"

"You'd be right about that," Jay said.

"You don't trust me?"

"Not to put too fine a point on it, but no, I don't."

The old man cackled. "I wouldn't trust me, either. Come on. Keep an eye on the trees, there's hanging serpents there look kind of like moss—one bite, you're done."

"Nice place."

"Only bad men get sent here, son. We're all guilty."

As they walked, Jay figured he had better get whatever information he was going to get sooner rather than later. He was a little ways behind Reef, ahead of Gauss. He dropped back a little more so he could talk to the bigger man.

"So," he said. "Stark."

"What about 'im?"

"You tell me."

Gauss shrugged. "Soldier. Killer. Got shot in the back trying for the gate when a supply flitter came in."

"I know that much. What else?"

"He hung with ex-troopers, mostly. Mercs, freelancers, guys who made money in shooting wars, guarding dopers or smugglers."

"Any names?"

"Groves. Russell. Hill. Thompson. Carruth. Couple others I never got to know. Special Forcers—Recon, green hats, Rangers. Badasses. Just as soon kill you as smile at you."

Ahead, Reef said, "We're almost—ah, shit!"

Jay turned his attention to the old man, who had dropped to his knees. What—?

There was something that looked like an arrow piercing the man, the barbed point of it coming from his back. As he watched, Reef was jerked off his feet and dragged along the wet ground. Jay saw that the "arrow" was actually the end of a long, vinelike tentacle, connected to a creature he couldn't immediately tell was animal or plant. Looked kind of like a squid, but squatter, and covered with what looked like scales or bark. It had a huge, circular mouth with lots of pointed teeth in concentric rows.

Whatever Reef had, there was no getting it now.

Terrific scenario, no question. Scared himself.

"FREEZE RIGHT THERE!" came an amplified voice.

Jay glanced up and saw a five-man flitter floating twenty meters above them, the snout of a plasma cannon pointed over the side at them. If it wasn't one thing, it was another. Crap.

"I'm not goin' back!" Gauss yelled. He started running, lumbering through the brush.

The squidlike thing fired a sharp-ended tentacle at Gauss, but missed.

The gunner in the flitter was more accurate. He opened up with the plasma cannon and when the bolt hit Gauss, like a tree being hit with lightning, Gauss's sap turned into superheated steam and blasted him apart—*ka-blam!*

"Euuww," Jay said. "Ick!"

Time to leave.

"End scenario," Jay said as the gunner started to line up on him.

Not much, maybe, but he had a few names. Something, at least.

Washington, D.C.

Lewis, at home, worked out the best way to deal with Carruth. There were a few risks, but she figured she could handle those. It was all in the setup.

First, she had to pick another Army base. Which one didn't matter, as long as she could convince Carruth he had every chance of getting in and out okay, and that ought not to be a problem. Then, it was just a matter of how best to make sure he wouldn't be captured alive.

She could use a vox-scrambler and make the call from a moving car in the middle of the city; she knew who to talk to to get the maximum response, and they'd never be able to get a fix on her in time.

She imagined how it might go:

"Listen, don't talk—the terrorists who have been hitting the Army's bases are going to hit another one." She'd fill in the blanks here—time, place, like that. "But here's the thing: the leader of the group, guy named 'Carruth'? He's an ex-SEAL who won't let himself be taken alive. He's already killed a bunch of GIs, plus a couple of civilian cops—he carries this monster handgun—and he has wired himself up with explosives. There's a button on his belt, if he pushes it, he'll take down half a city block when he goes. . . ."

She smiled at the scenario she was creating. She could easily imagine that she was the officer in charge of security. They wanted these suckers, bad, but they sure as hell wouldn't let Carruth and his boys get within a hundred meters of anything they didn't want to see blown up. So the ideal place to take him down would be in the middle of nowhere. But if they stopped him before he got onto the base, they'd have to bring in the civilian authorities—local and state police, FBI counterterrorism force, Homeland Security, maybe even the National Guard. The Army wouldn't like that for a bunch of reasons, not the least of which would be the lack of control.

If, however, they could channel Carruth once he was on the base—a detour into an artillery range would be good, like that—then they could surround him somewhere relatively safe, and if he went nova, too bad. There were some stiff antiterrorism laws on the books these days, but if Carruth was simply captured, eventually he'd get a day in court.

An Army security guy would almost surely be thinking that it would be better for a bunch of killer terrorists to go up in smoke than maybe having some bleeding-heart liberal lawyer convincing a jury to let the clowns off because they had unhappy childhoods or some such crap.

That Carruth wouldn't be strapped with bombs wouldn't matter. Some Army sniper who could shoot out a bug's left eye from a kilometer away would be perched somewhere with a scoped rifle and when Carruth tried to run— believing that he could get away, because Lewis had convinced him there was a secret bolt-hole he could use—then Carruth would be no more. . . .

Shoot, she could even set it up that he had to go into the base alone—that since he was just going to collect a colonel, there wasn't going to be any shooting necessary. . . .

She smiled again. She was good, she knew it. Good enough to pull this off.

Carruth didn't have a prayer.

31

Something was wrong.

Carruth couldn't put his finger on it, but it felt . . . off, somehow.

He had the information Lewis had given him, codes, orders, specific and detailed directions, same as always. The gate-check had gone smooth as silk. The sun was shining, felt almost like spring was in the air, getting close to shirt-sleeve weather.

Lewis hadn't screwed up yet—the time that things had gone south was something nobody could have figured, some GI who wasn't supposed to be where he was, an X-factor for which it was impossible to calculate, and certainly not Lewis's fault.

This would be easier, it involved stealth, and nobody would think twice about seeing him until he grabbed up the target. And even then, all he had to do was show the colonel the gun and keep it hidden, they'd be two guys walking to his car, nothing to see here, move along.

Once he drove onto the base, there was a roadwork sign blocking the main drag a couple hundred meters in, and the detour wasn't on her plans, but that could have started this morning and even so, it shouldn't matter. He ought to be golden.

But something was not right here. This place was so new the paint wasn't dry. Why wouldn't the road be in good repair?

Could be anything. Laying electrical lines, water or sewage pipes. Or maybe they just hadn't finished paving yet. It was the Army—they didn't do things like everybody else.

Could be anything.

But it didn't feel like that. It *felt* like somebody he couldn't see was out there, he could *feel* their gaze on him, tracking him. Stalking him . . .

Nothing reasonable about it, this feeling, nothing whatsoever to confirm it, but it was as if there was an invisible cloud of doom hanging over him, gathering itself to hit him with a monster lightning bolt that would blow him out of his shoes.

He'd had this sensation a couple times before. Once, it hadn't been anything he could ever tell. The feeling came, he looked around, didn't see anything, and eventually it passed.

The second time, he had been walking outside a camp in Iraq and he felt a panicked urge to stop right where he was. In that instance, he had halted, cold. Looked around, didn't see anybody outside the camp within rifle range who might pot him. Then he'd looked down.

Another step, and he would have put his foot smack on the trigger of a terrorist-rigged mine planted by some local scumbag, what turned out to be an old artillery shell with a spring-loaded striker that would have no doubt blown off a foot at the least and probably killed him. IED, they called 'em. Improvised Explosive Device.

How had he known that? What sense had been tripped? It wasn't dependable, this feeling—he hadn't felt squat when the two cops had braced him, nor when the shooting had started in Kentucky. But he felt it now.

If he kept going, he was going to die. He knew it right to the marrow in his bones.

He pulled the car into a hard U-turn, breaking the back end loose, laying rubber and noise over the road. As soon as the car's wheels regained traction, he tapped the gas.

Two things happened: Three men in field gear with M-16s at the ready came into view to his left, running in his direction.

A car started up behind him, a flashing light bar lit, and a siren screamed.

The M-16s opened up, their sounds reached him about the same time as the first rounds hit the car—*clunk-clunk-clunk!*—and punched through the metal just behind him. Part of a shattered bullet spanged around inside the car and blew out a back window—

"Shit—!"

He ducked instinctively and stomped the gas pedal.

The rental car wasn't a Formula One racer, but it did surge a little. He turned the steering wheel sharply to the right, zig, then back to the left, zag. Soldiers kept shooting, but he couldn't worry about that. They'd either hit him or they wouldn't.

He saw a camo'd Hummer heading toward the gate, angling to cut him off.

The only weapon he had was a SIG side arm, a fucking nine, but he pulled it, aimed through the closed passenger window, and cooked off three fast shots, aiming at the other vehicle.

The first shot shattered the window, and it and the other two were damned loud in the car, but there was no help for that.

The Hummer's driver hit his brakes. Too much to hope for that he'd hit the guy, but at least he'd slowed him down—

He saw sparks from the road in front of him. They were trying for his tires. He wouldn't make much speed running on the rims.

He swerved the car again, slewing back and forth.

The gate was ahead, and a counterweighted pole was the only thing blocking the exit, though the guy in the kiosk had triggered the rolling gate and it began to close—

The pedal was floored, he wasn't going to make the car go any faster, but it looked as if he might make it—

The guy in the kiosk ducked as Carruth pointed the SIG and let one go in his direction—

Why weren't they closing on him? It was like they were hanging back on purpose—

The car threaded the gap, though the gate scraped the back passenger panel with a steel-fingernail-on-a-chalkboard noise. He had to be doing fifty, and in a few seconds, that went up to seventy.

Off the base!

Nobody was out here waiting for him—why the hell not?

Carruth uttered a steady stream of curses as he drove, watching the rearview mirror for pursuit. Another half a block into the base, he'd have never gotten out, even if he'd turned around and tried. His instinct had saved his ass—at least temporarily.

But—what the hell had happened? How had they gotten on to him?

Worry about that later, too. Right now, he had to drive like his life depended on it. Because it sure as shit did.

32

Thorn stepped out of the shower in the Net Force gym he had pretty much turned into his private practice *salle,* dried himself, and began to re-dress. Other people still came by to work out, but almost never when he was here.

He didn't expect he would be working out here that much longer. As his grandfather used to say, you don't need to be a weatherman to know which way the wind blows. The zephyrs of change were about to start roaring through Net Force like a small hurricane. What had started out as a civilian-run group under the aegis of the FBI had been co-opted by the DoD into another arm of the military, and its mission had radically changed. A tank just didn't run the same way a Corvette did.

So far, the military had left most things as they were, but eventually they would alter things. It was in their nature. Like a corporate raider forcing a company merger, the powers-that-be were going to look around and notice there was a lot of duplication of effort—and it would be cheaper, simpler, and smarter to eliminate that duplication—why have four when two were plenty?

Why have two when one could do the job?

Thorn finished dressing. He checked himself in the mirror, ran a comb through his hair. He had come out of private industry, he had been involved in his share of buyouts and takeovers, and he knew how things worked. Things changed, and for all kinds of reasons: Buggy whips weren't made anymore because there were no buggies. There came a time when the old gray mare was put out to pasture because she couldn't keep up. That was how it had always been, and Thorn didn't see that stopping anytime soon.

When the DoD took over Net Force, the agency's days were numbered, and, as he looked at it, that number wasn't very large. Six months, a year, maybe longer, but his guess was sooner rather than later. It didn't make any sense otherwise. Net Force would be broken into components and the chunks sold or traded or given away, and in the end, nothing would be left. The name might stick around for a time, but the heart and soul would be gone. It wasn't about the hardware, but about the people, and if they left, the party was over.

Thorn had an older cousin who had been a paper company manager twenty-five years or so past. The company, thinking ahead, always replanted the trees it harvested, put three in the ground for every one they chopped down. They were cutting third-growth, fourth-growth wood now. And they were adding new kinds of trees that grew faster and made better pulp, but now and again they would screw up the timing. A region would start to be harvested and trees replanted as they went, but they would cut down all the viable timber before the new plantings matured. There would be a five-year, sometimes a ten-year gap. When that happened, all the local loggers and support people were laid off. Thorn's cousin had been the manager of one such area, up in Alaska. He'd had to shut the operation down to a few caretakers; a couple hundred workers, most of whom had been working the woods all their lives, thirty, forty years some of them, were let go. The little mill town had no other industry, and property values went into the toilet. Those people who couldn't make it farming or fishing or hunting had to leave and find work elsewhere. The town effectively died.

Thorn's cousin would tell the story at family gatherings, how the heart went out of the people who worked for him. How there had been suicides, divorces, vandalism against the company. It was a terrible experience, his cousin would say, taking another drink from his beer. Awful to be part of, depressing to watch. A way of life being lost. Much like what had happened to the Indians.

The listeners in the room would mutter and nod, and take sips of their beers. Yah, but who could have sympathy for the white men who went through it? Their own fault. Not like being herded onto a reservation and kept there by force.

Even though it was nearly as dramatic in this situation, Thorn wasn't going to do that with Net Force. He had no intention of leading a funeral march. The party was winding down. It was time to think about getting his coat and taking his leave.

Pentagon Annex

Lewis called Jay, using the private number to his virgil this time. She was past trying to rattle Jay's wife. It was time to get down to serious business.

"Rachel?"

"I need to see you," she said. "I've got a break in the hunt."

"Now?"

"As soon as you can. I figured out who designed the game. But I can't ship you the file."

"I'm on my way. It'll take me an hour or so."

"I'll be here."

She leaned back in her form-chair and smiled. She had a another red herring for him. Roy "Max" Waite, a fellow student who had graduated the same year she had. He'd

gone into design for one of the big entertainment companies, built a couple of movie-tie-in games, had several
other good game credits. In one of those lovely bits of good
luck that sometimes happened at just the right time, Max
Waite had been killed in an auto accident recently—only a
few weeks ago. She had come across this just yesterday;
somebody sent her an e-mail of a posting on an alumni
website, lamenting the man's early departure from life.

Big, fat, ole Max was dead. What a shame.

She'd seen immediately that she could use this. She'd
gone through the system files, through her backdoor into
the original game, and found what would look like a clue
pointing to the dear departed Max, whom she remembered
as a very stout man who'd spent most of his time in the
computer labs perched precariously on a sturdy, but com-
plaining, chair. It wasn't real, the clue, but Jay wouldn't
know that, and he'd have no reason not to believe her. And
even better, it would be almost impossible for him to check
it further. Perfect.

Earlier, it could have been another wild hair for Jay to
hunt down and tug at, but that wasn't the reason she wanted
him to come and see her. Once she got him behind the
locked door of her office today, she was going to go for
something much more primal. And she was sure he would
be up for it.

Jay's escort tapped on Lewis's door. "Come on in."

Jay did, and the sergeant ambled away. He shut the door
behind him. "Gear up," she said. "I'll show you what I've
got." All crisp business, which was good.

He went to the guest chair and started slipping into sensors. He was already wearing his mesh under his clothes.
He had taken the time to put it on so he wouldn't have to do
that here.

He jacked in, and the scenario blossomed. This time, it
was a 1950s version of a big-city newspaper's newsroom—
copy boys bustled back and forth carrying typed sheets of
papers; reporters, mostly men, smoked cigarettes or cigars

at their desks and pounded away on old manual typewriters. The place even smelled like pulp paper and ink and cigar smoke. Nice.

Rachel said, "This way."

Jay followed her down the hall to a door with a brass plate on it bearing the word MORGUE.

They went inside. An elderly woman in a gray wool suit and sensible shoes behind a scarred wooden counter smiled and handed Rachel a manila file folder. Rachel led Jay to a nearby table, and sat in an armless wooden chair, then patted the seat of the one next to that. He sat.

She spread the file out on the table in front of them. It was full of newspaper clippings in black and white.

She tapped one of the clippings with a fingernail. "Here."

Jay read it. It was dated about three weeks ago:

NOTED GAME DESIGNER
DIES IN AUTO ACCIDENT

Jobsville, CA—Roy B. "Max" Waite, 31, died in a two-vehicle traffic accident at the corner of Herman Avenue and Ishmael Road in Jobsville early this morning. Witnesses say that Waite's car, a Volkswagen Beetle, was struck when a tractor-trailer driven by Al Huxley, 43, ran a stop sign and hit the VW broadside. Police say alcohol was not a factor, but that Huxley's truck was traveling at an estimated 40 mph when it crashed into Waite's car.

"I spilled my coffee on my lap and I was trying to blot it up—I didn't see the sign until too late," a tearful Huxley said, according to witnesses at the scene. Police are investigating the incident. No arrests have been made.

Waite, unmarried, worked for ICG Corporation, headquartered in Lucasville, and was the creator of several popular and best-selling computer games, including "Tentacles" and "Lords of the Galaxy."

This is the third traffic fatality in Jobsville
thus far this year, the second at this location. Local authorities are considering the installation of
a traffic signal at the intersection.

If the trucker hadn't stopped at the stop sign, would a
red light have made any difference?

Jay looked at Rachel, whose leg was, he noticed, now
pressed warmly against the side of his own leg.

"Graduated MIT/CIT same year I did," she said. "And
look at this."

She slipped a flat color photograph out of her purse, and
slid it over to where Jay could see it. It was a video still
lifted from the bug game. There was an alien standing by
some kind of machinery, a vehicle, parked on a raised platform. The bug was looking at a readout of orange, alien hieroglyphs on the edge of the platform.

"What am I seeing?"

"That's a scale. The bug is weighing the car. See what it
says on the read?"

Jay frowned at her. "It's in what I assume is *bug*," he
said. "Not a language I know."

"It translates to a number—thirty thousand. And the last
part says, 'Maximum Weight.'"

"Ahh." Jay got it immediately. The dead programmer's
nickname—"Max Waite." Of course. Every programmer
signed his or her work. But if you didn't know who had built
it, it was often hard to find, much less decipher, the in-joke.

Even taken as a whole, this wasn't anything you could
take into a court of law and prove, but it all fell together:
Game designer who built space games, his nickname hidden in a glyph? This was the guy. He would have had the
chops. Shoot, Jay even remembered *Tentacles*. It had been
all the rage when it first came out.

Of course, Waite being dead wasn't going to help them
a whole lot. He wouldn't be telling them anything unless
Jay could find a spiritual medium who could reach beyond
the grave. . . .

Crap.

It was good work, though. He told her so.

"Thank you, Jay. That's something, coming from you."

At which point she slid her hand up his leg to his crotch.

Startled, Jay bailed from the scenario.

But that wasn't much help. Rachel squatted next to his chair in her office, and her real hand was on his real lap.

"Rachel! What are you doing?!"

"Clever man like you can't figure that out?" She smiled. Rubbed a little.

Jay shook his head. "Not a good idea," he said. He tried to back his chair away, but the wheels seemed stuck.

"Oh, it's a great idea. The door is locked. Nobody will interrupt us."

"I'm married!"

"Good for you. This won't hurt your wife, Jay. Nobody but us ever has to know. I won't tell." She squeezed him again. "You want it."

She was right—he did want it—and that fact was more than a little obvious to her, given where her hand was. And nobody would know. . . .

For a few heartbeats, Jay sat balanced on the razor edge of choice. She reached for his zipper, smiling. . . .

He caught her hand. "No. I can't."

"It's already evident that you *can,* Jay. And that you definitely *want* to." She leaned in, to kiss him. . . .

He got the wheels working on the chair, and it rolled back suddenly, leaving her a couple feet away as he slammed into the wall, hard.

He leaped to his feet. "I'm sorry, Rachel. I just can't do this!"

He practically ran for the door.

And part of him kept saying, *"Idiot! Go back! She wants you! And you damn sure want her!"*

Yeah, and that was the problem!

33

The Bizarre Bazaar

Jay had bagged the sci-fi convention scenario to try something different. He was still rattled by his visit with Rachel, really rattled. He felt as if he had developed a sudden case of some tropical fever; he was alternately hot and cold and on the edge of throwing up. He didn't want to think about it, and work was the best way to avoid that, but even so, it kept coming up in his thoughts.

How close it had been. Way too close. He was ashamed of himself for letting it get that far. For even considering it.

So here he was, in fantasy Arabia, looking at a hookah when the alarms went off. The hookah was big, maybe three feet tall, and VR text hanging in the air in front of it advertised it as suitable for flavored tobacco or "other substances." The hose of the hookah had been customized to look like snakeskin, and the mouthpiece had been molded appropriately to match.

"Other substances." Yeah, right.

The alarms sounded like air-raid sirens. All around him vendors grabbed their cash boxes and headed for the exits.

The VR commerce center had been modeled like a cross between something from the Arabian Nights and a 1940s Hollywood movie about Damascus in Glorious Living Technicolor—baskets, tables covered with colorful cloth, and brightly decorated awnings inside a huge, cavernous, walled marketplace. A bizarre bazaar, indeed . . .

It was mostly a gray market—products which were illegal in some countries, but not here, as well as questionable transfers of supposedly legal items.

Like, say, firearms.

If he could figure out for sure who bought the BMF, they'd be one step closer to nailing the terrorists attacking the bases.

Unfortunately, while the information was here, the site containing the information was international—which meant he had no jurisdiction to demand anything. How what he wanted had come to *be* here, Jay didn't know, but he was sure that it was.

The problem was the way the records were kept. There were hundreds of vendors, each of whom had their own unique files. And most of those were only internal—to follow the money outside the market, their transactions had to be cross-checked with the site's commerce engine. He could easily hack the individual sellers, but getting to the money transfers was somewhat more difficult. The guy who had bought the gun had used a swiped ID, but he had come, for some odd reason, through here to do it. Jay was betting his real name was here somewhere.

The data he wanted was kept behind a major firewall—one designed to Net Force specifications. Which meant that even being Jay Gridley wasn't enough to get into it.

If only I could get the good guys to protect their stuff like that.

So he had followed what one of his professors had called the "Prophet Tactic"—if you couldn't go to the mountain, maybe you could get the mountain to come to you. . . .

He'd run two quick tests, triggering the site's security.

During each test he'd seen the site's crisis measures in action.

Rather than wiping every dangerous piece of data, the site database was split and fired off into different directions. After a set time the pieces would be reassembled and business would begin as usual at YAVA—Yet Another VR Address.

Jay had twice watched the burnoose-wearing VR metaphor for the cash records haul ass down a dark alley toward the back of the market and out through an arched doorway.

So all he had to do was trigger the alarms again, grab the records from the avatar—who looked like a middle-aged accountant in faux-Arabic robes—and he'd be in good shape.

There he goes. . . .

Exactly as predicted, the cash records guy hustled out the firewall entrance—which looked like a concrete bunker pasted with advertisements in Farsi or something—and toward the rear of the marketplace.

And here I go. . . .

This was where it could get iffy. Up until now, he'd been a bystander, no one who would catch the attention of site security.

If site security ID'd him quickly enough, they could start unraveling his net disguise and track him back to U.S. law enforcement.

Which would be embarrassing.

Not that the United States wasn't *used* to being embarrassed—but Net Force's top VR jock certainly wasn't.

And I don't want to start now.

Jay ran past the hookah vendor's long table toward an intersection the records carrier would cross before turning into the alley. By not following the carrier directly, he hoped he was less likely to catch unwanted attention.

But—no. Someone had programmed the marketplace's security with a predictive network filter. They weren't common, and ate up a lot of processing power, but apparently the site's owners were willing to spend it to protect their records. He'd been identified as a threat. Dozens of black-robed security avatars, each carrying long, shiny scimitars, came running toward him. They sounded like extras from Ali Baba and the Forty Thieves. . . .

Damn!

The carrier was still a good twenty yards or so ahead and the blade-wavers were coming up fast.

Bullet time . . .

Jay triggered a subroutine he'd prepared as a "just-in-case" and instantly everything slowed—including himself.

He was in the air, running, front foot on the way earthward again. All around him everything had slowed to a barely perceptible crawl. . . .

Although he couldn't move any faster, he was able to sit back from his avatar and examine the scene like a three-dimensional model—himself running, the carrier ahead, the security guys closing in.

He only had a few seconds—the slowdown routine would be blocked by the VR site, since speed was to their advantage—so he had to think fast.

Come on, Gridley!

He could see he wasn't gonna make it. The security team would have him trapped before he intercepted the carrier.

Should he abort?

Normally, he wouldn't even consider it. But being caught raiding an international site in U.S. colors would be ugly. Real egg-on-the-face stuff. Crap!

Unless there's another way—

There were too many guards, and too many bystanders between himself and the carrier. The spacing of the tables in the marketplace funneled things too tightly. He couldn't get to the carrier fast enough going around the tables—

But nobody said he couldn't go over them.

He jumped up onto a table holding a variety of decorative daggers and kicked a display out of the way. Blades flew left and right and he saw one of the security guards duck.

The seller yelled what was surely a nasty curse.

Jay jumped to the next table, this one full of cartoon collectibles, and knocked over boxes filled with mugs and figurines as he kept moving. He glanced down and saw a red-garbed dog with a black U on its chest go flying.

Do not fear, I am here. . . .

The guards couldn't recover fast enough. The network predictor was confused just a hair, and that was enough.

By running the tables, he gained enough time to be just in front of his quarry at the mouth of the alley. He leaped, knocked the guy down, grabbed the papers and started shuffling in a big hurry. *C'mon, c'mon—!*

All he needed was—there it was, the name!

Carruth. He recognized it from the prison scenario. *Gotcha!*

As the guards closed in to behead him, he laughed and gave them the finger. "End scenario!" he yelled.

Net Force HQ
Quantico, Virginia

Jay knocked on Thorn's door, and didn't wait to be invited in.

Thorn was on the com, but he said, "Let me call you back."

Jay said, "Boss, I got one of the terrorists ID'd. And it's the guy who iced the Metro cops, too."

"Carruth," Thorn said.

Jay looked as if he'd been punched in the gut. "How did you know? You got spyware in my system?" There was a scary thought. What else might he know? About Rachel?

"No. The Army got an anonymous tip about another base going to be hit. The caller identified Carruth and gave Army Intelligence particulars—where and when. Said the guy coming in would be wired with explosives and was not going to let himself be captured."

"Damn. All that work and somebody just . . . gave him up?"

"The confirmation is important, Jay. The guy just hit the base, right on schedule."

"He dead?"

Thorn shook his head. "No. He got away."

Jay frowned. "What? How'd he do that if they knew he was coming?"

"I don't know. According to what I just heard"—he nodded at the com—"he was on the base and heading toward his target—supposed to kidnap some colonel—when all of a sudden he spun his car around and boogied. They weren't expecting that. They hadn't sealed things up tight yet. He got off the base and they couldn't catch him."

"Crap. What morons!" Yeah, he was still upset about the Rachel thing, no question.

"We have a location," Thorn said. "In the District. The tipster called back and gave the Army an address. The FBI and local police are rolling on it. Abe Kent and a team are going along as 'advisers.' We'll collect him if he went home."

Jay nodded.

"You can ride along with General Kent in the mobile command center if you want. He's leaving in about two minutes."

"Thanks, but I'll pass. Not my area of expertise, and this guy has a gun that will drop a charging Kodiak bear. I don't want somebody explaining to my wife how I was hit by a stray bullet that will require a closed coffin at the funeral."

Especially before he had a chance to see her and come clean about Rachel. He had to do that.

"Smart," Thorn said.

"Some days I think so. Other days, maybe not. Lemme know how it goes."

Jay stood.

"What are you working on now?"

Jay shrugged. "A loose end. Probably not anything, but a thought came up I want to run down."

"Break a leg."

"Not mine, I hope."

There was no need to build a complicated scenario for this, and Jay didn't really feel up for it. What he felt was sick, and what he hoped was that he was wrong. He wasn't looking to entertain himself; he just needed the facts.

Carruth, however many people he might have killed, wasn't the brains of this operation. That became obvious the more Jay looked at it. The guy didn't have a net presence to speak of, and nothing in his background indicated any great computer skills. He was an ex–Navy SEAL. He could stomp you to mush, or shoot you, or blow you up, and he could do it falling out of a plane, on the ground, or underwater, too, but there was just no way he had built the alien-bug game, and no way he could have hacked into Army computers and gotten squat. That a dead guy made the game and might have been running the show made sense, but it was awfully convenient—maybe too convenient—and now Jay wasn't so sure about that, either.

Carruth was a pawn, maybe even a knight, but not the king for whom Jay had been searching.

Or, as it had finally dawned on him, maybe he wasn't looking for the king at all.

Maybe he should have been trying to find the queen. . . .

Jay used a stock VR library, went to the front desk, got the location, and went to find the biography of Captain Rachel Lewis, United States Army.

He took to the book to a table and opened it.

The facts and figures were there—DOB, family, schools, like that, but what Jay wanted was going to be beyond the public facts; fortunately, he had access to things most people couldn't get to, and the index in the Book of Rachel was very thick.

Some of it came from odd angles, but there was a lot of information there if you knew how to look, and certainly Jay knew that.

It bothered him that he was doing it. No, that wasn't

strictly true—what bothered him was that he believed he had a *reason* to do it. It was an ugly suspicion, and maybe he had it for the wrong reasons.

Was it just guilt? At how he had felt as she was rubbing his crotch? Or shame at how hard it had been to jump up and run out of her office?

Because that had been tempting. Lord, it had. He could have just . . . let go, pretended it was VR, that it wasn't really happening, and he had a feeling it would have been absolutely dynamite sex, too. Blond, beautiful, brainy, everything to like . . .

But the image of Saji holding their child had bloomed in his mind, and he couldn't see past that to the woman wetting her lips for him and reaching for his zipper. . . .

Sure, a lot of men had affairs after they were married. None of them seemed to think it was that big a deal, a little on the side, but Jay realized that he wasn't like most people. He had been a computer geek for a long time—he'd had a couple of girlfriends—but nobody had ever loved him like Saji. She had been there for him while he was lying in a coma, she had given him a son, and what he felt for her was beyond his ability to put into words.

Yes, Rachel Lewis was smart, she was sexy, and she wanted him, no question, but if he had gone down that road, how would he have felt about himself afterward? Were a few minutes of sexual pleasure, no matter how hot, worth his self-esteem? Worth risking his marriage?

The answer was simple: No.

Once he had realized that, once he had made that decision, even in the panic in which it had taken place, things had . . . shifted. There was an old saying he had seen somewhere, from the I-Ching or the Tao or something: "The Truth waits for eyes unclouded by longing."

When it had been a fanciful possibility that he might have fallen into bed with Rachel, he hadn't looked at her as critically as he might have done otherwise. He didn't like that, but he had to accept it. She'd had a free pass.

On some level, he had been enjoying the flirting, the

idea of it, the risk. But when push came to shove, he couldn't do it. It would have been *wrong*.

And now? Now his vision wasn't being blocked by the image of Rachel lying naked on a bed. And he had started wondering.

Now, all those little things he had accumulated that he had ignored? They suddenly seemed bigger than they had before.

Who had given him the information on the URL that he'd wasted so much time chasing, only to find it a red herring?

Who had been with him when his scenario crashed as he was about to catch the Alien Cowboy?

Who had access to all the Army's sensitive information, and the ability to use it without being suspected?

From whose unit had the original information supposedly been hacked?

Who, if she hadn't been beautiful and sexy and smart, would have been at the top of Jay's check-'em-out list, once he got rolling?

The answers to all the questions were the same.

There was a tendency to separate people into good guys and bad guys, and since Lewis had been on the same side— and gorgeous—that made her ipso facto one of the good guys. But there had always been bad cops, and they were harder to catch because nobody started out looking at them.

Now, there were too many fingers pointing that way for Jay to stay blind any longer.

He came across the entry on Rachel's father. He turned to that page, began reading. A career Army man, just as she had told him. Died young . . . hmmm.

A sub-index on Sergeant Robert Bridger Lewis turned up the cause of death: suicide.

As Jay read the file, he felt a cold sensation begin gathering in his belly.

Sergeant R.B. Lewis had been court-martialed and convicted of killing a soldier, and had been awaiting sentencing when he shot himself.

Records of the trial told the story: The soldier had allegedly assaulted the then-seventeen-year-old Rachel Lewis, a date rape. Her father had gone to find the young man and had killed him with his side arm.

The cold in his gut turned into a hard and icy lump.

Jay leaned back and stared at the book. That might tend to make for a screwed-up view of the Army, that they prosecuted your father for taking out your rapist. But it wasn't proof.

Jay thumbed back to the index, and to the medical records section.

There was no record of Rachel Lewis ever having a child. That didn't mean all that much—could be she had avoided giving her real name. He could strain the records looking for live births about the time it would have happened, and death certificates due to the cause she had told him, a burst aorta. That would take a while. . . .

No, wait, hold on. Here was a sealed record of a medical exam just last year, a routine physical, and a copy of the doctor's exam notes: "Well-developed, well-nourished sthenic Caucasian female, gravida 0, para 0, appearing to be about the stated age of . . ."

Jay grabbed a medical dictionary and leafed through it.

Gravida and para . . .

Pregnancy and delivery . . .

Whoa.

If, after a physical examination and lab tests and all, a doctor had written down that Captain Lewis had never been pregnant, much less had a baby?

That meant she had lied to Jay about her baby. Why?

Well, if she had been trying to get his sympathy, certainly that had worked. He had wanted to hug her and comfort her when he'd heard that, and if she had designs on him to keep his mind from churning along a certain path—

If? All those sexual images in her scenarios? That fallen towel during that phone call? Her hand in his lap?

She wanted to sleep with him—but not because she thought he was God's gift to women. It was to put him off her trail!

What a moron he was! Why hadn't he seen that before?

Jay was certain of it in that moment. Rachel Lewis was behind the attacks on the Army bases. The only question was, how was he going to get enough evidence to prove it?

Maybe Carruth, if they got him alive, would roll over and give her up. But Jay couldn't depend on that. He had to get what he needed in case Carruth blew himself to pieces when the authorities came to call.

Then again, once you were convinced of something, once you knew it was the truth, finding evidence to back that belief was easier than fumbling around in the dark looking for it in the first place.

Well. He had plenty of material to look at. Everything she had told him needed to be checked. She had been lying to him all along, and somewhere in that mess might be just the thread he needed to unravel it.

Rachel was the bad guy. Damn.

34

The roar of the BMF revolver was a noise to rival Thor's hammer smashing a mountain of granite, a scream that stunned both the ear and the mind. He wasn't worried about his hearing or ballistics at this point—it was his ass on the line. They were here, they knew who he was. All bets were off.

He pointed the handgun at the front door, not bothering to aim, and squeezed the trigger again, and the second blast from the firing chamber blew sideways hard enough from the cylinder to blast paint chips off the door frame in the hall where he stood.

If that didn't make them duck, nothing would.

Even with his ears ringing from the shots, he heard: "Holy shit! He's got a fucking cannon in there! Get down!"

He assumed they had both the front and back covered, and there was only one way out. He ran to the bedroom and jerked open the door to his closet. He had a moment of regret when he looked at all the stuff he'd have to leave behind, but that's all he had time for, that brief moment. He could buy new stuff if he got away. If not, he wouldn't need it anyway. He'd either be dead or on his way up the river for a long damn time.

How had they found him? Only one way he could see— the same way they had known to set a trap at the Army base. Somebody had ratted him out, and there was only one person who could have done it.

Why? Had she gotten spooked over something and wanted to throw him to the wolves so they wouldn't follow her? Had that business with the terrorist's brother rattled her? She seemed so cool and so smart, he'd never figured on that. Was she getting greedy now that the payout was getting closer?

And how stupid did she think he was, that he wouldn't eventually figure it out that she'd given him up?

Unless maybe the reason they had hung back at the base, and weren't storming in here like gangbusters, was because she'd told them something else? Like maybe he was suicidal? She didn't want him alive and talking, did she?

Crap. What a screwup this was.

There were D.C. cops, FBI, and at least a couple goddamn Net Force logos out front, all of them armed, some with subguns, some with LTL beanbag guns and tasers. He had to assume there were that many of them in the backyard, too. They wanted him alive, obviously, the way they were waving those beanbaggers and electrical shockers, but once he'd cooked off a few more rounds from the honker, they'd rethink that. If it was him leading the assault and somebody coughed as loud as the BMF at him? The take-him-alive plan would be right out, and it'd be into just shoot the bastard first chance, and game over.

One against eight. Not good odds, even if he'd had the element of surprise—and he sure as hell didn't have that.

He had one chance, and it wasn't much. His only hope was that he had rattled them before they had a chance to get everybody into position. If not, he was probably a dead man, because he wasn't going to just give up.

The trapdoor to the crawl space was in the floor of the

closet. He jerked it up, grabbed the flashlight hung on the nail on the back wall, and dropped into the opening. They'd find the door eventually, but it was covered with carpet to match the closet's floor, and he tugged it back into place. It would take them a few minutes to get into the house and realize he wasn't there. A few more minutes to find the crawl space, if he was lucky.

After hearing his gun, nobody would want to be the first guy through the door, just in case he was sitting there maybe wanting to go out in a blaze of glory and see how many he could take with him.

The crawl space was just that, less than a meter high, and he dropped prone and started ass and elbows and knees working. He'd done a modification to the house when he'd rented it, built an exit to the side that opened up in the narrow corridor that had once been a dog run. There was even an old doghouse there, and Carruth had taken out one wall of it and shoved it against the side of the house, to cover the trapdoor leading to the yard.

The place was dirty, full of spiderwebs and God knew what other bugs, but that wasn't high on his list of worries at the moment.

He came out inside the doghouse, which was big enough to hold a St. Bernard. He looked out through the door, didn't see anybody in the backyard looking his way, and that was because there was a wooden gate to the dog run and it was closed and padlocked. That would change soon. They'd be watching the back door, checking windows, and looking at the gate to the dog run. With a six-foot-high fence running down the side of the yard, they'd figure they'd see him if he hopped it. Sooner or later, though, somebody would get a bolt-cutter for the locked gate and come to check the side of the house.

He had to hurry.

The fence between his house and the next-door neighbor was a two-meter-tall wooden privacy deal. Fortunately, the neighbor had cats and not a dog, and didn't know that Carruth had dug a hole under the fence, covered it with a thin sheet of Masonite, and spread bark dust over the top on both sides, so it looked just like the rest of the ground. His next-door neighbor wasn't big on yard work; his side of the fence was thick with weeds, which was good—he had never notice the disguised pit.

No time to sit around here thinking how clever you were to do that, Carruth. Git!

He lifted the edge of the doghouse up, reached across the half a meter, and grabbed the edge of the Masonite, pulling it toward himself. A certain amount of the bark dust scraped off the other side and fell into the hole, but there was enough room, even for a big man in a hurry, to wiggle into the hole and undulate underneath the fence. He moved.

He had a bad moment when the back of his belt snagged on the wood, but he jerked free and came out into the neighbor's yard. He couldn't cover the hole from this side, but by the time they found it, it shouldn't matter.

He stayed crouched low and duck-walked along the side of the neighbor's house. They had a TV going inside, with what sounded like a ball game of some kind on.

Once he rounded the corner and started away from the fence, Carruth came up some and started to sprint. If the fence didn't hide him from view, he was screwed; there wasn't any real cover in this backyard, a couple of short bushes and thin-trunked trees, nothing to hide behind until he got to the other side.

He ran, hard. Passed a sliding glass door and caught a quick glimpse of his neighbor and his two teenaged boys watching the big-screen television. He didn't think they saw him, but that didn't matter, there wasn't anything he could do but run.

Idiot cops should have cleared this house—ought not be risking civilian casualties—first thing they shoulda done was get the families on both sides of my house out and away.

Well, if they screwed up on this, maybe they would screw up on other stuff. He could hope.

He rounded the corner, ran toward the fence on the other side of the house, and launched himself over the top in a high-speed high jump, not the Fosbury Flop, but with both hands on a four-by-four post and a sideways vault.

He cleared the fence, hit, fell, rolled up, and kept going.

This neighbor did have a dog, a yappy little Pomeranian that went into a conniption. Fortunately, it was inside the house, and not likely anybody on the street would hear it.

He made it across the yard and hopped the next fence. Banged his left knee hard when he didn't lift it quite high enough, but cleared it and damned near came down in the next neighbor's swimming pool. It was covered for the season, but that would have been a bitch to get out of had he stepped onto the plastic cover.

The next fence was the last—this was the corner lot. Carruth ran around the pool to it, stopped, stood on his toes, and peeped over it.

Traffic on the street, but nobody standing around in urban camo with weapons he could see. He'd have to chance it.

He made ready to climb up and over.

"Hey! What are you doing?!"

He turned, and saw the house's owner, a short, florid, fat man in a sweat suit, standing there with a garden hose, washing down a barbecue grill.

Carruth's gun was in his holster and hidden under his thin Windbreaker, but if he cooked the guy, he might as well go out front and jump up and down to attract the cops. They'd hear the shot half a mile away.

"Chasing a guy broke into my house!" Carruth said. "Better stay inside, he's got a knife! Cops are on the way!"

He hopped over the fence.

The fat guy washing his grill stared. He knew Carruth to look at, and while he hadn't seen a burglar running around back here with a knife, it was the kind of thing that he'd have to think about for a while. If there *was* somebody Carruth was chasing and he had a *knife*? Maybe he *should* go inside and wait for the police to arrive and sort it out. A lot safer than facing down a knifer with a garden hose . . .

Carruth turned to his right and started jogging down the sidewalk. If he could get to the next block without being seen, he could maybe swipe a car or—wait, look at that, there was a Metro bus, right there.

He ran toward the bus.

The driver was about to pull away when he saw Carruth running. He stopped and waited.

Carruth climbed up the step. "I'm all out of change," he said. "Can I buy a pass?"

"Sure, at your local Safeway."

"Come on, we can do a deal here, can't we?"

The driver wanted to get on his way. "How long?"

"A week?"

"Thirty dollars for the Short Trip, forty for the Fast Pass."

Carruth pulled out his wallet and removed two twenties. "The Fast Pass," he said.

The driver took his money. Carruth took the pass and went to find a seat. A few blocks, and he could get off and find wheels.

After that? Well, that was going to be a problem, wasn't it?

The shit had definitely hit the fan now.

He sat, and adjusted the big gun on his hip. He needed to hit the road. Go to his storage unit where he had the old clunker car, charge up the battery, grab his go-bag with the new ID and haul-ass money, and get gone. This time tomorrow, with luck, he could be six, eight hundred miles away.

That's what he should do. But he wanted to do something else before he left. His life had just taken a bad turn, and it wasn't ever going to be the same again. And it was Lewis's fault.

Lewis needed to pay for that. Big-time.

Half a block up the street from Carruth's house, in the tricked-out RV that served as a mobile command post, Kent listened to the lieutenant's report without saying anything.

"Yes, sir. He went out through the crawl space—there's an access in the bedroom closet. Came up in the side yard, hidden behind a wooden gate, and had a tunnel predug under the fence into the neighbor's yard. We must have just missed him."

Kent nodded. If he'd been leading the op, it probably wouldn't have gone any better. The operation had been run by the FBI with backup from the Metro police, and Net Force's team was just here as "ride-along guests"—though they were armed guests. Given that they were Marines, albeit a special unit, operating on U.S. soil, even like this, was iffy. The Posse Comitatus Act had been around since the 1870s, passed during the Administration of Rutherford B. Hayes. The Army, Navy, Air Force, and Marines went over *there* and kicked ass. At home, the civilian authorities were supposed to catch the bad guys. If the cops weren't enough, there was the National Guard. Military units were not supposed to police American soil, save in very specific circumstances. And the last time he looked, martial law hadn't been declared.

The old law was slowly changing, given the war on terrorism and all, but it hadn't been really tested yet. The guy they were after was a civilian, and he'd be prosecuted as a civilian—if they ever caught him. Hard to justify calling out the Marines to bring him in . . .

They'd had the front, back, and one side of the house covered immediately, and when that handgun went off—two rounds blew holes through the front door of the house and sent the slugs, fortunately, into a thick tree near the front walk—everybody ducked. They all knew that this guy had killed a couple of police officers and several Army guys and he had nothing to lose by taking a few more with him if they got careless. And there was that story about him being a walking bomb, too.

By the time they got back to cover the side of the place, Carruth would have already been gone. Didn't sound to Kent like a man who was in a hurry to die, but there was that possibility.

He reached for his virgil, to call Thorn. This wasn't the first time an operation had turned into a snafu and the bad guy had gotten away, and it wasn't even Net Force's fault, but still, Kent hated to make the call.

Not as much as he hated losing the bad guy, though.

And this way of doing things? Sitting in the RV as an observer? That stunk. If his troops weren't going to be able to go out and do what they had been trained to do, what was the point?

Well, he could sort that out later.

He reached for his virgil.

35

Washington, D.C.

However macho and narrow Lewis thought Carruth was, she didn't think he was completely stupid. When he'd escaped the Army's trap, she'd known it would only be a matter of time before he realized she had set him up. She had just heard from one of her sources that he'd gotten away from the cops and FBI who'd gone to his house.

Dead, she was safe. If they took him alive, he would serve her to them on a platter. *Eat up, boys. Here's your main course. . . .*

She still had a chance, a small one, but it was better than none.

She called him on the throwaway cell.

"Yeah?"

"We need to meet."

"Oh, yeah, damn straight about that."

"Whatever you're thinking, it's wrong," she said. "Net Force got to you through Stark."

There was a moment of silence. "What are you talking about?"

It was a risk, speaking on an unscrambled cell, but it was digital and nobody should be looking for the sig. Besides, that was far down in the pile of her worries at this point. She had to sell him on this. She said, "Gridley. The FBI ID'd Stark from dental records and DNA—Gridley found a connection to you. He ran it down. Then he found out about that gun of yours. The gun you shot two cops and an Army guy with and didn't get rid of. Somehow Gridley figured out where you lived. They followed you. Realized you were going to the base, and set a fast trap to catch you."

"Bullshit!"

"Think about it. If they'd had time to get ready, you'd be caught."

This was iffy, and didn't play that well if you *did* think about it too long, but she was banking on his guilt about the gun keeping his thoughts murky. It could have happened the way she'd said.

The silence lasted longer this time. "Shit," he finally said.

Did he buy it? Maybe. It didn't really matter, if he would meet her—and he didn't show up shooting. "Yeah, my thoughts exactly."

"What are we gonna do?"

She had him! "You have to go to ground. I have some money. Enough so you can live for a while. When the deal goes through, I'll get your cut to you."

"What are *you* gonna do?"

"They aren't looking for me."

"All right. Where?"

Here was the tricky part. It needed to be somewhere that would not make him any more suspicious than he already was. Someplace public, but where nobody would pay any attention to them.

"The Mall," she said. "In front of the National Archives. That's between the Natural History Museum and the National Gallery of Art."

"The old skating rink?"

"No, the lawn, other side of Madison. How soon can you make it?"

"Maybe an hour."

That was good, it would take her thirty-five, forty minutes this time of day—she didn't have to cross the river from her place.

"I'll see you there."

After they discommed, Lewis sat and took several deep breaths. This was going to be a bitch to pull off, but she didn't have any choice. The only gun she had was the snub-nosed .38 Special and, fortunately, it wasn't registered to her. She went and found the gun in her bedside drawer, emptied the cartridges from it, and sprayed it with Break Free. She wiped it down carefully, then wiped the shells with the lubed rag, using it to avoid touching the brass when she reloaded the gun. No prints on anything.

She put on a pair of thin leather gloves, picked up the revolver, and dropped it into the jacket pocket of the coat hung on the bedroom door.

She put a pale blue skirt and white blouse and flats into a shopping bag, along with a darker blue sweater, then dressed in gray sweat pants and shirt, with white running shoes. Put her hair up and under a Baltimore baseball cap, slipped her jacket on, added a pair of shades.

In the bathroom, she took a Band-Aid and put that across her nose, under the sunglasses' nosepiece. If anybody looked at her face, what they would notice would be the bandage—that's what they'd remember. Skinny kid with a bandage on his nose. Or her nose.

She looked at herself in the mirror. Took another deep breath and let it out. Grabbed her coat and shrugged it on.

Go.

The National Mall
Washington, D.C.

When Carruth had first come to D.C., way back when, he had, like millions of tourists before him, gone to the monuments and museums that lined the lawn. He'd scoped out the old Smith, the Air and Space Museum, crossed over a couple streets to the Navy Memorial. He'd hiked down to the war memorials, seen the thousands of names on the Wall and the Korean Monument, walked along the Reflecting Pool, all that. It had been a while since he'd spent any real time there, but he knew his way around enough to get to the lawn between Madison and Jefferson.

He parked his run-for-it car in a lot—didn't want it towed—and walked a few blocks. It was cold, but there were still tourists around even so.

He wasn't sure about Lewis anymore. Could be she'd set him up, but it could be the Net Force geek had made the connections she'd said. She had warned him about how good the guy was. He should have gotten rid of the gun after the cops, and if that was what had nailed him, it was his own damn fault. Couldn't blame anybody for that.

And if Lewis had some cash, he could use it. He only had a couple thousand, and that wasn't going to go far. There was a cabin he'd rented a couple times in Montana. They knew him there from before, and nobody would bother him if he could get there. Way out in the boonies, lotta survivalists out there didn't have much use for newspapers, TV, certainly not the government. They minded their own business, expected you to mind yours.

Lewis would have to pay him if she made the deal, because he could bring her down, and she wouldn't want to risk that. Could still turn out okay, maybe.

Maybe he'd been wrong. It could have happened like she'd said. One thing for sure, if he killed her like he'd been thinking, that wouldn't make him a dime. Alive, she might still help him become a rich man. He could live in Mexico or Brazil or somewhere forever with a couple million, and live well. Lots better than some of the other options. State murder charges. Federal rap for treason.

If she didn't come through, he could always turn her in, or pay her a visit and drop her.

The Mall was a good place to meet. Nobody would pay

any attention to them, and a cop searching for him wouldn't put the lawn next to an art galley on the top of his go-look locales.

He could collect the money and head out. Get away, get set up, see what happened. If worst came to worst, he could always find a war zone somewhere and get work. Better than a kick in the gonads. Better than prison or the chair.

He headed across Madison toward the lawn. The Smith Castle was off to his right. He didn't see Lewis.

Lewis, across the corner of Seventh and south of Madison, close to the National Gallery West, watched Carruth amble across the lawn, his back to her. Too far. She'd have to get closer.

She started that way.

She was maybe forty meters away when Carruth stopped and turned around, as if he'd sensed her. Any sudden moves, he'd jump.

Crap. Well. It was what it was. She already had the gun in her hand, still inside her jacket pocket. She raised the shopping bag in her left hand and waved it at Carruth. Kept walking that way. She smiled real big.

He raised his right hand to wave back.

Good. His hand was as far away from his hip as it was going to get.

She pulled the S&W snubbie from her pocket and pointed it. Stopped walking and lined up the rudimentary sights. One-handed. Forty meters. Not the best.

When Carruth saw Lewis wave a shopping bag at him, he waved back. Her breath made fog in the cold air. Bag full of cash? that would be nice—

Then he saw her pull her other hand out of her pocket—

Holding a *gun*—!

Jesus! He jerked his hand down for his piece, jumping to his left as he did—

She had to adjust her aim, she swung her arm to her right—

She was too far away, she'd never make the shot with that stubby piece at this range, he was okay, he had time, he had time—!

He grabbed the BMF's butt, pulled the heavy gun clear, and thrust it toward her, bringing his left hand up to catch it in a two-handed grip—he had her, the stupid bitch—!

Lewis held the revolver one-handed, like a target shooter, but she finally had Carruth under the front sight. Take it easy, don't jerk. . . .

She squeezed the trigger, once, twice, three times—

The gun didn't seem all that loud out here in the open, though it made a lot of smoke in the cold air—

Carruth felt the bullets slam into him, in the chest, *thump-thump,* at least two of them. He was stunned. How could she hit him that far away with that gun?!

He tried to line up on her, but as he pulled the trigger, his arms felt weak suddenly, and they sagged. Came the monster *boom!* and the recoil, but he saw where the bullet hit the ground and kicked up a divot of grass ten feet in front of her, a miss—

Crap, crap—!

He struggled to raise the gun again. So heavy—

The blast from Carruth's gun was loud, it sounded like a bomb, but his arms drooped as he fired, and she didn't feel the impact of the big bullet, so she was still golden—

Lewis squeezed off the last two rounds in the S&W, was sure that at least one more hit Carruth, this one higher, at collarbone level. At least three hits, maybe four, center of mass, mostly. Best she could do. Surely he'd die before they could get him to a hospital—the bullets she'd used were hot-loads that should blow up any major organs they hit. Heart, liver, lung, he should bleed out fast.

She dropped the gun, turned, and walked quickly—not a run—toward the National Galley of Art.

* * *

Carruth felt cold as he collapsed to his knees. He tried to cock his gun, but he didn't have the strength to pull the hammer back.

Lewis was walking away from him, not looking back.

The bitch! The fucking bitch! She had shot him! And from so far away . . .

His vision grayed out; all he could see was the green grass next to his knees. He felt his consciousness ebbing. Must have hit the heart, no blood getting to the brain.

He looked at the big revolver in his hand. It fell from his grip. Hit the grass.

That was his last sight as he fell forward onto his face. That gun. That goddamn gun . . .

Inside the museum, past the huge marble columns, Lewis smiled at the guard who was heading for the door to see what the commotion was about outside.

"Somebody shooting off firecrackers," she said to him when he looked at her.

She headed for the bathroom.

Inside, she stepped into a stall and stripped off her gloves, jacket, cap, sweats, and shoes. She put on the skirt and blouse, the flats, and finally the sweater. She pulled a comb from her purse and peeled the Band-Aid off her nose. She turned the shopping bag inside out and put the old clothes in it. She would burn them when she got home.

She combed her hair in front of the mirror, smiled at her reflection, and left the bathroom, a different woman altogether.

People searching for a slightly built man or a woman dressed as she had been wouldn't look at her twice. She was a citizen, an Army officer, and if anybody stopped her—which they wouldn't—she would smile and talk her way past them.

She left the gallery through an east entrance.

She walked briskly north, away from the Mall, to where she had parked her car. Her biggest problem had just been solved. The rest of it, she'd figure out as necessary.

36

The Virtual Library

Jay was blurry from all the input. He had run down every fact and factoid on Rachel that he could find. He was sure he knew more about her than anybody alive did—if anybody had put data into a system that was linked to the web anywhere, he was pretty sure he had seen it, from her grades in primary school to her date for the junior high school prom, to every posting she had ever made to Usenet under her own name.

It had been like wading through a heavy surf. It would surge, roll in, and just about knock him down. He would regain his footing, and in would come another wave. Even skimming, it was a lot to see. And the little things kept piling up.

Item: Rachel had been in school when the Troy game had been posted on that server, and she'd had both the access and the skill to have done it.

Item: There was no translation on any fan website of the bug language that supposedly was Max Waite's signature, zip, so that splotch of hieroglyphs could say anything—or nothing.

Item: It needed somebody with very good access to the Army computers to have gotten the information about the bases. And there was still no sign of an external hack.

Item: Jay's version of the bug game, saved from an old site, was slightly different than the new version in which Rachel had supposedly found that old desert-scenario web page. That bit was missing from the older version, indicating it had been put in later. Somebody with a hidden door could do that, and backdate their input. It was easy if you knew how—and if you had a back door into the program.

She had never been pregnant, much less had a baby. She had no reason to love the Army, which had convicted her father of murder.

She had been actively trying to seduce Jay, and, let's face it, he knew he wasn't God's gift to women.

She was the bad guy. That sucked, but he was sure.

None of it was solid proof. Yeah, she was a liar, but that wasn't enough to put her away. Jay was sure—he *knew* she was the one behind all this—but his certainty by itself wasn't nearly enough, and he hadn't found a solid link to anything criminal.

He shut down the library. He was tired. He would go home, get some rest. Talk to Saji, much as he wasn't looking forward to that, and hit it again as soon as he could. If it was there, he'd eventually find it. If it wasn't there, he was screwed.

His com beeped.

"Yeah?"

"Jay? Can you come to my office?" Thorn.

"On my way. Good news?"

"Yes and no."

At Thorn's office, the boss waved him in and at the couch.

"There was a shooting today on the Mall. Park rangers and local police found a dead guy on lawn," Thorn said.

"Shot four times with a .38 Special revolver by a tall-short-fat-thin-black-white-man-woman-teenage-boy-or-girl, depending on which tourist you believe."

He paused, his gaze steady on Jay. "The good news is, the corpse is Carruth, and he's all paid up for his crimes. The bad news is, he won't be helping us with our investigation."

"Aw, crap," Jay said. "What time?"

Thorn looked at his holoproj's clock. "A couple hours ago. It took a while to ID him. They found a gun lying next to him they are pretty sure was the one used to kill the Metro cops and Army guy, but they're waiting on FBI ballistics to get back to them."

"Where was Captain Lewis when this happened? Can we get the Pentagon Annex logs?"

Thorn frowned. "Captain Lewis?"

"Yeah. She's the one behind this."

"Really?" Thorn sat up straighter in his chair. "You have something we can take to the Army and FBI?"

"Not enough."

"But you have good reasons to believe it?"

"Yeah."

Thorn waited.

"She . . . came on to me," Jay said.

"Well, yeah, I guess that's reason to hang her for treason." He smiled. He started tapping his keyboard.

"I'm serious, Boss. I started doing some backtracking. Every time I hit a dead end, she was behind it. She's been leading me around by my . . . nose. When I was about to out Carruth, she was with me when my scenario mysteriously crashed. She lied to me about all kinds of things. She had the skill to build the game, she had access to the information that was supposedly grabbed by a hacker. She has a reason to hate the Army. I don't have a direct link between her and Carruth, but I know she did it."

Thorn looked at his holoproj screen. "I just got the logs from the Annex. Captain Lewis checked out shortly after you did. She's not back yet."

"She went to meet Carruth and she iced him," Jay said.

"I'd bet every computer I'll ever own on that. But I don't know if there's any way to nail her on it. I've been reading stuff for hours, and so far all I've got is a bunch of circumstantial stuff. She didn't leave anything obvious lying around."

Thorn said, "Maybe that's all we need."

"What do you mean?"

"I mean I have to call this in. Now that you've brought this to me—which is exactly what you should have done, of course—I can't sit on this. But if I call General Hadden and tell him we are sure that Captain Lewis is behind the attacks on his bases, he'll have his MPs grab her right away. After all, he doesn't need absolute proof. She's in the Army, and not subject to the same search-and-seizure protections as a civilian. Hadden will most likely have her reassigned to sentry duty inside a maximum-security prison until he sorts it out. If she tries to run, there's surely some antiterrorism statute he can unlimber and hold her on. At the very least, it would stop her from doing whatever else she might have planned."

Jay nodded. "Yeah . . ."

"But—?"

"It's a slippery slope, Boss. I know she's guilty, but if you can just throw anybody into jail that you want without due process, who's next? If they can do that to her, then somebody could look at you or me and decide we are bad guys and put us away for years, too."

"Like I said, she's in the Army, so it's not quite the same thing, but I understand your point, Jay. I even agree with you, but I don't see an alternative here. It's an imperfect system, Jay. Some folks'll tell you that sometimes the ends do justify the means."

"And sometimes they don't."

"That's true, and I know you'd rather have ironclad evidence. So would I. But you're sure she's guilty, which means she's still a threat."

"Yeah. But I could be wrong. Wouldn't be the first time, much as it pains me to admit that." *Like he'd been wrong about Rachel, up to a few hours ago . . .*

"You don't think you are, though."

Jay shook his head. "No. I know what I know. But—"

"What do you want, then, Jay? Would you rather see her skate? Get away? Maybe swipe a tactical nuke from the Army next time and blow up half a city full of innocent people?"

"No, but—"

"If we err, shouldn't we err on the side of safety? If Captain Lewis has to spend a few days in detention, is that worse than ten thousand people going up in a fireball?"

Jay sighed. "Of course not, but that doesn't mean I have to like choosing between evils. Either way, they're both still bad choices."

"Do you have a better choice to offer?"

Jay shook his head.

"Then I don't really have any choice, Jay. I'm sorry." Thorn waved his hand over the com. "Get me General Hadden," he said.

Jay got up. He was going to head home, but his virgil blinked, indicating he had an incoming call. He looked at the caller ID.

He felt a deep chill.

Thorn looked up at him.

"I'll be in my office," Jay said. "One more thing I need to do before I go."

The Perfect Beach
The Perfect Sea

It was her scenario, and Jay was invited, but he hacked in without using a password, brute-forcing. He'd been there before, he knew where to hit it. No way he was waiting for her to open the door.

It was the beach, with the warm sun and white sand, the breeze, the perfect waves rolling in from the electric blue sea. He saw Rachel, sitting at the waterline, her knees drawn up to her chest, her arms around her legs, staring into the far ocean. She looked mostly bare from this angle, though she could be wearing a bikini.

Gulls soared and wheeled and *craw*ed and he heard the sound of the gentle waves as they lapped on the beach. So peaceful. So serene.

So big a lie . . .

He walked barefoot through the sand, listening to the little squeaks his feet made. It really was a well-built scenario. She really had talent. It was really too bad.

He stopped ten feet behind her.

Without turning to look, she said, "Well, well. Smokin' Jay Gridley has arrived. Took you long enough. I left a hole in the wall big enough to drive a train through."

He didn't say anything.

She stood. As she uncoiled, he saw that she was completely naked. Slowly, she turned to face him, her stance going wide. She smiled, stretched her arms out into a dramatic pose. She did a slow three-sixty turn. "Take a last look, Jay. This is who I am. Just like I am in the RW, no airbrushing, no augmentation; what you see is a near-perfect copy of the real me."

She ended up facing him, smiling real big.

Jay's mouth would have been extremely dry in RW, he knew. He nodded, still not speaking.

"You could have had me. In the Real World. It would have been the best you ever experienced—the best you ever *would* experience."

She certainly was gorgeous, no argument. But he shook his head. "No. No matter how great you are in bed, it would have been missing something."

She lowered her hands and laughed. "What?"

"It was all a sham. You would only have done it to keep me from looking too closely at you. Fake. Bogus. Just like this beach."

"You're wrong. Maybe that's how it started, but along the way, I got to like you. I would have enjoyed it. You would have, too. And you wanted me."

"Yes. But that still wouldn't have been enough," he said.

"Oh, really?" Her voice was thick with sarcasm. "What else was missing?"

"Love. That's something you can't replace."

She laughed. "Love is bullshit, Jay. My boyfriend said he loved me, but then he couldn't wait for what I was going to give him anyway and he took me by force. My father said he loved me, but then he killed himself. 'Love' is just 'sex' prettied up, a fairy tale to keep the masses entertained. It doesn't compare to a warm and willing body lying next to you, ready to do anything you want to make you feel good."

He shook his head again. "I'm sorry for you, Rachel. Life handed you some hard hits, but what you did was wrong. You lied, cheated, stole, and you killed people. You shot your partner in the middle of the damned Mall, gunned him down like it was nothing. That's cold."

"Not admitting anything here, Jay, but this Carruth was a killer, right? He had a gun, didn't he? He would have shot whoever killed him if he could, so whoever did it—they were just better than he was."

"Whoever. Right," he said.

"I'm not any worse than anybody else trying to make her way in the world."

"Yeah, you are. You're bright, talented, you could have risen to the top on your own merit, but you got bent. You could have gotten a job at a civilian company making three times what you do in the Army, been running the place in a couple years. You threw it all away. That's worse than if you never had anything going in the first place."

She laughed again. "You think?"

"Yeah, I think. I wanted to see you first, but you're about to have visitors coming through your door. It's all over, Captain."

She gave him that angelic smile. "What makes you think I'm on the other side of any door that 'visitors' are about to kick open?"

Jay shook his head. The bad guys always thought they were going to get away.

"You know, you are always going to wonder about how it would have been with us. It will always be somewhere in the back of your mind, the road not taken, the field not plowed. You won't ever be completely rid of me. When you are an old man, sitting in your rocking chair, you'll remember me, and you'll wonder if you made the right choice. I know you will."

She lowered her arms. "Good-bye, Jay."

She kept smiling. A second later, her scenario vanished.

Net Force HQ
Quantico, Virginia

Back in his office, Jay stripped off his gear. What a waste. So smart, so talented, so beautiful. And now going to prison for the rest of her life.

He looked up and saw Thorn standing in the doorway. "Boss?"

"The FBI and local police just raided Captain Lewis's home. She wasn't there. It appears she packed up and left."

It took Jay a second to process that. "She got away?"

"For now, that's what it looks like."

Jay blinked. She was a user, a killer, she would have caused more death and destruction. She was dangerous, and she needed to be put where she couldn't hurt anybody. He knew that. But, for just the briefest of moments, something in him wanted to smile.

She'd gotten away.

He was ashamed of the part of him that felt that. He had to try and make up for it.

He would have to catch her.

37

Rachel knew her car would be spotted pretty quick, so she had used her computer skills to have a military vehicle checked out to somebody else; she was in that. By the time they missed it and figured out what had happened, she'd be far away. They'd be watching local airports and train and bus stations, so she needed to get out of the area before catching a ride elsewhere. Baltimore was a good place—she could head for New York, then transfer to a flight heading west. Carruth had that place in Montana he didn't know she knew about. She could be his girlfriend, waiting for him to meet her there; that would be good for a few days.

She needed a place and some time—she had to see if she could still broker the deal for her stolen data. If she didn't do it quick, though, it wasn't going to fly—now that they knew who she was, they would take her system apart and eventually unravel it and shut everything down. It would take a while, even with the best hackers working it, but they'd crack it in the end. It hadn't been designed for an all-out armored attack, but for stealth. That was gone now.

Her own best chance to come out of this with something was to contact her potential buyer, tell him there was a ticking clock, and offer a cut-rate deal. A couple million for a door that was going to be open for a few days? At least that was something an enterprising man could do something with.

She could still pull that off, maybe.

And if not? Well, at worst, she had still cost the Army a lot of grief and a lot of money. Certainly there had been plenty of payback in that even if she didn't make a dime herself.

If she could stay out of their hands for a little while longer, she'd be okay. She was too smart for them. Even for Gridley, the stupid bastard. She still couldn't believe he'd turned her down.

What an idiot.

Baltimore? As good a direction as any. They weren't going to set up roadblocks looking for her. She knew how the Army thought. They were always training to fight the last war. She was going to get away. No question.

Probably what was the most disappointing was not getting it on with Jay. She'd really been looking forward to that.

Ah, well. His loss.

38

Midtown Grill
Washington, D.C.

Kent sipped at the wine, which was considerably better than the house red—he had called Gino and arranged for that, and also spoken to Maria for the other little surprise he had in mind.

Set it up well in advance.

Jen chatted about the handmade-guitar show she'd attended last weekend, with mini-concerts provided by the luthiers to showcase their new instruments.

"—amazing that brand-new spruce-top classical could sound that good after what the player said was forty-five minutes of playing time. In another four or five years, it will open up and probably sound so good you won't be able to listen to it without crying."

Kent nodded. Said, "Uh huh."

"I asked one of the makers what the difference was between a guitar-maker and a luthier. 'Luthier,' by the way, comes from 'lute,' but has come to mean anybody who makes fretted instruments like guitars, lutes, ouds, and the like. He said that the difference was about two thousand dollars. . . ." She stopped and looked at Kent. "Where did you go?"

"Nowhere. I'm right here."

"No, your mind isn't. What's up?"

He took a deep breath. He had once stutter-stepped across a field littered with bodies, charging a Colombian machine-gunner trying to chop him down; once, had crawled into a dark underground tunnel in which he knew an enemy soldier with a shotgun was waiting. As a first lieutenant, he had, once upon a time, told a bird colonel to go to hell, and what to do to himself when he got there. He wasn't a coward when it came to risking his ass, and he had been living on borrowed time for years. He didn't worry about a lot of stuff.

He was worried now.

"Abe?"

"I've got a question for you." He glanced away, caught Maria's attention where she was on standby. He nodded, giving her the signal. She started toward their table.

"Yeah? I'm right here. Anytime."

"Give me a second. I've only done this once, and it was almost forty years ago."

She frowned, trying to make the connection. If Maria didn't hurry, she would, too.

Maria arrived. She set a covered plate on the table in front of Jen. Jen looked up. "What's this? We haven't ordered yet."

Maria smiled. She pulled the metal cover from the plate. . . .

Lying on a piece of black velvet was the engagement ring Kent had bought. It was white gold with a half-carat blue-white diamond mounted in a solitaire setting. He'd had it sized to match the ring he'd found in her medicine cabinet. He hoped it fit.

She blinked, stared at the ring. Then looked back at him.

"So, what do you think?" he said.

She smiled and shook her head. "What do I think about what, General?" She locked gazes with him, waiting.

He managed another breath, his heart pounding as if he

had just finished the obstacle course. "Will you marry me?"

Her smile got bigger. "Sure." She picked up the ring, slid it onto her finger. It seemed to fit okay. She put her hand back down, picked up the menu. To Maria, who was grinning like a pack of happy baboons, Jen said, "So, what's the special tonight?"

Butter wouldn't have melted in her mouth she was so cool.

"Miss Jen!" Maria said. She sounded horrified.

"I thought the wine was better than usual," Jen said.

"Does this mean I'll get a break on the cost of my lessons?" Kent asked, smiling.

"Only after the wedding," she said.

Kent laughed. If he thought he was going to one-up her, he realized, he was wrong.

London, England
1890 C.E.

Jay walked through the grimy streets, the vile, choking miasma of coal smoke and fog so thick you couldn't see half a block. He was following a short man wearing an opera cape and silk top hat. So far, he was getting nothing more than dogs-not-barking-in-the-night, and he could have used Conan Doyle's master detective and his doctor sidekick to help out here.

Rachel Lewis had been a dead end. She was too good to leave obvious clues that he could find.

Carruth had spent hardly any time on the web; there were few net-trails to find, and most of those didn't go anywhere useful.

Jay was about ready to pack it in, but he figured he might as well follow up this last line of inquiry.

The figure fading in and out of the reeking smog was headed somewhere, and he might as well see where.

It wasn't a direction connected to Lewis, as far as Jay could see.

Ahead, the caped man paused, then turned into an alley.

Probably Jack the Ripper's turf.

Jay followed, and was rewarded by seeing the fellow enter a low doorway with a fitful oil lamp mounted on the wall next to it.

Jay went in, and found himself in a pub of some low standing. Thieves, cutpurses, trulls, sailors, a hard-looking lot drinking bitters and gin.

Rachel Lewis wasn't here. Even in disguise, he would have known her, he was sure. Ah, well. That would have been too much to hope for, he figured.

"End scenario."

Net Force HQ
Quantico, Virginia

Jay leaned back in his chair, shucking gear a piece at a time. So what he had found in the killer London smog was nothing more than an address for a cabin that Carruth had rented a couple of times, way the hell out in Montana. No sign that Lewis had anything to do with that, and Carruth wasn't going to be using the place again.

Jay voxaxed the cabin's rental site. It took only a few seconds to find out that it had just been rented. Details of the renter were not available for public consumption, but, of course, Jay wasn't the public. He hacked the website and found the name of the person renting the place:

"M. Lane."

Jay frowned. Something about that rang a bell, what was it . . . ?

He scrolled down, found a handwritten signature on the rental agreement. It was pretty much an unreadable scrawl, looked like it said "Margie," or maybe "Margaret," or . . .

Margo? Margo Lane? Lamont Cranston's friend?
The Shadow's girl . . . ?

"Holy shit!" he said. He reached for the phone. He needed to talk to the rental agent, to find out if the person in the cabin was, indeed, a woman. And if so, what she looked like . . .

39

Thorn nodded. "Looks pretty good, Jay."

They were in his office—Thorn, Jay, and Abe Kent. "What do you think, Abe?"

"I've looked at the aerials. There's a shiny new OwlSat footprinting the place. Couple feet of snow on the ground, but it is approachable. Small team, a quad, that would work. We could mount up, be there this afternoon, hit it after dark."

" 'We?' "

"I'm a lousy desk jockey," Kent said. "This is what I do."

Thorn smiled.

Jay said, "I want to go, too."

Thorn regarded him. "I thought you didn't want to risk field operations."

"This one I do." He paused. "This is personal, Boss. She suckered me. I want to see her face when she realizes she's caught."

Thorn nodded again. "Okay."

"I need to mention there are some legal issues," Kent said.

"Posse Comitatus," Thorn said.

"Yes, sir."

Jay blinked. "Posse who?"

"In the earlier days of the Republic, the civilians got worried that some sleazy politician might get himself elected and use the military to kick ass and take names," Thorn said. "So Congress passed a law that forbade the use of the federal military, save the National Guard, from police activities here at home. The Posse Comitatus Act. General Kent is a Marine, as are his troops. They aren't supposed to be traipsing about in the woods hunting people for civilian crimes."

"Lewis isn't a civilian, though. You pointed that out yourself earlier."

"Even so. The FBI has jurisdiction, or the local police, not the Army. Certainly not the Marines."

"So, does that mean we can't go?"

Thorn grinned. "Oh, no. That just means we have to be very careful. We're going."

Kent nodded.

"You could get fired," Jay said.

"I don't think that's gonna happen," Thorn said. "I think the Chairman of the Joint Chiefs would make a whole lot of things disappear if we deliver Captain Lewis to him. As long as there isn't a big, smoking crater in the ground out there when you get done, I don't think there will be any record that General Kent and his Marines ever set foot in Montana, except to do a little fly-fishing."

Kent grinned at that.

Thorn stood, as did Jay and Kent. Thorn extended his hand to Kent. "Good luck, General."

"Thank you, sir." He turned to Jay. "Let's go. We've got places to go and terrorists to catch."

After they left, Thorn considered his course of action. He had places to go, too. He took a deep breath and let it escape slowly. Should he call Marissa?

No. He'd made his mind up. He had to do what he had to do. She'd understand that.

40

In Hadden's office, Thorn sat across the big desk from the general. The chairman of the Joint Chiefs had listened to what Thorn had to say without interrupting.

Now he said, "Are you a student of history, Thorn?"

Thorn shrugged. "I know a little."

"What would be the most famous duel in the U.S.?"

"Burr and Hamilton."

Hadden nodded. "Two men who didn't get along politically and who hated each other personally. Burr was Jefferson's Vice President. He blamed Hamilton for all kinds of things, not the least of which was being dropped from the ticket for the reelection campaign. So, the sitting Vice President challenged the former Secretary of the Treasury to settle things once and for all. Since dueling was illegal in New York in 1804, they barged across the river to the Weehawken, New Jersey, dueling grounds. There were seconds, a doctor. The two men loaded their single-shot pistols—.56-caliber, I believe they were. They squared up at ten paces, were given leave to shoot. Burr fired and hit Hamilton. Some say Hamilton fired into the air rather than at Burr; some say he was simply a lousy shot. In any event, Hamilton's wound was fatal, though he lingered, dying the next day at his home in Manhattan."

Thorn nodded, wondering where this was going.

Hadden continued: "Hamilton was shot in New Jersey, but died in New York, and Aaron Burr was indicted for murder in both states. He was never prosecuted in either. Burr left town, went to the Carolinas, and then back to Washington, where he served out the last of his term as Vice President. I do believe that's the only time a sitting VP was under indictment for murder while he was in office. He traveled after that, but eventually returned to New York, after the heat had died down.

"Burr's fortunes sagged—a few years later, he was arrested for treason in connection with some land scheme connected to the Louisiana Purchase, but he got off. He didn't die until 1836, making him about eighty."

Thorn looked at Hadden. "Fascinating."

"And why in hell am I telling you this?"

"Exactly. Not to put too fine a point on it, sir."

"RHIP. Rank has its privileges, son. Aaron Burr killed a prominent man, but he had powerful supporters, and was at the time the Vice President. However unhappy his life might have been after his duel, he had more than thirty years of it left after Hamilton was laid beneath the cold ground. Three decades wherein he was able to eat, sleep, make love, travel, all the things that the living do. He got away with what the state called murder. He wasn't the first. Won't be the last. Had he been an ordinary citizen, that probably wouldn't have happened."

Thorn nodded.

"As the Chairman of the Joint Chiefs, I have a lot of privileges not available to most men. I try and use them for the good of these United States of America as best I can. Sometimes I step over the line, and because I am who I am, I get away with it. That doesn't make it right. I need all the help I can get, and people who will stand up to me and call it like they see it? They are hard to find. You're an asset, son. I respect a man who will fight for his principles, even if I don't always agree with them."

Thorn nodded again. "I appreciate that, General."

"But you're leaving anyway."

"Yes, sir. Net Force as it stands isn't what I signed on for. I'm not a soldier. I didn't like some of the end-justifies-the-means choices I had to make. I want to be able to look at myself in the mirror and believe I am part of the solution and not the problem."

Hadden nodded. "That's what I figured."

"I don't envy you your job. Rank does indeed have its privileges, sir, but with great power comes great responsibility."

"Carl von Clausewitz?"

"No, sir. Spider Man."

It took a second, but then both men grinned.

Hadden stood and extended his hand. Thorn took it.

"I appreciate your service, son."

"Thank you. Good luck on finding somebody to run things."

"It was good work, uncovering the terrorist we wanted. I'll keep you posted on it, let you know when we catch her."

Thorn smiled.

"Something?"

"No, sir. Nothing."

Trooper's Trail, Montana

The cabin had a solar panel that fed batteries, and once you scraped the foot and a half of snow off the cells, you could get enough trickle to run a computer and a cell-phone Internet connection okay, with a few lights thrown in for good measure. Even out here in the middle of nowhere, the phone worked most of the time—one of the joys of civilization. Lewis could reach her hidden server using a laptop, and that was all she needed.

She had been working the connection to the buyer, and it looked as if they had a deal. Less than she had hoped for, but she couldn't really push it too hard. The Army might not crack her systems for a while, and even if they did, she didn't care if the buyer got burned when he tried to break into a base, but she couldn't give any more demonstrations, and that was that. He was firm on a million-five, and she was going to have to take it. Not the ten million it might have been once, but better than nothing.

She'd have to hire some muscle, but she thought she could manage that okay. She knew a couple places where mercs hung out, and all she needed was somebody who could look menacing and shoot if he had to.

The sun was going down. Lewis shut the computer off and went out to collect firewood. The only heat the cabin had was a potbellied wood stove smack in the middle of the main room, and she had to keep it going all the time. Aside from that, there was a wood-fired range in the kitchen, and no heat source at all in the single bedroom, just a mound of quilts and comforters on the bed. She left the door to the bedroom open at night to get the stove's warmth. She didn't want to be fumbling around outside for more firewood in the middle of the night, in the dark and at twenty below. Bad enough if she had to go to the bathroom, which required a trip to the outhouse—no indoor plumbing, and you had to get water from a hand pump outside the cabin—after you thawed it out.

Primitive, yes. On the other hand, nobody was going to accidentally stumble across her here—she was a long way from a major road.

It hadn't snowed for a few days, wasn't supposed to for a few more, so the AWD SUV she'd rented under a fake name would get her out okay. She could firm the deal up in the morning, and take off.

Not exactly as she'd planned things, the way they'd turned out, but she was still ahead of the game. Better that than not.

* * *

"You sure you want to do this?" Kent asked.

Jay nodded. "I came this far. I want to be there at the end."

Kent said, "From here, we have to snowshoe. It's a couple miles. People out here will notice us and word will get around pretty fast, so we want to go in while it is dark, to minimize chances of being seen. We'll use IR lights, cold-weather snow-camo clothes, and hike in on the double."

"I'll keep up."

"I expect you will."

"I heard you were thinking about getting married, General."

"Not thinking about it, son, going for it. I'll send you an invitation to the wedding."

"Congratulations."

"Thanks. Best we gear up and get ready."

Not long after midnight, Lewis half-heard a sound on the cabin's front porch. She came awake fast, listening. In the two nights she'd been here, she'd had a few animal visitors, foxes or wolves or raccoons. She had to keep a heavy lid locked into place on the trash can to keep garbage from being strewn all over the place. Probably a coon out there trying to get a free meal.

She grabbed the flashlight next to the bed, and the gun that Carruth had stashed under the mattress, an old Beretta 9mm pistol.

Probably, it was a hungry critter, but best she go and make sure.

When she opened the door, she saw a man standing there, dressed in white camo and a hood. She jumped, startled, covering him with the pistol as he pushed the hood back. . . .

"Jay?!"

"Hello, Captain."

She steadied the gun, kept it aimed at his chest. "How did you find me?" She looked past him, didn't see anybody else out in the dark.

"I found Carruth's records, rental receipts for this place. I followed it up. Margo Lane? Come on."

She shook her head. Amazing. "What, did you think I was just going to . . . *surrender* because you figured it out? Come out here like the Lone Ranger to take me in? I can shoot you dead where you stand and bury you in the snow. They won't find your body until spring."

"You would do that?"

"Did you really think I wouldn't?"

"Probably not a good idea," said a voice from behind her. "Do you really think a civilian computer guy like Jay hiked out into the cold Montana woods all by himself?"

She froze, then turned her head, not moving her body.

An older man stood there, also in snow gear, and he had a Colt .45 pistol pointed at her. Not wavering a bit, that gun.

Kent, she remembered. General Abraham Kent. A Marine. They weren't supposed to be doing this, the Marines.

"And if you think you're Annie Oakley and you can take me out, I've got four crack shots outside with M-16s covering your car, which won't run right now, both cabin doors, and the windows. I get killed, I'd guess your chances of leaving here alive are close to zero. But if you blink funny, I'll shoot you, and I don't think you're good enough to get me anyhow. Put the piece down."

"Shit," she said, letting the gun sag and hang by her side. She released it and it clunked on the rag rug over the wooden floor.

They had her.

She looked at Jay.

"Why are you here? You're not a field guy."

"I didn't want to miss it," he said. "It was the least I could do."

"What if I'd just shot you without a second thought when I opened the door?"

"General Kent tells me the ceramic and spider-silk armor I have on under this poncho will stop anything you could have carried to the door. It ought to, it's heavy enough."

She shook her head. Damn.

Damn.

EPILOGUE

There were half a dozen new faces in the gym. Thorn had put the word out that he was expanding, and Jamal's success had helped bring in a few more students. It would grow further, he knew, now that he had the time to put into it.

He and Marissa stood off to one side, watching Jamal demonstrate the guard position, the first simple parries, and the basics of footwork.

"He's a good kid," she said.

"I think he's gonna do fine. He's smart, talented, disciplined. He learns from his mistakes. And I think helping teach these new kids will be very, very good for him."

"And this is what you want, Tommy?" She gestured around them at the ratty old gym, refurbished but still run-down.

"It won't always be like this," he said. "But right now, it fits. And, yeah, this is what I want. Well, as long as you're a part of the package, but you knew that already."

She smiled, but then grew serious again. "You've officially resigned from Net Force?"

Thorn nodded, still watching Jamal's retreating back. "There's no reason for me to stay. We caught Lewis, and they'll put her in a room so deep it'll take daylight a week to get there. Nothing else on my plate."

He sighed, then turned to look at her. "I'm not a military man, Marissa, and I don't want to be one. My position isn't really necessary in the new chain of command, but then most of the people who work for Net Force aren't necessary. There's too much duplication of effort. Kent commands a Marine unit, though. They can at least find a place to stick him and his troops, those who want to stay. Or he could retire as a general, get a job in private industry, if he wants. Jay probably won't stick around unless they offer him something he can't get elsewhere, which they can't. General Hadden knew all along, I think, that I would be leaving. Sooner or later, it would have come to a pissing match, and I'd have lost. Better to retire a winner in your prime than hang on and get knocked out by some young and hungry fighter on the way up as you are going down."

He paused again, then asked her, "So, are you okay with this?"

She nodded. "Yeah. I didn't want you to quit for the wrong reasons—ego, mostly—but you make good points."

"Now and again, even a blind squirrel finds an acorn." He paused. "You heard that Abe Kent is getting married?"

"No, really?"

"His guitar teacher."

"Wow, seems like everybody is getting married, doesn't it?"

He took her hand. "Everybody important, anyhow."

She smiled at him. "So, Tommy, are we going to live happily ever after?"

He reached up and touched her cheek with his other hand. "Believe it," he said softly.

And kissed her.